Wild Lavender

NICOLE ELIZABETH KELLEHER

DIVERSIONBOOKS

Diversion Books
A Division of Diversion Publishing Corp.
443 Park Avenue South, Suite 1008
New York, New York 10016
www.DiversionBooks.com

For more information, email info@diversionbooks.com

First Diversion Books edition March 2016.
Print ISBN: 978-1-62681-934-4
eBook ISBN: 978-1-62681-933-7

This book is dedicated to my mom,
a practical woman who loved a good story
as much as she loved a good recipe.
I miss her every day.

Prologue

In the Thirty-First Year of the Great Peace in the Realm of King Godwin of Aurelia

King's Glen

She would pay dearly if her family discovered that she had slipped from their quarters, but it had been worth the risk. When would she ever be at High Court again and have a chance to see the royal stables? Her stolen two hours were over, and it was time to return before her absence was noted. Navigating the many corridors of the castle undetected would be simple enough; her training included the art of stealth. And as long as her younger sister Claire had not wakened, none would be the wiser.

Voices brought her back on point, and she slowed her pace as she approached the King's Royal Hall. It seemed the lords and ladies at court and the men of the Royal Guard never slept, preferring rather their games and flirtations.

Light spilled across the cobbled floor in a broadening wedge. She ducked behind a tapestry and flattened herself against the stone wall of the passageway, turning her toes inward lest they peek from beneath the wall hanging and betray her presence. Just in time, she thought, as she heard the gentle patter of a lady's slippers racing past. When the light in the corridor dimmed, she knew the Royal Hall's door had been closed once more. Anna darted past, heart galloping in her breast.

The safety of her room was nigh; only two more deserted corridors, and no one would know of her forbidden adventure. She was congratulating herself on her own success when an arm struck out across her path. With the collision, her breath exploded from her chest in an unladylike grunt, and before she could collect herself, she was drawn into an alcove and pressed against its wall. Her mind reacted instinctively, gauging all possible means of escape. Damn her long cloak, for it kept her legs from kicking out at the man who held her. Patience, she told herself, an opportunity would come.

"Shh," he whispered to her, "you'll wake the castle." His voice seemed to bore into her heart and soul, resonating deep inside.

Anna stretched her neck to see over his shoulder. She was taller than most, boys included, but this man, as she pushed at his chest ineffectually, towered over her. Exposing her neck to him had been a crucial error on her part, and in the dark of the alcove she saw the outline of his head dip down. Lips and whiskers met her skin, creating the most unusual sensation. Far from finding it unpleasant, she found herself tilting her head to better give him access. It was then that she noticed how hard the muscles of his chest felt under her fingers, and she pressed her palms against the beat of the heart racing in time with hers.

She knew she should stop him, and she would, soon. It must be the thrill of her earlier foray, she determined, that kept her from calling out. She was sixteen, after all, old enough to marry though not yet promised. His fingers traced down her back, and his lips lifted to nibble at the bare lobe of her ear. His hands came around to open her cloak.

He nipped gently along her jaw, searching for her lips while his fingers sought to undo the ties of her breeches. Never in her life had she been kissed by a man, Anna thought with growing anticipation. His lips were so close to hers; she held her breath. But no kiss was forthcoming, and when the warmth of his exhalation cooled, her eyelids fluttered open. Eyes as dark as sin stared back at her.

"What game is this?" the stranger all but seethed under his breath. She felt the sting of each word. He must have thought her frightened, for he swore an oath.

"Do you comprehend how dangerous—" he started, taking a step back, and then closed his mouth as she edged warily away. "You need not worry; I am no ravager of maidens." He eased farther away, trying—and failing—to appear less menacing. Only, Anna was anything but daunted, and he must have sensed her mettle, for his appraising gaze washed over her.

He leaned out of the alcove and peered down the deserted passageway, and she could tell from his bearing that he was a noble. "Well, as you are not who you are supposed to be," he scolded, "you had best return to where you belong."

She felt her face go hot, and she narrowed her eyes at him in what she hoped was a scathing look. He mirrored her expression, and then raised his eyebrow in amusement. Anna gave him a wide berth, skirted the recess, and backed her way down the corridor. She glared at him even as she turned on her heel.

"Wait," he called to her, and she stopped, shifting her weight to her toes, poised to flee like a deer if necessary. "What is your name?" he asked.

"Anna," she said breathlessly, her grin as mischievous as it was sweet. His return smile, barely visible in the dim corridor, had her heart tripping in time with her feet as she dashed away.

"I'm Lar—" he called after her, but she did not quite hear. She turned to ask him what he had said, but when she noticed a flickering light approaching from the opposite direction she realized that fortune was nipping at her heels. Every second she delayed was a risk that her nighttime escapade would be reported to her mother. She spun around and raced to her quarters.

CHAPTER ONE

Two Years Later

They headed north to the old forest, six men and Aubrianne of Chevring. Well, no longer Aubrianne of Chevring, she admitted to herself. She was now Lady Aubrianne of Stolweg. Her husband of half a day, Lord Roger of Stolweg, rode next to her. Much like their betrothal and wedding, their pace was quick and without impediment. The fields and crops passed behind them as the distance to the Chevring forest shortened. No one spoke, leaving Aubrianne to her thoughts. She allowed her steed to fall back from her husband's so as to gaze discreetly at him.

Like everything else about him, his profile was perfect. His nose was straight and sharp, but not pointed. His mouth was set in a firm line with lips that were neither too full nor too thin. Strangely, the bright day did nothing to lighten his blond hair; instead, his golden streaks deepened in the sun. Aubrianne was reminded of harvest time at Chevring, when the wind blew over the wheat fields and caused the heavy stalks to undulate and shine. She wanted to reach out and touch his hair, knowing that the strands would not feel silky like so many with fair coloring, but strong and thick. Like the wheat, it would bend; it would not yield.

She remembered the first time she had seen him. It seemed like years ago, but in truth it was only months. It had been a beautiful day, much like this one.

She and her destrier Tullian had been galloping for the sheer, heart-bursting joy of speed. Tullian, over nineteen hands, was a gray blur against emerald pastures. His ash-colored coat was dappled with charcoal smudges, as if he'd rolled in the sooty remains of a campfire. His mane, tail, and fetlocks were as dark as charred wood. Aubrianne remembered how her long braid had trailed behind in the aftermath of their passage and how she had laughed aloud.

Anywhere else in the realm, she and her war horse would have seemed outrageous. But not at Chevring. The people of Chevring were horse people. With no male heir to carry on generations of horse breeding and training skills, her father had turned to Aubrianne. The family's rigorously guarded secrets of producing the finest destriers would not be lost. No other family in the realm could be trusted to breed the mounts destined for the King and his Royal Guard. It came as no surprise that Anna had a way with the horses not seen since the days of her great-grandfather. Horses were in her blood.

Aubrianne smiled at the memory of Tullian's hooves pounding the fertile ground. The air around them had been filled with the sounds of rending stem and root, and grating horseshoe and soil. Wild grass and loam had exploded below like shot from a trebuchet, great clods thrown to the sky.

Her mother had told her not to go for a ride that day. She was to remain near the castle. But Aubrianne had never been one to listen to another's counsel. It hadn't been half past ten in the morning when she turned back; hours yet remained before the first meeting of betrotheds. Returning from her ride, she had spared only a moment to check her appearance: mud-spattered. At least her mouth was clean, she had thought, and then grimaced, feeling the grit in her teeth.

She had felt the drag of decorum growing stronger with each stride closer to the castle, her momentary sense of freedom gone. In one last act of defiance, she opened her arms and embraced the buffeting wind.

Already eighteen years of age, Anna hadn't been surprised that her parents had arranged her marriage. At the time, she had only thought her wedding would be more romantic, perhaps to the dark and dangerous lord who had haunted her dreams for the last two years. Hadn't her grandmother promised that *love* would find her?

A ghost of a smile touched her lips as she continued to reminisce: that morning, she'd nudged Tullian into a high-stepping trot as they entered the confines of Chevring's wall and found her intended groom waiting in the courtyard, her impatient mother next to him. Under her mother's glare, Aubrianne had remembered herself and quickly masked her doe-eyed surprise at seeing such a well-made man. She sat taller in her saddle under his scrutiny. There had been a flash of disapproval in his eyes, but then he strode forward to greet her with a smile.

The sound of stumbling hoof on root drew Aubrianne from her reverie. Her husband was still ahead of her, paying her no mind. He would be surprised if he knew just how different she really was from other girls, she mused. Yes, she knew how to be a chatelaine; her mother had made sure her instruction was complete. As such, she was well versed in the healing arts, for it would be her duty to help the sick and wounded of her new home.

Additional lessons included a thorough history of Aurelia and Nifolhad, two countries separated by the Western Sea. It had been the Great War between these two realms that had shaped the kingdom of Aurelia. Once, there had been many territories, all ruled by lesser kings, but to overcome the powerful and united Nifolhad, a High King had been chosen. His descendant, King Godwin, now sat upon the throne. Of the two and twenty regions that had once existed, only eight remained; most had been absorbed into the area surrounding King's Glen, King Godwin's seat. Although they each kept their own castles, the lords of these smallholds spent most of their time at court.

The remaining eight regions accounted for more than two-thirds of the realm, the largest being Whitmarsh. Stolweg, to which this road now led, was second in size. Each region had its own castle, and each castle was the center of commerce for its region. Their lords and ladies were the meters of both justice and care. Anna sat straighter in her saddle. She was the Lady of Stolweg, and its import finally penetrated her mind.

Of her education, her husband knew that she was practiced in such skills as were needed to run his castle, Stolweg Keep, as it was called. And he also knew of her unconventional abilities with the horses. In fact, that was one of his reasons for wishing their union. For with their marriage, he had secured what no one else in the realm had—the secrets of breeding and training Chevring destriers. In return, he had loaned her father enough coin to keep Chevring from ruin. The years of peace between Aurelia and the kingdom of Nifolhad had whittled away the family's once-great fortune. With no battles to be fought, King Godwin no longer required stables of destriers for his lords and Royal Guard, and the demand for war steeds had dwindled.

Roger had explained that the King was establishing a series of tournaments to keep the many unlanded noblemen in Aurelia occupied, and those men would require proper mounts.

"Aubrianne. *Aubrianne.*" It took her a moment to realize she was being addressed. She just wasn't accustomed to her formal name of Aubrianne. Everyone at Chevring had simply called her Anna. From every word spoken to her thus far, Roger was proving himself to be a man who preferred formality.

He dropped back next to her. "We shall make camp in a few hours." His expression was mild, but his eyes searched her face. "What has occupied your thoughts so thoroughly?"

"I was thinking of the King's tournaments," she replied. "Will you compete?"

"Most likely," he answered. "Of course, doing so means I will have to leave Stolweg Keep often. I am pleased to see that you do not appear to be worried. Your mother assured me that you were up to the running of the keep in my absence. And, you have yet to meet my arms master, Cellach. He is quite capable." Roger looked back at his men. "Everyone at Stolweg is capable of their assigned duties. You see, even my stableman has your dowry in hand."

Anna regarded Gilles with an assessing eye. The stable master *was* doing well. It was no easy task controlling Anna's dowry, five prime broodmares from Chevring. When she turned back to Roger, he had pulled ahead, once more leaving her to her thoughts.

Her husband seemed a traditional man. One who would want his wife in her proper place, a true lady to run his castle. He impressed her as a man who was practical both in mind and in heart. Despite this conservative nature, he had chosen her, a woman more apt to ride astride a horse than sidesaddle, as she did now in her split-skirt riding habit.

For once, Anna would heed her mother's advice and not divulge her other talents to Roger. Even now, the tools of Anna's training were following behind in the cart, concealed in a secret compartment in one of her trunks—armor, centuries old, sized for a woman and handed down through the generations of women in her line. Not only armor, but sword and shield too, specially balanced for a woman's weight. And bow and quiver. Few in the realm knew of Anna's ancestors, for their names had changed as they married into other noble families across Aurelia. Anna could name them. She had studied every one of these leaders who had risen to fight alongside men in the upheavals that had peppered the history of the realm.

But she had her father's line to thank for her innate ability with horses, and her favorite weapon, a dagger once wielded by her father's father. Her mother's side had gifted her with a talent for weaponry skills—the likes of which hadn't been witnessed since her great-great-grandmother. She prayed that her skills did not foretell some major change in the realm.

She gazed upon Roger's straight back and proud stance. No, she would not reveal her secret yet. Still, she hoped, perhaps the King's tournaments would come to Stolweg. It was not unheard of for ladies to enter archery competitions. Mayhap her husband would not mind if—

"Your Tullian looks as if he's aching for a gallop, Aubrianne," Roger said, interrupting her thoughts once more. "What say you to a good run?"

Hearing Roger's voice, Anna was pulled from her memories of Chevring and focused instead on his words, "...it is perhaps two or three miles to the forest."

She was glad for the distraction. While she felt that she could ride forever, Anna was tired of the monotonous scenery. Hill after rolling hill, on a road that ran as straight as a mason's rod, had her mind running in circles.

"Tullian has wanted to gallop since we departed," Anna replied. "He's never thrown me, but I think he might if I don't give him his head."

Roger clucked his tongue, and Anna watched as he dug his heels into his horse. Tullian held himself in check until receiving his signal from Anna. When she subtly shifted forward in her saddle, her horse shot out after Roger's, catching the roan-colored destrier in only ten strides. She reined in her horse, for something inside her warned against making this into a race, especially one Roger had no chance of winning. Though his mount was a noble steed, it was not of the Chevring line. Tullian and his ilk were kings and queens among horses. To prove it, Anna's steed gave a disgruntled snort and nipped his competition's rump, disrupting its smooth gait. Roger deftly pulled his horse back under his control, taking no note of the equine power struggle.

CHAPTER TWO

Rivals

Lady Caroline's breath came fast as Lark's hands skimmed down her waist. "And here?" he asked, kissing her collarbone as he reached lower, lifting her skirts. Oh, what he planned to do to her.

"Larkin," Lady Caroline moaned.

He pressed her against the wall of her chamber, and then lifted her, wrapping her legs around his waist. "The bed," he demanded, and carried her across the room to the waiting platform.

"Now, Larkin, please," she pleaded. "I can't wait one more moment."

Always willing to oblige a lady in distress, Lark took Lady Caroline until both were sated. He held her in his arms and listened as her breath calmed.

"Such a gentle name you have, Larkin," she said, turning to him. "A true misnomer if ever there was one. You are rarely tame, especially in bed. The pleasure you give is cruel, for it spoils a woman for all other men."

He started to worry that Lady Caroline's thoughts were turning toward something more permanent. She was smiling at him now, and he was surprised to hear her throaty laugh.

"Oh, Larkin, rest easy. I am *not* looking for a husband," she stated, guessing his thoughts. "Being a young widow has too many benefits— the freedom to do as I choose being first on the list. And speaking of freedom, are you at liberty this evening?"

"I am at your disposal, m'lady, but it will be late." He stood to secure his clothing, and then helped Lady Caroline with her gown. Bowing as he discreetly left her chamber, he bade her goodbye.

• • •

It had taken Warin and Lady Beth nearly two hours to track down Lark. And now, as Warin saw Lady Caroline in the corridor, he knew why. He quickly assembled a scheme to thwart any plans Lark might have made for the evening.

"Whoa, m'lady," he said with just the right touch of velvet in his voice. Lady Caroline barely avoided colliding with him. "You nearly toppled me. Why such haste?" He and Lark knew that the ladies were cognizant of their game of hearts, but being ladies, they kept their own counsel. Lately, their favors had gone more to Lark. The man was as clever as a bramble-bird, capable of escaping any situation with nary a ruffled feather. But not this time, for the snare that Warin was about to set not even Lark could evade.

"M'lady?" Warin prompted.

"But I'm in no hurry," she replied, studying him with interest.

"Everyone rushing about," Warin complained. "I was nearly tackled by my good friend Larkin as he and Lady Beth rushed off."

'Twas no lie he told to Lady Caroline, but neither was it the full truth. He and Lady Beth *had* sought out Lark, and Lady Beth had rushed off with him. Not to her chamber, however, but to the Queen, who had summoned him. He allowed Lady Caroline to come to her own conclusion.

She narrowed her eyes. "As I said, Warin, I'm in no hurry. And I find myself unengaged this evening." She took his arm and batted her lashes. "Perhaps you are free as well." Warin gave her his cockiest grin and ushered her down the corridor.

• • •

In her royal apartments, Queen Juliana did not look up from her work as the door clicked closed. She could sense Larkin watching her from the other side of the room. Finished at last, she folded the letter she had penned and pressed her seal upon it. She stood and faced the man she'd summoned. As he bowed low, she appraised him: darkly handsome and as graceful as a cat, he was tall with long, lean muscles. He took after his father in every way except for his raven hair and dark coloring. Those attributes came from his mother.

The last few years at court had matured more than his looks; his twenty-five-year-old mind was sharper than any guard's in Aurelia. Her husband often sought Lark's recommendation.

"What is this formality, Lark?" she demanded, striding across the room.

Lark humored her and took her in his arms. "It was a summons from the Queen, was it not?"

"Lady Beth tends to exaggerate. I should have sent Lady Caroline, but she was nowhere to be found." She caught his eye after he was a bit too late in hiding a knowing smile. She would have to have a word with Lady Caroline. "I don't want to know!" the Queen exclaimed as she pushed Lark away.

"I think you have nothing to worry about, my Queen. I've a notion that my evening's plans have been foiled once again." His tone held not a pinch of regret.

"Warin?" she asked.

"Who else, Auntie?" he admitted.

Queen Juliana's heart warmed; he called her Auntie only when they were alone. "Why do you play these games, Larkin? You could marry any noblewoman of your choosing. I promised your mother that I would—"

"I'm only five and twenty. There is time aplenty to hitch my cart to another," he asserted.

Queen Juliana would not be put off-topic. She remembered when Lark had arrived to join the King's Royal Guard. He had sought her out and asked that she and the King not reveal the blood-link between them. For that reason, few in court knew that Lark's mother was the Queen's half sister, Lady Kathryn of Morland. "But if you were presented as my nephew, many landed nobles would seek you out. Lord Gervaise of Chevring, for instance. His youngest daughter is nearly of age." She thought of the eldest daughter, now married to Lord Roger, and tried to mask the distaste she felt for the man.

"Are you ill, Auntie?" Lark asked her and led her swiftly to the chair at her desk. Queen Juliana marveled at her nephew; he could see past all pretenses faster than a starving vulture scenting fresh kill.

"No, no," she assured him, "I'm quite fine." When he raised his eyebrow, as he was oft to do, and peered at her with his ebony eyes, she added, "I was thinking of the Lady of Stolweg and her husband." Now, *there* was a true vulture, she thought. "You, on the other hand, I would like to see settled before I'm old and gray. One word from the King and—"

"I want no special treatment because of our relation," he pressed again. "I've survived this long without it; I daresay I'll last awhile longer."

It was her turn to cock an eyebrow. "Careful you don't become too hard, Larkin," she warned. "Others have made that mistake and lost what mattered most. You do not want to live a cold life with nothing but regretted days to keep you company."

She was, of course, referring to Lark's father, Lord Aldred of Sterland, whose first wife, after a decade of illness, had passed quietly in her bed. She remembered how his mourning had lasted for years. Chance took Aldred near Morland Keep, where he met Queen Juliana's half sister, Kathryn. Attracted to her youth and vitality, he fell passionately in love. They married almost immediately. But her sister was always one to speak her mind. Lord Aldred, twenty years her senior, soon found that he preferred quiet subservience. They quarreled fiercely and often. Six months into the marriage, Lord Aldred sent her back to Morland Keep. When Kathryn found herself with child, she sent a letter to Aldred, asking to return to him. Lord Aldred, too proud for his own good, never responded. Fifteen years passed, and he died, lonely and bitter.

Juliana wondered how much of this Lark knew. Most of it, she judged, for his face had become impassive. No matter how much he loved his Auntie, he could shutter his emotions in an instant. She rarely trespassed onto this forbidden subject. His father's abandonment had impressed an indelible mark upon Larkin. But her nephew had shaped his anger into a useful tool. With no father present in his youth, Larkin had learned all that he knew by observing others. He was an expert at tying together seemingly random facts. Moreover, he was fearsomely loyal to his mother and all those he held dear.

Yet, Queen Juliana worried for her nephew. He rarely dropped his guard low enough to allow others to get close to him. Only once, two years ago, had he expressed more than a passing interest in a woman. He'd asked her if she knew of a young noblewoman answering to Anna. When she did not recall anyone by that name, he had looked crestfallen and quickly changed the subject. But she had glimpsed the spark in his eyes. A rare moment indeed.

"I have a letter that needs to be delivered as soon as possible," she stated. The queen may have lost this skirmish with her nephew, but his mother was about to enter the battle. There was no stopping her sister when she set her mind to accomplish something. "How would you like a respite from court?" she asked, knowing he wouldn't refuse her.

"Where are you sending me? And why do I feel that I should surrender now?"

"Too late, my dear nephew," Queen Juliana replied. "Fate has other plans for you."

CHAPTER THREE

Roger had offered her this chance to ride, but much too soon Anna saw its end. The forest loomed ahead. At least Tullian seemed satisfied, she thought, but she would have preferred charging through the woods.

"There's a clearing ahead where we can camp," Roger said as they entered the trees. "My men know where to go."

Anna knew of the clearing: level and grass-covered, with a creek mere paces into the woods. She and her father had used it many times. She took stock of the familiar surroundings and, under the shade of the trees, where the air was cool and damp, she breathed in the rich, loamy scents.

She loved these old woods of oak and maple. The road that cut through was straight and clear of underbrush. As long as anyone could remember, the highway had been as much a part of the forest as the trees themselves. It was perhaps even older. Neither encroached upon the other, save when the wind gleaned the dead limbs, and autumn loosed the leaves from the vaulted canopy above. The people of Chevring believed that the route had been laid by an ancient race and that deep under its surface was pounded iron. No precious ore could be seen today, for hundreds of years of decaying leaves covered any trace. It was an ill omen to be caught on a road such as this in a thunderstorm.

Roger pulled ahead, leaving Anna's thoughts to wander more. Her grandmother had oft recited the lore of the old forests and of the rings of stone scattered throughout the realm. Nothing like the watered-down fables told to scare children, but the true stories as sung by the minstrels. And to Anna, each tale held romance.

Anna sighed, her eyes lingering on the perfect figure of her husband just ahead. She was married now, she recalled with a touch of sadness. It was time to put girlish reveries away.

She wondered about their coming wedding night and if he would be gentle with her. He'd been married before, so she knew he must be practiced in the art of lovemaking. He was a fine-looking man, and she was surprised to find in herself the slight stirrings of attraction.

Roger's build was muscular, and try as she might, Anna could not detect the paunch that afflicted most men of thirty. When he spoke, his voice possessed a pleasant timbre. Perhaps one day, they could come to love each other. Then she remembered seeing Roger's eyes for the first time, hoping against hope that they would be as dark as night. But their hue matched the sea's slate-colored ice that forms only on the coldest of days. Like the ice, she found no warmth in his gaze.

Anna suddenly realized that Roger had been studying her. Her cheeks flamed with color, and she snapped her focus to the path ahead. From the intensity of his stare, he seemed able to read her mind. Roger smiled and clucked his tongue, putting his horse into a canter. Anna composed herself before following.

The newlyweds pulled up in unison to the trail leading to the campsite. The path was just wide enough to ride two abreast. More than once, Roger's leg brushed against hers. By the time they came to the clearing, Anna was as skittish as a newborn colt, simultaneously afraid and hoping that he would ravish her.

Roger dismounted first, and then came around to lift her from her saddle. His hands encircled her slim waist, and he set her lightly on the ground. When he did not immediately release her, Anna peered up at him through her long lashes. She did not know what to expect, but she wanted something, anything, to happen. The tension was too great, and her breath caught as she tried to calm her nerves. She was sure he would kiss her.

"We have only a few moments before the others arrive, Aubrianne, and I want to make something clear," he murmured. "I have decided that we will not consummate our vows until we reach Stolweg Keep." When she lowered her face in embarrassment, he lifted her chin with his knuckle. "I am only telling you this to ease your nerves. You've become a bit anxious since we reached the forest. It is not becoming of the new Lady of Stolweg."

Anna had not expected this. Moments ago, she had believed that he was about to ravish her once they were alone. Instead, he was instructing her on how to behave. He pulled her a fraction closer. She saw fire in his eyes and a hint of future passion. An instant later, he stepped away to lead their mounts to the far edge of the clearing.

"Would you mind taking the horses to water?" he asked, unperturbed. "There is a brook just along that path," he explained, pointing into the trees.

She cleared her throat discreetly and answered, "Your request is my pleasure, m'lord." The corner of his mouth lifted, and she took heart in the fact that her words had amused him.

Anna found the creek easily, for she'd oft been there before. Leaving the horses standing in the shallows to drink, Anna gazed about. Mossy boulders, timeworn and sleeping for centuries, beckoned her to the brook's edge. One rock in particular was flat and dipped into a natural pool made by a curve in the stream. The dark green, living carpet was thick and soft and cushioned her knees as she knelt over the clear pool. In the waning light, she could just make out her reflection on the water's surface. Her golden-brown hair, so neatly plaited earlier in the day, was a mass of wild tresses. With a sigh, she began the process of braiding her thick mane once more.

After the horses had drunk their fill, they returned to the bank, where they nibbled at the tender green shoots growing there. Tullian lifted his head suddenly and snorted. Anna turned to see Roger striding toward her, his previous good humor vanished.

"Are you almost done?" he asked—his tone was polite, but Anna could see the impatience etched in the tightness of his jaw. "My men need to water their mounts."

"I'm just finished now," Anna replied cheerfully. He held out his hand to her as she stepped lightly from her perch. They led their two horses to the clearing and handed them over to the stable master.

Anna was about to assist when Roger took her elbow. "I assume that you have refreshments in your saddlebag. It was a long ride, and you should retire now," he suggested, directing her to a newly erected tent before stepping away to his men.

Something about his dismissal worried her. She had seen the passion in his eyes earlier; perhaps he was pushing her away for that reason. She sat alone inside her tent, staring at the thick bedroll and the small trunk atop which a lantern sat. When she opened the screen for more light, the flame illuminated her wedding ring: a band of silver, thickly made to accommodate a cabochon ruby, fat like a plump raspberry but as red as flowing blood. She couldn't help but frown at the gem, terrible in its beauty. She would have to be careful, for rubies were known to shatter.

CHAPTER FOUR

Lady Kathryn of Morland set the letter down and gazed at her son. Queen Juliana was right to send Larkin from court. His game with Warin was cause for trouble. And as clever as the Queen's ladies thought they were being, hearts would be broken, and scandal would mire the workings at King's Glen. It was time for Larkin to settle.

"Finding court to your liking, my son?" she asked innocently.

"Didn't the Queen say in her letter?" he replied, a little too shrewdly for his years. "What are the two of you contriving?"

Lady Kathryn merely smiled. "My dear Larkin," she praised him, "the Queen writes only of your virtues." They both laughed at her wit.

"Shall I wait for your reply before returning?" he asked.

"So eager to return?" She sighed as only a mother could. "Be patient. I'll have it ready in a few days. For now, I have a gift for you." She went to the cupboard in her waiting room. "This belonged to my grandfather. It's time it had a new home." She placed a dagger in his palm, and he examined it by the light of the fire.

"Onyx?" he asked, fingering the detail work on the hilt and butt.

"Yes. And just as it was with my grandfather, it's as dark as your eyes."

"These markings are much older than your grandfather's time," he stated, touching the runes etched along the blade.

"Our family's line is an ancient one, as you well know," she responded.

"And what do these symbols mean?"

She would have to tread carefully here, for her son knew that deciphering runes was her passion. "Some old prophecy," she answered lightly, seeing a spark of interest in his midnight eyes. "It's nothing, really, something about blood and stone. I've copied it down somewhere. If I find it, I'll send it to you. For now, dear boy, I must finish some translations for the Queen."

"I hope you and Auntie are not plotting my life again," Larkin said, leaning his tall frame against the wall and crossing his arms in front of him. "An ancient prophecy won't encourage me to wed any faster than would a formal command from the King. I'd rather be banished to Nifolhad."

"Larkin! Hold your tongue," she cried. "You kill me with such words."

"I spoke in jest, Mother," he said soothingly. "I did not mean to worry you. I would never wish to be sent to such a place. But understand this: I will not marry. It would be better for all if you mentioned that to the Queen in your letter."

"Stubbornness runs through your bones, Lark, just like your father," she stated, and instantly regretted her words. For not only had his father never taken an interest in Lark, but by marrying him, Lady Kathryn had surrendered Lark's birthright and title to Morland Keep to the whims of a bitter man.

Morland, the smallest territory in the realm, was a peninsula jutting into the Summer Sea. Sterland, the only region to touch Morland, was to the north. No ship could approach Aurelia from the south and escape detection by the watchmen upon the walls of Morland Keep. Though still a territory in its own right, and Lady Kathryn its keeper, Morland fell under the protection of Lark's half brother, Lord Hugh of Sterland. An ancient treaty, one not dissolved when the regions of Aurelia had consolidated, stated that if ever Morland and Sterland united in marriage, the lands of Morland would be absorbed by Sterland.

When Lady Kathryn realized there would be no reconciling with Lord Aldred, she petitioned King Godwin to dissolve the pact. The King had allowed that if Lord Aldred would relinquish this right, Lark could retain his inheritance. But Lord Aldred would not be swayed.

She looked at her son, thinking about what she'd just said to him. "Being sorry for my words doesn't make them any less true, Lark. But perhaps there still is hope for you. Your brother has embraced marriage and family life."

"Half brother," Lark grunted, as if she needed the reminder.

She knew his memories of Hugh were not always pleasant, for Lord Aldred had pitted the two against each other. It was a mutual enmity that she was trying to remedy.

"I have no dispute with Hugh, Mother," her son averred. "He takes his responsibilities toward Morland seriously. I am even grateful to him that you are under the protection of Sterland Castle. But do not think that I too wish to be tamed by a wife."

Lady Kathryn sighed. It was futile to try to change her son's mind now. But it would matter not in the end; Larkin would have no choice. Fate would intervene, and he would lose his heart to one as strong as he. It was written in the stars, if she and Juliana had read them correctly.

Her son was astute enough to realize that the Queen had a motive for sending him away from court, and that she, his mother, was colluding in some scheme. She gave him her coolest gaze and narrowed her eyes to match his. "There was a time when you sought out another," Lady Kathryn reminded him. "What was her name? Anna, was it not?"

"I tell you once more, she was nothing," he stated, refusing to admit that the name still haunted him.

"Go," Lady Kathryn ordered her implacable son. "Find some food and drink and leave me to my writing. You'll soon be back at court." He kissed her cheek before leaving her to her letter.

Lady Kathryn worked long into the night to chart the stars, searching for some portent of the future. She stopped only when the sky brightened with the new dawn. Two more nights she toiled, barely sleeping, barely eating. When at last she finished, she summoned her son, and whilst waiting for him, she reread her final words:

...I'm afraid there is no denying that the realm will face its greatest trials since the Great War. When this will occur, I have yet to discover.

As for the other matter, I have translated the runes from the dagger:

Black as Night this Blade is Forged,
Seeking Red in Stone and Blood,
Tempering Hearts in Field of Stars

I am sure this is prophetic. The ancient race had better methods than we in foretelling. And so, we must find Larkin's match. Whether she is at Court or in some other corner of this realm, I know not. So much has been lost during the peace. The bloodline has been forgotten by all save those touched by it. Perhaps fortune will bless you in your own search of the Royal Archives.

My Queen, my sister, my friend, the day is not long away when we must divulge all that we know. Until then, keep an eye on my boy for me. He dwells yet on the girl named Anna.

Your loving sister,
Kathryn

CHAPTER FIVE

The Crossing

Anna awakened feeling refreshed. She was determined to impress Roger with an improved comportment. They broke camp early, and like the day before, her husband set a brisk pace. The misty shadows of the woods dissipated as sunlight filtered through the branches above, heralding the end of the forest, and so too the end of Chevring lands and her former life.

The trees gave way to fields of wildflowers of every color, and the road, for so long as straight as an arrow, now meandered at the whim of the low hills. As their trek steepened, the wide swatches of tall grass yielded to rockier terrain. On and on they rode.

To break the monotony, Anna attempted to draw Roger into discourse, but he seemed content to survey the never-changing scenery. She tried starting a conversation with the stable master, but he only replied with quick nods of his head, or "Yes, m'lady" and "No, m'lady," and avoided meeting her gaze. She had hoped he would be friendlier, being a horse person. Perhaps he was loath to accept equine advice from a woman.

The landscape did nothing to help Anna's sinking mood either. Gone were the stately hardwoods of the forest and hills. And the stands of aspen growing in the dells had given way to twisted conifers. Anna searched the horizon for something to take her mind from her growing lassitude. Finally, as they topped yet another hill, Anna beheld a beautiful open vale with a wide river snaking its way through.

They stopped when they reached the broad, easy-flowing water. Anna waited while Roger gave orders to his men before riding up to her. "We'll cross here, and then take a short rest," he explained. "The water is shallow enough even with the spring runoff. I assume your steed has forded a river before." Before she could reply, Roger turned his mount and rode down the bank. Anna followed with ease.

Midstream, the water was clear, and the riverbed was scattered with smooth rocks as big as gourds. After crossing, she slid from her saddle and set Tullian free to graze upon the stray clumps of grass. There was not much to be found. It seemed as though the area had been well traveled of late.

So after leading her destrier downstream to find fresh grass, Anna sat on the bank. Hidden in the tall reeds, she removed her boots and stockings to sink her toes into the cool water. From where she rested, she could just see Gilles leading the mares and pack animals across the river. One of the packhorses stumbled on a rock and reared. Its burden came loose, falling with a great splash into the moving waters. Roger charged past the stable master, nearly knocking the man from his saddle, to retrieve their belongings.

Anna was too far away to hear, but she could tell by the way Roger was gesturing that he was furious. Gilles lowered his head. Then something happened so quickly that Anna wasn't sure if she'd witnessed it at all. Roger struck the stableman hard and fast, catching him on the cheek and knocking him into the river. Her husband stiffened and scanned the area around him. Anna ducked further into the reeds. After drying her feet, she slipped on her stockings and boots, then hurried to find Tullian before rejoining the others.

Gilles was holding a wet cloth to a bleeding gash just below his eye. She dropped Tully's reins and hurried to the cart, feigning surprise at Gilles's injury. She could tell that he was badly shaken. "I have just the thing for that," she said in a soothing voice. "Keep that cloth to your face. The pressure will slow the bleeding." There was a tremor in the man's hand, and she thought he shook his head at her. "Do as I say, Gilles, and we'll have you patched up soon enough."

As she walked back to Tullian, she ignored the curious looks from Roger's men, caring little that they did not seem to approve of her actions. Gilles was hurt. What good was she to anyone if she couldn't help with a simple injury? Anna pulled a small earthen pot from her saddlebag, fitting it neatly in her hand. She pivoted on her heel, and stepped right into Roger. She might have tumbled back if it were not for Tullian behind her. Her horse shifted his weight and set her aright.

"What are you doing, Aubrianne?" Roger asked. His men were observing the exchange with interest.

"Did you not see, my lord? The stable master is bleeding. My family has used this salve for years to treat small scrapes and cuts. Why, I've even used it on the horses."

One of Roger's men was overly keen on the conversation, so Anna lowered her voice. "I apologize, m'lord. I should have asked you first if I could help, but my mother taught me that one duty of a lady to her people is to treat the injured and sick. My mother—"

"You may help him if you wish, Aubrianne," Roger cut in. "Do not take overlong."

Anna hurried back to Gilles. The wound was shallow but long; Roger's ring must have caught him, straight and clean. With a dry cloth, she delicately patted the area and was pleased to see that the bleeding had slowed. When she uncorked the earthen pot, Gilles eyed the small container with suspicion. He squinted, and his nose crinkled as if something rotten were contained within.

"This will only hurt a little. There's not much I can do about the flowery smell, but at least it will keep the flies away," she said, hoping to garner a smile from the injured man. He flinched. "You won't even have a scar," Anna promised, smiling as she dabbed at the cut.

"Thank you, m'lady," he mumbled under his breath.

"You are welcome," she replied, happy to be useful. She hurried back to where Roger held Tullian by the reins.

"I'm afraid you'll not have time for refreshment," he said, peering down at her from his saddle. "I suppose that comes with the responsibility of being Lady of Stolweg."

Once seated securely in her saddle, she regarded her husband with a bright smile. "I'll have to make do with dining atop Tully-boy. His gait is smooth enough even to pour tea, m'lord."

Roger clucked his tongue, and his mount started at a brisk pace. Anna wasn't sure if she'd said something wrong. No one made eye contact with her except for one soldier, and he stared at her with a sly gleam in his eyes. She frowned at him before looking ahead and nudging Tullian forward.

That day and the next four, they rode on. On the seventh morning of their journey, Anna rose early, packed her belongings, and went outside to find Tullian. He'd been well tended to and was already saddled. The group began its trek through the mountain pass that would lead them to Stolweg land. They rode single file on the narrowing trail.

To Anna, after the lush and verdant fields of Chevring, this landscape was horribly stark and menacing. The trees, at least those still living, grasped tenuously at the barren soil, their roots clutched white-knuckled on the craggy earth. The slopes rising on either side were a tangled mass of knife-edged rocks. Above, the outcroppings were sharp and cracked, like great broken teeth waiting for a meal. Now and then, small pieces of rock would come dislodged and skitter heedlessly down the banks, spooking the horses that were not of Chevring stock. Oddly, Roger and his men grew lighter in spirit.

"We've just crossed into Stolweg," her husband told her. Anna gazed at the bleak scenery and had her first qualms about the success of his breeding program. If all of Stolweg was so devoid of vegetation, there would be little chance of the mares foaling.

To Anna, the unforgiving surroundings of this leg of the journey seemed interminable. The steady beat of horse hooves put her in a trance. So it came as a surprise when she noticed that the landscape had changed. The vegetation clung less desperately to the earth. Their group threaded its way for some time, single file, along the path, until Roger pulled to a halt for the midday break.

Anna excused herself to check on Gilles, taking her balm with her.

"Don't be too long, Aubrianne," Roger instructed. "I'm eager to start again."

As she cleaned the wound and reapplied the salve, Gilles waited patiently, staring forward at the mountains. Perhaps it was because no one in their group apart from Roger had actually spoken to her that it came as a shock when Gilles said quietly, "Be careful, my lady, the path ahead is unsure." His eyes darted to her husband before quickly turning back to her. "A careless move could prove dangerous." Then he averted his gaze as if he'd said nothing at all.

It was late afternoon when they began their descent from the mountain pass. The land transformed; Anna was amazed at the beauty surrounding her. The steep slope, at first sparsely wooded, grew thick with trees and plants. She could hear the rushing of rapids, and once beheld a dazzling waterfall. The lush dells and sheltered canyons could provide year-round protection and nourishment for the mares.

"M'lord, Stolweg is breathtaking," she declared, as they entered yet another forest. "There are so many places for the mares."

"We are south of Stolweg Keep. As long as you confine the grazing to this area and to the east, you may come here as you see fit. The west can be treacherous, and you will heed me when I say do not venture there."

Unabashed by his brusque warning, Anna asked, "How far to the keep, m'lord?"

"We'll camp one more night before arriving at the castle next midday," he answered.

The trail had widened enough that Anna was able to ride alongside her husband. Thick trees grew on either side. These were not the ordered woods of Chevring, however, but wild in their beauty. The forest floor was lush with ferns and shade-loving trillium. Thick vines, trailing with moss, climbed the massive trunks before hanging like ship rigging from the branches. Other areas were choked with brambles and underbrush. The route widened more, and the enveloping growth stretched open like a great mouth, spitting the travelers into a broad valley.

"Do you think Tullian has enough wind for another gallop?" Roger asked. "This valley boasts some old ruins that you might find interesting."

"I think Tully is not used to such a tranquil pace," Anna answered, and laughed for the first time in days, happy to be able to do that which she loved best.

"Good. We'll stop at the ruins. Our camp is located near the tree line. My men will catch up to us while you explore the henge."

"A henge on Stolweg land!" Anna exclaimed. "It must be very old."

"It is. You may have noticed that we are keeping to the edge of the forest. The men will not admit that they fear the ruins. Superstitious, the lot of them."

"You are not afraid, then?" Anna asked.

Roger smirked. "Why should I be afraid of boulders so ancient that no one remembers their use? Are *you* afraid, Aubrianne?"

"Certainly not," she replied jovially, encouraged by Roger's good humor. "I am simply respectful. My grandmother believed that there was still much power in such rings of stone."

"She sounds superstitious to me," he said, "like my men." He kicked his horse into a gallop, leaving Anna to follow.

She was struck by his sudden change in mood; Stolweg must be good for his temper. As Tullian was straining to go, she leaned into his neck, and he lifted his front legs to paw the air before taking off after the other horse. Perhaps this time she could let Tullian show his true speed.

CHAPTER SIX

The Stones

Roger scanned the clearing, admiring the efficiency of his men. He thought about the progress he had made. But it wasn't the journey about which he mused. It was his life's work, nearly done. To the northwest, his home of Ragallach had grown prosperous, and its keep had been refortified. He left the running of its castle to his late mother's cousin, a witless man who followed Roger's every command. Ragallach was truly under the thumb of one of Roger's more capable captains. Ragallach thus secured, Roger had been able to marry Lady Isabel of Stolweg and now controlled the lands in the center of the realm.

Stolweg was a vast region, and strategically placed. During the Great War, the army of Nifolhad had been held at bay by the men of Stolweg and of Chevring, and never allowed to cross into Whitmarsh. Part of their defeat was due to their inability to navigate through the intricate landscape of Stolweg. Too accustomed to the broad, open expanses of Nifolhad, the forests and hills confused them and the waterways that turned back on themselves left them stranded in ravines and canyons. When the Nifolhadajans finally made it to the great basin surrounding Stolweg Keep, the Chevring riders on their war steeds and the Royal Guard, likewise mounted, were lying in wait.

Roger had spent the few years of his marriage to Lady Isabel exploring every inch of Stolweg. Once widowed, he'd wasted no time and looked to the south, to Chevring. Aubrianne's father had been shortsighted indeed to accept so much coin. He would soon find that more than his daughter and a few mares would have to be paid. Roger's men would insinuate themselves across Chevring. If Lord Gervaise did not like it, he would find his loan come due.

He turned his thoughts to Aubrianne and her dowry. Chevring horses were critical to his plan, and he would use her skills to reach his

NICOLE ELIZABETH KELLEHER

goal. She was a spirited girl. But as with horses, sometimes you had to break a spirit before you could control it.

As if considering a horse at auction, he analyzed her attributes in precise detail: high cheekbones; clear skin; a fine, straight nose, despite the unfortunate freckle on one side; well-formed lips, the lower being slightly fuller; and a cuppable chin, one with a small indentation that was most engaging. She would have to do something with all of that hair, however. Thick and wavy, the golden-brown tresses never stayed put. But her eyes, he decided, were her best feature: ashy brown and flecked with gold. Long eyelashes and delicately arched eyebrows completed the picture.

She was taller than most girls, with a body lithe and toned from riding each day. Her hips were narrow, he thought critically, but pleasantly curved. She would not have trouble breeding, if he happened to get a brat from her.

His new wife was both beautiful and spirited, the best of combinations. And she belonged to him.

That morning, they had made an earlier start than usual and rode steadily toward their goal until the sun began its descent into the western sky. When Roger suggested that his new bride and he gallop the rest of the way, she agreed before he could finish speaking. He knew the destrier she rode was superior to his own mount, but she tactfully allowed him the lead.

He turned slightly to see that she had gained on him. The wind whipped through her hair, pulling burnished tendrils from her braid. On either side, a rainbow of greens ribboned past: teal and emerald for the shadowed forests' leaves; the pines and mahoganies of the trunks, so dark in places they were nearly black; and soft chartreuse for the spring meadow growing in the valley. Up ahead, he could just make out the gray megaliths as they rose out of the ocean of grass.

When Roger slowed, his wife pulled up next to him. She took in the lush valley, and he could see her measuring its worth in terms of the broodmares. He'd made a good choice marrying the Chevring girl.

It was only mid-spring, and already the wild grasses grew high, almost to the bellies of their horses, and they rose and fell in the breeze as if the meadow had breath. Patches of wildflowers spilled paintlike on a canvas of foxtail and meadow barley.

The stones towered above them, and they pulled to a stop. Aubrianne dismounted and gazed in awe at the megaliths. Great billowy clouds whisked overhead in the cerulean sky, and she reached for his arm to steady herself. "It makes one feel quite insignificant!" she exclaimed, looking at him with wide, innocent eyes.

He led her through a large gap in the henge, supplying her with detailed measurements and distances. As they entered the ring, she pressed her palm to one of the surfaces of the weatherworn stone. "It's warm," she stated, half to herself. "How did they get them here?"

"No one remembers," Roger answered. "This land, especially the land where Stolweg now sits, has changed hands many times. King Godwin's followers were not the first to occupy it. And they probably won't be the last. Why don't you explore while I water the horses?" he suggested, peering at his bride. Her skin was flushed. "Aubrianne, are you well?"

"Oh yes," she replied, fishing a kerchief from her sleeve, "just warm from the sun."

"There's some shade near the southern stones," he suggested as he left the circle of stones. "Do not tarry overlong, though. Camp will be set, and you'll want your rest after this long day."

• • •

After he was satisfied that the horses had had their fill, Roger secured them. His mood had much improved since they'd stepped on Stolweg land. Now that he had Aubrianne, he hoped to add much more to his holdings. His goal, decades out of reach, was finally in sight. One more year, perhaps two, and he could make his next move.

At Stolweg, he could be himself and not worry about outsiders questioning his methods or authority. Aubrianne would learn her place soon enough. He'd told her not to take too long, to follow him to the campsite, yet she lingered at the henge. She'd had enough time to explore.

He approached the stones from the southeast. The shadows were deepening with every minute, and it took him a moment to find his young wife. She was on the ground, almost hidden in the grasses near the stone to his left, and he thought she was asleep. But her features were far from restful, and she was mumbling to herself. Could she be dreaming?

He knelt down next to her, and just as he lifted his hand to caress her cheek, she sighed. On her breath, a single word floated from her lips: "Larkin."

Roger shook her shoulders none too gently, and her eyes fluttered open. She immediately sat up in alarm, only to swoon once more as the blood rushed from her head.

31

"Are you injured, Aubrianne?" Her eyes were wide, her pupils enlarged. Her confusion seemed genuine. "What is the matter with you?"

"I—I'm not sure," she answered him, brow knitted. "I was exploring, and then—I don't know. Could I have fainted? I've never done so in my life, m'lord."

Roger held out his hand to help her to her feet, and she stood, albeit unsteadily. He continued to study her. Thus far, she'd been so easy to read. He saw her guarded look and decided to question her later about what she had said when she was dreaming. His mind did naught but imagine the worst.

CHAPTER SEVEN

Homecoming

The next morning, when Anna emerged from her tent, she regarded the men working doubly hard to break their camp. For once, even her husband could find no faults in their efforts. Their home was within reach—*her* home, she amended. Everyone went about their duties with such efficiency that they started earlier than anticipated.

Roger rode ahead of the group, mulling over some matter. He'd yet to say a single word to her, and the uneasiness she'd felt upon waking from her faint grew. When the trail widened, she pulled alongside him. He remained focused on the path ahead.

"Good morning, m'lord," Anna started.

He nodded to her but kept his silence.

"I was hoping to speak with you earlier, but there was no time. Yesterday—"

"How fare you this morning?" he asked, interrupting her. "No more spells, I hope."

"No, m'lord," she stated, trying to make her tone light in an effort to ease her nerves. "In truth, I know not why I fainted. It must have been warmer than I thought." Anna didn't quite believe this, for she'd never experienced anything even close to a spell. That was an affliction that troubled her sister.

"Your malaise, had it anything to do with Larkin?" Despite his casual tone, he scrutinized her face as if his question were some sort of test. She had no idea to what he was referring.

"M'lord? What larkin?" Her bafflement must have been the answer for which he was searching, for as soon as it was uttered, a satisfied cast stole across his face.

Before she could say more, he muttered a curse under his breath and wheeled his horse around. "Damn. The stable master needs my help again." He rode abruptly away, even though it appeared that Gilles had the broodmares perfectly in hand.

When Roger later returned to her side, she listened while he pointed out various grazing locations. And as he told her of his expectations for his breeding program, the valley yielded to a gently rising plain. He suggested they pick up the pace, and they cantered up the incline. As they reached the crest, Roger reined in his horse. Anna followed suit. Below them sat Stolweg Keep.

It was perhaps a half-league away, at the bottom of a broad basin. But it was not the keep that captured her attention. It was the wide, smooth-flowing river meandering through the land. The water flowed from the northeast and continued southwest until it curved around the keep. After flowing back upon itself, it finally widened to form a serene, almond-shaped reservoir. A peppering of cottages was spread along its northern bank. A structure, most likely a mill, pinched the southeast end of the lake back into a river. From there, the water flowed east before disappearing in a jumble of rolling, forested hills. Was her new home similar to Chevring, with all village life spread around the fortress and contained in the immediate lands around it?

Stolweg Keep sat to the northwest of the lake. The castle and ramparts were cleverly placed. The river created a natural moat, and the resulting peninsula within its girth was several hectares wide. Every bit of land within the river's belt was used: arable fields, small orchards, and walled grazing areas filled alternately with milk cows and sheep. Here and there, herders' cottages and farmers' crofts provided shelter. Despite the strict order imposed on the land, the effect was comforting, like a patchwork blanket.

Anna scanned the region to the west. There, the land was thickly wooded and savage. Her gaze shifted east, to the forested hills, much gentler than their brothers across the basin. These forests were much like those of Chevring, open and airy, not choked with wild brush.

All of these details Anna soaked in. The rise atop which they were perched was verdant in grasses and was in striking contrast to the opposite edge of the basin. There, a small band of green followed the water's outer curve. But too soon, the lush green gave way to a gray, lifeless landscape. Except for sparse patches of trees, the northern side was barren. Its slope rose to about the same level of the ridge upon which they'd halted and then transformed without break into steep, desolate hills. The uninterrupted terrain lay smoky in the afternoon sun. Austere and forbidding, the hills blended seamlessly into the mountains behind.

Anna's chin tilted up to better view the peaks. A sound between a whistle and an oath escaped her as her eyes widened in awe.

"The snow *never* melts on that range," Roger told her.

"Have you been up there?" Anna asked.

"Several times. There's interesting hunting to be found in those mountains, if you're brave enough," he added. "Of course, most men will only venture there during high summer. Any other time, it can be devilishly cold. And extremely perilous. You're just as likely to be devoured by the wolves that roam there as you are to fall into an ice crevasse."

Anna tore her eyes from the north as she and Roger rode over the basin's brim. The afternoon sun reflected off the river, transforming it into a ribbon of molten gold. Roger pointed out various features of the land, including a massive bridge that spanned the narrowest part of the river. He told her how its builders had defense on their minds during its construction. Sections could be lifted and rolled back, cutting off entry to the lands around the castle. There was a second, smaller crossing near the mill that could also be quickly dismantled. If an enemy found the main crossing retracted, it would take an hour's hard ride to reach the mill. From there, it would be another hour to make the main gate. By then, the people of Stolweg could be safely ensconced inside the curtain wall.

As they drew closer to the keep, Anna gazed at the castle in the distance. Located on the northwest side of the peninsula, it was constructed atop a large rock formation. "I see only the one gate, m'lord. Surely there are other entrances than just the one."

"There's but one other, though much smaller," he replied. "It is just large enough for one horse and rider to pass through at a time, making it easily defendable. During the Great War, Stolweg Keep was all that stood between the armies of Nifolhad and the heart of Aurelia."

"I can see the stable and paddocks," she said, "but what is that large building to the east?"

"The barracks," Roger answered. "Most of the servants are housed within the curtain but not within the castle. There are a few exceptions, including my master-at-arms and your maid."

They rode to the bridge, passing herders tending to their beasts and field hands working their parcels of land. Anna nodded to them all, and smiled. They nodded back, though not at her, it seemed. She sensed that they surreptitiously studied her, but their eyes mainly focused on Roger. He ignored them. As soon as he passed, they resumed their labors. No words were spoken, no songs were sung to ease their toil.

Anna couldn't help but compare the silence to the liveliness she'd left behind at Chevring. Here, the lack of happiness was incongruous to the well-tended land.

When they reached the bridge, Anna marveled at its construction. Stretching nearly twenty paces, it had ropes, as thick as a man's thigh, running to wheeled structures on either side. And the workings—gears, chains, and cables—had the appearance of careful maintenance.

Over the bridge, they rode toward the massive wall, passing more dwellings nestled under its protection. They were well maintained, each with a small garden patch. A few homes boasted flower boxes, though nothing yet bloomed there. Anna noted that the stoops were all swept and the roofs in good repair. The few people at home who had stepped outside to greet their lord and his new bride gave polite nods before returning to their tasks. It was quiet here, too. The familiar sounds of women chatting, children playing, and babes crying were absent. It dawned on Anna that there were no young children; only boys and girls of a ready age to work with their parents could be seen.

She was on the verge of asking Roger about this when they came to the large archway at the southeast corner of the curtain wall. Looking up, Anna saw gigantic wooden beams wrapped in iron plating, their pointed tips deadly. She imagined that the heavy timbers, when lowered, could withstand any siege. Roger's people had kept the workings in excellent condition. The wheel axles were oiled; the chains and pull ropes were new.

As they entered the courtyard, not a single person stepped forward to greet them. There were men and women present, to be sure, she noticed. But after a fastidious nod to their lord, they went back to their work. Roger's people were healthy, well fed, and well shod, but silent.

She and Roger dismounted in front of the stable. A boy, perhaps fifteen years of age, approached the horses with an easy confidence. He looked familiar, Anna thought. And when the rest of the group entered the yard, she made the connection. He had to be Gilles's son.

"Show Lady Aubrianne the stable," Roger ordered. "No doubt she will visit often." He strode toward several soldiers emerging from the barracks, leaving her alone with the young man.

Following the stable hand, Anna led Tullian into the structure's cool sanctuary. The clean scent of hay, oats, and horse manure floated in the air of the two-story building. Anna breathed deeply, relishing the sweet ambrosia, and thought, *I'm home.*

She stood in the center of the long, open stable, analyzing its details with great interest. There were at least twenty stalls on each side, and an opening to the paddock on the far end.

"I'm called Will, m'lady," the stable boy told her as he removed the saddle and gear from Roger's horse.

Curious, thought Anna. Although he hadn't made eye contact with her, he couldn't keep his eyes off Tullian. She recognized a kindred spirit when she saw one.

She noted that there was a large tack room and that each stall had a split trough for both clean water and grain. Above her head, the lofts were well stocked with fresh hay and straw. The ladders were sturdily made, with wide rungs so as to be more like stairs. Trapdoors running along the center beam were propped open, letting in not only light but fresh air as well.

"This stable is more than perfect, Will. It's expertly designed," Anna commented. "Not a single detail has been overlooked." For the first time, Will looked at her. And Anna saw that his eyes were filled with pride. *So, she thought, not everyone here is so cold.* Mayhap she could get the boy to speak more than just his name. When she noticed a small opening to the right, she asked him where it led.

"To the farrier's shed, m'lady," he replied. "'Course, my da can shoe the horses better than Quinn—that's the farrier." Sweeping his arm wide, Will continued, "My da's the one to credit for all of this. Those roof vents were his idea, and the ladders. Lord Roger consulted with him a long time before construction began." Will was about to continue but stopped short. Tucking his chin into his chest, he retreated behind the horses. Anna turned around and saw that Roger had entered the stable, followed closely by Gilles.

"Well, do you think this stable will do?" Roger asked.

"Yes, m'lord, this stable will most definitely do."

"It's been a long journey, Aubrianne," her husband said, taking her by the elbow. "Perhaps you should rest awhile. Your maid is waiting outside. You'll have ample time later this week to take a full tour, if you're up to it."

Before leaving the stable, she turned to her husband. "Her name, m'lord? My maid, I mean. Does she have a name?"

"What? Yes, of course she has a name," he replied curtly and, after a brief hesitation, he added, "Grainne. Her name is Grainne."

CHAPTER EIGHT
Anna's Wedding Night

Anna stepped into the bright courtyard. She didn't have to search far to find her maid—she was right outside the door. Easily two heads shorter than Anna, her posture was stooped like a much-kicked dog. And, as with everyone else, Grainne wouldn't look directly at her. She gave a slight acknowledging nod before hastening back to the castle. Anna quickened her pace to keep up with the diminutive woman.

It wasn't until they entered the fortress that Grainne finally found her voice. Her words were clipped and so obvious that she needn't have bothered speaking at all. "Great hall. Kitchens. Stairs to my lord's quarters." Anna moved in that direction, but Grainne blocked her path. "My lady, your chamber is this way."

A blush rose on Anna's cheeks; she was glad that Grainne walked ahead. They entered a narrow passage and began climbing a long flight of steps. "There are four sets of stairs, Lady Aubrianne. One for each tower."

There were slits in the thick stone walls, allowing fresh air and light to penetrate the keep. Through them, Anna caught glimpses of green pastures and blue sky. Grainne finally stopped by a heavy wooden door with scrolled iron fittings. The entrance's keystone was marked with a carved rosette. Ahead, there was another arched passageway with more stairs, and Anna asked where they led.

"To the battlements, Lady Aubrianne," her maid answered tersely. "There are similar stairs in each of the four towers. Each set of steps cuts diagonally from tower to tower."

Despite her maid's queer demeanor, Anna was excited. She couldn't wait to explore every nook of the castle. Knowing how to reach the roof and the promise of open skies would allow her to take in the view and familiarize herself with the surrounding land.

Grainne opened the heavy door, surprisingly smooth and silent for its weight, and entered. Anna followed and was delighted to find that her corner suite boasted a large living space, complete with a fireplace and a partitioned area for her toilette. The room had high ceilings and three tall windows. The multipaned center window cut across one corner of her room and faced south. Its mullioned glass was a luxurious rarity so far from court. Flanking the large center window were two tapered arches, angled to offer views to the southeast and southwest. The smaller windows were shuttered, open at present, but not fitted with glass. Thick woven fabrics were suspended above the windows and tied back to allow the day's light to flood the room.

The interior walls were covered in thick tapestries, and there were piles of throws on the sleeping platform. The hearth was located on the inner northwest wall. In front, there was a low table and a worn but comfortable-looking couch flanked on either side with cushioned benches. Anna tested her bed, so firm she was sure it was filled with horsehair. Just like her bed at Chevring, she thought wistfully.

"If you're hungry, Lady Aubrianne, you'll find wine with bread and cheese near the hearth," Grainne offered while staring at the floor. "Your possessions will be delivered shortly. Warm water is coming for your bath."

Hoping to be on friendlier terms with her new maid, Anna commended her. "Thank you, Grainne, you've been thorough. But I must ask you to do one more thing."

"If it is in my power to do so, Lady Aubrianne."

"I would prefer for you to call me Anna. We did not stand for so much formality at Chevring," Anna explained.

Grainne peered nervously from beneath her lashes and stammered, "I—I am sorry, m'lady. Lord Roger has already instructed us on his preferences. It would not do to disappoint his lordship."

"That would be a problem, wouldn't it?" Anna mused, not hiding her irritation. She could see that she'd made Grainne uncomfortable, so she hastened to add, "Perhaps when we know each other better."

Grainne was saved from having to respond when Anna's trunks were brought into the room. Anna was happy to see her belongings again. She liked this room but longed to make it her own. From the few feminine touches, it was clear that this chamber had belonged to Roger's departed wife, Lady Isabel.

When a scullery maid peeked in and explained that there would be a delay with the hot water, Grainne was forced to excuse herself. Anna took her time surveying her new accommodations and thought upon the cold welcome she'd thus far received. Perhaps they were just more formal here. When they got to know her better, she assured herself again, things would be different.

Her maid returned, followed by servants carrying heavy pails of water. Grainne ordered the servants to fill the bathing basin behind the partition. After the water bearers departed, Anna stepped behind to the bath and, with Grainne's assistance, stripped herself of her travel-soiled clothes. She lowered herself into the large basin and found the water deliciously hot. Her skin tingled as she submerged her body from the top of her head to the tips of her toes. Grainne stood by, head lowered and hands outstretched, offering a cloth, and—*miracle of miracles*, Anna thought—*cake soap!* While she washed, her maid bustled about the rest of the room.

When the water cooled, Anna reached for the thick wrap left by Grainne. Her maid had started a fire, and Anna sat near the hearth, settling her head back on the couch. Grainne lifted her heavy tresses and began to comb her wet hair. It was so soothing that, as she rested, Anna fell asleep. Her hair was dry when she woke to Grainne's gentle nudging.

"Apologies, m'lady. Lord Roger will be here soon, and he'll want you prepared."

"Prepared? Ah, yes. My wedding night," she said unsteadily. "When will he arrive, Grainne?"

"In an hour, I should think," Grainne answered. "I've laid out your sleeping attire. And you still have time to eat before his lordship arrives."

Anna touched her bridal bed raiment: a white garment with flowing sleeves, a loose neckline, and drapes that cascaded to the floor. Grainne had poured her another cup of wine, and Anna sipped the sweet concoction before picking at a piece of cheese. Preoccupied with the coming night, she did not notice that her maid had left the chamber.

Strangely, Anna felt more at ease than she had in days. She sipped a little more of the heady wine and, leaning back against the padded cushions of the couch, she thought of her hasty marriage and new life. The warmth of the fireplace and the soporific effects of the drink conspired together, and Anna closed her eyes to allow her mind to wander. Visions of romantic embraces and gentle caresses slipped in and out of her thoughts. Instead of the shadowed man with eyes the color of ink from her dreams, she tried to picture her fair-haired husband. She closed her eyes, imagining her wedding night.

Making no sound, Roger entered his bride's chamber and found her in repose near the fire. This wedding night would be quite different from the first; there would be no meddling father-in-law tottering about to curb his appetite. He studied his new bride, and at first glance, he thought her to be sleeping. But then he smiled, seeing her flushed face, imagining what she was expecting.

"Aubrianne," he whispered, and watched as her eyes fluttered opened. Seeing him so close, she blushed; he chuckled and held out his hand. Still smiling at her, he led her to the bed, where he removed her gown, allowing it to fall to the floor in a soft puddle. She held her breath as he circled around, examining her from every angle.

Her blush had warmed her skin, flushing the tops of her breasts with pink. Still, she stood proudly, his equal. Her tall form was classic in its lines: straight shoulders, perfectly shaped breasts, each just a handful, and a tapered waist that rounded out sensually to her hips. And her backside. Roger's breath caught in anticipation. He felt the beginnings of his arousal. From the way her breathing heightened, Roger could tell that his wife's blood was stirring too. She would be a passionate lover.

He listened to her as she sighed. No doubt she was fantasizing about a loving husband. His hands skimmed her waist to allow her anticipation to grow. But the expression on Roger's face as he stood behind her was anything but loving. Roger had enough passionate lovers as it was. What he wanted from Aubrianne was much more stirring to his blood.

Gracefully, yet with terrifying speed, he shoved her onto the bed. One hand moved to the back of her neck. He suppressed an almost gleeful shout when he heard his wife's surprised gasp. Beyond excited, his hand shot down to undo his breeches. She was truly magnificent, muscular and smooth, with curves that promised to develop as she grew to a more mature woman.

• • •

At first, it was as though her dream was coming true. And then, suddenly, it was real, and ugly. She couldn't move. He'd knocked the wind from her chest. When she regained her breath, she found herself pinned to her bed. Though she could not see her husband, she heard his breath growing thicker with each passing moment. Why would he not let her go so that she could show him her willingness to be his wife?

He levered her legs apart with his knee and forced himself into her unprepared body. When she bucked in protest against his violent entry, she heard him groan with pleasure. Pain followed then. An excruciating pain that she could never have imagined. Her body clenched against his relentless attack.

As he plunged deeper, the thin barrier that held her innocence was rent. And still he went on, withdrawing and thrusting, again and again. Anna's voice abandoned her. He held her neck to the bed and, in his frenzy, pressed her face into the blankets. She couldn't draw breath; black spots crept over the edges of her vision.

And then her neck was free. She felt him grab her hips to force himself deeper one last time. When his seed exploded, she screamed. Finished, he withdrew as quickly as he had entered and reached for her discarded sleeping gown.

So stunned by the rapidity of his assault, Anna could form no clear thoughts. She tucked herself into a ball, drawing a blanket over her battered body. Was this how it was between man and wife? She closed her eyes against the truth of it: she was his to do with whatever he wanted; it was his right as her husband.

Over the roaring in her head, she heard him speak. "I'll be riding out tomorrow, and when I return, I will summon you to my chamber."

Anna watched through tear-swollen eyes as he cleaned himself with her sleeping gown. He threw the garment on the bed next to her face. She closed her eyes against the sight of her blood.

His hot breath was suddenly on her face. "Aubrianne. Aubrianne!" His expression was benign. "You were everything I imagined. Please don't worry yourself. I'll return to you soon." After securing his breeches, he strode from her chamber.

The pain inside was so acute she mewled like an injured animal. It pulsed with her every heartbeat. She was afraid to move. Finally, she slipped into unconsciousness.

Hours must have passed, for when she woke, the embers of the fire had gone out and the room was cold. She slid off the bed, then half crawled to the other side of her chamber. Each throb of pain reminded her of every vicious thrust she'd endured.

She found a pail and vomited. When all the food and wine was ejected from her body, she vomited again, willing the bile from her stomach, all the while praying that Roger's seed would be purged as well. It was then that she remembered that the bath was still full.

Anna lowered herself into the bracing water, then scrubbed herself raw to be clean of Roger's seed. She forced her head under, coming up only after her lungs screamed for air, and then let her head rest against the basin's edge. After the initial shock of her cold bath, her pulse slowed and the pain that came with each heartbeat drifted farther and farther away. As her breathing calmed, she sank deeper into the basin's chilly water.

Her husband's face as he'd left her chamber had been horrific in its passivity. Behind the frozen blue ice of his eyes, there was a promise of the nights to come. Anna's mind darkened, and she slipped under the surface of the bath, staring at the world outside her watery cocoon. Her body succumbed to the numbing cold; try as she might, she could not escape its embrace. Before her eyelids closed, a soft glow surrounded her. At least there would be light, she thought. And her final breath bubbled to the surface.

• • •

"Don't interfere. Don't interfere," Grainne chided herself. "Your heart broke when Lady Isabel died. Don't attach yourself to this girl. Help her. See her to bed. Feed her and nurse her in the morning. Do not befriend her."

She'd done too much already, truth be told. Still, there was no harm in giving help when it was not expected, especially if she hid her actions from Lord Roger and his soldiers. She thought about the wine she had given her new mistress. Her lady hadn't noticed the faint trace of fairy cup in the drink, for Grainne had added a touch of honey to cover the bitterness of the sense-dulling herb.

Upon entering the chamber, Grainne noticed the cold first, and went to the hearth to stoke the fire. She turned to the bed and saw her lady's bloody gown. Panic seized her heart, and her eyes raced to the windows. They were shuttered and latched.

Then she noticed the trail of blood on the floor. Grabbing her lantern, she raced behind the partition. The stench of vomit and the coppery smell of blood reached her nose before her eyes beheld the basin. Her lady, eyes open but unseeing, was under the water. The warm cast of yellow candlelight did nothing to diminish the blue tinge on Lady Aubrianne's lips.

With a strength belying her size, Grainne lifted the woman from the freezing water. Lady Aubrianne's head came up with a satisfying intake of breath—her heart struggled yet to live.

"Good thing you don't listen to yourself, Grainne," the maid muttered aloud. "You were well on your way to losing your second mistress."

Grainne pulled her mistress onto a thick rug. She grabbed the corners of the carpet and slid her to the couch. With the utmost care, she dried Lady Aubrianne in front of the fire. *Lord save us*, Grainne thought, when she discovered the bruising on her lady's neck. She then spread a clean blanket over the couch. Using all her strength, she pulled her lady onto it, then covered her with another blanket.

She piled more fuel onto the fire. Satisfied that her mistress was as warm as possible, Grainne began removing all traces of violence from the chamber. She had never imagined that Lord Roger had escalated to such cruelty. Her lady would not soon forget this night. But she would, in time, think of this room as a refuge. Quietly, just as she had done years before, she removed a bloodied gown, stripped the bed, and cleaned the floor. Then she dumped the stained bathwater into the privy hole that would eventually deposit its crimson contents to the ground outside.

After Grainne left the room, she made her way to the kitchen to find a kettle. There was a candle already burning on the work block.

"I'm so very sorry, Grainne," spoke a soft, female voice.

"Yes, well, I'm a little more prepared this time around, Doreen. I won't allow my heart to be broken as it was with Lady Isabel."

Grainne's longtime friend smiled sadly and put her arms around her. "Of course, you'll try, but I know you. You'll care for this one too."

Grainne sighed and looked at the tray on the table. Doreen had prepared tea. There were other items there, too, that she would need to nurse her new mistress. The road ahead would be a long one, and it helped knowing she was not alone.

CHAPTER NINE

The King's Consideration

Queen Juliana handed her sister's letter to her husband, King Godwin. He read the pages, then sat heavily next to his wife. She could see the worry in his eyes. It had been growing over the last two years, as word from his allies in Nifolhad lessened and eventually ceased. Their latest emissaries had never returned and were considered lost.

Her husband was examining the documents on her desk, a mixture of ancient scrolls and their translations, many in her own hand. They'd pored over the parchments for hours. "Kathryn has given Lark the dagger?" he asked, plucking from the table another ancient blade and turning it in his hand. The handle was worn, but the knife's edge was keen. Juliana nodded.

"And you agree with your sister's translation of the charts?" he asked, testing the blade with the pad of his thumb.

"Yes, my lord," she answered. "And we both believe that such a girl's existence heralds an upheaval for Aurelia."

"This dagger's prophecy, you're sure it is linked to the other's?" Godwin asked.

"I am, my love," Juliana maintained. She pointed to the handle of the dagger and the intricate metalwork. Though ancient, bright silver stars gleamed from their bed of lapis lazuli. "Look, here, along the blade, most of the etchings are worn off. But in the fuller, you can still make out the runes. '...*with night do stars find strength.*'"

"No more than that," Godwin mused. "This is thin advice indeed to plot our course."

"What is coming will not be deterred," she said. "Even without the translations, we know that strife is brewing, and the cause is Diarmait, Steward King of Nifolhad. We must grasp every advantage. And if mating the two blades will strengthen our cause, then it needs be done."

NICOLE ELIZABETH KELLEHER

Her king handed the dagger to her, nodding solemnly. She thought of her nephew Larkin, the most talented of the Royal Guard, and his determination to remain a bachelor.

"Have you traced the girl's lineage? Do you know her identity?" her husband asked.

"This blade has long been absent from its home," the queen noted, for its sheath was missing. "Its brothers, shield and sword, are somewhere in this kingdom, and intact, I believe. As to with whom they reside, there are a few possibilities. The strongest connection to the old bloodline lies with Lady Estelle of Chevring and her two daughters." Juliana thought about the simple escutcheon of silver stars in a field of blue, not seen for generations. There was worry in her eyes when next she spoke. "My correspondence to Estelle has gone unanswered."

"I've received word that the road between Chevring and Stolweg has been traveled much of late," her husband added. "And so it comes back to Roger of Stolweg, for he is married to the eldest Chevring girl. Perhaps it is time to learn more about the man."

"A mission is a goodly reason to keep Larkin from court," Juliana agreed. "But he should not be alone, I think. Perhaps Trian and Warin should go as well—so opposite are their temperaments that Larkin may find himself moving to a middle ground. Too long has my nephew dallied with my ladies."

Her husband chuckled. "Methinks your nephew's mind is strong enough to not be swayed by Warin; he has always made his own decisions." He patted her hand reassuringly when she frowned. "But I agree," he added. "We shall send Warin and Trian too. The hot and the cold may temper Larkin."

Late into the night, they discussed Aurelia's future. Queen Juliana told him more of that which she and Kathryn had read in the stars. He in turn spoke of the rumors circulating throughout their kingdom, rumors that only confirmed the Queen's predictions. The next day, Larkin and Warin were sent to Whitmarsh and to Larkin's mentor, Lord Baldric. Trian would join them there, and together they would ride to Ragallach, Lord Roger's birthplace.

CHAPTER TEN

Awakenings

Anna woke, and in that instant between sleep and waking, her mind was blessedly blank. But as her senses sharpened, the horror of her wedding night coiled around her head. And like a snake, it spit its venomous images across her mind. Her cry broke forth. Oh, she ached, deep inside. The pain crested, and she gave it voice with a moan. She felt a gentle touch on her shoulder and tried to shrink away. "Shhh, be still, m'lady," a woman's voice soothed. "You're safe now."

She tasted warm tea, sweet, and smelling of mint and chamomile. Her mind cleared for a moment, and she recognized Grainne.

"Here, m'lady, drink a bit more. It will help you sleep." Anna felt an ebbing of the pain.

When she woke next, the sun was already making its way west. The windows of her chamber were open, and a soft breeze played about the room. The pain she had suffered earlier had changed to a dull ache. The memories, though, were jagged and sharp. For the first time in her life, Anna was afraid. She did not belong here. She would have to escape to Chevring. Tully would take her there in half the time it took to arrive. She could camp simply, a blanket under the stars, or not camp at all and sleep in her saddle.

Roger would be gone for a week. Plenty of time to make the ride south. Her parents would protect her. But then she remembered that her parents were indebted to Roger. What would he do to her family? They could lose everything.

East, Anna thought next. She could plead her case to King Godwin. But they would send her back. Roger would smooth things over and make her look like a foolish girl.

West. No one would know her in the west. She could hide in a seaside village. She could work. West, she decided. Anna had been so intent on planning her escape that she hadn't noticed that Grainne was standing beside the bed.

"It won't work, m'lady," Grainne said sadly. "Whatever it is you're planning. I can see it written all over your face. You think you can run away," Grainne said as she prepared more tea. Anna felt dismay that her thoughts had been so obvious on her face. *Damn that door, too*, Anna thought. It was much too quiet.

"He'll make it his mission to find you, m'lady. And after he tortures everyone in your life that you care about, he will kill you."

"Grainne, what are you going on about?" Anna asked with forced ease.

"You've probably been thinking about where to hide," Grainne carried on. "Not south, he'll hurt your family. Perhaps east, with the north being impassible. But the best option is west. And if you do manage to elude him, what then?"

"I could work," Anna stated, lifting her chin proudly. "Or, I could keep moving."

"And your horse? Such a mount would not be noticed? Are you willing to leave your horse? Sell him perhaps? And then there is your family. Lord Roger is cruel beyond imagining. What do you think will happen to them?"

Anna shook her head and placed her hands over her face. "Why are you telling me this? I don't want to hear it. There has to be a way, for I cannot endure another night with him." Tears streaked down her face. Grainne sat down next to her and pulled her hands away.

"There is something you should know, m'lady," Grainne told her. "It will help you to understand why you must not flee."

Anna listened as her maid told her the story of Lady Isabel, the daughter of the former Lord of Stolweg. About how she resided in the castle with her father. But her father was old and ailing; he wanted his daughter safely wed, and to a man he could count on to take care of Isabel and Stolweg Keep.

Lord Roger's arrival was the answer to his prayers. Isabel was wooed and courted. They fell deeply in love, and a short betrothal followed. Their marriage was an idyllic one. Content, Isabel's father died peacefully in his sleep.

"Lord Roger had long been handling the daily management needed to keep Stolweg profitable, m'lady," Grainne explained. "We embraced him as one of our own. He had toiled side by side with us. So when the liberties we'd enjoyed for so many years slipped through our fingers, we never even noticed the leak. He put a stop to the celebrations and made it difficult for us to worship. But the change was so gradual that no one thought to speak out. We were well fed, well housed, and well clothed. An occasional lashing could be endured.

"And Lady Isabel, so in love with Lord Roger, refused at first to see what he was becoming. When summoned to his chamber, she went willingly. She never told me what was done to her, but I could see that she was hurting. She stopped leaving the keep, afraid to go outside. Later, she never left her chamber, except when ordered to Lord Roger's room. I waited for her on those horrible nights. I gave her tea to help her forget.

"Then one night, I helped her to retire," Grainne continued. "She was so calm that evening. She dismissed me before I could give her the tea. Perhaps if I had stayed…"

"What happened, Grainne?" Anna asked.

Grainne sighed. "She was found the next day on the ground below this chamber." Anna stared at the window while Grainne relived the morning. "I was here, delivering her breakfast, and thought it odd that she'd already arisen. Even more so that she was gone from her chamber."

Grainne grabbed Anna's hands and cried, "Lord Roger burst into the room. He was so angry, yelling at me for my negligence. He grabbed the back of my neck and pushed me to the window. He unlatched the shutters and forced me to look down.

"Lady Isabel was crumpled on the ground below." She swallowed hard before continuing, "Oh, dear God, I didn't know what I was seeing. After I realized, Lord Roger lost all control. He almost pushed me out the window after her. If he had not been interrupted…"

"Grainne, what am I supposed to do?" Anna pleaded. "I cannot stay. I cannot leave."

"You must grow stronger, m'lady. You must find a way to live with what has happened. With what *will* happen."

"I can't, Grainne," Anna cried.

"No, m'lady, you can," she insisted. "You are here for a reason. And I will help you any way I can."

Something shifted deep inside Anna's heart, and she worried about its portent. "Do not count on me overmuch, Grainne. I do not think that I am the savior for whom you are questing." A sudden resolve came over her, and she moved with care to the edge of her bed. Grainne protested, saying that she should rest, it was too soon. She should drink more tea.

"No more, Grainne," Anna ordered. "Your tea dulls my senses. If I am to survive, I need to feel alive. Please help me to dress. I want to check my horses before the sun sets." Her horses would keep her strong, Anna vowed to herself.

After dressing, Anna walked unaided to the door. She studied its smooth hinges. "Hand me the stoking iron from the hearth, Grainne."

Her maid did as bidden, and Anna grasped the cold iron in her hands. She raised it and swung down at the middle hinge with all her strength. The metals sparked against each other, and Anna swung at the hinge a second time. Not satisfied with her work, she struck once more. With a satisfied smirk, she gave the dented poker back to Grainne.

They looked at the hinge and saw three identical marks, each perfectly scored into the joints where the hardware was married. When Anna pulled the door open, it still moved effortlessly, but the sound of metal grinding against metal screeched in protest. Never again would another enter her chamber unremarked. Anna ignored Grainne's astonished face until she realized that, finally, someone at Stolweg was smiling at her.

CHAPTER ELEVEN

Pasties

With Grainne at her side, Anna made her way to the courtyard. "Are you sure you're up to this, my lady? No one would think poorly of you if you kept to your quarters a few more days."

"They know?" Anna exclaimed. Her maid lowered her eyes. Anna realized why everyone had avoided making eye contact with her. She had mistakenly thought their behavior was due to their loyalty to Lady Isabel. But no, the people knew firsthand of her husband's cruelty. Their fear had kept them silent. Anna wondered how much abuse they'd already borne.

She held her head high. "Don't answer, Grainne. Of course they know. And it is for that very reason that I must continue on my way."

Anna released Grainne's arm, stood taller, and left the cool comfort of the stone fortress. Each step left her aching, but she refused to be slowed. She entered the stable, and Tullian let out a pleased whinny. Anna scratched him just below his forelock, his favorite spot. "You look much like the king rooster of the coop here, Tully-boy. Enjoying yourself?" Tullian rested his massive head on Anna's shoulder as she patted his neck. "What do you say we go for a nice ride tomorrow? Get a feel for our new home." Her horse nickered companionably.

Anna stepped down the line of stalls to check the mares. At least two would be in season within the week. Tullian would have a busy schedule. She turned and was greeted by Will.

"Good morning, m'lady. Can I get you anything?" he offered with a tentative smile.

"Not today, Will. I'm just stopping by to say hello to my friends," she answered. "But I'll need Tullian saddled for a ride tomorrow."

Will was saved from having to reply when his father arrived. "We would be pleased to escort you," Gilles said. "There are some excellent grazing areas nearby that I'd like you to see."

NICOLE ELIZABETH KELLEHER

Anna considered his offer. Until now, Gilles's only words to her had been a warning. His tone was conciliatory, at least. Could she trust him? "All right, Gilles," she replied, deciding to give him a chance to prove himself.

She walked with the stable master and his son and introduced them properly to the Chevring mares, noting their specific traits and personalities. "Great care must be taken when choosing mares to breed with our stallions," she explained to Will. "The Chevring chargers have distinct characteristics that set them apart from other horses, the dappled coat of silver and gray being the most prominent."

Anna looked outside. The sun had dipped below the curtain wall. All of a sudden, she felt exhausted, so she gave Tullian one last scratch. To father and son, she offered her goodbyes. "I'll see you both on the morrow."

It had been foolish to spend so much time on her feet, she thought. But she would not let those at Stolweg see her weaken. The dull ache inside her grew worse with each step. When Grainne arrived and took her arm as if directing her to the castle, Anna sighed with relief.

They reached the foot of the stairs, and Anna groaned in dismay. "Never you mind these stairs, my lady," Grainne ordered. "We'll go slowly, and I'll support you."

Her maid's arm encircled her waist and pulled her forward and up. Anna would lay wager that Grainne could carry her all the way, slung over her shoulder if necessary. It was funny how her first impression of Grainne had been that the maid was a small, slightly plump woman in her forties. But Grainne was all strength underneath her clothes—her arms were like iron bands. And her age was younger than Anna had first deduced, perhaps on the cusp of thirty. Grainne's skin was clear, her face heart-shaped, and her nose as pert as her new demeanor. Anna realized that it was her maid's eyes that aged her. Grainne's eyes had seen a lifetime.

They reached the door to her chamber. The metal squealed, making them both jump, then titter nervously. Anna swept her eyes across her room and marveled at its transformation. Grainne had been busy. Her belongings had been unpacked, bringing some cheer and a small amount of homesickness to her heart. A second table had been procured and placed in one corner of the room. Anna discovered that her small chest, wherein lay the ingredients for her special balm, had been placed on top. A wooden dowel, strung with the many herbs and flowers that she had collected during her journey, hung above. The largest bunch, lavender, hung on a separate rod nearby.

Grainne gave her a cup of warm tea. And although Anna took the drink willingly enough, her maid read the question in her eyes just the same.

"Simple herbal tea, m'lady. Chamomile, mint, and only a tiny hint of fairy cup," Grainne disclosed. "Not enough to make you sleep."

"I'm curious about the tea yesterday, Grainne. It was extremely sweet. Honey?" At her maid's nod, Anna queried further. "You used it to cover another taste, did you not? There was a hint of something bitter."

"Wormwood, m'lady, and a goodly amount at that."

"Ah, that explains the deep sleep."

"Are you learned in the healing arts, m'lady?" Grainne asked, examining the dowel with the drying plants. "You've collected some herbs whose properties are not commonly known: king's clover and horsetail are oft overlooked. Is that what you used for Gilles's cheek? He has nary a mark."

"Horsetail, yes. And calendula. My grandmother was responsible for that part of my education," Anna replied. "She instructed me on where to find the rarer herbs and wildflowers." Anna directed Grainne to her pot of salve.

"It smells lovely," Grainne said. "That'll be the lavender, of course."

Anna sat near the fire where Grainne had set out her evening tea. On her bed, she noticed a small sachet containing her favorite purple bloom. It was a thoughtful touch, and she regarded Grainne with fresh eyes. "You seem to have noticed my penchant for this delicate flower."

"Well, yes, m'lady, from your handkerchiefs," Grainne noted, picking up a folded kerchief to study the fine embroidery: a tiny, pale green stem with a purple bud. "Why did you pick lavender?"

"I didn't, really; it chose me," Anna explained between sips of tea. "My mother said that I was an active babe, hated sleeping because I wanted to see what everyone else was doing. She and my grandmother hung bouquets of the stuff around my cradle to soothe me. Since then, I have always loved the smell."

Anna finished her tea and ate a little off the plate that Grainne had provided. She was bone-weary and had much to accomplish in the next few days. It was time for rest. When Grainne asked if she felt fit enough to ride the next day, Anna was ready with an answer.

"Riding tomorrow and being with the horses—that is where I will find my strength. I promise," she added, "no galloping. Just smooth, easy gaits."

Grainne had turned as white as the linen she was holding. "You needn't worry about me, Grainne. If you would be more at ease, you could ride with us."

"Ride? With you? Oh dear me, no! I could never. Please, no, m'lady. I could never get on one of those monsters."

"You don't mean to tell me you don't like horses!" Anna exclaimed, astounded by the idea.

"I think more that they do not like me, m'lady. The beasts can sense my fear."

"We'll see, Grainne," Anna encouraged her. "I can help you to come to terms with the *monsters*. I'll not make you ride them," Anna amended when she saw her maid's frightened face. "Only touch them. For a start."

"Perhaps, m'lady, perhaps," Grainne conceded, pulling a sleeping gown from one of Anna's trunks. "But for now, you need to sleep."

• • •

The next morning, Anna woke feeling stronger. The pain was present but manageable. There was a soft rap on her door, and then it screamed as Grainne entered. She carried a breakfast tray with tea, cheese, a hefty chunk of bread, and tender spring carrots. Anna munched happily on the carrots to freshen her breath, then pocketed a couple for Tullian.

She asked Grainne to inform Gilles that she would meet him at the stable in an hour. First, she wanted to explore. Reluctantly, her maid left her on her own. Anna climbed the stairs leading to the parapets at the top of the castle.

After the dimness of the narrow steps, the bright daylight dazzled her eyes. She stepped out into the sunshine and breathed in the fresh air that swept across the top of the west tower. The wild woods below continued as far as she could see.

She turned to survey the lands around the keep. Moving northward, she spared only a moment for the distant and foreboding mountains. She had once thought them beautiful in their harshness. Now, they only reminded her of Roger.

Anna walked along the wide parapet to the eastern tower. Turning toward the wooded hills below, she had to shield her eyes against the sun glaring off the lake.

Finally, she made her way to her own tower, south. Below her, the land cascaded in terraces to the southeast before gently climbing again. The hills rising beyond the lake were soft and rolling and forested in trees whose spring leaves were so light they glowed in the morning sun. To the distant south, Anna saw the rise whence her first view of Stolweg was beheld. The fields below were perfect. But she could no longer gaze upon them and think of a comforting quilt. Now they were too orderly.

Anna would have stayed atop the tower all day, but she didn't want to be late for her ride with Gilles and Will. On her way past the east tower's corner chamber, she noticed that the door was ajar. If she hurried, she had just enough time to take a quick peek. She pushed the door open and gasped. The armory lay before her. Every type of weapon, from sword and staff to crossbow and quarrel to longbow and hammer, was neatly arranged on supports throughout the room. Shields bearing the standard of Stolweg, a four-petaled rose encircled by a thorny vine, were hung with precision along one wall. And some of the most beautiful armor Anna had ever beheld sparkled as if polished daily. Everything gleamed in the sunlight that flooded the chamber.

"Ahem!"

Anna whirled around at the sound and instinctively lifted her hands, both to protect herself and to strike out if necessary. A barrel-chested man whose height measured no more than her own stood in front of her, hands on hips. He had startling blue eyes, made more so by the reddest hair she'd ever beheld. But his skin was smooth and tan, not ruddy like one would expect. It was an exotic combination.

"You shouldn't be in this room," he stated. "These weapons are dangerous. If mishandled, they could injure you."

Anna was fully aware of the picture she presented. After all, few women in her position felt comfortable enough to walk around in riding breeches, even if the long panels of her overtunic looked more like a skirt than a coat. She steeled herself, bringing her eyes level with his. "I am well acquainted with the proper use of the tools here."

At his raised eyebrow, she added, "I don't think we have been introduced. I am Lady Aubrianne. And you are?" *Good*, she thought, *that captured his attention*. By his dress, he was clearly a soldier. "I have met several of Roger's men, but I have not had the"—she paused; the word *pleasure* was unacceptable—"occasion of meeting you before." She didn't miss the dark flash that passed over his eyes at the mention of Roger's soldiers.

"Please excuse my brusqueness, Lady Aubrianne. I am Cellach, *Stolweg's* master-at-arms."

"I see," she replied, noting that he allied himself with the keep and not the master. "Then this room is your doing." Seeing his puzzled face,

Anna added, "You take great pride in your duties; I have never seen an armory so well kept. There is a great deal of artistry in the placement of each item, and I would not dream of disturbing a single thing. Now, if you'll excuse me." His scrutiny of her was making her uncomfortable.

"Lady Aubrianne, I meant no offense," he said. "These weapons are my responsibility, yes. But when Lord Roger is away, my responsibility grows to encompass the people of Stolweg. To have someone injured on my watch, especially his lordship's new bride…"

Anna turned and regarded him. She had been ready to think the worst of him, but his graciousness halted that decision. "No harm done to either party, Cellach. Let us forget this small misunderstanding." She departed then, leaving him to his own thoughts.

• • •

Her escorts and horses were ready and waiting at the stable when she arrived. Once mounted, Gilles took the lead, Anna followed, and Will brought up the rear. They rode through the courtyard, out the main gate, and then turned southeast. Their pace was too slow.

"A nice canter would be faster, don't you think?" she suggested to Gilles. Reacting to some imperceptible movement from her, Tullian leapt forward, and before they knew it, they had reached the mill. The crossing was made of sturdy wooden planks, its span wide enough that a pair of oxen yoked together could pass over. When a man stepped out of the building, Gilles lifted his hand in salute. "Hail to you, Carrick."

"A good day for a ride, friends," the miller answered, nodding in deference to Anna. "Maggie," he called out to a young woman standing in the doorway, "come meet the new Lady of Stolweg. M'lady, this is my daughter, Maggie."

She was a pretty girl, Anna thought, perhaps the same age as she. But there was an odd gleam in her eye, as if she were assessing her new mistress. After the girl curtsied, Anna tilted her head slightly and smiled, then nudged Tullian forward.

Once past the mill, Gilles pointed east. "There are fine grazing pockets to the south, m'lady. Today, I thought we should stay closer to the keep and find a few quiet groves for Tullian and the mares."

True to his word, the places Gilles showed her were perfect for the horses. They climbed the next hill and dismounted to rest. From Tullian's back, Anna removed the saddlebags containing their lunch. Will had brought a blanket and spread it on the grass. Will and Gilles sat opposite Anna on the blanket, and she passed out their meal. To her delight, Grainne had packed half a dozen meat pasties. They were a shade hotter than warm, and she breathed in the deliciously rich aroma.

"Cook must be in a good mood today," she announced. Gilles grinned, and Will elbowed his father's ribs. "What aren't you telling me?" Anna demanded.

"Well, Cook is me mum, m'lady," Will explained. "Her mood's always improved when the lord's away." She noted that Will's father was suddenly on edge and wondered if he was nervous that his son's words would be reported back to Roger.

"These are the finest beef pasties I've ever tasted," Anna announced, hoping to ease the wariness from Gilles's face.

"You know," Gilles finally confided, "she rarely makes these. It drives Lord Roger to distraction because he loves them so much. I think my Doreen is the one person at Stolweg that he's afraid to order around."

• • •

In the days that followed, her Tullian and a few of the mares were set loose together. Anna would know in less than a month if he'd managed to get one of them with foal. But more than the breeding program was on Anna's mind. Her husband was due to return the next day.

CHAPTER TWELVE

Lord Roger's Return

Even with Grainne's tea, Anna didn't sleep on the eve of Roger's return. Thoughts wheeled in her head like great flocks of starlings, darting again and again in different directions. She tried everything to clear her mind. When nothing helped, she alighted from her bed and, in the dull light of the fire's banked embers, found and lit a candle.

Even though her body was at her husband's disposal, her soul was her own. She swallowed hard, thinking about her wedding night. She'd been naïve, but refused to blame herself. With a shudder, she blocked out the much-too-peaceful image of her almost watery grave. She'd nearly died that night. Not because of the assault, but because she permitted her mind to sink into an unfathomable darkness. Had it not been for Grainne, she would've drowned.

The thought caused a surge of rage to wash through her. Rage was one emotion she could and would control. It made her feel alive. Her other emotions were now safely locked away in what was left of her heart. She sat near the warm hearth, remembering every detail of that evening, and swung the memories away from the fire burning inside her, leaving them to simmer out of the flames.

She had tricked herself into believing in fairy-tale romance and passionate embraces. Some pain was natural when a woman's maidenhead was pierced. But Roger had not made love to her, had he? Next time she would be better prepared.

The herbs, roots, and wildflowers were still neatly arranged above the small table next to the door. Physical healing was another area she could control. Anna said a prayer of thanks that her grandmother had taught her so well.

Suddenly, the look in Grainne's eyes the day after Roger's attack came to mind and gave her pause. That same expression had come from

Gilles and, now that she thought about it, was in Cellach's gaze as well. They all had looked at her expectantly, as if their long years of waiting for a miracle were over. Was this the purpose of her training? Was this the duty of which her grandmother had spoken?

"Duty to my people?" Anna asked herself. "First, duty to myself." While solving the physical problem, Anna had unconsciously fortified the emotional wound as well. Stone by stone, she would erect a wall around her heart.

• • •

It was around midday when Roger returned. She witnessed the people— *her people* now—wither back to nothing. Her husband came through the main gate and into the stable where she was checking on a mare named Rina.

Gorman, Lord Roger's right-hand man, dismounted and yelled for Will. He gave the young man a hard cuff to the head. Gorman was a cunning soldier, and Anna had heard that he took pleasure in hurting others. He was currently making sport of bullying Will.

As soon as Roger dismounted, Gilles stepped forward and led the horse away for its rubdown. Her husband approached her, smiling as if nothing had happened, and her blood froze.

"Which of the mares will breed first, Aubrianne?" he demanded.

"We've already begun, m'lord," she replied with forced calm. "Tullian and Rina have mated, and I believe that we can expect a foal by early spring next year. Dragonfly will be next."

Anna had worked on masking her emotions during his absence. She stared blandly at her husband's surprise and doubted not that he had expected to see her cower.

"Very good, then," Roger spoke. He left the stable, throwing one last remark over his shoulder. "I expect you in my chamber in two hours, Aubrianne."

Anna stood in the center of the stable, the ice in his words having immobilized her. Thankfully, Gilles and Will pretended that they hadn't heard her husband's menacing tone. But Gorman loitered near the entrance. She made a show of checking on Tullian and the mares, humming soft nonsense words as she went along. She glanced under Tullian's neck and through his long mane. Gorman followed her every move. He was waiting for her, playing some devious game. Anna squared her shoulders, lifted her chin, and walked purposefully to the door. When he lurched forward as she passed, she halted.

"Isn't there something you should be doing, Gorman?" she demanded. She could see that he had meant to scare her, and his disappointment at not doing so was as plain as day on his face.

He fumbled for a moment before offering a lame excuse. "Beg pardon, my lady. I was just resting a moment. I seem to have pinched my neck while standing here."

Anna stepped closer to him, boldly meeting his rude stare. He smelled of two and twenty foul things, and she lifted her hand to cover her nose. "Perhaps next time you will attend to your duties instead of loitering here. Standing the way you were, one would think you were needed to hold up the walls of this structure. I suggest you mind your assigned business instead of mine, and give your neck no opportunity to pain you."

"As you say, my lady."

She had called him to task. Checking the urge to gloat, she spun on her heel, her braid whipping out at him, and walked to the castle.

Anna made her way to her chamber quickly, cursing Gorman for delaying her with his malicious game. She now had little more than an hour before her presence was required in Roger's chamber. It was barely enough time to ready herself.

She headed behind the partition to bathe. When her door protested, she didn't jump, so inured was she already to its noise. Grainne carried a tray to the table near the fire. "I've brought you some food. And tea, of course. Would you like me to prepare a plate and cup?"

Steadily, Anna answered. "No, thank you. You see, I've been summoned to his lordship's chamber this eve. If I have time, I'll eat before I retire."

"As you will, m'lady. Can I bring you anything else?"

"No, Grainne, I'll see you tomorrow. In the morning." Grainne retreated reluctantly but held her tongue.

It was almost time to go, and Anna realized she had no idea what Roger expected her to wear. She couldn't very well walk to his chamber in her sleeping gown. And then it came to her. There would only ever be one thing that she could wear to Roger's chamber: her wedding gown. She would not willingly sully any other garment.

• • •

Roger sat at his desk, his head bent in the study of one of his many ledgers. At his feet, his black mastiff slumbered. He bent down to rub his head affectionately and was rewarded with a contented growl. He remembered the day his father had given him the mastiff. He'd named him Garamantes after the great war dog of olden times.

His brother had been miserable with jealousy that day, and if Roger had not returned to Ragallach, he was sure that his pet would have suffered some fatal accident. He and Garamantes had bonded from the start; the dog only snarled and snapped at his brother. Their father clapped Roger on the back that day, and laughed. And for once, Roger was his favorite child, and Garamantes went unpunished for his transgressions. In fact, Roger encouraged his beast, training him to protect his person at all costs.

Gorman, assigned by his father to protect him, was no match for Garamantes's instincts. The man always gave the dog a wide berth. Roger knew he was reporting everything he did to his father, and it was just as well. His father ruled over his people with a heavy hand, and would certainly approve of Roger's treatment of the people here.

He ruffled the mastiff's wiry coat. "My poor brother," Roger said to the beast, "having to live under our father's thumb. Couldn't have happened to a better person, right, boy?" Garamantes lifted his massive head and licked his master's fingers.

Roger straightened up and closed the ledger on his desk. His wife was due any moment; it would be interesting to see her reaction to Garamantes and his to her. She still hadn't learned her place in the hierarchy of Stolweg. As his father had treated all of his wives, so Roger would treat Aubrianne. To do otherwise would risk losing the respect and fear that he held over the people of Stolweg. And keeping them afraid was integral to all that he wished to accomplish.

There was a tentative rapping at his door. His wife, no doubt. Garamantes sat up, alert to any threat. Roger bade her enter.

• • •

Anna hadn't known that her husband kept a dog; she smiled hopefully at the beast and felt a lessening of the panic gripping her heart. His tail thumped in greeting. Roger whispered a command to the dog. It immediately rose to all four paws and a low growl rolled from its throat like distant thunder. Her husband patted the dog's head with affection and, without looking up, spoke, "You will remain still and silent, and wait until I have need of you."

She stepped to the center of the room to stand as told, facing his bed, with her back to Roger's desk, and waited. Periodically, there was a rustling of parchment and the scratching of quill and ink. The shutters were open, allowing the frigid night air to enter. The small glow in the hearth offered no warmth. Anna began to shiver.

And still she waited, at least two hours judging by the dying embers in the grate. Her legs were stiff and her back ached. Lack of movement made her colder. She stifled a scream.

What was he doing? It occurred to her that she would rather he came at her all at once than making her stand there, unknowing. But that was exactly what Roger wanted her to feel: helpless and frightened. No, she decided, an attack like before would be much worse.

"You may go." Roger had spoken so unexpectedly that she jumped. "I expect you back at the same time tomorrow." She hadn't even realized that he'd risen from his desk, and now he stood before her. He lifted her chin with his finger. "What was it you said once, in the clearing? Ah, I remember now. 'Your request is my pleasure.' I would like to hear you say that when I give you an order. Now, go. I will see you tomorrow evening." His finger remained under her chin.

Anna focused on her husband's handsome face. He was waiting for her to do something and was growing impatient. She swallowed and spoke almost inaudibly.

"What was that?"

"Your request is my pleasure," she managed to choke out. A queer look came into his eyes: part satisfaction and part something else that she was too afraid to name. But she had to know. She couldn't stop herself from asking the question that had haunted her since the consummation of their vows. "Why? Why did you...?"

"Because I can," he answered when it was clear that she could not finish her question.

"But it doesn't have to be that way between us." Terrified, she blundered on. "We could find pleasure in each other's company."

"I have whores for pleasure. You are nothing more than property. My chattel." His fingers plucked at the velvet of her gown. "Even this dress belongs to me. You are mine to do with as I wish. And that is the most pleasurable thing I can imagine."

CHAPTER THIRTEEN

Larkin patted his great Chevring steed as he turned him toward the place he now thought of as home: Whitmarsh. Weeks ago, Lord Baldric had given him this mission, wanting information on Lord Roger. Few in the realm knew much about the man. And those who had met him, Larkin included, hadn't liked him. So Larkin had ridden out, along with his fellow guards Trian and Warin, northwest to Ragallach, to the place where Roger had been born.

It had taken them weeks to reach this small but vital region. Nowhere else in Godwin's kingdom did Nifolhad come so close to touching Aurelia. With a strong wind, it was only days by ship across the Western Sea. Ragallach's coastline was to Godwin's realm as a watchtower was to any stronghold.

On Ragallach's western and northern borders, impenetrable cliffs dove hundreds of feet to the ocean below, a natural curtain wall; its eastern border consisted of near-impenetrable mountains. Down the length of the territory was a narrow strip of pasture, perhaps only a few miles wide, continuing down the coast for leagues. It was this strip of land that gave nourishment to the one industry of Ragallach: sheep.

After the Great War, Roger's ancestors hadn't resumed trade with King Cedric of Nifolhad. The former Lord of Ragallach, Roger's father, had a long memory and had lost friends and family alike to the violent battles, more so than any other region in the kingdom. The refusal to barter continued until Roger's parents passed away and Roger took over. He immediately grasped the opportunity to trade, and soon Ragallach was rich from its prized wool.

"Baldric will be disappointed," Warin groused, interrupting Larkin's thoughts. "Either the people of Ragallach, and therefore Roger, have nothing to hide, or else they've been threatened into such subservience that they are afraid to speak, and by an absent lord, no less."

"I'd wager odds on the latter," Larkin said to his longtime friend. Though not his closest confrere, Larkin trusted Warin with his life.

When none of the men of Ragallach were inclined to speak frankly, Larkin and Warin had tried their hand with the fairer sex. But the women of Ragallach had been impervious to their charms. He cast his glance at Trian, his most trusted friend, and as usual, the great bear of a man remained silent. But Larkin knew his friend as well as he knew himself. He had something on his mind. So he waited, knowing Trian would speak when he was ready.

Warin, on the other hand, couldn't stop complaining. "This rain is interminable. I'll not be happy until we cross the mountains and into a fairer clime."

Larkin smirked, enjoying anything that made Warin uncomfortable. Experience had taught him that the best way to quiet Warin was to agree with him. "This is a miserable place," he concurred, "and a waste of time." They rode on, the hooves of their mounts making the only conversation, a sucking and splashing of mud.

"They were broken, those people," Trian said, finally letting go of what had been gnawing at his mind. "Did you see? Especially the women."

"What women?" Warin growled.

And there it was, thought Larkin, the crux of what had bothered him. He waited for Trian to put to words what he'd noticed but not recognized.

"Even the girls, they were clothed head to toe. Did you notice they all covered their hair with scarves? Not completely, but enough to act as guimples," Trian noted.

It was true, Larkin realized. Women hadn't covered their hair in Aurelia since before the Great War. He knew of only one place that continued the tradition.

"Nifolhad," Warin supplied, as if reading his mind. "I'll be da—" He was stopped from saying more by what sounded like a woman singing. Soon, the smell of roasting meat filtered through the rain. The soft glow of a window drew them forward like oil through a wick. "I will be damned," Warin repeated, "a tavern!"

• • •

If Warin weren't careful, Larkin thought with a small amount of relish, the pert little barmaid sitting in his lap might migrate to Trian. She'd already cast a longing eye in Larkin's direction, but he'd warded off her affections, leaving her fluttering eyelashes wilted. He hadn't been as interested of late in the game of hearts that he and Warin played, and was content to listen to the local gossip, hoping to hear something of worth to take back to the king.

The tavern keeper's welcome had been so warm when they'd shuffled in from the rain that Larkin wasn't sure if they were still within the borders of Ragallach. Thus far, they had been placed near the great hearth with its roaring fire, been fed a hearty stew, hot enough to warm their bones, and were kept supplied with one of the best honey meads that he'd ever tasted. Trian was so satisfied that he'd broken into song. His beautiful tenor voice rang true and clear through the tavern. The barmaid couldn't keep her eyes from him.

Larkin had heard this sad ballad from Trian's northern home of Cathmara before. It spoke of the legend of Fishwife Point, a perilous outcropping that stretched into the Northern Sea. Many a ship had been wrecked on the jagged rocks hidden under the surface of the waves at high tide. At low tide, a person could walk to the tip of the natural jetty, a quarter league from the coast. The lyrics told the tale of the young wife of a fisherman. Newly married, he vowed to return to her every night; she vowed to wait for him. Out to sea he sailed, and his wife watched until his boat disappeared. Each evening, at low tide, she would walk to the point's end and await his return. One evening, as the ballad went, she waited, but he came not. Hours passed, and she kept her vigil even as the tide rose around her. Finally, she saw his boat. But it was too late; the rising sea had cut off her return to the mainland. The waves swept her from her perch, dashing her upon the rocks hidden below. Her husband, seeing her perish, scuttled his boat and joined his beloved in a watery grave. At low tide, the farthest rock of Fishwife Point resembled a woman leaning toward the sea.

As Trian sang the final verse, there was not a dry eye in the room.

...they keep their vows, yet ev'ry day
For still she stands, and waits for he
Whose wat'ry arms encircle she.

Larkin finished his mead and used the end of the song as his cue to head out to the stable where he would bed down in a pile of hay. He nodded to Trian, who had been unsuccessful in turning down another mug of drink. Warin would no doubt find a cozier bed, Larkin mused, as he bade all good night.

Stepping over the threshold, he tucked his chin to his chest in anticipation of the pouring rain. Only, the deluge had ceased. A fine mist hung about him as he made his way to the stable. His destrier, Rabbit, nickered upon hearing him enter, and Larkin scratched his horse affectionately before stretching out in the fresh hay. He was still awake when Trian came in and found a dry spot to spend the night.

Larkin's rest was habitually brief. When he finally fell asleep, it was anything but restful. He dreamed of a young woman with golden-flecked eyes and beautiful hair that curled down her back. He pulled her into his arms and tasted her velvety skin. Her hair smelled of flowers, though he couldn't tell which bloom, and the scent was subtle and fresh and made his lust grow.

But she slipped from his embrace, and the more he stretched his hand to reach her, the farther she seemed to be. He woke, sitting straight up, and peered into the dim stable that the dawn was just illuminating. "Anna," he whispered to himself, shaking his head to clear the image of the face that had haunted him for so long.

He stood and brushed the hay from his clothes, waking Trian in the process. Together, they walked back to the tavern. The scent of smoked pork and fresh eggs poured into the courtyard when they opened the door. Surprisingly, Warin was awake and halfway through his breakfast.

It was early when the three guards started out for Whitmarsh. Still troubled by his dream, Larkin rode behind his friends. Baldric would be disappointed, he thought. Ragallach had given up naught but a tavern with good mead. Warin's jovial manner and running commentary on the barmaid's attributes further darkened Lark's mood. That is, until he focused on the words slipping so easily from his friend's tongue.

"...at least this quest wasn't a total waste," Warin was saying. "That little bird likes to sing."

"What mean you, Warin?" Trian asked. Larkin pulled up next to his fellow guards.

"It turns out that yon pretty thing's grandmother was no less than the midwife at Roger's birth. She's an old woman now, but her mind is still sharp."

"You spoke with her! She's still alive?" Larkin demanded.

"Alive and kicking, but in hiding for years. She believes that her daughter was killed in an attempt by Lord Roger's men to find her. The tavern keeper hides her in a cottage in the woods. In return, she concocts that mead we drank." Warin patted his bulging saddle bag. "A goodly sample for Baldric."

"Out with it, Warin!" Trian ordered in a rare show of impatience. So Warin began the crone's tale of how Lord Roger was delivered into the world and how his mother died soon after.

"But Lady Ascilia did not die. She was alive when Roger was a toddler," Trian countered, remembering what Baldric had told them.

"I said much the same thing. But the old woman insisted, mentioning a name long since forgotten. She told me of Lady Ulicia, daughter to Lady Ascilia of Ragallach and the jewel of her father's eye. She was lost to the sea during a great storm," Warin retold. "The midwife insisted it was Lady Ulicia who gave birth to Lord Roger."

Larkin pondered this strange tale as they rode out of Ragallach and into the northern reaches of Cathmara. Weeks later, they cantered into the courtyard of Whitmarsh Castle and went directly to meet with Lord Baldric.

"So, Lady Ulicia did not perish as believed," Baldric marveled. "She died after bearing a son, leaving her father and mother to raise Roger as their own."

"The midwife revealed that there was no love between Roger and his grandfather," Warin explained. "After Roger's grandmother died, they argued constantly. Then Roger disappeared. He was eighteen or nineteen at the time. When he returned seven years later, he was wealthy, and very much the prodigal son."

"Or prodigal grandson," Larkin quipped.

"The woman's memory faded slightly after this," Warin went on. "Soon after his return, Roger's grandfather died. Trade with King Cedric of Nifolhad was reestablished. Ragallach's coffers filled, and Roger was able to push his suit with Lady Isabel of Stolweg."

Baldric was worried, Larkin observed. His mentor looked at each of the assembled men before settling on Larkin. "Tomorrow, we ride for King's Glen."

CHAPTER FOURTEEN

Nature's Bounty

A pattern emerged during the first year of Anna's marriage. Her husband would disappear every few weeks and, upon his return, she would be summoned to his chamber. Anna lived for the days—three, four, five at a time—when her duties with the horses would take her afield. Weeks could go by when she would not see Roger at all.

When she was at the keep, she would visit the cottages each week, checking on the health and welfare of her people. They were slow to accept her aid, but she persisted. Trust grew, and before long, they would seek her out with each new injury or illness. In this way, Anna came to love all of the people of Stolweg, and they in turn loved her.

As summer turned to autumn, Anna noticed that her stock of herbs had dwindled, as had Grainne's. So it came about that during her excursions with her horses, she collected plants and wildflowers. Grainne would mention some herb that she required, and Anna would make it her mission to seek it out while with the horses. Will and Gilles were so used to her stopping to pick at weeds or to dig for roots that they began to recognize the plants and would dismount to harvest them as well.

Anna had yet to hear from her family. On her first day at Stolweg, when her life had drastically changed forever, she'd written to her sister. Claire had never answered. And she now doubted that the other letters she'd written to her family, carefully omitting any details regarding her marriage, had ever left the keep. Perhaps it was for the best that the months passed with no word.

One morning, she and Will had taken the mares into the hills to allow them to stretch their legs and graze on the lush grasses growing in low glens. It was in one such clearing that they discovered three wizened apple trees that were early in producing their fruit, the clime being slightly cooler than in the tended orchards within the keep's wall. To Anna's surprise, the fruit trees yielded pomerois, an old variety, and usually held in reserve for the King.

"These trees could be the last of their kind in Aurelia," Anna explained. "King's apples, they are sometimes called." She pulled the dead branches from around the trunks. "When I was a child, an apple blight swept through Aurelia. The pomeroi orchards were decimated. If we could take some cuttings—"

"We could give King Godwin a tribute he wouldn't likely forget," Will finished for her. They cheered each other on as they picked as many apples as would fit in their saddlebags. Still too early for fully ripened fruit, the poms, as the fruits were called, were small and misshapen.

Anna bit into one and her mouth puckered at its tartness. But after eating the soft, mealy apples from the previous harvest, the crisp fruit with the promise of sweetness to come was wonderful. Happy with the day's toil, they rode back to the keep. Will transferred the apples to a large burlap sack. "I'll help you carry them, m'lady."

"Why don't you give them to your mother?" Anna suggested. "I'm afraid Grainne has depleted her supply from last season." Grainne had noticed Anna's affinity for apples, and had kept her in good supply. It was no small feat to take anything from the kitchen, Anna thought, and she had yet to be welcomed into Doreen's domain.

"But Lady Aubrianne, it—it was your idea to gather them," he stammered.

"It would mean more to her coming from her son. Have you ever given your mother a gift?" Anna asked.

"Well, no, come to think of it. I think she may likely faint."

The next day, Grainne brought Anna's dinner as usual to the south chamber. As was their custom when Lord Roger was away, they ate together, enjoying capons stuffed with leeks and topped with a sauce delicately laced with rosemary.

Grainne uncovered a small plate and held it out to Anna. "Doreen made sweets, m'lady."

Anna took a small pasty from the proffered dish. When she bit into the flaky treat, she was delighted to find it filled with tender apple slices laced with honey, spices, and wild onions.

"She's no fool, m'lady," Grainne commented. "She was beside herself that Will was so thoughtful, but she knows that you had a hand in it."

"I have no notion to what you are referring, Grainne."

So it became Anna's habit to search out useful foodstuff that could be taken back for Doreen as a gift from her son. They stuffed sacks in their saddlebags, never knowing what they would find—mulberries, gooseberries, blackberries, wild onions, woodland mushrooms, and chestnuts.

But Anna's favorite days were spent near the many streams sewn throughout the fabric of the hills and forests. "Too bad we didn't bring our fishing rods," Gilles said sadly, gazing longingly at one of the streams. "Who needs a fishing pole?" Anna asked. She fashioned an alder branch into a long spear and stepped into the cool shallows.

Once the silt settled, she waited patiently for a trout to swim near. She held her breath as a large fish swam steadily closer, her weapon poised for action. With a light flick of her wrist, the alder branch was gone from her hand.

Pulling the spear from the water and holding aloft a neatly skewered trout, she grinned sheepishly at her openmouthed companions. If they only knew of the summers spent fishing in the streams that flowed through Chevring, she thought, they would not have been so astounded. She had inherited her love of fishing from her father and her excellent aim from her mother. Anna was a dead shot every time she threw a spear, knife, or dagger. It had driven her mother to distraction that she could be so lethal.

That evening, they enjoyed fresh fish peppered with herbs and butter. The fruits of Anna's and her friends' labor were so prolific that it was not long before Doreen started smoking their surplus. Thus, Anna's tentative friendship with the cook began.

One afternoon, Grainne confessed that Lord Roger demanded weekly reports on Anna's health, appetite, and cycle. He was most curious about the latter, wanting to know immediately if Anna had missed her courses. Anna had assured Grainne that anything she told Lord Roger was not a betrayal. In truth, she thought, if her husband knew when she was having her courses, she would gain a few additional days' respite.

It was one of her greatest fears that Roger would get her with child. So every night she drank a tea infused with loveroot, feverfew, and a goodly amount of chamomile. Although the concoction might not prevent a pregnancy, the daily intake would help maintain her regularity. Grainne, without acknowledging its constant use, kept her supply of these herbs fresh and full.

One day there was a small burlap sack on Anna's workbench. The bag was filled with a whitish, powdery substance. When Anna's supper came that evening, she asked her maid what the bag contained.

Grainne cleared her throat nervously. "It's saltpeter, Lady Aubrianne.

My mother called it fool's pipe." At Anna's confusion, Grainne added without preamble, "It's for your great horse, m'lady, in case he has some difficulty, erm, dismounting. You boil the powder with wood ash to purify it, and mix it into an ointment. Be careful, though. Prolonged use and he'll likely stop acting the stallion and take on like a gelding."

"But Grainne, it would not work when breeding horses," Anna pointed out. "To approach a stallion in that state of, well, readiness, it would be too dangerous. And then to attempt an application of ointment or balm—it would be impossible!"

"Oh dear. Well, m'lady, the ointment can be applied to the mare. Over time, the stallion feels the effects," she explained with frankness. "There are a number of uses for fool's pipe, m'lady. It's rumored that many a monk depends on its effects."

When comprehension dawned, Anna's mouth dropped open. "For my stallion, I see. And the mare, Grainne? Any side effects for the mare?"

"None that I've heard, m'lady."

CHAPTER FIFTEEN

Circle of Conspirators

The crops had been reaped, the fields long since mowed, and fruits and nuts and root vegetables stored. Autumn thus passed uneventfully into winter.

One cold morning in early January, Anna awoke to sunshine streaming through a slit in the tapestries covering her windows. For weeks the weather had been dismally cold, unusual even for Stolweg. Each day had dawned gray and dark. Or hadn't dawned, in Anna's opinion, so dreary were the mornings. The sodden skies were an endless expanse of pregnant clouds. But this day, a crackling of light knifed its way across her room and lost itself in the folds of her blankets. She jumped from her bed with an energy she had not felt in weeks.

Walking to her window, she trailed her fingers in the wedge of light, disrupting the floating specks of dust. The luminescent motes tumbled wildly in the turbulence she caused and winked out as they left the bright shaft. Anna yearned to be as free and unencumbered.

A year ago, she was a naïve maiden; now, she felt as though she'd lived a lifetime. She drew back the heavy fabric that covered the large south-facing window. Frost was etched on the lower corners of each pane in fantastic patterns of barbed spikes and feathery swirls. Although the sun had yet to spill its light over the distant hills, its rays kissed the mullioned glass of Anna's high tower window. She stared up into the heavens. The sky was an unadulterated shade of blue, the rarest of colors seen only on very clear and cold winter mornings, its brilliance intensified by the endless sea of blue-shadowed white that covered the ground. The swollen gray sky of the last few weeks had finally opened and dropped its crystalline treasure on the muddy land below.

Anna sighed, looking at the landscape, virginal in the early morning. The snow that had fallen during the night was a heavy blanket that offered no warmth to the sleeping land. Early as it was, she was still surprised that no one had marred the perfect canvas. She spied one or two trails in the courtyard itself, brave souls who had ventured out, in the confining space between the castle wall and an encroaching snow drift.

A need grew in Anna's chest, that irresistible, all-too-familiar urge to take Tullian for a ride. She quickly bundled herself in her warmest riding gear before racing to the stable. The gray light from the dawning morning spilled into the dark stable as Anna pulled open one door and slipped through. Inside, the horses rested, content to continue their slumber in the warmth of the stable. Not surprisingly, though, over the edge of Tullian's stall door, the charcoal nose of her steed poked. Anna walked to her good friend and saw his nostrils flare before he blew out a frustrated explosion of air. She stroked his velvety muzzle, sensing that he wanted to be free of the structures of the keep as much as she. Her own compulsion to fly over the pristine fields was so overpowering that she didn't bother with bridle, reins, or saddle. Once outside the curtain wall, they turned east toward the rolling hills.

They raced forward to greet the sun as it lifted its face over the approaching rise. She could make out the trees, their branches unmoving and black against a brightening sea of blues and purples. All around, sound was suspended, blotted out by the thick snow. The only noise was Tullian's heaving breath and the dull pounding of his hooves. The hood of her cloak had long ago flown back, and her eyes streamed with tears as together they raced over the landscape. Her fingers, entwined in Tullian's mane, remained warm. The first hill was before them. Riding bareback, Anna felt the raw power of her steed's muscles as they bunched and extended, his strides lengthening to take the incline without slowing.

They crested the first hill, and the sun's rays speared into the sky and through the bare trees, sending a million arrows of light to the west. Anna pulled up and turned to witness its flood spill into the basin below. The bruised blue-white fields changed before her eyes into a jewel-encrusted robe. Except for their lone path, the snow was unspoiled. Shadowed pockets of opalescence gave the expanse texture. Anna gazed at the mournful path, at once beautiful and sad in its solitude. Her path, she thought.

Tullian, eager to move again, blasted his breath from his nostrils in steamy explosions. "All right, Tully-boy, let's go," she said, and they wheeled back to the east to descend the first hill before climbing another. And many more, until they had their fill and turned for home.

Riding up to the stable, she saw Gilles frowning, hands on hips. Will, carrying a bridle and blanket, ran from the stable upon hearing Tullian. He stared at Anna with relief.

Warning bells sounded in her head, so she jumped from Tullian's back and ran to Gilles. "What's happened?" she demanded. "Tell me at once." Gilles made no reply but tilted his head toward the stable where, just inside, Cellach waited with an angry scowl.

"You'd best go into the stable, m'lady," Gilles suggested, casting a nervous glance around the courtyard. "It'll be warmer."

Once inside, she asked again what had happened, directing the question to Cellach, who was still frowning menacingly.

"What happened, you ask? You happened!" Cellach bellowed. "Will found Tullian gone. Then Grainne said that you were not in your chamber. The soldiers at the gate had changed, and the last watch had to be tracked down before we discovered that you had ridden out. Alone!"

Anna's first instinct was to laugh. Cellach's posture was so exactly like her mother's that she found it difficult to squash the knot of mirth. But Cellach was *not* her mother. He had no right to question her doings in so abrupt a manner.

Her hackles rose. "Am I to understand that I am not allowed the freedom to leave the keep as I wish?" she seethed. "Has Lord Roger ordered you to follow me?" *Hah*, she thought; she could see Cellach reining in his temper at the mention of Roger. "Should I give you a daily schedule or would you prefer a weekly diary?" She glared at them, daring them to answer.

Cellach stiffened. Gilles looked away uncomfortably. It was Will who finally broke the heated silence. "There is no such order upon us, m'lady. We were worried. We wanted to..." He fumbled to find the right words.

Gilles intervened. "Cellach, don't you think it's time? She has a right to know."

"Fine. But not here." His jaw set, and he turned his attention back to Anna. "Lady Aubrianne, if you have time this morning in your *schedule*, might you give me a moment of it?" There was a steel edge to the sarcasm in Cellach's voice, one she'd not heard ere now.

"Mind your tone, Cellach. I will not be spoken to in such a way," she answered, matching her mettle against his. "We'll speak now."

"Please, m'lady," Cellach quietly urged, "we should speak privately. Perhaps in the armory." Anna could tell it took great effort for him to speak politely, even if it was done so through gritted teeth. She nodded and followed him from the stable.

"M'lady, you must give me your word that what is said in this chamber will not be repeated to anyone. Gilles may trust you, but it is not only his life that I am protecting." He watched as she took stock of the weapons before stepping over to his worktable in the corner.

"I see. And do you trust me, Cellach?" she asked.

"Aye, Lady Aubrianne." He looked directly into her eyes. "Your comportment this past year has earned not only my trust, but my respect as well."

"You have my word, Cellach, on my family's name."

Cellach exhaled in relief. "Simply put, it is not safe for you to ride out alone. I've seen signs that many strange riders have been on Stolweg land. Riders who have taken great care to hide their tracks."

"Have you told Lord Roger?" she asked.

"I believe him to be aware, m'lady. I can recognize any track made by any horse in our stable, including those made by Lord Roger's horse and those of Gorman's. Many times the tracks of their horses were among those of the strange riders. I do not as yet know what it means and have not risked following them. Until we can ascertain who these riders are, please let us know when you leave. It is your choice, of course"— Cellach searched for the right phrase—"but it would greatly ease our minds knowing you are safe."

Her eyes narrowed. "Your mind, and Gilles's? Are there others in this clandestine circle?" she queried.

"Aye. Will, Doreen, Grainne, and some others. There are those who curry favor with Lord Roger and would happily provide him with details of any suspicious behavior on our parts."

"This group has the makings of a cabal, Cellach. I ask you again: how many are you numbered?"

"*Cabal* is too strong a word, m'lady, for we are not plotting to overthrow Lord Roger. We formed our circle to protect ourselves and those loyal to King Godwin. But to answer your question, there are four and thirty in our group."

"Including Carrick the miller?" Lady Aubrianne asked. "He has always struck me as honest."

"He is, m'lady. But we have not included him."

"Because of Maggie, his daughter," she said bluntly. "I don't trust the girl. She's always lurking about, especially near the north tower."

Startled, Cellach wondered if his lady had discovered the relationship between Carrick's daughter and Lord Roger. He didn't reckon so, or she would not have said the name so easily. Still, he was impressed by her intuition. "It would be wise to steer clear of that girl. She is not to be trusted."

"All right, Cellach. This circle of yours, how do you meet? Surely Lord Roger's men would report any gathering."

"We take great care, m'lady, and do not meet often. Instead, we pass word to one another. When we meet, we do it in small groups in the chapel."

"When Lord Roger is away?" she asked.

"No, m'lady," Cellach said, and he saw the surprise in her eyes, followed by a nod of understanding. "You've guessed why, I see. Your husband would never imagine that we would conspire right under his nose. He has little use for the chapel; when our clergyman passed away, Lord Roger never bothered finding a replacement. We have continued to use the chapel as a place of worship and reflection. So our presence there is not in question."

Lady Aubrianne stepped to the window and peered down at the courtyard. "Cellach," she said as she turned back to him, "what exactly do you think my husband is doing? Does it have anything to do with his absences?"

"We don't know. But he has been fortifying Stolweg since he first married Lady Isabel," Cellach replied.

"Grainne has already explained some of this, how Lord Roger's behavior changed once Lady Isabel's father passed away."

"I suppose Grainne has confided many things," Cellach said. "She wasn't exactly correct when she said that Lord Roger changed. I believe he stopped pretending to be someone else, and reverted to his true nature, one that is inherently cruel."

"Grainne told me the story of Lady Isabel," Anna began. "But something in her tale has always bothered me." Cellach listened as she repeated Grainne's words. "'Lord Roger grabbed the back of my neck and pushed me to the window. With his other hand, he opened the shutters and forced me to look down at the scene below.' Cellach, if Lady Isabel truly jumped from her window, how could the shutters have been latched?"

CHAPTER SIXTEEN

Carrick's Wife

A day did not pass that Anna didn't think upon the dangerous web in which she'd been captured. Years ago, when it became evident that she was different from other girls, her father had bestowed upon her a dagger that had once belonged to his father. She began tucking it into the folds of her overtunic, carrying it whenever she left the keep. At night, she made sure it was always within reach.

The blade was with her right now, although she didn't think she would need it. She was in the great hall, and today was the day that the people of Stolweg could come to her for treatment of pain, illness, and injury. Grainne had suggested this, for the recent weeks had been bitterly cold, and her people could come for winter supplies as well.

Anna had just helped her last patient, an elderly man with pain in his joints. She was packing her basket of supplies when she noticed a woman enter the hall. It was Lia, married to Berwick, one of Stolweg's farmers.

"Good day to you, Lia," Anna said while searching Lia's face, skin, and eyes for symptoms that might explain her presence. Lia burst into tears and dropped to her knees.

"Oh, m'lady," she said between great sobs. "I think I'm with child!"

"But this is wonderful, Lia. Berwick must be so pleased."

"No, m'lady. It is the very worst thing that can happen to a woman here."

"What do you mean?" Anna asked as gently as she could, for she could see the fear in Lia's eyes that they might be overheard.

"Ever since Carrick's wife died," Lia started, stopping when she heard the sound of boots in the corridor. "I'm sorry, m'lady," she whispered. "I shouldn't have come here. Please, say nothing to your husband."

"I'll keep your secret, Lia," Anna promised. "But I'll come to your croft next week. We can talk then." This put the woman at ease, and she left the hall as quietly as she had come. What did Carrick's wife have to do with Lia's fear? Anna wanted answers and knew exactly where to find them. She headed to the kitchens.

Grainne was there, chatting with Doreen about the garden. "...been warmer than usual. And the snow's almost all gone. I think we might get an early start on cleaning the herb beds," she was saying. When she saw Anna, she gave her a welcoming smile.

"Tell me about Carrick's wife and the absence of young children here," she said. Grainne and Doreen turned to each other and nodded.

"I was going to tell you, m'lady, to warn you," Grainne began with a sigh. "But then I saw what you put in your tea each day. Forgive me if this is too forward, but it's to avoid being with child, is it not?" Anna nodded. "I know this because I supply all of the women here with the same herbs," Grainne continued. "The women are afraid to have children, m'lady. Ever since Carrick's wife."

Before Anna could ask, Grainne explained. "It was right after Lady Isabel died. Carrick was away, and his wife was out sweeping the causeway by the mill. She was trampled to death. Gorman and two soldiers were riding home; they claimed not to have seen her."

"Bah!" Doreen interjected. "You've seen the mill crossing; it's broad and straight. How can you not see a person at the opposite end, and a pregnant one at that?"

Anna's heart sank, thinking of Carrick's loss. "What happened next?" she asked, knowing the tale was not complete.

"Upon his return, Carrick confronted Gorman in the courtyard. Many had gathered to see justice done. Lord Roger deemed it an accident. He warned us to be more careful, else the same could happen again." Grainne took Anna's hand and continued. "It was horrible, m'lady. Carrick launched himself at Gorman. If Gilles hadn't been there to restrain him, to remind him that he had young Maggie to care for, I don't think Carrick would be here today."

"A wife dead, and an unborn child, and what did Carrick get?" Doreen demanded, then answered her own question. "A lashing ordered by Lord Roger and given by the man who murdered his wife!"

"When it was over," Grainne finished, "I heard Lord Roger say, 'One less Stolweg brat to deal with.' M'lady, please tell me you are not with child."

"No, not me, thank heaven," Anna answered. "But Lia is, and we have to protect her." They spent the rest of the afternoon assembling a plan that would take Lia east, to the border of Stolweg and Whitmarsh.

Doreen had cousins there who could shelter the woman.

When Anna retired that night, she realized that she needed more than her horses to survive, and more than her herbs and flowers. She needed moments like the one spent in Doreen's kitchen. Working together for a common cause, with good friends, gave her new purpose. It was time to do more than watch as her husband tightened his grip on the people of Stolweg; it was time to take an active role in the shaping of her own life and of those around her.

CHAPTER SEVENTEEN

Loyalty and Retribution

Will looked on as Lord Roger interrogated Lady Aubrianne about the mares. She faced her husband without fear as he cornered her in one of the empty stalls. Her strength gave Will newfound, but dangerous, courage.

Rina, Dragonfly, Sea Star, and Willow had foaled in the spring; three more were expected over the summer. Will couldn't understand why Lord Roger was impatient to have the mares mated again so quickly. Lady Aubrianne explained that she had already done so with Rina and Dragonfly, but that only Dragonfly had conceived. The results of Rina's matching would be clear in the next few weeks.

"And Jessa?" Lord Roger demanded menacingly. "Why haven't you tried with Jessa?"

Will had been with Lady Aubrianne the day that she'd attempted to breed Tullian with the skittish and high-strung mare. Jessa had lashed out wickedly at the stallion. So before Lady Aubrianne could answer, Will jumped to her defense. "But she has tried. Jessa is too nervous to let Tullian near her, er, sir. Beg pardon, m'lord."

Lord Roger glared at him, galled that a servant would interrupt him. He raised his hand to strike, but stopped when Lady Aubrianne stayed his arm. Will cowered back regardless, so delighted was Lord Roger's face. "So, you care for this whelp. How very fortunate for him."

It was the first time that Will had ever seen fear in his lady's eyes, and he felt panic catch hold in his heart. "Please, m'lord," she started, "he didn't mean to—"

Lord Roger sneered. "Lady Aubrianne," he cut in, "if you'll excuse me, I have another matter to which I must attend." He headed to the barracks.

Lady Aubrianne leveled a look of sheer frustration at Will. "How could you be so careless!"

"But he was blaming you, m'lady. I just wanted him to know that you tried."

"He'll never let this go. That you even spoke to him he considers an offense." The dread in her voice did nothing to ease his fear. "I won't be able to protect you, Will. I shouldn't have even tried."

"But, m'lady, when he left, he didn't seem angry."

She looked out to the courtyard where Lord Roger had gone. "He'll plan and prepare. He'll hurt you. He'll do it because by hurting you, he's hurting me. I don't know when, but he will. Go. Now," she ordered. "Tell your father what has happened. And, for your own safety, stay away from Lord Roger. And Gorman."

"M'lady, I'm sorry. I—I didn't realize," he stammered before racing out.

That evening, his family prayed that Lord Roger's grudging respect for them would soften his temper. After a month passed without recriminations, Will's worry lessened. Perhaps Lord Roger had forgotten the incident, unlikely though it seemed.

Then, one day when Will was mucking stalls and his father was away with the mares, Lord Roger entered the stable with Gorman in tow. Will heard his name called and, upon recognizing Lord Roger's voice, picked up the heavy slop bucket and stepped from behind the partition. Gorman's foot shot out, tripping him so that he fell to the dirt floor.

There was nothing Will could do but watch as manure and urine-laden sludge flew from the bucket and onto Lord Roger's boots. Before he could rise, a hand seized the back of his collar and hauled him roughly to his feet. Gorman gave a satisfied grunt and twisted Will's collar, choking him and blocking his attempts to apologize.

Will blanched, hearing Gorman's next words. "Ten lashes, m'lord? That ought to make this pup more careful. Perhaps twenty," Gorman amended when Will tried to twist free.

"Twenty would likely kill the boy," Lord Roger said as if bored. "A compromise: fifteen. One blow for each of the fourteen words that he spoke out of turn that day, plus one for my boots."

Gorman grabbed a rope and dragged Will, still struggling to get free, to the hitching post in the courtyard. He forced Will to his knees, and then bound his wrists to the hitch's high crossbeam.

• • •

Cellach was in the armory with Lady Aubrianne. She was standing at the window when she cried out in horror. She raced past a startled Cellach, shouting over her shoulder, "Protect Doreen!"

Cellach flew to the window. He took in the scene and sped to the scullery to head off the cook. He was just in time to grab Doreen by the waist as she started out the door to protect her son. He suspected that someone had told her knowing she would do anything to protect her son. But who would be so malicious?

. . .

Anna made it to the hitching post in the time that it took to execute six cracks of a whip. Will's thin shirt offered no protection against the lash, exposing blood and strafed skin to all who had gathered. Before Gorman could strike the seventh blow, Anna jumped between him and the young man. She didn't flinch as he brought down the whip a hair's breadth from her face.

"Aubrianne!" Lord Roger bellowed. "You will remove yourself immediately. This boy will be taught a lesson."

"Lord Roger, I beg you, a word in private." Only after he nodded did Anna move from Will.

"What is it?" he demanded.

"Please, Lord Roger, spare the boy. I know he offended you, but there must be some other way." Anna glanced at the kitchen's entrance where Cellach had an iron grip on Doreen. Grainne was there, too, whispering something to Will's mother. "Please, Lord Roger."

She lowered her head submissively, pleading quietly so that only her husband could hear her. "Surely there is something that would give you greater pleasure than inflicting pain on this boy."

"You do not understand, as usual," he replied as if she were a simpleton. So that those assembled could hear, he then pronounced, "I have ordered that fifteen lashes be dealt today. So far, there have only been six. What would the good people of Stolweg think of their lord? Nay, Lady Aubrianne, fifteen lashes must be dealt."

Before Gorman could continue, Anna called out in a clear voice, "Lord Roger states that nine more lashes still must be paid and someone must bear them." Roger's eyes narrowed at her. "Very well, m'lord. Your *request* is my pleasure."

Before he could stop her, she rushed back to the unconscious Will, shielding him with her own body. Grasping the ropes, she twisted them around her wrists.

Her husband nodded to Gorman, for he would never back down and risk losing the respect he thought he had. Anna heard the whistling of the lash seconds before it slashed across her back. She did not cry out, biting deeply into her lip as the second and third stroke came down. A searing pain radiated through her frame and by the fifth blow, she lost count. Waiting an eternity for the telltale sound of the strap slicing air, Anna realized that the last blow had been laid, and her body sagged against Will's bloodied back.

A heavy weariness threatened to pull her to the ground. She gathered what strength she had and forced herself to stand. Anna never knew how she was able to remain upright; it felt as though the earth tilted with each step she took. Halfway to the castle, she passed Roger. His hand shot out and grabbed her arm. She ripped it from his grip and staggered.

"I will expect you in my chamber tomorrow at the usual time, Lady Aubrianne," he commanded, his voice cold with fury. She glared at him with every bit of intensity she had, willing him to understand that if she ever had the chance, she would kill him. Her eyes glimmered with satisfaction when he took a step back.

Then, she focused on the entrance to the castle. Her only goal was to reach it before collapsing. Someone rushed past her. Doreen? Then another. That would be Cellach, she thought. He did not slow; he could not risk showing his loyalty to her.

Anna reeled her way to the entrance and rounded the corner. When her hand reached out for support, she discovered that the wall had disappeared. The floor seemed to race up. Grainne caught her before she fell, and then supported her as they climbed the mountain of steps to her chamber. She reached her bed and collapsed on her stomach.

• • •

When Anna next woke, it was day, her quarters entombed in shadows, the heavy drapes drawn to block out the sun. Her first thought was to find her dagger. She espied it on a low table pulled next to the bed. Her maid must have found it and placed it there. Although Anna doubted she could move to lift it, she took comfort knowing it was at hand. Across her chamber, near the hearth, a weary-looking Grainne slumped on the couch. Gilles sat next to her on a bench. Anna tried to move, and a sigh escaped.

Grainne was immediately by her side. "M'lady, you're awake."

Anna smiled weakly.

"Gilles is here, m'lady. He wishes to speak to you. I can tell him to come back later."

Anna's voice croaked from lack of use. "Now is fine, Grainne."

Her maid tipped a cup to her lips. "Only water for now, m'lady. Drink slowly."

Gilles knelt before her. "Lady Aubrianne, I have no words to express—" He choked. "What you did for Will, for all of us. I…"

"It's all right, Gilles. You would have done the same for me."

"That's just it, m'lady," he said, noticing her dagger and picking it up to study it. "I don't know if I would have had the strength to do what you did."

"I know," Anna stated simply. "You would have found the courage. You and Doreen and Will, you must let this go. To do otherwise, I—I don't think I could survive again."

Gilles lowered his head and whispered, "I pledge my life to you, Lady Aubrianne. If you ever need it, it's yours." He held her dagger between them, and touched it first to his lips, then his forehead. It was an old oath, usually made with sword, though any blade would suffice. It was the strongest a person could give, an oath reserved for kings. Anna closed her eyes, accepting his promise of fealty, hoping she would never have to call upon it. Grainne pulled him away, pushed him from the room, and returned to Anna.

"How is Will, Grainne?" Anna asked.

"Healing, m'lady," Grainne replied, "Now drink this; it will help you sleep."

"I can't, Grainne. I must go to Lord Roger's chamber this evening."

"What nonsense is this, m'lady? Lord Roger is gone. He'll not return for a week."

"Gone?" she whispered.

Grainne caringly smoothed the hair back from Anna's cheek. "M'lady, 'twas two nights ago that I sent him word that you were not yet revived. He came to see for himself. Of course, I stayed; I would not leave you alone with him. He left just this morning."

"I have been senseless for three days? It is not possible."

"Three and a half, m'lady," Grainne amended. "You woke many times but were incoherent. I've been dosing you with this tea. Today is the first time that you did not wake screaming."

Anna took a deep breath, refusing to forestall what she needed to know. "How bad is it?"

"You've been healing for several days, m'lady, so you've slept through the worst of it." Grainne frowned as she evaded the question.

"Grainne, how bad?" Anna asked again.

Her maid lifted her eyes and, with a voice tinged with rage, hissed, "It is—was—very bad. Nine lashes by that devil. I saw him do it, m'lady. He doubled his efforts when you stepped in, laughing as each stroke fell.

"The wounds smell clean. There's no rot," Grainne went on. "I used Doreen's entire supply of honey to prevent it. But you'll wear the scars for the rest of your days. I'm so sorry, m'lady." Tears coursed down Grainne's cheeks.

Anna's eyes lost focus as if she were searching for a dream long forgotten. "It seems to me, Grainne, that I owe you twice now for my life. I will find a way to repay you before this is over. That is *my* oath to you."

Grainne grew angry. "You owe me nothing, Lady Aubrianne. I had been dead those years before you came here. I died with Lady Isabel. It is you who have given *me* life. All of us our lives. Please, speak not in such a way again."

"If you will not let me express my gratitude, may I at least have more of your tea, Grainne?" Anna asked, humbled by her maid's words. She accepted spoon after spoon of the intoxicating tea, and it wasn't long before she fell back into a numbing sleep. Her last thought before she gave in to the comforting dark was this: pain or no, she would rise from her bed on the morrow.

The next morning, Grainne was sleeping when Anna attempted to do just that. She found she had not even enough strength to roll to her side. She'd been lying on her stomach for days, and her arms lacked the power. Anna sighed in frustration, and Grainne, upon hearing the noise, blinked and immediately looked to her mistress with concern. Before Anna could tell her to rest, her maid hovered at her side.

"I cannot get up on my own, Grainne. Can you help?" Anna asked.

"Why don't we roll you to your side first, let your blood get used to flowing in a different direction," Grainne suggested. "Then we'll work on sitting."

It was as good a plan as any, Anna thought. As she rocked forward, the scabs across her back stretched dangerously, but Grainne assured her that the wounds hadn't opened. The pain was barely tolerable; she'd been lucky to have passed through the worst of it unconscious.

"Another day, m'lady, and you'll be able to move without risk of opening your wounds. Sit here, and I'll run to the kitchen for you. I think you can handle some warm broth this time."

"This time," Anna repeated to herself as Grainne hustled from the chamber.

Later, Anna sipped her broth in silence while Grainne bustled about the room. Her maid had not told her everything about Roger's visit, she was sure. Anna had but six days before his return. Six days to recover. Six days to prepare. She gazed with new intensity at one of the trunks that she'd brought from Chevring.

CHAPTER EIGHTEEN

Weapons and Armor

During Anna's recovery, Gilles had seen to it that the mares and foals were exercised and allowed to graze in the hills. Tullian, too, had been taken out, but on a lead, as he would not let any but Anna ride him.

Anna was just finishing her lunch one day when Cellach paid a visit. He surprised Grainne by asking her to leave the chamber so that he could speak privately with his lady.

"I have observed, Lady Aubrianne," he said, then cleared his throat, "that you have been quiet of late." She arched an eyebrow at him, and he forged ahead warily. "I saw the look you gave Lord Roger after the lashing. If you had had the strength, I've no doubt you would have tried to kill him. I can see you calculating just how best to dispose of him."

"You can stop there, Cellach," Anna warned. "Do not think me so naïve that I would risk my life and attempt something so foolish. Do not presume to know my thoughts."

"No offense was meant, m'lady, only"—Cellach paused—"I do not think that such an attempt would be entirely foolish."

Anna was momentarily stunned. He'd read her strongest desire at her weakest moment, a desire she had intentionally not hidden from Roger. Realizing her error, she worried about the consequences. She sat down, a little too heavily, and winced.

"Lady Aubrianne, Lord Roger's return is imminent. I worry that your life here is about to worsen." She waited while he tried to find the right words. "Of late, Lord Roger and his men have been watching me more closely, visiting the armory often. Their reasons are overcontrived."

"Cellach, I understand that you are unable to intercede on my behalf. Lord Roger would have you killed if he knew where your true loyalties rested."

"My loyalties. Yes. That is a good way to begin the conversation that we have both been avoiding. My loyalties lie with King Godwin and Aurelia, as do yours. I have not wanted to bring this notion to light, but I think we can both agree that Lord Roger has been involved in a plot to undermine our King's rule. Would you agree, m'lady?"

"It explains his many absences, and the strange men who have been passing through Stolweg." At Cellach's surprise, Anna continued, "I have seen them too, Cellach, coming in at night and leaving before first light. Who are they?"

"Not Aurelians, I suspect," he replied. "But we must have proof before acting, m'lady."

Cellach squared his shoulders before continuing. "I've been meaning to approach you about another matter. For a long time, I have thought that you should be taught some means of self-defense. Unfortunately, I cannot train you directly. You are being spied upon, and so too anyone who has contact with you. Do you remember the conversation we had regarding Carrick's daughter?"

Anna thought of a day not so long ago, when she and Will had ridden past the mill. Gorman was standing outside the home that Carrick and his daughter shared. He was holding the reins of his horse and those of Roger's. Anna had thought it odd, for she knew Carrick to be on an errand outside Stolweg. As she and Will drew near the cottage, they heard what they at first thought was shouting. Then they recognized the noise for what it truly was: rutting.

Roger had orchestrated the entire spectacle. He'd made sure that she knew Carrick was away, and he had, that same morning, demanded her schedule. Will had been the first to kick his mount into a gallop; Anna, mortified, followed. Gorman's raucous laughter gave pursuit.

"Maggie," Anna guessed.

"That's the girl, yes," Cellach said. "You see, before you came here, Maggie had set her eye on Will. But Will never returned her regard. Whether of her own accord or so ordered, it was Maggie who told Doreen about Will on the day of the lashing. How was Maggie able to see Will's predicament and make it all the way to the kitchens in so short a time?"

"She had foreknowledge," Anna stated flatly.

"That is not all she has, m'lady," he added with an awkward expression. Anna knew the best way for Cellach to make his point was to remain silent until he was comfortable enough to speak. After a long pause during which he was unable to look her in the eye, he at last continued, "She has aspirations as well."

Anna snorted in an unladylike fashion. "Aspirations, is it? Such a pleasant way of telling me my husband isn't faithful. But, Cellach, this is old news. It's a relief, you know. I am not sure why that is true, but it is. Perhaps now my guilt for wanting him gone will abate."

"Your guilt?" he cried. "You have done nothing wrong."

"You, Cellach, would not understand," Anna replied with a sigh. "*You* are not a woman."

Anna turned the topic back to Maggie. "I don't know how she can be so duped by him. Doesn't she realize it was his men who ran down her mother?"

"M'lady, I watched your husband woo Lady Isabel; he was attentive and charming. He fooled Lord John. He fooled me," Cellach admitted. "And everyone else here. What young maid would not fall for his affected gallantry?"

"Does Maggie truly think he holds her in such esteem? He is only using her, as he uses everyone: Lady Isabel to obtain Stolweg, and now me, although I have yet to fathom the purpose. Surely something other than the horses." She paused a moment. "Can we protect her?"

"Protect Maggie? You are overly generous, m'lady."

"We must try for Carrick's sake," she explained. "One day, Cellach, this horrible state in which we find ourselves will end. This I believe in my soul. I want as few casualties as possible." Anna brightened. "In the meantime, we can take advantage of this situation with Maggie. If Roger desires information about our doings, let us make sure he hears what we want him to hear."

"There is one more item to discuss, m'lady. I said that *I* could not prepare you, but Gilles can. When you are off with the mares, he can teach you the rudiments of self-defense. I can slip you a few weapons from the armory."

"That won't be necessary," she told him. "I'm well enough equipped."

He raised a ruddy eyebrow but forged ahead. "I may appear to be distancing myself from you in the months to come. But please know that your safety is my first priority."

After Cellach departed, Anna stared at the massive trunk with the secret compartment. Her thoughts traveled back to a day when she was but eight years of age and had just finished wrestling with three boys near the stable. They'd insulted her by saying she was a useless little girl. She took on all three at the same time, besting them all. Fists still clenched, a triumphant Anna saw her mother marching toward her. Her five-year-old sister Claire had tattled.

Anna had known Lady Estelle would not be happy about her torn sleeve, nor overjoyed at seeing her bloodied lip. What she did not expect was her mother's sad resignation. She uttered not a word, just motioned for Anna to follow to her grandmother's room.

"Wait here," she'd been told, and then had stood dejected outside the door while they privately conversed. But she heard some of what was said.

"She's all yours, Mother."

"Are you surprised?" Anna's grandmother had asked. "You knew this was probable."

"Why one of my daughters? And in a time of peace."

"We must honor the old ways. The traditions are not for us to question."

That day, Anna had seen both fear and hope in her mother's face when she had turned her over to her grandmother's tutelage. Her studies began with the history of the women in her line—ancestors who, in times of peace, were singled out to be healers; in times of unrest, warriors. On her twelfth birthday, her grandmother had summoned the Chevring master-at-arms, Osbert. He was to instruct Anna in all manners of weaponry.

Osbert had soon found that Anna's aim was exceptional. She never failed hitting the center of the target. It had taken only days to teach her to use a bow and then mere weeks for her to capture the subtle nuances of wind and moisture and their influence over trajectory. After the initial lessons, she'd practiced for hours, building strength and endurance.

Anna recalled her grandmother's final days. She had held her frail hand for hours while her grandmother gave one final assignment: the recitation of the names of all the women in Anna's family. She received a piece of parchment upon which each name had been put to ink in her grandmother's spidery script. Anna's last lesson was to memorize the names and, once they were secure in her mind, give the list to her mother.

Just before her grandmother died, she'd given Anna the chest that now sat in her chamber. It contained a treasure of weapons and armor. Her grandmother's final words echoed in Anna's mind as if they'd been spoken yesterday: "One day, you will leave Chevring. You must keep yon chest with you wherever your life leads. These weapons and this armor date back farther than any in our line can remember. Perhaps they are as old as the stones to the north. They have been used only by the women in our family."

And when Anna had asked why she had been chosen to receive

them, her grandmother's words had both chilled and excited her: "Because, dearest Aubrianne, you are marked. I do not pretend to foretell the future, but in your life, there will be dark days. These weapons will protect you and those you hold dear."

So far, no one at Stolweg knew she possessed such a treasure. She had told Cellach only that she was equipped to defend herself. Anna glanced at her door; Grainne was not due back for another hour. She chanced a look at her armament. She pressed the secret latch at the bottom of the enormous trunk, and the bottom panel popped open to reveal several bundles wrapped in thick fabric. One by one she unwrapped them. First, a beautiful bow and a quiver of arrows—she would need fresh catgut for the string.

A shield came next. One of remarkable quality, light enough for a woman to carry but hardy enough to take the strongest blow. Anna's fingers traced the scratches and dents from long-ago battles. The shield was married to a helmet, likewise enameled in the deepest blue and inlaid with pure silver stars. Breastplate followed, then cuisse and greave for leg protection and pauldron and vambrace for arms.

She gazed sadly at the smallest bundle before lifting it from the compartment. An empty dagger sheath, cracked and malformed from years of disuse. The missing piece of the set, gone for generations. No matter—she had her grandfather's blade.

Finally, Anna lifted the one remaining bundle from the trunk. She carried it as if holding an infant and tenderly placed it on her bed. She unfolded the fabric to reveal a belt, scabbard, and sword. Stepping to the center of her chamber and holding the sheath, she pulled the sword out in one smooth motion. Its blade gleamed in the sunlight, its metal untarnished. For the first time in her life, the hilt felt natural in her hand. Her arms remembered the lessons taught to her by Osbert, and she swung the blade in a high arc, coming down and across, thrusting forward and pulling back only to lift and cross down again from the other direction. It was but one of many practice drills hammered into her.

Anna's bosom heaved. She felt invigorated. As her breath calmed, she took stock of her scarred back. There had been some tightness, but none of the wounds felt as though they had ruptured. She repacked her trunk, shutting the lid with a satisfying thump just as Grainne bustled into her chamber with her evening meal.

"M'lady, you should be resting," her maid counseled.

"I am finished with resting," Anna affirmed, relishing the new sense of purpose that filled her.

CHAPTER NINETEEN

Threats and Oaths

When Roger finally returned to Stolweg from his latest foray south, he brought with him gifts from Chevring. His wife had not even known he was visiting there. And why should she? His marriage had nothing to do with love, and everything to do with advancing his grand plan. She was simply the means to his end. The gifts from her family were intended for her: several gowns and a few baubles from her mother. And from her father, additional broodmares, a few already with foal.

And there she waited, standing so stoically in the center of his chamber, ready to do his bidding. He been gone nearly a month and had hoped to see a growing abdomen upon his return.

Aubrianne might be proficient at breeding his horses, but she was a complete failure at giving his seed a home in her womb—he pressed the nib of his quill too hard, and it collapsed, leaving an untidy ink splotch on the ledger. His father had sired so many bastards, Roger had lost count. Even his brother, still unwed, was rumored to have a brat or two. Roger patiently cut a new quill, and made some notations regarding the lumber he'd sold to his wife's father, dragging him further into debt.

Everything had gone according to plan, everything except getting Aubrianne with child. He closed the ledger, set down his quill, and pulled out the latest letter from his father. He'd already read it, had it memorized in fact, but there was something about his father's penmanship that tugged at Roger. For as tyrannical as his father could be, Roger worshipped him.

Which was why he hadn't yet replaced his wife. He was within his rights; no man would argue the point. She was barren, and therefore was in breach of the marriage contract. But his father ordered him to be patient, for Aubrianne was still useful in her capacity as a horse breeder. And he couldn't fault her management of the keep, though she was too familiar with the servants. One year more, his father had written, or two, and Roger would be free to dispose of her as he wished. In the meantime, he should continue to try to plant his seed, in his wife or any other woman for that matter.

Before Roger could think about the replacement he'd chosen for his wife, there was some important business that needed tending, and he folded the letter into a neat square before tossing it into the hearth. He turned toward the object of his consternation and saw the highlights in her untamed mass of hair glint brighter as the letter took flame.

• • •

As Anna waited, she asked herself what Roger had given her family in return for the additional broodmares; she prayed her father was not more indebted to him. When she'd entered the room, she had noticed a new trunk in the corner behind his desk and recognized it as one of her mother's. She might not ever know its contents.

A flash in the hearth brought her abruptly from her ponderings, and she was startled to see that Roger was walking toward her. She shivered in her nakedness, but not because she was cold. Her husband wished to examine the scars on her back. Anna's skin twitched in protest as he touched the wounds. Surprisingly, he bade her dress again. She had no sooner refastened the ties of her wedding gown when there was a knock at his door.

"Enter," her husband ordered. "Ah, Gorman, on time for once. What think you? The Lady of Stolweg seems restored."

"I didn't expect to see her so quickly recovered, m'lord," he replied, his tone etched with disappointment.

"I have been wondering about you of late, Aubrianne," her husband said. "You have overstepped your bounds a number of times. And I have been patient, amused by your spirit. But the lesson for the stable hand proved to be one for me as well. Do not pretend to me that you do not wish me dead. I would like to hear you admit this truth."

She lifted her chin and looked him straight in the eye. "Your request is my pleasure, m'lord." He slapped her hard across the face, and she tasted the blood inside her mouth where her teeth had cut into her cheek.

"Before you plan my demise, know this, *wife*: I have soldiers stationed at Chevring. They have been ordered to kill every man, woman, and child upon hearing of my death. You have a sister, do you not? Claire, I believe. Should I send word that you need her? Such a beautiful girl. Do you think she would adapt to a new life here?"

Gorman snickered. With so many soldiers moving in and out of Stolweg at night, Roger could easily have sent some to Chevring.

"You may want to know why I have invited Gorman into my chamber this evening," her husband taunted. "It is so I can be sure that you understand the consequences of any actions that you, or others, might take against me."

He looked at the brute standing next to her. "Gorman, I ask you to swear this oath: should I die, by accident or foul means, you will take my lovely wife, Lady Aubrianne, and kill her. However, if you find yourself tempted by her beauty, I would understand a few hours' delay."

Anna stood, unwavering, as Gorman repeated the oath. *Checkmate*, she thought.

"Good night, Gorman," Roger said, dismissing him before coming to stand behind her. "I think you now understand your position here, Aubrianne," Roger whispered. "You may return to your room; come back to me two nights hence."

Defeated, Anna made her way back to her chamber. Roger now controlled her completely; the fate of her family rested in his hands. She prayed for them.

Two nights later, she returned and waited for Roger to acknowledge her. "Step over to the bed, Aubrianne," he politely ordered, stripping his breeches as he followed her. And as he took her, he whispered into her ear, "Do you think your sister will enjoy her time here?"

He said *will*, Anna realized, not *would*.

After he finished, Anna made her way to her chamber. This night, like all the others, he had taken her from behind. She was amazed by his lack of foresight, for gazing into his loathsome face would be a torture she could never survive. And except for the day they were married, she had yet to suffer a single filthy kiss from his wretched lips. Even then, he had only kissed her forehead.

In the safety of her rooms, two thoughts crystallized in her mind: one, her husband's perversion knew no bounds, and two, perhaps it was finally time to try the saltpeter.

CHAPTER TWENTY

Winter's Tapestry

Winter was coming early; Anna could taste it in the air as she rode ahead of the mares. She studied the gray landscape. Barely November, and the once beautifully colored foliage was no longer lying in soft mounds upon the earth but crackling and blowing wildly with each passing gust. She thought of Lia, sent far from the keep. Her babe would've been born by now, and Anna wondered if it was a boy or girl. She patted Tullian's neck as they watched over his brood.

Her efforts since arriving at Stolweg were noteworthy. Seven additions to Roger's stable, and four more expected. At Chevring, Anna had memorized the old breeding journals. There had been times when the mares had been bred from one year to the next, in some cases spanning a decade. It had been the Great War that had spawned such an aggressive breeding program. So why did Stolweg need so many horses? Roger's answer pointed to the King's tournaments. As excuses went, his was feeble. Anna saw no indication that he'd ever entered a single tournament, and according to Cellach, Roger's armor hadn't left the armory in years.

Her own reasons for such a prolific success were much less complicated. If almost every mare in the stable were with foal, Roger would need her. She pushed this depressing thought aside.

Of late, he had been pressuring her to complete the training of the foals early; he wanted the first two to be given to the King and his heir. Anna had explained that it would take at least three years to produce a true Chevring steed. He gave her two. Although she had no choice but to accept his terms, she managed to give one of her own. Her time away from the keep would have to increase in order to spend more time preparing the young horses. An added benefit was that she wouldn't be subjected overmuch to her husband's evil predilections.

NICOLE ELIZABETH KELLEHER

She'd been using the saltpeter, and although its effects were slow to manifest, her husband's virility was suffering. It had taken her awhile to overcome her embarrassment when using the fool's pipe, for it had to be applied to the area that would come into most contact with her husband. Even now, Anna blushed thinking about it. Mixed with her balm, Roger hadn't noticed; the scent of lavender always lingered about her.

• • •

In the quiet of her room, Anna gazed at the tapestries covering the thick stone walls of her chamber. She began pacing in front of one. It was the third of five in her chamber, and together they told a story of love and courtship. She'd always hated them.

The first tapestry showed a lady traveling with her escorts at the exact moment at which her party was beset. The second depicted a lord coming to the rescue and assailing the enemy. The lady sat her horse with her hand over her heart, gazing at the man who battled to save her. Next in line was the largest; it depicted the courtship of the lord and lady.

Upon the fourth tapestry was woven the story of a hunt. It was one of two flanking the fireplace. A great stag had been stitched upon it, head alert, body poised to bound away from impending danger. The lord had his bow at the ready, but his lady's hand rested on his arm. Anna had always found this tapestry most intriguing. Did the lord spare the stag or did he loose his arrow?

The final tapestry, in front of which she now stood, showed a great wedding feast. In the center was a bonfire. The lord and lady presided over the gathering, their hands clasped. It was the most romantic of the tapestries, she thought ruefully. It annoyed her completely.

Anna studied the fourth wall hanging again, the one she dubbed "The Hunt." About to move on, she noticed a peculiarity. The lady looked at neither the stag nor her lord. Instead, her face was tilted toward the upper left corner of the tapestry. Anna searched the scene on the tapestry, trying to locate the object of the lady's attention. There was nothing but the decorative border.

But the design on the upper corner was oddly familiar. With a stool and standing on tiptoes, Anna could just make out the image. It was a bird's-eye view of Stolweg Keep. Along the interior square of the castle, a purl of silver had been stitched, neatly linking each of the four corner towers. The towers holding her chamber and the western chamber were wholly outlined in the same thread. When the stool tottered, she reached for purchase, pushing the tapestry against the wall. The shadows shifted over the weave's surface to reveal another gilded strand. Amazingly, through the years of wear, she could see a thin, silver line trailing outward from the west tower in the direction of where the chapel stood.

Anna's heart beat faster. Could these tapestries have hidden an age-old secret all these years: hidden passageways in the keep? And what of the thread that extended from the west tower? Anna studied the tapestry again—not the scene, but the construction and materials that made it. The woven threads were probably as old as the keep itself. Had the architects added secret passageways and sewn the clues into the tapestry?

With racing heart, Anna walked back to the courtship panel and examined the corners. Only one corner was different. The pattern was an exact match to the outline of her chamber. In the dim light, she could see a faint purl on the upper right edge of the square.

Taking her bearings from the tapestry, she deduced that if there were a passage, the entrance would be behind the tapestry to the right of the hearth. She walked over to "The Wedding Feast" and looked at the panel's four corners. Each depicted the same image: a four-petaled rose with a door in the center. She pulled the heavy hanging away from the wall and discovered a recess, perhaps only a foot deep. But the mortared stones showed no seam, nor crack, nor hinge. But there, set high above her head—a carved rosette with thorny vine! The same Stolweg rose pattern that was prevalent throughout the castle.

Anna raced back to the courtship tapestry again. In the center of the diamond depicting her chamber was a four-petaled rose complete with vine. She looked anew at the upper corner. A symbol resembling a keyhole was centered in the rose.

There had to be a release of some kind to open the passageway. She had to be missing something. Anna stood back and took in the wedding feast tapestry as a whole. The lord and lady stood between a great bonfire and a table laden with food. The lady's hands were open and extended as if bidding her guests welcome, directing them to the flames. But why not to the banquet table?

She peered at the stitching that made up the fire. The wood appeared to be wood. The smoke curled like smoke, replete with bits of ash floating to the heavens. The oath that Anna let out was neither quiet nor proper. The dark bits were not specks of ash, but miniature keyholes. Fire and smoke, another clue!

She flew back to her fireplace. Ornately carved, the Stolweg rose flourished on the mantel and along the sides of the hearth.

"Aha!" she exclaimed upon locating a rosette with a keyhole symbol. It was about the size of her palm. When she pushed at the carving, the stone moved a finger's width, and so easily that she thought it had not moved at all. She had expected to hear some click of a latch, a grating of stone upon stone. She did not even feel a draft.

Anna peeked behind the tapestry, half afraid that she would find the alcove as solid as it was before and half afraid of seeing a dark, gaping void. As it turned out, she saw neither. But the alcove *had* changed. There was now a distinct delineation of an entrance carved into the stone. She pushed against the wall, and it moved effortlessly.

She took a deep breath and passed through the opening. Just as quickly, she stepped back into her chamber. An irrational fear swept through her: the entrance could close, leaving her locked in the stone passageway forever. She grabbed a log from the hearth and wedged it in the gap, only to laugh at her overcautiousness once she found the matching release inside the opening.

The passageway turned to the left where a short flight of stairs ascended behind her fireplace. Forcing her racing heart to slow, Anna stepped carefully up the stairs and found a short stretch of hallway to the right followed by two sets of steps going in opposite directions. Imagining the design of the keep, she deduced that the steps hugging the chimney had been created to take a person up and over the hallway that connected the four chambers. It was the only way that such a connecting passage could exist along the inner square of the castle.

Anna skipped down the steps. She walked to the east tower, to Cellach's quarters and the armory. Exactly where she thought they would be, she found another set of steps. But she continued and found the descending steps to the right, leading northwest. All in all, there were four passageways leading to four sets of steps, ending at the four main chambers of the keep.

With Roger away, she could secretly enter his chamber with no person the wiser. She took a deep breath and walked to her destination. In her mind, she counted off the same number of steps that it took her to reach Roger's chamber all those nights before. *One, two, three, four...* Soon, the lantern's glow revealed the steps that would take her over the corridor and into the north chamber. She touched the stone on the back of his hearth. The wall was reassuringly cool, confirming his absence.

Anna raised her light and located the release that would allow her entrance to the room that had been her private hell. Setting her lantern on the floor, not wanting its light to alert anyone who might be below

Roger's windows, she pulled the door open.

Anna needn't have worried about her lamp, as the window shutters were sealed, and thick drapes had been drawn over the large leaded glass window. Still, she was cautious when retrieving her lantern and thrice-shuttered the candle's glow through the translucent horn panels. She stepped over to Roger's massive desk, and then stared down at the neat piles of parchment and ledger books. With utmost care, she rolled back the documents one by one, keeping an anchoring fingertip on the bottom edge of the stack. She was halfway through the second pile when she saw one of Cellach's drawings. But she had barely registered the notations regarding materials and measurements when her eye caught something much more dear.

In a neat script, as familiar as her own, was her father's writing. Pages and pages of it. She realized that what she was seeing were torn-out sheets from one of the many ledgers at Chevring. Notations concerning mares and their offspring and debts paid to Roger were meticulously entered. And on the last page, next to a payment of lumber, a pen different from her father's appeared. The letters were long, deeply scrolled, and elegant: Roger's hand. There was only one word and a number: *Mordemur 10*.

She whispered the word, a person's name perhaps. In the silence of the chamber, her hushed voice echoed in the corners of the cavernous room. She glanced down at the desk, checking to make sure she had left everything as she had found it. The hour was growing late, and not wanting to push her luck, Anna walked quickly to the secret passage.

When she returned to her chamber, she thought about her discoveries and what they could mean. Why had her father parted with his ledger sheets? And who on earth was Mordemur? Had he anything to do with the lumber?

Anna thought again of the silver thread on the tapestry that indicated an egress from the castle to the chapel. There *had* to be another secret passage, and she was determined to find it.

CHAPTER TWENTY-ONE

King's Notice

As the storms of March continued to roar, the horses became restless. Weeks of being kept to the paddocks and stable were taking their toll on man and beast alike. When the first sunny day appeared with its brilliant skies, Anna, Gilles, and Will took the herd straight to the southeast hills. They remained away from the keep for seven days and nights, before returning to find Roger gone already for six. When he didn't return the next day, or the next after that, the group of conspirators decided to meet. They chose to rendezvous in the Chapel. Word was spread.

Arrangements were made to keep the unwanted away, a detail left to Grainne and Doreen. Cellach eyed the group. Clearing his throat, he suggested, "Shall we commence?"

"Not yet, Cellach," Anna stated. "I've asked one other to join us." The door opened. Every voice fell silent as Will entered, followed by Carrick. Many a curious eye went from the miller to Doreen and Gilles and back.

Anna motioned for him to take a seat next to her. Carrick regarded everyone, daring them to challenge his presence. He saved Will's parents for last. "Doreen, Gilles," he started solemnly, "I am sorry for my daughter Maggie's part in your family's pain."

Doreen managed a smile. "My thanks for your words, Carrick. You are as welcome here as any of us."

At Anna's nod, Cellach began. "I've been tracking the number of men coming through Stolweg, strangers all. Lord Roger has even made a point of speaking openly about them from time to time, claiming that they are wool merchants from Ragallach."

Carrick harrumphed. "Wool merchants, my arse. Pardon, m'lady," he apologized after being elbowed by Grainne. "Ev'ry merchant I've met carries samples of his wares. Those crossing the mill's causeway carry nothing but metal strapped to their belts, though they try to hide it."

"I've seen some of them. Soldiers," Anna stated. "Cellach, do you know where they go after leaving here?"

"Not for certain, m'lady," he said. "I've followed their tracks as far south as the mountain pass into Chevring. Some have gone back in the direction of Ragallach, though they take the treacherous route to bypass Cathmara. And a few have gone west."

"And the men not bothering to disguise their trade?" Anna asked. "How many of these soldiers are still here at the keep?"

"Nine, at least," Gilles stated. "We've been seeing to their horses."

"More like fifteen," Doreen corrected, "judging by the food I've been sending to the barracks. Not all soldiers ride, my dear."

"Double that number for the men he sends on regular patrols," Anna said. "Cellach, Stolweg has how many strongholds along the coast? Four?" He nodded. "Are they all manned?"

He nodded again. "Lord John, Lady Isabel's father, awarded the strongholds to his most trusted men, all lesser nobles of Stolweg who fought valiantly during the Great War. Their families still live there—at least, they did when last I toured the strongholds with Lord Roger. Each has its servants, farmers, and tradesmen, as well as its own complement of soldiers."

"When was the last time you visited one of the strongholds?" she asked.

"Three months before Lord Roger married you, m'lady," he replied. "He has kept me tied to the area around the keep and has sent Gorman instead."

Anna was silent for a moment, half listening to the others share their opinions on the number of men her husband was moving into and through Stolweg. "It is only natural that he would want some of his men from Ragallach here," she mused. "No one would think it odd. He could slowly replace all the men who were once loyal to Lord John, one by one, moving them to the remote strongholds." She glanced up, surprised that every eye was on her. "Lord Roger has been doing this since before I came to Stolweg, hasn't he?" Cellach nodded. "And how many men here—the soldiers, I mean—are from the old watch?"

"Maybe five," Cellach replied dismally.

"It'll be four tomorrow," Gilles amended. "Old Tom's son, Jorah, is leaving in the morning."

Anna turned to Cellach to speak but was interrupted by a chirp of warning. Will had been posted near the entrance to the chapel and had given the signal that meant there was movement near the barracks. "We've been here too long," Doreen worried. Anna nodded, and the group dispersed.

• • •

Cellach waited until only he and Lady Aubrianne remained. His respect for her grew every time he met with her. "That was either the most dangerous stunt that you pulled with Carrick or the most brilliant. What made you think to include him?"

She pondered his question before answering him. "Call it a hunch," she said with a shrug. "What do *you* think, Cellach?"

"I've wanted to include Carrick for the last year or so. I only hesitated out of deference to you, Lady Aubrianne. It was a good thing you did today. He is an honest man and can be counted on despite his foolish daughter. What did you say to him?"

"Actually, he brought up the subject." When Cellach raised his eyebrows in alarm, Lady Aubrianne continued, "Rest easy, Cellach. He started by telling me how he'd heard about Maggie's involvement in Will's flogging. He asked how he could approach Doreen and Gilles to express his sorrow over his daughter's lack of judgment."

"And this led you to invite him into our circle?"

"I admit it was part of it," she answered. "Then he shared an interesting story with me."

Cellach listened as Lady Aubrianne related Carrick's tale.

"He rode east a few weeks ago, needing a part to repair a piece of machinery. The only person he trusted with the job was a blacksmith just within the borders of Whitmarsh. On the way, he saw the tracks of a single rider, tracks going east. He only noticed them because they seemed to appear from nowhere. The next day, he stopped at the Crossroads Inn rather than camping in the woods. He was spooked and wanted company.

"While eating his supper—and these are Carrick's exact words—'A bear of a man entered the inn. He scanned the empty tables, then chose to sit with me. It was his eyes that gave me pause. Everything about his hulking figure reeked of violence. Everything except his eyes.' Carrick told me that the innkeeper went to great lengths to please the man."

Cellach had been hoping to hear some news to this effect. "Did he tell you the man's name?"

"Yes," his lady replied. "His name was Trian."

Cellach leaned back against the wall. A rare and thoughtful smile played on his lips, and his mistress inquired, "Do you know him, Cellach?"

"No. But I've heard of him. He's of the Royal Guard. What else did Carrick say?"

"He said that this man, Trian, was interested in the goings-on at Stolweg and asked what news could be had. He also asked that his interest not be imparted to the wrong ears upon the miller's return. Trian offered Carrick some coin for information, coin that Carrick refused."

Cellach's elation plummeted.

Lady Aubrianne continued, "Carrick said that he was taken by Trian's forthrightness. And knowing the innkeeper was a good man and a sound judge of character, he offered information freely. Our wonderful miller told Trian all about dear Lord Roger, his frequent departures, his abuse of the people, the strangers coming and going at all hours from the keep. Bless Carrick, he even told this Trian that despite the spring, the days were still too dark at Stolweg."

"You realize what this means, m'lady?" Cellach said as he walked with her through the courtyard. "Not only has the King taken an interest in the activities here, he is now aware of our plight."

"Carrick said almost the same. It was right afterward that he asked me if he could do anything. Not ready to reveal our group, I asked him what he meant and he told me this: 'There's change in the wind; I can smell it. Trouble's brewing, and I want to be on the right side when it comes. Like I told that man Trian, loyalty and trust come cheap if the right person asks. It's only the wrong side that finds those qualities expensive.' I told our miller that I would send word if I needed him. So today I sent Will to ask him to join us."

Lady Aubrianne paused outside the entrance to the keep. "Cellach," she said quietly, "we must have more information if we are to protect ourselves. If Roger is acting against the good of the realm, we mustn't be implicated. Do you trust Jorah enough to do reconnaissance for us?"

Cellach nodded, seeing where his lady was going. "It could work," he said. "Yes, yes, it could work."

"Excellent," she stated. "I'll leave you to it and bid you goodnight."

Before she could step through the door, Cellach added, "Thank you, m'lady. It is good to finally take action after all these years."

She agreed, but added, "This is only the beginning, Cellach."

CHAPTER TWENTY-TWO

Escape Route

They had risked much in meeting together with Roger's return imminent. Anna was pleased that her friends were preparing for the worst, but she wanted more than a plan based solely on defending herself. She needed something much more tangible: an escape route, one she could share with the others if necessary. So, while she and Grainne supped together, Anna asked her maid about the tapestries.

"Lady Isabel loved these old tapestries. She told me they were a gift from the first lord of Stolweg to his wife. This has always been the lady's chamber, you see. And the story depicted is true."

Grainne pointed to the second tapestry. "Yon lord came to her rescue, defeating the ruffians. It turned out that the lady was the youngest daughter of the King. He was so grateful to have his daughter safely returned that he awarded the lord with title and the lands that are now Stolweg. The King also gave the lord his daughter as wife. They fell in love while the keep was constructed.

"I always liked to believe that the lady's favorite flower was the rose," Grainne added wistfully, "and that is why it is carved everywhere."

Anna smiled at Grainne's romantic streak. "It may well have been her favorite flower, but I think its meaning goes much deeper." Anna pointed to the four petals. "Each of the four petals represents one of the four corners of the castle. And the thorny vine gives three-sided protection, like the river flowing around us."

"I never noticed that, m'lady. Too much of the old history has faded," she said with a sigh.

"But you are right too, Grainne," Anna added. "Without fail, the lady on the tapestries either is holding a rose or has the flower embroidered on her garments. She would've been a kindred spirit with my mother."

After Grainne departed, Anna slipped into her most serviceable breeches and tunic. She picked up her lantern and hurried to the tapestries for one last look. The purled corners, she knew, revealed the secret passage like a legend on a map. Perhaps there was more to learn, she thought, kneeling to study the details along the bottom edge for further clues. The lower right corner showed the outline of what had to be the west chamber. Stitched into the center of the rosette was a cross. Anna brushed the dust from the tapestry and held her flame closer. There, she thought, a gilded stitch that must certainly represent the chamber's great window.

Next, she went to the lower left corner's design. Although there was no silver thread, the rosette offered one last clue: in its center, a table with three lines underneath. Perhaps the west chamber would reveal its meaning. Anna walked determinedly to her fireplace and pressed the special rosette that would open the passageway behind the tapestry.

Before long, she silently entered the vacant west chamber, dimmed her light, and crossed the room to the window. If the silver thread on the tapestry in her chamber represented what she believed, she would find some sort of latch on the window seat below the mullioned glass of the great west-facing window.

The moon, gibbous-waning, barely pierced the slit in the heavy drapes, so Anna moved her lantern closer and ran her hand over the ancient wood of the bench. Smoothed by years of use, its patina was rich and beautiful even in the dim light. The seat back featured the Stolweg rose, but something had once been carved in its center. All that remained now was the outline of a rectangle with two curved lines below it. Anna then studied the carved rosettes that ran under the lip of the seat, feeling for one that was different from the others. She found it, moments later, on the left side. Within its center, a flame had been carved. She pressed it.

The banquette tipped forward to reveal another passageway. In the space below the seat were steps so steep she mistook them for ladder rungs. After pulling the seat closed above her, she climbed down cautiously and stood breathlessly on a narrow landing. Only by turning sideways was she able to move behind the staircase and descend a second set of steps, then a third.

Her light revealed a tunnel with a ceiling supported by wooden beams so old they might have been made of stone. The air around her was stale and dry, without the slightest stirring.

She peered ahead into the darkness but was unable to make out the end of the tunnel. A wood planking system had been laid down, smothering any noise of footfall as she moved forward. The only sound came from her heartbeat and her excited breath.

Finally, Anna saw steps. After walking up the short flight, she found herself in a small alcove. Anna found the release latch and pressed. The outline of her egress silently emerged. She took a deep breath and pulled at the door.

After her travels through the dry and dusty underground corridor, the smell of beeswax and incense assaulted her senses. In front of her was an ornately carved panel. Seeing it from the reverse, it took Anna a moment to recognize that she was standing behind the wood backdrop for the devotional candles. The passage had delivered her into the chapel.

Except for a few sputtering votives, the church was deserted. The moon was high now, and its beams streamed through the windows, illuminating the colored glass, infusing the air with soft jewel tones. It was beautiful, she thought, as if she'd stepped into a rainbow.

Where would the next passageway lead her? The chapel was within the curtain wall and offered no chance of escape. Anna stared across the vaulted room. The sanctuary was simple in design, with a plain altar of veined marble resting upon two stone piers. Her gasp echoed through the space as she realized that the form was identical to the depiction on the tapestry in her chamber. Not a table, as she had guessed, but an altar. Mayhap the three lines represented the steps behind it.

The pull of discovering a link to yet another tunnel was too great. There was one last clue to unravel: the rectangle with the two curved lines. She stepped quickly behind the altar, then allowed her fingers to do more work than her eyes. They better recognized the oft repeated carving of the rosette as she ran them over the cool stone. If the architects had hidden another tunnel, they would have placed its release as near to the opening as possible.

The pattern under her fingertips was intricate. Carved in stone, the rosettes' vines trailed and interlaced with one another. To the far right, one rosette was different.

She scanned the expanse of the chapel one last time. Assured that she was still alone, she pushed the carved stone button. In the empty church, a barely audible *snick* sounded. Following the noise, Anna returned to the front of the altar and lowered herself to the main floor. And there it was, after two years, the secret that had been right in front of her each and every time she came to pray for succor.

The panel on the right had shifted to reveal a small gap. The carved wood glided smoothly to the side. She moved her lamp into the opening and peered into the shadowed pocket. The space was about as wide as the platform supporting the altar. Anna crawled through the opening and discovered a dark hole with steeply carved steps, mere toe- and handholds cut into a nearly vertical wall. The air was cool and damp, and the farther she climbed down, the moister the stone surface became. She breathed a sigh of relief when her feet touched flat rock. The stone floor descended at a shallow grade, a hundred paces at least, before gradually changing to an incline.

When she reached yet another set of steps, she climbed quickly to the landing and held her lamp aloft. Carved into the lintel of an arched door, she read aloud, "Be Not Afraid to Enter Our Home. Unlike You, We Are at Rest." Releasing the latch, she stepped into the darkness. The barracks! Her mind screamed, and she stepped quickly back and away from the sleeping men. She suddenly realized where she stood. This was the old crypt. The supine men and women were carved of stone.

Months ago, she had explored this exact spot. She stepped to its inner, solid oak door, opening it to reveal an old metal gate, its latch long broken from disuse. It was probably the only mechanical thing that was in disrepair at Stolweg. She waited until she was in the safety of the tunnel before shouting with joy. If the time came, she had the means to escape the keep and its curtain wall undetected!

In the coming months, she explored the passageways whenever she was able, formulating plan after plan only to discard them. Each plan resulted in the death of her family. It wasn't until spring came around once more that Anna realized what would be required of her. She shivered. The cost due for saving her family would be more than Roger's life.

CHAPTER TWENTY-THREE

King's Glen

Lord Baldric of Whitmarsh, the King's most trusted adviser, was troubled. He'd been at King's Glen and in council with King Godwin for a week now. Like weeds, the answers they sought only served to propagate new questions. Everything circled back to Lord Roger. Stolweg was too important an asset to the realm's protection to have someone with questionable motives in place as its leader.

Baldric sat next to King Godwin at the large table in Glen Hall. With him were assembled the elite of the Royal Guard: Larkin and Warin, Trian and Tomas, and Ailwen. In times of war, these five men would be Baldric's captains. They had gathered to discuss Lord Roger.

Trian, Larkin's closest friend, had returned from his mission and was reporting his findings. He had just finished describing the group of people moving horses to different grazing areas, explaining that the herd was always confined to the fertile hills and woods to the south and southeast of Stolweg Keep.

With a nod from the King, Baldric finally spoke, choosing his words carefully. "Let us start with the most obvious. Trian, do you believe the group with the horses could be doing other than that which they appeared to be doing?"

"The riders always numbered two or three," Trian expounded. "One rider was a man and the other a boy—rather, a young man. I had thought the third rider was a boy as well. It became obvious by the way the other two deferred to him that *he* was instead a *she*."

"Must be the Chevring girl," Baldric said. "It makes sense that she would be with the horses. I've heard that her prowess in breeding and training exceeds that of her great-grandfather's. Roger chose well his wife."

Trian nodded his agreement. "They've bred more than a dozen

foals. From the tracks of the mares, more are on the way, three or four, at least. The horses are all of Chevring stock."

"That is something to consider, isn't it?" King Godwin commented. "Everyone at this table would agree that the Great War was won because Nifolhad's lords were outhorsed." After a pause, he added, "It is time to speak of Lord Roger. What think you all? Is he treasonous?"

Warin, Tomas, and Ailwen glanced at one another uncomfortably. It was one thing to suspect treason, Baldric thought, another to accuse. Trian, always one to keep silent unless he had something of import to relate, cleared his throat as if to speak, then lowered his head to think. But Larkin stood abruptly. "If Lord Roger is suspected of treason, we must act," he charged.

A look passed between Baldric and the King. "It's time that you heard the rest," King Godwin said patiently. "To understand Roger, we must discuss Nifolhad. Baldric?"

Baldric took a deep breath and began. "When King Cedric of Nifolhad died three years ago, and his brother Diarmait declared himself Steward King, we realized there would be repercussions in the state of peace between our two realms. At first, diplomatic ties went on as usual. Cedric's daughter, Aghna, was to marry a favorite of Cedric's, a man who shared his desire for a kingdom unmarred by the hardship of war." Baldric, seeing Larkin's impatience grow, gave him a hard look.

"You may already know this story, but you do not know that Princess Aghna, Cedric's only heir, has died. The details are not clear. Her betrothed, Lord Ranulf, managed to get us word: he believes that Diarmait is culpable. Diarmait's son, Bowen, now has a clear path to the throne. With Nifolhad still mourning the loss of King Cedric, they are now torn apart over the death of Princess Aghna. Their people are clamoring for Bowen's coronation."

"And this *Bowen*," Larkin asked, "how does he view the peace that has reigned for so long? His father has long voiced his objections to the treaty between our realms."

King Godwin spoke then. "That is what we have been trying to ascertain. Unfortunately, the envoys we have sent have not returned and are considered lost. For now, assume Bowen is of a like mind to his father."

"How does Lord Roger fit into this puzzle?" Trian asked.

Baldric steepled his fingers and cleared his throat. "A good question, that."

"Interesting, isn't it?" Larkin asked no one in particular. "Ragallach's only strategic value is that it can alert the kingdom of any invaders from the west. Roger returns to Ragallach, and his grandfather conveniently dies. Then, Roger obtains control of Stolweg by marrying Lady Isabel, giving him a stronghold in the center of the realm." Larkin continued, "Soon after, the Lord of Stolweg dies. Again, conveniently. After Lady Isabel dies, there is trouble at Chevring. And who comes to the rescue with the necessary coin? Lord Roger. In return, he is given one of the Chevring daughters and access to Aurelia's greatest weapon: the Chevring destriers."

Larkin addressed his fellow guards, bringing the point of his observations to bear on their minds. "In just six years, Lord Roger's influence reaches from the northwest clear to the southwest, a wide band across the kingdom."

"I see you *have* been listening at court these past months," Godwin said with admiration. "Have you any other thoughts?"

Larkin gave King Godwin a respectful nod before brandishing one final question. "I do, if it pleases you, my liege. The question we should all be asking is this: Just who is Lord Roger's true father?"

"Who indeed?" echoed the King.

A plan was drawn up. Lord Baldric, with the cream of the Royal Guard, would ride west to Whitmarsh, then on to Stolweg. There, they would question Lord Roger and his people, and determine once and for all if the man was plotting against the King.

CHAPTER TWENTY-FOUR

Horses

The date of Anna's third wedding anniversary came and went. She celebrated that Roger had not remembered. However, Anna always remembered, for the passing of each year since coming to Stolweg was never far from her thoughts.

So much had changed, she thought. She had many friends now, and the breeding program had exceeded her expectations. And she'd been practicing with bow and quarterstaff, and was feeling stronger than she ever had before.

And so little had changed, she realized too. Despite all of her accomplishments, she and the others had yet to discover what Roger was plotting. He'd just returned from his latest journey and summoned her to his chamber. She stood patiently in front of him as he demanded an update on the foals. "They are to be ready to present to the King in the fall," he ordered.

"If you want to present steeds such as Tullian," Anna retorted, "it takes years."

"They do not have to be saddle ready, Aubrianne," Roger countered with a pained look. "I just want them to have the heart of a Chevring destrier. The King has an entire staff of trainers. Tullian's little tricks are amusing, but not especially useful; he has yet to be tested in battle."

He was so condescending that Anna's ire was pricked. "The colts were *born* Chevring steeds," she maintained heatedly. "Heart in a warhorse comes from breeding, not training."

A satisfied coldness settled over her husband's face. She had unwittingly driven another nail into her coffin by giving Roger the idea that her training skills were no longer necessary. As he walked away, she wondered just how many weeks she had left.

Days later, this question still occupied her thoughts as she rode back to the keep. She'd been in the hills with the mares and returned to a stable in shambles. Will raced from the paddocks to intercept her. It seemed that Lord Roger had procured more mares and a few geldings in her absence. Anna followed him to the corral. At first she thought her eyes were deceiving her. The horses were from Chevring, every last one.

Had her family arrived? Where was her father's stallion and her mother's gentle mare? Where was Rebel, Claire's steed? She raced from the stable and was breathless by the time she reached Roger's door. Only by sheer force of will did she manage to stop herself from barging in. She rapped firmly on the door. It swung open, and Gorman leered wolfishly at her before leaving her alone with her husband. Roger sat near his hearth. She strode forward and demanded news of her family. Roger's mastiff leapt to his feet, growling and snapping his jaws, ready to protect his master. Anna drew back as the dog advanced.

• • •

Roger watched her quell her urge to flee, half hoping she would make a run for the door. If she did, his beast would attack. But she held her ground, ignored the dog's low growls, and waited for an answer.

"Ah, Aubrianne," Roger drawled, "I assume you have seen the horses." He stood next to his dog and placed a loving hand on its massive head. "For nothing else would cause you to be so rude as to come here uninvited."

His wife said nothing, probably for fear of provoking the still-growling Garamantes.

"Your father had some trouble with his stable again. It caught fire," Roger explained. His wife shuddered. "Your father wanted the surviving horses cared for."

"A fire. Is my family—"

"I suppose that some good has come from this," Roger interrupted. "We now have more broodmares."

He grinned at his wife, relishing her repulsion at his callousness. "You may leave now, Aubrianne. I expect you back this evening.

"And do take care around Garamantes. He is trained to follow certain command words but will also attack on his own if he senses a threat to my person. For example, if I were to say his name and *lladhund*, you would be dead in minutes." Garamantes had bristled and crouched down as if stalking prey. "*Bakea*, Garamantes," Roger commanded, and his dog immediately sat down and thumped his tail. "You can go now,

Aubrianne," Roger said. "Garamantes has hunted enough this month."

When his wife departed, Roger squatted down in front of his dog and scratched the thick fur of his neck with affection. Garamantes shifted forward, toppling his master, who laughed as the dog took advantage of him and licked his face. "Good boy," Roger encouraged him. "And don't you worry; you'll have prey enough in the coming year."

CHAPTER TWENTY-FIVE

Ride to Stolweg

Lord Baldric, along with King Godwin's most trusted guards, departed King's Glen. They traveled with great haste, stopping at Baldric's home, Castle Whitmarsh. They rested one night, and then departed the next morning. His men—Larkin, Trian, Warin, Tomas, and Ailwen—were unusually quiet as they pressed on at top speeds. On the eve of the final day, they rode well past sunset. When they finally stopped, weary from the day's grueling pace, they tended to their horses, and bedded down for the night.

• • •

Larkin was checking on his horse one last time when Trian took first watch. Warin had second, followed by Tomas. Larkin knew Warin would wake Tomas early. No doubt Tomas would finish Warin's duty without complaint. So when Tomas's watch was only halfway through, Larkin relieved him. "Get some sleep. I'll take over now."

Tomas was the newest of the five guards appointed to this mission. In appearance, the young man was everything Larkin was not: fair, blond, blue-eyed, and baby-faced. But Tomas's angelic face hid a mind-boggling talent for the quarterstaff. Larkin had seen many an opponent at the tournaments misgauge Tomas and end up on his back. He counted himself among a numbered few who had not been bested by the young guard. But for all of Tomas's skill, he was still inexperienced, and he cast a worried glance in Larkin's direction.

"Something on your mind, Tomas?" Larkin asked.

"No, not really," Tomas replied.

Larkin cocked an eyebrow and waited.

"All right, Lark," he conceded, using a name that only those closest to Larkin could. "I was only wondering if you've been on many of these missions before."

"No. Of course, no one here has, save perhaps Baldric. The peace has gone on for so long, there hasn't been a need. You've seen how King Godwin has been increasing the Royal Guard's numbers; he recognized long ere now that trouble from the west has been brewing. I finally understand why he's been so keen on the tournaments. He's been training his guard for something greater. I imagine by next year there'll be dozens of young men looking up to you as a fixture in our ranks."

"But do you believe Lord Roger has committed treason?" Tomas asked.

"I only know what you know," Lark answered, and saw that Tomas had more on his mind. Somehow, Lark realized, he'd taken on the role of mentor to his young friend.

Tomas cleared his throat. "But what do you *think*, Lark?" he inquired. "Will Lord Roger hang or be beheaded?"

"Perhaps both," Lark responded, and smiled ruefully when his young friend's eyes rounded. "I believe he's guilty. But treason is difficult to prove." He put a hand on Tomas's shoulder. "Be on alert at all times, Tomas. Lord Roger is at best a dangerous man. If he's cornered, he will be a deadly one as well."

Tomas swallowed. "What will become of the Lady of Stolweg?"

"We don't know yet that she is complicit, although it is likely," Lark answered. "Her fate will be determined by King Godwin. Our mission is to discover if Lord Roger is treasonous, and to deal with him if he is." Lark ordered Tomas to get some sleep while he still could. As Lark rarely needed more than a few hours' rest, he often took on more than his own shift. Tonight, Ailwen too would get some extra sleep.

CHAPTER TWENTY-SIX

Stolweg at Daybreak

Dawn was yet hours away as Lark saddled Rabbit, and Lord Baldric sought him out in the darkness of their camp. Lark studied his mentor and took note of the worry in Baldric's eyes. "I'm sorry, Baldric. You are good friends with Lord Gervaise of Chevring; it must weigh heavily on you that his daughter is caught up in this treachery."

"Never think it, Lark," Baldric said vehemently. "I've known the girl since she was a babe. Granted, I haven't seen her in years, but the girl I once carried around on my shoulders would never hurt her family. Not Little Aubrianna."

"Aubrianne," Lark corrected, but Baldric was no longer paying attention.

"You didn't wake Ailwen for his watch. Are you all right, Lark?"

"I am," he replied, then nodded in Ailwen's direction. "It was quiet, and I'd had enough sleep. Everyone else awake?" Lark asked.

"Yes. Except Warin. Trian's threatened to dump water on him," Baldric joked without mirth.

"Warin will be fine. We've seen him do this before, and he always manages to come through." They both chuckled upon hearing a soaked Warin sputter awake.

Not long after that the six riders left their camp. A two-hour hard ride brought the group to the last hill. Once that was crested, the vast basin below would be revealed along with a view of Stolweg Keep. Larkin and the others followed Baldric up the slope. They came to a halt at the hilltop, waiting for the sun to send its rays streaking over and around them. From their vantage, they overlooked the deep bowl of land where the heart of Stolweg was situated. If Baldric and his trusted guards expected to see anything amiss, they were disappointed. Below them, the hill's incline fell softly into the basin. The lake, as yet unlit by the day, was dark and murky.

Finally, the sun touched their backs. Its shafts kissed the peaks of the mountains to the north and the hills to the west. The six men watched as the top of each tower caught the light. The castle's granite surface sparkled as if constructed of some translucent stone, like the iridescent nacre found in cast-up shells on the beach.

Larkin gazed at the keep, ignoring the surrounding land. He had the strangest feeling that their arrival had not gone unnoticed. The reflected glare from the large window on the east tower blinded him to the details surrounding it. But the south tower—the glass there was not directly angled at the sun. The hair on his neck stood on end, and Lark shifted uncomfortably in his saddle.

CHAPTER TWENTY-SEVEN

Sunrise

Grainne bustled around Anna's chamber, efficiently setting out a breakfast of fruit and baked goods. It was Grainne's habit to remain quiet on the mornings after Anna had spent time with Lord Roger, helping her to dress in silence. But Anna was already garbed for the day. Truth be told, she'd been up for hours. After securing Will's promise to see Tullian outside the wall, she'd gone to find Cellach. For if she were to act against Roger, she had to at least try to help her family. Doing so meant finding someone she could count on to warn them. Cellach had surprised her by suggesting that he himself go to Chevring, for he trusted none other with the task. An unexpected bit of luck, Anna thought, seeing the benefit of his absence, for he would be clear of any suspected involvement in her deed.

She greeted Grainne warmly, having decided in the minutes it took to return from the stable that, as this day was possibly her last, she would make every moment count. Who knew when she would ever again have the benefit of the company of her friend? When Grainne went to the hearth, Anna saw her puzzlement. The tray that had held her repast from the night before was empty. Anna had never eaten a bite, not in three years, either before or after a night with Lord Roger.

She turned back to the view, breathing the sweet air that flowed through the open shutter. The dawn sky was painted deep magenta, and Anna waited for the sun to spill its light over the hills. Mere heartbeats passed, and the firmament transformed into a sky of roses. At the point where the sun would rise, the blooming pinks melded with soft orange, only to change to fiery yellow a moment later.

Behind her, the embers in the hearth had been rekindled but had yet to chase away the early morning chill. Anna molded her hands around the warm mug of tea Grainne had given her, and her mind wandered to Cellach. If he could warn her father in time, her actions might not cost them their lives. For years, she had kept them safe by acquiescing to Roger's demands. But Roger had made it clear that her usefulness was at an end. What then of her family? She shuddered to think of Claire in Roger's grip. And there was her new family to think of as well. She looked at Grainne. Her success this evening would secure her maid's safety. And that of Doreen, Gilles, and Will. Will was the brother she'd never had, for that was how Anna thought of him. When he gave her his promise earlier, even before knowing what she would ask, her heart broke at his trust. She took comfort in the fact that her beautiful horses would be left in Will's capable and caring hands.

Grainne was straightening the bedclothes when Anna spoke. "I can't remember if I ever thanked you for the saltpeter, Grainne. It has been quite effective."

Grainne regarded her mistress, straight-faced and serious, and tried to find a suitable response.

Anna's lips curved as she turned back to the window. Outside, the spectacular colors of the sunrise gave way to blinding light as the sun rose above the wooded hills. Its warmth kissed her cheeks, and she breathed in deeply as if the radiance could bolster her strength.

As she gazed again at the hills in the distance, her eyes almost missed the movement in their sweep of the panorama, barely catching the shifting of silhouettes against the sky. On one bare hill to the east, moving boldly over the apex, were six riders. Anna stepped back, ridiculously afraid they could see her.

In the shadows of her deeply set window, Anna tracked them as they cantered down the slope, losing them in the shadow of the hill. Even at a fast pace, she calculated, their arrival to the gate would take at least an hour. Her heart pounded. She searched her chamber, unsure of what to do next.

"Grainne, it is imperative that we are in the courtyard within an hour! No, halve that. There are riders, from the east," Anna explained breathlessly. "Find Doreen, spread the word. I'll warn Will." Anna realized what the riders might mean, and she grinned. "I do not think Lord Roger is expecting these visitors. Be sure that he is not awakened."

"King's men?" Grainne asked excitedly.

"Perhaps. Either way, we'll want to see for ourselves, won't we?" Grainne hastened from the room to find Doreen, and Anna wasn't far behind. Throwing her cloak over her riding clothes, she ran to the stable. She *had* to be near the courtyard when the riders arrived, if only to know how and if her plan was to be affected.

CHAPTER TWENTY-EIGHT

Gate and Courtyard

Lark turned to study the man leading them. The coming days would be dangerous, for Baldric most of all; he was King Godwin's right arm. Lark would keep a steady eye on him.

They had held their position on the crest of the hill, awaiting Baldric's signal to advance. He suspected his mentor anticipated trouble as they moved forward and down the slope, but there was no way of guessing Baldric's thoughts. If he wished it, he could be as unreadable as Lark. And this was not a social visit. Whatever Lord Roger was up to was sure to be harmful to Aurelia. He'd not take lightly Godwin sending Baldric to investigate.

They approached the bridge, crossed over, and still were unmet by Roger's men. No warning call could be heard from the wall. The few workers in the fields and pastures kept to their business. Those people who lifted their heads nodded in greeting only, eyeing the riders with anticipation.

"I'm quite looking forward to this," Baldric said cheerfully. "Lord Roger has always been a bit of a prick in my side. If he's up to no good, well, even better!" They angled and turned their way through the patchwork of fields and pastures, riding steadily to the curtain wall.

• • •

Preoccupied, Roger had been unable to sleep. He had planned on wasting the morning away in his bed, Maggie nestled against him. A loud banging interrupted his thoughts. "What the devil?" Roger muttered and sat up. Over the pounding on his door, he recognized Gorman's voice. He whipped off the blankets, annoyed that Maggie had been able to sleep through the commotion, and scrambled out of bed. "This had better be important, Gorman!" he growled, throwing open the door.

"Riders, m'lord," Gorman began without preamble. "Six men, most riding Chevring steeds."

"King's men." Roger swore. "When will they arrive?"

"They're already at the gate, m'lord."

Roger wanted to strike someone, so black was his anger. Gorman must have sensed it, for he took a wary step back. "Who was on watch?" Roger bellowed. "Never mind, I don't care. Make sure they don't live another day to miss something so important again. Damn!" As he pulled on his breeches and tunic, he instructed Gorman to stall the riders. He wanted to be in the courtyard when they came through. Roger rubbed his face and grimaced at the stubble grazing his palm. Worse, he thought, he probably still had sleep lines etched across his cheek from where it had rested on the cushion.

Once in the courtyard, he stood facing the gate and surveyed his surroundings. His assembled men looked as haggard as he felt. There was nothing left to be done save signal his men to open the gate. He waited impatiently as five riders halted in front of him; the sixth rider had broken away from the main group, continuing to ride some twenty paces off to the side. "What brings you to Stolweg on such a fine spring day, Baldric?" Roger all but seethed.

Baldric didn't answer him, but at least he dismounted. When Will rushed forward to take the steed, Baldric's men alighted from their horses as well, all save one. He continued to sit his horse, infuriatingly out of Roger's view. If he wanted to see the man, Roger was forced to turn his head.

"Now, Roger," Lord Baldric reproached him, "I realize it's early, but surely you can offer a better welcome, not to mention being more hospitable to an envoy from King's Glen."

Roger scanned the area. Aubrianne and Will had led the five horses into the stable. "You're probably hungry," he grumbled. "We'll take some breakfast and then speak civilly. I myself am not a pleasant man when hungry, and I've yet to eat this morning."

• • •

Larkin sat his horse, taking in the scene. He didn't miss the frustrated glances thrown in his direction by Lord Roger. He studied the man, and the ruffian next to him. The soldier had a malicious gleam in his eye.

He next cast a curious eye at the stable hand's partner. She was

121

covered neck to toe in a long, worn cape. But she handled the horses expertly, taking three to the stable hand's two and confidently leading them away. Strange—why did she hide her face? Her thick brown hair was caught up in a braid and stray tendrils escaped and curled forward. The loose wisps only added to the mystery, concealing her visage better than any mask could. Even Rabbit was distracted by her, pricking his ears in her direction and tracking her every move.

• • •

When Will had left the stable to retrieve Lord Baldric's mount and that of another guard, Anna studied the rider sitting off to the side. She fought an unshakable urge to retreat into the shadows of the stable, the same instinct that had had her backing away from her window upon first spotting the riders. She'd thought his attention was fixed on Roger, but then he'd homed in on her. For once, she was grateful for her untamable hair; he made her nervous.

From between her loosed tendrils, she dared a quick glance his way. He sat his horse in a way that displayed his long form, slightly slouched to demonstrate how at ease he felt. His hair was coal black, and with a loose curl that caused the length to fall forward onto his forehead in chunky locks. He had a closely shaved mustache that framed the sides of a broad mouth before trailing down to a trim beard on the lower half of his chin. His bottom lip was weighted by a small triangle of whiskers.

Returning to the stable, Anna could feel his eyes upon her again, and she risked another peek to confirm her suspicions once in the embrace of the shadows. Yes, he was staring in her direction.

"Who's the fellow still ahorse, m'lady?" Will asked, following her gaze.

"I'm not sure. He is making an impression, though. Look at Lord Roger. He keeps checking on the man. I would say yon brooding guard is purposely antagonizing my husband."

She tore her eyes away. "The older man is Lord Baldric," Anna pointed out. "From Carrick's description, I would guess that the man to Baldric's left is the guard Trian."

Roger swept his arm toward the area under the oak tree. Food and drink, Anna guessed. Unbeknownst to Roger, Grainne was with Doreen, putting the final touches on an impromptu feast. They had been working on it for the past hour. Roger would be ill-put when he saw Doreen's famous pasties served to his unwelcome guests. Anna retreated deeper into the coolness of the stable to finish tending to the horses as Baldric and the other guards followed her husband toward the keep.

Over the back of Lord Baldric's horse, Anna called excitedly, "Five of these horses are Chevring bred, born, and trained. The stallion in the courtyard—I named him. Rabbit, he's called."

Anna regarded Will. "I need to speak with Roger before he settles in with Lord Baldric. With Cellach gone, it'll be important to have Gilles here, especially if trouble is brewing."

She sneaked a look out of the stable's entrance in time to see that the group was dispersing. There was but one obstacle to her leaving. "I'll go now. You can follow a moment later and distract the man still waiting on his horse."

"Is there something wrong, m'lady?" Will asked, concern etched across his brow.

"Not at all," she replied easily. "But it's better if Lord Baldric's men are not involved."

Anna left the stable with lowered head. No sooner had she walked five paces when she felt Rabbit's rider studying her. She peered through her masking tresses and at the man on the horse. Something about him set her on edge. Best not pique his interest, she thought.

But her color rose upon realizing that she was certainly interested in him. She couldn't help it. In fact, as soon as the riders had entered the courtyard, her gaze had been drawn to him. She hoped he was a true friend to Rabbit. The stallion, now five years old, had been a superb colt, one of the best to ever come out of the Chevring stable.

She remembered how Rabbit had earned his name and smiled wistfully. As a baby, he would hunker down and then dart quickly from side to side. They would play a game of catch the colt. But the young horse was too fast, as impossible to catch as a wild rabbit. Her father had made a gift of Rabbit to King Godwin, as was Chevring tradition. The man riding him must be held in high esteem indeed for the King to give him such a treasure.

• • •

The woman exited the stable again. She inserted herself between Roger and his soldier, and Lark could have sworn Roger's man smirked appreciatively. The woman turned and faced the sneering brute.

Lark listened as she skewered the oaf with a voice that held no fear. "Should you not be doing some other task for your lord, Gorman?

NICOLE ELIZABETH KELLEHER

Perhaps watching for more surprise guests."

Lord Roger glared at the woman, clearly exasperated. "Gorman, I want a full sweep of the outlying fields and hills. Do it. Now! After, I want you to…" He stopped, aware again that one of Baldric's men continued to observe him. He whispered to the man named Gorman, walking away from the woman so that she also would be unable to hear his orders. Lark strained to better see her face.

Roger was walking to the castle and Baldric when he stopped abruptly and turned to the woman. His words brooked no patience, and he spoke harshly, "What is it, Aubrianne?"

So this was Baldric's Little Aubrianna, Lark realized, and leaned forward in his saddle.

"Sir? Excuse me, sir? May I take your horse, sir?" The voice came from behind him. He glowered at the stable hand addressing him. "Can I take him for you? He looks as if he's itching for a good rubdown."

"Yes, of course, one minute," Lark answered impatiently, turning back to the scene unfolding in the courtyard. The woman was already walking back to the stable. With a beleaguered sigh, he dismounted and handed the reins over. "Mind his teeth and hooves. He's a mite puckish, today more so than usual."

Lark wanted nothing more than to go into the stable, if only to see the face of the Lady of Stolweg. Something about her captured his attention, and he disliked unknown variables. But Baldric would want him present when he expressed the King's concerns to Lord Roger.

CHAPTER TWENTY-NINE
Trouble in the Stable

Lord Baldric was seated at a long trestle table under a great oak tree. Its leaves, not yet fully unfurled, offered no shade from the steadily rising sun. It was just as well, Lark thought—the air still carried a chill. Lord Roger was returning, followed by several servants carrying baskets of bread and jugs of what had better be cider or beer.

"Our cook is preparing a meal for you, Baldric," Roger announced with false courtesy as one of the servants filled the mugs that had been placed on the table. "In the meantime, why don't you tell me what brings you so far from Whitmarsh?"

"Let us eat first," Baldric replied. "We'll have time to discuss the reasons for our visit after." Another servant came to the table bearing a tray. "Ah, perfect. Pasties and"—lifting his mug to his nose and sighing in appreciation—"cider."

Baldric raised his drink and, managing to keep the sarcasm from his voice, gave a toast. "To our gracious host, Lord Roger of Stolweg." But before Lark could raise his cup, a loud crashing noise came from the stable, followed by a high whinny.

"You'd better see to that beast of yours, Larkin," Baldric ordered.

Roger whipped his head around, but Lark ignored him. Instead, he strode to the stable. He should have tended to Rabbit himself, knowing how mulish the beast had been all morning. When he walked into the structure, the stable hand was off to one side, calming the other horses. Unbelievably, he'd left the woman, Lady Aubrianne, to settle his stallion. Lark started forward but paused when he heard her speak.

She was doing her best to calm his horse. Rabbit let out a pained whinny and reared. Aubrianne continued soothingly, clucking her tongue and whispering, "Shhh. Hush now, friend."

Upon hearing her voice, the destrier stopped bucking, but his head and neck continued to dip up and down violently. "So you do remember me, boy. I was beginning to feel slighted."

His horse calmed even more. She placed her hands on each side of Rabbit's head and touched her forehead to his. "That's it, good lad. I'll fix whatever ails you."

Larkin cleared his throat. "His name is—"

"Rabbit," she supplied tersely, cutting him short.

"How do you know his name?" he demanded. The stable hand glared at him and moved closer to protect the woman. Brave lad, Lark thought.

With her forehead still pressed to Rabbit's, she answered, "I'd better know his name. I gave it to him. How've you been, Bunny? Do you still like to be scratched here?" She inserted her fingers under the bridle strap that fit along and behind Rabbit's cheekbones. When Rabbit snorted in pleasure, she laughed. "What's hurting you, boy?"

She gestured to Will to approach, and Rabbit gave a threatening nicker. "Come now, Rabbit. He's a good friend. Say hello to Will. Will, this is Rabbit." Will reached out his hand to the horse's neck. Rabbit nickered again, this time without the warning. "What were you doing before our Rabbit caused the ruckus, Will?"

"I pulled the cinch tighter, to loosen it, m'lady. He jumped sideways, crashing into the other horses. Lucky he didn't jump my way."

"You're too smart for that, aren't you, boy?" she said, patting Rabbit's neck.

Lark had yet to see the face of Roger's wife, the Lady of Stolweg, but she'd removed her cloak. The breeches she wore left little to his imagination. Baldric might be interested to know that Little Aubrianna was no longer. She was a grown woman. Something inside him tensed; he felt like a bow string pulled too far and not released.

She was running her fingers down Rabbit's neck, along his withers, and over his barrel, never once lifting her touch, tracing lazy circles over his ash-colored coat. She stepped closer to Rabbit's side and carefully lifted the stirrup, fixing it over the pommel of the saddle. Lark took a position in front of Rabbit where he could observe Lady Aubrianne. Her fingers trailed delicately along the cinch, and Rabbit turned his head to nudge her. She shushed him again, murmuring something under her breath. Her hands had made the trek about three-quarters of the way down when they stopped. She sighed heavily.

"Will, fetch my bag. And a swatch of leather, too." She nodded to Will after he arched an eyebrow in Lark's direction. "It's all right. Go ahead."

"Right away, m'lady," he called and ran to the tack room.

Lark had been watching Will and hadn't noticed that Lady Aubrianne had rounded on him. When he did, he saw the fury in her eyes.

"Had I known Rabbit would go to such an uncaring clod of a man, I would not have troubled myself to train him." The temper in her voice matched the fire in her eyes. "Did you not notice that he was hurting? Or worse, you noticed, and you continued to ride him." He put up his hands and opened his mouth to speak. Before he could, Will stepped protectively in front of Lady Aubrianne, shouldering Lark a step back.

"What is it, m'lady?" the young man asked. "A burr?"

"A nasty one," she answered angrily. "A bogburr. I showed them to you once, remember?"

"Aye, brownish-red, almost an inch long. Poisonous, too."

"I hope this one hasn't burst," she said.

They'd dismissed him, Lark realized, unused to being ignored. So he held Rabbit's bridle straps and continued to scratch his horse. That she had questioned his loyalty to his steed had irked him, but more so that she'd been right to do it. He'd known something was wrong but hadn't wanted to delay the others.

After they'd broken camp, they'd found themselves in a small fen. Rabbit's tail had caught on some burrs, and he'd spent nearly a quarter hour removing them. He still had the thorn in his finger to prove it. And damn it, his finger was swollen and hurt like hell. When Rabbit had grown skittish, Lark dismounted to search once more, signaling the others to ride on. Apparently, he had not been thorough enough. He swore to himself.

"Will, I need you to pull the cinch away while I slip this patch underneath," she instructed. "Gently. Right here, where the burr is caught." Will did as asked, and Lady Aubrianne plucked the burr off Rabbit's coat and slipped the soft leather swatch under the strap.

She patted the great horse and rubbed his side again. "Good boy, Bunny," she commended him.

Lark's attention to Rabbit seemed to surprise her. He was cradling his horse's massive head, murmuring soft noises in the stallion's ear. "Go ahead, Will," Lark whispered. Will unfastened the cinch and quickly removed the saddle.

Rabbit's skin twitched as Lady Aubrianne peeled away the leather patch and probed the area, a raw spot the size of a thumbnail. She pulled first one, then two ugly barbs from the shallow wound. From the bag hanging over her shoulder, she brought forth a small, stoppered pot. A pleasant scent filled the air as she tenderly applied some sort of salve to

Rabbit's coat.

His destrier snorted in relief, and Larkin leaned back to look his horse in the eyes. "Sorry about that, Rabbit. I thought I found them all. Do you forgive me?" It seemed that Rabbit accepted the apology, for he nudged Lark's chest playfully, nearly knocking him on his seat.

Lady Aubrianne gazed at him speculatively. At least she had ceased glaring at him. And in that instant, when her features softened, he recognized her: Anna.

He took a step back as if someone had struck him in the chest. She studied him for a moment. When it became clear that she didn't recognize him in return, his disappointment was humbling. What did he expect, Lark thought, that she would rush into his arms, and finish the kiss that he'd started? He was acting like a lovestruck boy.

She pulled an apple from her bag and tossed it to him. "It's for Rabbit."

He caught it deftly but winced. Unwilling concern flitted across her face, and Lark took a moment to really study her. Despite the dark circles under her eyes, she was quite beautiful. Her eyes were as he remembered: light, sooty brown, and like her hair, dusted with gold. And, she still had what Lark liked to think of as a kiss-worthy mouth: full lips that begged to be teased and nipped.

As for her hair, more tendrils had escaped the long braid. He resisted the urge to wrap one around his finger. His gaze rose to follow the curve of her cheek, and he noticed for the first time a greenish-yellow tinge under her eye, as if she had just overcome some illness.

Roger was a lucky man to have married this woman. A surge of jealousy coursed through Lark, and he forced himself to pull his mind away from her attributes. When he looked at her again, he found himself condemned by her knowing eyes. She gave a snort of disgust. That she had found his regard distasteful bothered him more than he cared to admit.

• • •

Anna was starting to believe that all noble-born men were cut from the same cloth. She was tired of being viewed as an object to be owned and used. This man, this Royal Guard, he was just like all of the others, wasn't he? He saw her skirt—breeches, she corrected herself—and decided there was nothing more of value except for that which was hiding underneath.

Exasperated, she held out her hand. "Let me see your finger. Come now, don't be afraid. I'll show you at least half the gentleness that I gave Rabbit." She masked her true emotions under a shield of ire.

Rabbit snorted, and the guard gave her his hand. She cupped it with her own to better examine his fingertip. There'd been a spark in his dark eyes, and she almost lost herself in his stormy gaze. Could it be him, she thought wildly, the stranger from so many years ago? Her heart beat faster at the thought, her inner turmoil at odds with the practiced expression on her face. His eyes remained steadily fixed on hers; she was first to turn away.

Willing herself to be calm, she took his hand in a stronger grip and forced herself to ignore the strange tingling she felt when their skin made contact. His fingertip was red and swollen. And when she touched the sore, he winced, and his fingers curled back protectively.

"Did you not think to wear gloves?" When he didn't answer right away, Anna glanced up at him. He was so focused on her hands touching his that he hadn't even heard her.

• • •

She did not seem to be conscious of the effect of her touch. Or perhaps she did know, Larkin thought, remembering how she did the same to Rabbit's shoulder as her fingers inched their way to the bogburr. Perhaps she was trying to distract him as well. He realized that he'd forgotten about his finger. A pleasant tingling sensation engulfed his hand. Lost in thought, it took him a moment to realize that she had asked him something.

"Sorry, what was that?"

"Gloves?" she repeated. "Did you forget to wear your gloves?"

"Yes. No," he fumbled his answer. For the first time, he saw amusement in her eyes. Only a hint, but it transformed her beautiful face into one that bordered on radiant. If his discomfort was the cause, he did not mind the embarrassment. As more time passed without an intelligible answer, the smile in her eyes traveled to her lips.

"I see. Yes *and* no," she said with a small laugh. "Yes, you wore a glove on your left hand: no burrs. No, you did not wear a glove on your right: a nasty barb in the finger. Have I got it right? Shall we fix your finger before it bursts?"

"No *and* yes," he quipped. "No, you did not get it right. I wore gloves on both hands, but only after the first barb pierced my finger." He enjoyed hearing her laugh. "And yes. Please fix my finger. I'm rather fond of it and would hate for it to explode."

She gave Will a quick nod. The young man picked up a broom to sweep the already-clean threshold near the stable's entrance. Before Lark could ask why they required advance warning of someone's approach, Lady Aubrianne spoke again.

"Please sit over there; the light is better." She opened her kit and laid out a few instruments. The implements were clean and sharp. He stared down at two small blades, then at a pair of sharp scissors, and she poised her hand above one knife as if that would be her choice. At the last second, she reached for a pair of tweezers. He sighed in relief, earning another smile.

"It won't hurt—well, not really. But if I don't remove the spine, your finger could become diseased." She touched the swollen tip again. "You could eventually lose it," she added with more gravity. When he nodded to her to proceed, she probed the swollen fingertip to find the offending barb. He flinched but held his hand steady.

She was right, he thought, his finger already felt as if it were on fire. She sat facing him, her knees against his. He braced himself, then noticed a delicate fragrance in the air. *Anna's* scent, he remembered, breathing in the familiar and intoxicating smell. Definitely a flower.

"I lied," she said. "This will hurt. Are you ready?"

He needed to hear his name on her lips. "Larkin. My name is Larkin."

She cocked her head at him. "Are you ready, Larkin?"

He nodded. *Roses?* he wondered. No, not roses.

She squeezed the swollen pad, and the head of the barb poked out. Heather? No again, he thought.

Will continued to stand guard near the entrance.

Lilacs? No.

As Lady Aubrianne bent her head to her task, Lark gritted his teeth to stem the coming pain. He saw the quick gleam of metal and felt a sharp, painful tug on the tip of his finger. "I've got it!" she exclaimed victoriously, brandishing the tweezers.

Lavender! She smelled of lavender.

Will hurried past them, shooting a warning to Lady Aubrianne. Before she could release Larkin's hand, Roger entered the stable, Gorman tagging behind like a hungry dog.

Her husband seemed as though he were attempting to assemble some excuse as to why his wife was sitting next to another man, holding hands, knees touching. There was a tremor in Aubrianne's grip. To her credit, she did not release her hold too quickly. Doing so would appear as if she'd done something worthy of shame.

Lady Aubrianne ignored her husband's scathing glower. She reached for her crock of salve and spread some balm on Lark's finger. She sounded composed enough as she instructed him in its further care. "You'll need to soak your finger in cold water for fifteen minutes or so. It will get rid of most of the swelling. After you're done, wrap your finger in something clean. It should be back to normal tomorrow." She released his hand and gave him a small cloth with more balm.

"Your name is Larkin?" Roger demanded.

Lark yawned as if bored. In an even voice, he answered, "How clever of you to learn it." While Aubrianne gathered her kit together, he stood, blocking Roger's view of his wife. His demeanor was casual as he waited in front of them, but his hand came to rest on his sword hilt.

It was odd, Lark thought, the way Aubrianne's husband's eyes kept flashing between his wife and him. Lark waited for Roger to comment, and seeing that the man was at a loss for words, he turned to Lady Aubrianne, putting his back purposely to the two men.

"Thank you, Lady Aubrianne, for your expert care." He was loath to leave the woman alone with her husband. In a voice intentionally lowered, he spoke to her alone. "If I can ever return the favor, simply ask."

She forced a smile to her lips and answered, "You are welcome, Larkin. If you have any trouble with your finger, ask for my woman, Grainne. And remember to soak it—*now* would be better than later. You'll find buckets near the fountain in the courtyard." Her tone was dismissive, and Lark bowed low before leaving the stable. Gorman followed.

• • •

Anna watched him depart, mentally comparing him to her husband. He was slightly taller. Broader across the shoulders, too. His build was at once solid and lean. No, she thought, lithe. How strange that after three years of marriage, she had never seen her husband naked. Larkin's clothing left no doubt in a woman's mind as to his form underneath.

A hard slap to her face brought her out of her comparison. "So, I finally meet Larkin," Roger seethed. "When were you first with him?"

"What do you mean?" she answered, her hand cradling her stinging cheek.

"Don't lie to me, Aubrianne. I know you were a virgin when we married, but perhaps you have been with him after. Perhaps on one of your trips with the mares?"

She remembered where she had heard the name before. It was the day after she had collapsed in the ring of stones. Roger had spoken it.

NICOLE ELIZABETH KELLEHER

"A better question, Roger, is how do *you* know him? Why this fascination with his name?"

He was staring at her as if she'd lost her mind to be arguing with him. He grabbed her shoulders and shook her. "Shut up, Aubrianne. Tell me. Have you lain with him?"

She could not fathom whence her husband could have gotten such a ridiculous notion and almost laughed. She thought of the miller's daughter and pushed him a little harder. But as the words passed her lips, she regretted her reply immediately. "Considering how you view our vows, why should it matter?"

Her husband was incensed. This time when he struck her, it was not with an open palm. He backhanded her, knocking her sideways to the wooden bench, still warm from where she had sat with Larkin. The metallic taste of blood filled her mouth. She touched the spot where his hand had connected with her jaw and winced. The blow had split the tender skin.

But Roger wasn't quite finished with her and hauled her up by her hair. Speaking quite calmly, he demanded, "Answer me, Aubrianne."

"No, I have not lain with him," she replied shakily.

He released her, and she stumbled backward. "You'd better hurry and retrieve Gilles and the mares, Aubrianne. The sun is already high." He smoothed his tunic back into place, ran his fingers through his hair, then left the stable.

Anna sat to collect her wits. He'd struck her so hard that she'd seen stars. His uncontrollable violence before he walked out of the stable only cemented in Anna's mind that she would have to carry out her plan, Baldric's arrival notwithstanding.

Will approached with a clean, damp rag. "I'm sorry, m'lady. I only returned as he struck you. If I had been here, I—"

"Hush, Will. He would have hit me regardless."

"Is there anything I can do?" Will asked.

"Naught but what I asked earlier," she answered.

He doffed his ridiculous-looking cap and handed it to her. "And tonight, m'lady, do you still need me to take Tullian to the crypt?"

"I'll let you know when I return."

Before leaving, Anna took one last look at the bench where she and Larkin had sat. Could he really be the man who had almost kissed her so many years ago? She'd seen nothing but his near-black eyes that evening. A hidden lock inside her heart felt as though a key had been forced into it. This man's eyes were the same.

CHAPTER THIRTY

Larkin's Promise

Anna left the stable by way of the paddocks. Her intuition told her that if Baldric and his men saw her, there would be no chance for her to ride out to Gilles. Baldric would certainly confront Roger. Or worse, he would do nothing at all. She had but one corner to round and remain unnoticed, and she'd be within the castle. It was not to be.

Of course, it was Larkin who had seen her. "Lady Aubrianne, a word. Please," he called. She was less than five paces from the entrance and repressed the urge to sprint the last steps. Instead, she stopped but kept her back to him. "Can you at least turn around?" he entreated.

That was the last thing Anna wanted to do. For years, she had walked freely among her people at Stolweg, unafraid and unashamed. She never worried that they would pity her when they saw the marks left behind by Roger, for they bore their own bruises along with her.

So why did she care so much what Larkin thought? Anna realized that she was worried, though not for herself. The truth was, she was afraid of what Larkin might do to Roger. And as long as she was being honest with herself, she believed that it was not his affair. Inflicting pain on her husband was something she wanted all for herself.

In the stable, her husband had been so interested in Larkin's name that he'd been blind to the man himself. She'd seen the danger signs rolling off Larkin. How when Gorman had tried to flank him, the guard's hand had fallen so easily to the hilt of his sword that Anna had held her breath. His fingers may have been relaxed, but she'd recognized the coiled tension in his neck and shoulders. Roger, so overly confident, had missed it.

She would eventually have to face Larkin. But allowing him to see the condition of her face would only cause him to regret that he hadn't stayed with her. *Damn*, she swore to herself, he wasn't going to give her a choice in the matter. Tired of waiting, he simply walked around until he stood facing her.

"Will you look at me!" he demanded when she fastened her eyes to the ground.

God's oath, she thought angrily. Would there ever be a day in her life when she would not be ordered around by some man? If he was so keen on seeing her, then fine, let him. She smoothed her hair back from her face, turning her head slightly to conceal the worst from him.

"You want to see me, Larkin? Well, take a good look. Then tell me what else you want from me. I am quite busy." Anna hadn't meant to let it out, but some of the fury in her heart escaped.

He seemed shocked. Good. She'd expected to see pity, had even searched his eyes for it. To her surprise and relief, she found none. But there was anger—she could see the tightening of his features around his storm-filled eyes.

"I'm sorry," he said.

"For what? Did you strike me?" she spat angrily. "Why should *you* be sorry? You did nothing." His eyes were bleak, and Anna realized she had hit the nail on the head: he'd done nothing. And now he probably felt guilty. This only stoked her ire more.

"Don't you dare take this upon yourself, Larkin. You offered to help me. I sent you away." And because he stood there without speaking a word, she continued to rage at him. She told him to quit being such a *man*. He was not responsible for her. On and on she went, until there was nothing left. When she had finished, he merely watched and waited, his expression serene. She opened her mouth to say more but shut it.

"Are you finished?" he asked calmly.

When she could think of naught else to say, Anna discovered that Larkin had given her exactly what she needed: someone to rail against. She hadn't felt this good in years. He was too smart by any measure, and she was immediately wary.

• • •

It was clear to Lark that Roger had struck Lady Aubrianne, and more than once. "I'm sorry if I caused you any trouble by allowing you to tend to my hand," he told her. "I would rather lose my finger than see you hurt."

When she spoke out again, her words sounded more weary than angry. "You must think very highly of yourself if you believe this was about you. My trouble started years ago."

He reached out and cupped her chin, tilting her face up. He'd been mistaken earlier. The sallow color near her eye was not from any illness. The sunlight told him a different story. He frowned at the red welt high on her cheek and the cut on her along her jawbone. She met his gaze steadily, daring him to speak.

When he daubed away a smear of blood on her chin, her eyes softened at the gesture, and his breath hitched. In that instant, his heart was lost. He would accede to anything she asked. "What would you have me do, m'lady?"

Her eyes told him everything: an overwhelming need to be protected, then a resolute denial of the very idea. Lark nodded and removed his hand. "Nothing, then. But know this: he will not touch you again while I am here. Not even if you beg me to let him. I swear this to you."

Before she could comment, a tiny woman inserted herself between them, the back of her head coming no higher than his chest. Lark could not help but smile. First Will, and now this speck of a woman. Lady Aubrianne had brave friends indeed. Used to making people cower, this was a new experience for Lark.

The woman—her maid, Lark guessed—studied Aubrianne's face. "If we put a cold cloth on that right away, it might not bruise this time," she stated, ignoring the man towering behind her. "He'll be one of the Royal Guard, then?" Grainne deduced.

"Yes. Larkin, this is my friend Grainne." Grainne beamed at him, squaring her shoulders.

"I'm her maid, m'lord." Lady Aubrianne rolled her eyes.

He bowed to Grainne. "It is a pleasure to meet you, Grainne. And I am no lord; that title has gone to my older brother." He wondered what had prompted his admission.

"Larkin, if your finger troubles you," Lady Aubrianne reminded him, "find Grainne."

He nodded, then leaned forward. "I meant what I promised you, m'lady."

"I know," she replied, and stepped away.

Larkin's only thought at the moment was to control the urge to beat Roger to a pulp. But she had turned back to him, and the pain in her eyes took the wind from his rage.

"Larkin," she began, "in the stable, you said if ever I needed a favor…"

"You need only ask, Lady Aubrianne," he prompted, and waited for her to give him permission to pulverize Roger into dust. Her request was not what he expected.

"I do not want the others to know. I say this not out of pride, nor even to protect him." She glanced at Grainne. "My people have withstood more years of abuse than I. I can bear them knowing. But Baldric and the others—I cannot fathom it would make a difference if they knew. Do I have your word that you'll not mention this?"

"Lady Aubrianne, surely you do not think that Baldric would..." Lark halted midsentence as disappointment filled her eyes. Reluctantly, he assented, "You have my word."

"Then I thank you, Larkin."

Lady Aubrianne then disappeared into the castle. Her maid scrutinized him a moment longer, and then followed her mistress. Lark stalked back to the others.

Baldric must have sensed his mood. "Come, Roger, let us walk off these fine pasties."

Lark's eyes bored into Roger's back as they walked away. Trian whispered to him so the others could not hear. "Just make sure we have proof of his treachery before you kill him."

"Am I so transparent?" Lark asked.

Trian grinned. "Only to me. And Baldric, of course."

CHAPTER THIRTY-ONE

Anna's Ride

"I'm off to find Gilles," Anna explained to Grainne once they reached her chamber. Grainne placed her hands on her hips in disapproval. "Say your piece, Grainne. I'm in a hurry."

"Will he keep his word, m'lady?" Grainne asked.

"I believe him to be honorable," Anna replied. "Now, if I am to return with Gilles before supper, I have to leave. Can you pack my saddlebag and send it to Will? He'll have already saddled Tully," Anna explained. "And, Grainne, I don't want anyone to know it's me going. Baldric would never allow me to leave, at least not by myself. He'll think I'm Will. We are the same height, and I've borrowed his hat to hide my hair. No one will be the wiser."

"Then why not let Will go, m'lady?" Grainne suggested hopefully.

"Three reasons," Anna stated. "One, he needs to tend to the horses. Two, Tullian is the fastest horse and he'll only let me ride him. And three, well, I feel the need to ride." Anna gave what she hoped was an engaging smile, trying to hide her worry. There was a fourth reason: she needed time to think about what she was going to do once she returned to the keep.

"You only needed to mention number three, m'lady," Grainne stated with a beleaguered sigh, then turned before leaving the chamber. "And I'll make sure to check in on your *friend* Larkin while you're away." She was gone before Anna could reply.

Something about Grainne's tone discomfited her, but she couldn't put her finger on it. Anna shrugged. She donned Will's floppy hat, pulling it low. She headed to the stable. When she reached Tullian's stall, she leapt onto her great horse's back. "See you later, Will. Remember, keep out of sight if you can."

"I will, m'lady. Ride safely." They laughed at how ridiculous he sounded, both knowing full well that she would ride as recklessly as possible.

As she left the stable, Baldric and his men turned their heads to watch her. How could they not? Tullian was magnificent. To distract their attention from her, Anna put him into a high-stepping trot. He performed beautifully. "All right, Tully-boy," she whispered, "time to run!" He lunged forward, and they galloped through the gate. In record time, they made it to the mill crossing. Anna chanced a look behind. No riders pursued.

CHAPTER THIRTY-TWO

Explanations

"Find Roger," Baldric ordered Ailwen. "I want to know where that rider is headed." But Roger was already walking over to the gathered men.

"I see that you were admiring my greatest horse," he said, "sire to all that I am breeding."

"Where is that rider headed?" Baldric demanded, in no mood for Roger's gilded tongue.

"There are broodmares in the southwest hills," he explained smoothly. "The rider you saw went to retrieve them."

Lark stepped closer, shouldering Roger out of the way to confer with Baldric.

"What is this about?" Roger shouted. "You arrive uninvited and question me as if you have a right to know what I do on my own land. I insist you tell me what is going on."

Lark raised an eyebrow in amusement. He would not have thought it possible, but Roger's face darkened to a deeper shade of red. "As I understand it, it is your wife who breeds the mares. And to *her* stallion, Tullian." He ignored Roger's sputtering and turned back to Baldric. "The rider headed to the mill, then crossed the river and continued southeast. It's consistent with Roger's explanation." Still, Lark was troubled. Something was not quite right.

Baldric nodded, then addressed Roger. "We'll speak later about the King's reasons for our arrival. For now, Roger, just know that the King believes men from Nifolhad have breached our shores. Do you believe your rider to have safe passage to the mares?"

"That rider, on that steed, is better able than most," Roger answered. "If there *is* any danger, I am not worried in the least for the safety of the mares."

It wasn't lost on anyone that Roger's concern was not for the rider,

139

only his property. Baldric suggested they meet in the great hall in an hour to discuss the King's reason for their mission. In the meantime, he and his men could be shown to their quarters.

• • •

Gorman was in the stable harassing Will when Lord Roger found him. "My chamber, Gorman. Now!"

Gorman followed like a dog at heel. He knew firsthand how cruel his lord could be when displeased. And right at this moment, Lord Roger was seething. "Report," he ordered, once they were in the chamber.

"I circled 'round the immediate area, m'lord," Gorman began. "The only tracks I found belonged to Baldric and his men. I followed the signs for over an hour and didn't see any divergent trails. Six riders total."

"Assign a man to ride farther east to make sure," Lord Roger commanded. "Anything else?"

"No, m'lord," Gorman stated. "Just Cellach's trail, riding south to the mares as was reported this morning."

Lord Roger sat and motioned for Gorman to join him. "Godwin suspects foul play. Why else would he have sent Baldric? Send someone you trust to relay what is happening here." His lord paused and stared into the dead ashes in the hearth. "The timing could not have been worse. My brother is waiting for me to join him not a day's ride from here. If Baldric sends one of the guards west…"

"Beg pardon, m'lord," Gorman ventured, "mayhap the timing is perfect."

Lord Roger's eyes gleamed. He leaned forward. "What did you have in mind?"

• • •

The earlier meeting in the great hall went as expected. As Baldric walked to the center of the courtyard, Lark kept close to his side. Near the fountain, Baldric reaffirmed his certainty that Roger was colluding with Nifolhad.

"The man played his part expertly," Lark said admiringly. "In one brief meeting, he explained away the mysterious tracks found in this region, and Ragallach's involvement with the Nifolhadajans. His offer of a list of the tradesmen who have had business dealings with the men from Nifolhad will work to our benefit, I think. We'll know who is loyal to him that much easier."

"Pass the word to the others," Baldric commanded. "I want a watch placed on our corridor while we sleep. I would also like to speak to Lady Aubrianne. She is Chevring-bred through and through, and my heart revolts against the idea that she is involved in this mess."

"I've met the lady, Baldric. Your heart speaks true. She knows something, but I think she has not trust enough to speak," Lark confided. "Her woman, Grainne, is loyal to her lady. And Will, the young man from the stable. He was ready to fight me to protect his mistress."

"Fight you?" Baldric demanded, "Please tell me you didn't mistakenly threaten Lady Aubrianne."

"Of course not—the boy protected her out of instinct." He looked at the stable and thought of his horse. "I'd like to check on Rabbit. I missed a nasty burr, and Lady Aubrianne tended to him."

"I'll join you," Baldric offered.

When they entered the stable, both men were surprised to find Will feeding the horses. The mares must have been close for him to have returned so quickly. A woman stood nearby, speaking in hushed tones. She wore a long white apron covered with food stains. Lark shook his head as Baldric, a man who loved his stomach more than anything save his family, introduced himself.

"Forgive my interruption," Baldric begged, approaching the woman. "From your attire, I see that you must be the person who prepared those delicious pasties." Patting his stomach, Baldric continued, "I'm embarrassed to say that I ate three." Lark held up five fingers, earning a scowl from Baldric. "Perhaps four, I lost count. Poor Lord Roger, we spared not a single one for him."

Lark smiled and left Baldric to his conversation, and went to see Rabbit. His horse had every amenity: clean water, oats, and fresh hay. His wound had been left uncovered, allowing the air to aid in the healing process. The sore was much improved. Behind him, he could hear Baldric talking to the woman—Doreen, she had said loud enough for him to hear. Lark checked the other stalls for the beautiful stallion he had seen earlier. The great horse was not there. Nor were the mares that were to be retrieved.

He felt the telltale prickle on the back of his neck that warned him when something was amiss. He'd had it in the courtyard when Will had ridden away on Tullian. Thinking back, Roger had never said that it was Will who had cantered out. And where was Will's absurd hat? It was on the head of the other rider, of course. It occurred to him then, he'd known it even as he observed the horse and rider galloping away—where Will's lanky frame caused him to move awkwardly, the long form of the rider had been graceful.

"Will, where is Tullian, and who was riding him?" But Lark already knew the answer.

"Out, m'lord," Will answered nervously, edging closer to the rear exit of the stable.

"I can see that he is out," Lark stated, taking a step forward. Will stopped retreating and stood his ground. "What I want to know is out where, and with whom?"

"Here now, sir, you leave off my boy," Doreen ordered. "He owes you no explanation."

"It's all right, Mum. She said not to lie if asked." The stable hand stood straighter and met Lark's darkening eyes. "There's but one rider Tullian will allow on his back: Lady Aubrianne. She's gone to fetch her mares."

"Lord Roger knew his wife was riding out on Tullian?" Baldric had come forward and nearly bellowed his question.

"Of course, my lord. It was he who sent her."

Baldric was incensed. "Lark, can you track her?" Lark didn't hear him. He was already pulling his saddle from the tack room.

"But m'lord, she'll be back with—"

"I don't care," Baldric shouted. "Her father and I go back a long way. He would do the same for my daughters if he thought they were in the slightest danger. If she is already returning Lark will just escort her the rest of the way. Now, help him saddle his horse."

"I'll take care of Rabbit, Will," Lark stated. "You can help me by collecting my gear from my room. On second thought, there's no time. I have my sword and knife."

"I'll go and question Roger," Baldric added.

"Pardon, m'lord," Will said. "He departed two hours ago."

Lark shot a meaningful glance at Baldric. "You didn't happen to hear where he was headed?" his mentor asked.

Will shook his head. "No, but it was he and seven of his men, m'lord. They rode off in pairs, northeast, northwest, southeast, and southwest." Baldric narrowed his eyes, and Lark was curious to know why a simple stable boy had taken time to note the exact details of his lord's departure.

"His man Gorman is still here," Doreen interjected, taking the attention off her son. "Probably in the barracks eating."

Will had reached into his pocket for a clean rag and was placing it between Rabbit's side and the saddle's cinch, while Baldric drew Lark aside to confer. "Smart, riding off in different directions. He knows I won't split up our group to go in search of him. We'll have to wait for his return."

"Stay close to Warin and the others," Lark cautioned. "We don't know who we can trust." He turned to see Will attaching a small bundle, a waterskin, and a bedroll to Rabbit's saddle.

"My supper, sir, in case you don't find her right off." Lark nodded and jumped onto his steed.

"M'lord, the fastest route is by the mill, then on to the valley," Will advised. "When it turns west, head east. We hid the mares in the fertile glens; you should be able to pick up the trail then. If you don't, cross over the first stream, then follow the second south. You'll see where the mares bedded down last night. If you miss Lady Aubrianne's tracks, you won't miss those left by the horses."

Sensing his master's impatience to be off, Rabbit pawed at the stable floor and snorted violently. "One more thing, sir," Will advised. "Ride as hard as Rabbit can take. Lady Aubrianne was in one of her moods. She won't spare any thought for a leisurely ride. More than likely, she's already reached the mares." Lark gave Rabbit his lead, and they bounded from the stable.

• • •

Will watched as Lark tore through the courtyard and out the main gate riding as expertly as his lady. His mother had turned to speak to Baldric, and he heard the worry in her voice. "My good friend Grainne has spoken highly of yon guard. If Lady Aubrianne is in any danger, he'll be able to protect her, won't he?"

Baldric nodded. "If anyone can, it is Lark. I would trust him with my own family."

"He'll have help. My man, Gilles, is with the mares," she said proudly.

"Let me escort you back to the castle, Doreen, and you can tell me what to expect for supper."

Before they left, his mother turned to him. "As soon as you're done here, Will, come along to the kitchen. I'll fix a new meal for you. Perhaps enough for two," she amended when Lord Baldric held out his arm for her to take.

"Thanks, Mum. I'll be along in a moment." He finished settling the horses and was on his way to the kitchen and the promise of his mother's cooking. He had almost made it when Gorman blocked his path.

"Was that the guard Larkin who rode out?" the brute demanded. Will nodded. "Why was I not informed? Tell me what you know!"

As quickly as he could, Will explained that Lord Baldric was concerned for Lady Aubrianne's safety and had sent the guard after her. He ducked his head as Gorman's hand shot out to box his ear.

"Is anything amiss?" Lord Baldric asked, standing in the doorway of the kitchen and holding a fresh piece of bread with a hefty slice of cheese layered upon it.

"The boy is too clumsy," Gorman lied.

"And striking him will teach him to be otherwise?" Lord Baldric left the entranceway and walked to Gorman, and Will was taken by the change from his earlier fatherly demeanor to one who exuded authority. Two other Royal Guards approached from across the courtyard, and Gorman tensed. When several of Lord Roger's men rushed out of the barracks, Will positioned himself closer to the entrance of the kitchen. "Well?" Baldric demanded, and Will didn't think for one moment that he was asking Gorman about trying to hit him.

"No, m'lord," Gorman conceded, and waved off Roger's men.

"I didn't think so," Baldric intoned. "Now, why don't you tell me where Lord Roger and the others have gone?" He started walking away from Will, forcing Gorman to tag along after him.

"Not gone, m'lord," Gorman said smoothly. "They are searching for proof that Stolweg has not been infiltrated."

Will didn't hear the rest as they walked away. When he turned around, his mother was standing behind him in the kitchen. Will took her hand, then gently pried her white-knuckled fingers from a large and sharply honed carving knife. "Not yet, Mum."

CHAPTER THIRTY-THREE

The Chase

"Gilles!" Anna called out when she spied her friend with the mares.

"M'lady, what brings you? Although it *is* fortunate." He craned his neck to see behind her. "Where's Will?"

"I rode out alone." Gilles's eyebrows shot up. "Cellach is gone," she explained, "and Will is needed at the stable. I came to bring you back to the keep."

"The stable?" Gilles asked, suddenly on alert. "But most of the horses are here."

"They've finally come, Gilles." Anna was too excited to relate the news in an ordered fashion and forced herself to slow down. "The Royal Guard. I mean, Lord Baldric from Whitmarsh, along with five guards. Roger was still asleep when they rode up to the gate. Of course, the rest of us were awake and had everything prepared to welcome them. Lord Roger was furious."

Gilles cocked his head, studying her. "Yes, I can see just how furious he was."

Until now, Anna had forgotten about her face. She touched her jaw gingerly and was relieved that the swelling had subsided. "It's nothing."

"It is *never* nothing, Lady Aubrianne. Your face is swollen and bruised. And this time, he split the skin. Did Lord Baldric comment?"

"He never saw me. In fact, they don't even know that I'm gone. I pretended to be Will when I rode out." Gilles looked askance at the floppy hat on her head. "We're about the same size, you know?"

"Hmph," he replied.

She remembered something that Gilles had said when she first arrived. "Why is it fortunate that I'm here?"

"Let's take a look at the mares, m'lady. You'll see soon enough."

• • •

They walked through the trees to the small clearing where the horses were grazing. He brought his lady to Rina. The mare was next to foal and not due for another week. But her tail and hips had dropped, and after every few bites of grass, she swung her head toward her swollen belly.

"Oh, Gilles, she's early. This does complicate matters." Lady Aubrianne paced a few steps before coming to a decision. "You return to the stable. If one of us does not go back this evening, Baldric will be sure to send out his guards."

"I could always stay, my lady. You could hop right up on Tullian and ride straight back the way you came." But Gilles knew that once she saw Rina's condition, she would be as immovable as the henge. He smiled—there was one way: he could hit her over the head, tie her to the saddle, and slap Tullian on the rump after pointing him in the direction of home. "I don't like it, my lady, leaving you here alone. I know you can protect yourself, but…"

"We've never found tracks in this area, Gilles," she reminded him. "You can take the mares, and I'll find a good spot to hole up with Rina. I can remain hidden if necessary, you know that."

"All right, but I'm not leaving until we have your camp settled. And, I am sending Will."

Gilles thought about the plan he and the others had discussed. Perhaps it was for the best that Lady Aubrianne and his son would be away from the castle for a few days. Feigning reluctance, Gilles agreed to leave.

"Let's give the mares an hour to graze," he suggested. "While we're waiting, we can practice quarterstaff. I'll leave you my bow and quiver, and you have your dagger. You will at least have some weapons to protect yourself, though I doubt you'll need them."

• • •

Lark raced through the fields on Rabbit. His horse's strides lengthened to eat up the distance to Lady Aubrianne. *Of all the reckless behavior*, he thought angrily. He found the second stream and half expected to see the mares when the water rounded back upon itself. Only their tracks remained, trailing deeper into the wooded hills.

Then he heard a familiar sound on the breeze. He reined in Rabbit and listened to the uneven clacking. After dismounting, he slipped silently through the trees, his uneasiness growing upon recognizing the cracking of quarterstaffs.

• • •

Gilles and Anna had fought together so many times that their sparring resembled a dance. They advanced and reversed, butted and guarded, each knowing the other's moves as if they were their own. Still, Anna thought, the practice was good for her. It strengthened her even as it fed her soul.

Gilles almost succeeded in surprising her with a move he seldom used. Almost. Switching his staff from one hand to the other, he attacked. Anna ducked as his rod whistled through the air above her head. She jumped over his return swing, a blow aimed below her knees. Turning to counter the blow, she was distracted by a movement near the edge of the clearing. She barely managed to block a butt to her ribs. Gilles cocked an eyebrow at her.

She engaged him again by moving to the right; the position allowed her a better view of the tree line. There it was again, only this time, a glint of metal.

She raised her staff, leaving her torso unprotected. All of her concentration was focused on the hurtling object aimed at her friend. She lifted her hawthorn stick up and under Gilles's arm, just in time to catch a nasty dagger before it embedded itself in his shoulder.

Not until she was staring at the quivering blade lodged in her staff did she notice the pain radiating through her side. While she'd been protecting him, Gilles had landed a heavy blow to her ribs. He immediately backed off, followed her gaze, and realized their peril.

"Come forward, coward," he shouted to the woods, pushing her behind him. "Come forward, and I'll show you that a man does not throw knives whilst hiding behind trees."

Anna tried to catch her breath as a figure stepped into the clearing, a good twenty paces from the dagger's origin.

"What in the world do you think you are doing?" she panted. "You could have killed him. If I hadn't seen you…"

"The throw was not intended to kill," Larkin answered easily.

Gilles, having pulled his dagger from his belt, continued to shield her. Anna put her hand on his shoulder and squeezed hard enough to capture his attention. "Gilles, stop." When he made no move to heed her, she urged, "It's all right. Put it away."

"Not quite yet, my lady," he replied, never once taking his eyes from Larkin.

"I take it, Lady Aubrianne, that he is another loyal friend of yours?"

"Larkin, this is Gilles, Stolweg's stable master. Gilles, this is Larkin of the Royal Guard," she managed in one breath, the words rushing out while she held her side.

Gilles lowered his dagger but did not return it to its scabbard. Keeping his eye on the armed man, Lark wondered aloud, "Why is it every time I meet one of your friends, they think me set on doing you harm? Is this some special Stolweg tradition?"

Ignoring him, Lady Aubrianne picked up her quarterstaff, pulled out the knife, then tossed it deftly to him, hilt first. "I see that Baldric was hasty in sending me to your rescue," Lark added. "You seem to have your own army of protectors."

"You have it wrong," Gilles fired back, finally sheathing his blade. "It is Lady Aubrianne who protects us. I'll gather the mares, m'lady," he said, glancing at the deepening sky. "There'll be just enough time to make camp."

"Whose camp?" Lark asked. "I'm here to escort Lady Aubrianne back to the keep."

Gilles chuckled. "You can try," he said, and walked off to corral the horses.

"What does he mean, I can *try?*" Lark demanded.

"I'm not going back tonight. Or tomorrow. Or the next day. I can't. Rina's about to foal."

He stared at her in disbelief. "And Gilles, he was going to leave you here? Alone?"

• • •

Anna was unused to anyone questioning her methods when it came to the horses. Even Roger had challenged her only a few times. "Really, Larkin," she said impatiently, "it's only for a few hours. As soon as you both return to the keep, Gilles will send his son. I'll stay with Rina."

"That was quite a trick you pulled, catching my knife like that." He managed to completely ignore her order. "You'll have to tell me later how a horse-breeding girl from Chevring learned such a skill."

Anna scowled at him. "What do you mean *later?*"

His grin stretched from ear to ear, and her heart skipped a beat.

She could not imagine that he shared this beatific smile often, and she would gladly pay a king's ransom to see it again. The way she was thinking, Anna wasn't sure Gilles hadn't managed to land a blow to her head. She tried to focus on what Larkin was saying, but her eyes kept returning to his mouth, hoping to catch more. He only obliged her with his habitual smirk.

She was a moment too late realizing that he'd asked her a question. Apparently, he'd repeated it twice. "Lady Aubrianne, are you all right? The blow Gilles landed was a heavy one. Do you need to sit?"

Her face flushed crimson. "It's nothing," she answered angrily. "I've taken harder hits before." Realizing what she had just admitted, she glanced up at him. *That* had erased his smirk.

"You're not going back tonight?" he asked flatly. She shook her head. "Fine," he stated.

"Well, I must say that's a relief," she admitted. "Thank you."

"You are welcome, m'lady."

"If you help with the mares," she suggested, "you'll be able to leave that much sooner."

"I'm afraid you don't understand, Lady Aubrianne. I won't be returning to the keep either." And he walked away to help Gilles with the horses.

Anna's jaw dropped. She hadn't considered this possibility. Well, he could just keep his distance if he knew what was good for him. Gilles approached and, not caring a whit that Larkin could hear, asked bluntly, "Do you trust him, m'lady? Say yes, and I'll go with an easy heart."

Larkin lifted an eyebrow in interest. "We can trust him," she replied without hesitation. "I'll help you get the mares past the streams. Larkin, you should fetch Rabbit."

At least he was savvy enough to know she wanted a private word with Gilles, because he didn't argue with her. "Keep Will at Stolweg, Gilles," Anna said. "You'll need his help."

"Are you sure, m'lady?" Gilles asked.

"I am. Tell Lord Roger why I can't make it back. And, Gilles, it would be best if you explained in the presence of Lord Baldric. My staying here will only exacerbate Lord Roger's bad humor."

"Can we trust Lord Baldric?"

"I think so. When the time comes, we'll make it clear that we are aligned with King Godwin. Safe journey, Gilles," she said fondly, and he was off.

She returned to the clearing and found Larkin already mounted.

Rina was behind him, her lead secured to Rabbit's saddle. Anna mounted Tullian, and Lark followed her to a small brook flowing south. She kept the horses to the streambed; any hoofprints would be impossible to see under the flowing water and ever shifting pebbles. Finally, Anna turned and followed a small rivulet of spring runoff. On either side, the banks rose sharply, eventually becoming solid rock.

Anna remembered the day she had found what lay ahead. The creek ended at a wide, flat boulder. The rock must have sheared away from the canyon wall, cutting off the stream. A beautiful surprise was about to unfold before Larkin.

"We can leave Rina for the moment," she said, and nudged Tullian forward. He lifted one great hoof and then the other onto the stone slab before making a small leap and landing neatly on the other side. She could hear Rabbit behind her and turned to see Larkin's reaction to the hidden canyon. It was perhaps twenty paces wide and three times that distance in length. Straight ahead, a sheer rock face rose magnificently. Both sides of the canyon were made up of tree-covered hills so steep that they were impossible to climb either down or up without ropes.

Lark blew out a long breath in appreciation. "How did you find this place? It looks as though neither horse nor human has ever been here."

"I've scouted out several secure spots for the mares. We've not had a chance to use this site. Rina should be able to make it over, if I lead her."

Lark swung down and held Anna's elbow to support her as she climbed atop the boulder. His touch had been meant to steady, but her balance abandoned her. He jumped to the other side and reached up, his fingers circling her waist. Anna was forced to put her hands on his shoulders lest she pitch forward. She barely felt her feet touch the ground and blushed when he held her a moment too long. Hastily pulling away, she moved to check on Rina.

Lark came up behind her so silently that she started like a skittish filly when he spoke. "You lead, Aubrianne."

Rina went over easily, as easily as an eighteen-hand mare that happened to be a day away from foaling could. But contrary to her enormous girth, Rina was as nimble as ever. She pranced haughtily away to a thick patch of grass.

Anna was still embarrassed by her reaction to Lark's touch. To show him that she was once again in control of her faculties, when he offered his hand to help her down, she took it graciously. "Let me show you around," she offered, and as she started forward, she realized he had never released her hand. His fingers tightened possessively, and he continued smiling at her as before. Unnerved, she walked away a little too fast. He didn't actually yank her to his side, but that was where she found herself.

"Fine." She sighed irritably. "Shall we?" He nodded, and they walked hand-in-hand along the course of the brook.

"There's a pool, hidden under that willow tree near the cliff," she explained, and then pointed to a place where the sheer wall hollowed out at the ground. "We can build a fire there." He agreed, offering to gather wood.

"There's no need. I've already done it. Months ago, in fact."

"Aren't you tired of being so self-sufficient?" he asked her.

His question was meant in jest, Anna knew, but she couldn't stop the coldness that gripped her heart. There was no one else upon whom she could depend, save herself.

• • •

The camp was quickly made, and the fire was built. He placed his bedroll opposite hers. With nothing left to do, an awkward silence pressed down around them. Lark reached into his bag and pulled out a small bundle of fabric. "Are you hungry?"

"No, not yet. You go ahead."

"I'm not either." The quiet stretched. "I interrupted your sparring," he said.

"We were almost finished anyway."

"You're pretty good, you know," Lark told her. "But you should try practicing with other partners once in a while. The change would sharpen some of your lazier moves."

"Lazier moves? Is that right?" she challenged, her eyes flashing with anger.

Lark ignored the warning. "Don't get me wrong, Lady Aubrianne. I only mean to say that it appeared too easy. When you practice with the same person, you learn their moves as though they're your own. It's a disadvantage if you find that you have to defend yourself. All at once, your opponent is not behaving as you expect, and it throws you off your balance."

"You didn't seem to think it was a practice bout when you threw your knife," Anna retorted.

When he chuckled and shook his head, she was held captive by the loose black curls falling forward onto his forehead. Her fingers itched to smooth them back into place.

"You're right about that," he admitted. "I didn't know who Gilles was and wasn't about to take a chance where your safety was concerned. I didn't aim to kill, only wound."

"Why do you care so much about my safety?"

"Duty, perhaps," he replied, studying her.

• • •

Anna was perplexed. She'd been married three years and until this day, had never felt such intimacy with a man. She didn't know what she would have done if he had gazed into her eyes. Her heart, walled up for so long, was now lodged firmly in her throat. She swallowed hard, forcing her emotions back down.

When he noticed that her clasped hands were trembling, he cupped them in his own. "As I said before, Lady Aubrianne, I apologize for interrupting your match with Gilles. If you are up for it, I would be a happy substitute. But be warned, it will not be so easy with me."

She decided to take the bait, knowing he was offering her an escape from the awkward moment. "I daresay, Larkin, you are very sure of yourself. Grab the staffs; it's time to show you some humility."

"If you think you are the one to do it, I look forward to being conquered," he teased. He opened his mouth to say more, as if regretting the flirtatious note in his voice.

But Anna grinned. "Tell me that again when you are lying flat on your back and I'm smiling down at you." He raised his brow a fraction at the unintended innuendo, and she blushed.

Chuckling again, Lark fetched the staffs, leaving her with a ghost of a smile upon her lips.

CHAPTER THIRTY-FOUR

The Wager

Anna sauntered to where Larkin waited with the quarterstaffs. He had chosen an ash stave for himself and offered Anna the hawthorn stave she had used earlier. They immediately engaged each other.

"Go easy on me, Lady Aubrianne," he teased. "It's been some time since I handled a staff in the presence of a lady." His grin spread as he gracefully twirled his pole. Still warm from their earlier repartee, Anna felt her blush deepen.

She answered him with a deadly swing of her quarterstaff. He easily deflected it. They went back and forth, and Anna realized that he had yet to make an offensive move. She'd been doing all the work while he'd been saving his strength. She backed off, waiting for him to advance.

He flicked out with his staff, and she blocked the blow with nary an effort. But before she could parry with one of her own, his staff twirled and twisted her hawthorn rod from her grasp. Unbelievably, it went sailing through the air. He'd been right, she thought, sighing. She'd become complacent.

Lark stepped back and arched an eyebrow at her.

"I see your point," she said for him. "I want a rematch."

"I don't know, Lady Aubrianne," he drawled. "I don't see the purpose."

"Worried that it won't be so easy the next time around?" she asked, trying to inveigle him.

"I've made my point, and you've learned your lesson," he lectured.

"Mayhap you are fearful of losing to a woman," she goaded him.

He ignored her gibe. "Truth be told, there's nothing in it for me," he admitted, as his gaze drifted to hers. "Now, if there were some incentive, a wager perhaps, I might reconsider."

"Whatever you want," she agreed. He might defeat her, she thought, but she would not twice lose her stave. She took a moment to analyze him, as any combatant would when facing an opponent. He was tall, but then so was she. And agile as a cat, but she presented a smaller target.

"Don't you want to know the terms first?" Larkin asked with a smug expression.

She contemplated what prize he might ask and was surprised to discover that it didn't matter. He was so cocky, so disarming. She would discover and use his weakness. And she would win. "Wager away."

"Suit yourself. If I win, you owe me a kiss."

"Then you'd best prepare yourself, Larkin."

His smile widened. "You are that good at it, then?" he asked, twisting her words as he had twisted her staff.

Anna returned his smile in equal measure, rounding on him, advancing. "I meant that you should prepare yourself for a lonely night. Your lips will have no company this eve."

She was actually flirting, she realized. She had never flirted before. No, that wasn't true. She *had* flirted once, long ago with Roger, before their wedding night. She shuddered thinking about how often he'd used her words against her: *Your request is my pleasure.* Too bad for Larkin that she conjured Roger's image in her mind. She would use her rage to his detriment.

They tested each other before combating in earnest. For a long time, they were equally matched. Larkin would show her a technique she hadn't seen before. Anna would counter with one of her own long-forgotten moves. Around and around they went, their quarterstaffs whistling as wood cut through air, then cracking like thunder as they struck.

It dawned on her that he was still leading in this dance. Instead of waiting for his next advance, she improvised and moved swiftly against him. A slight upturn at the corner of his mouth was his only reaction. His counterblow was fluid.

He was forcing her to stretch her skills, and it felt *good.* When she smiled back, he showed, for the first time, a little surprise.

Around them, dusk crept in, and the azure sky darkened to the bruised-plum color that would herald the night. What would it be like to continue the bout forever? Advancing and blocking, she could see no end to it. And she wanted to win.

She thought of ways to gain the upper hand. It came to her that the one advantage she had over Larkin was not one of her strengths. Rather, her edge was his weakness: she was a woman, he was a man.

When next he advanced, she would be ready. Larkin brought the lower end of his staff up and forward. Anna purposely fumbled as she moved to block the blow.

"Oof," she exhaled when his staff connected with her waist.

He dropped his guard and his staff. "Lady Aubrianne! Are you hurt?"

She thrust her quarterstaff between his calves and twisted the hawthorn stick sideways and up. With her stave behind one of his knees, she pushed against his other leg. Upsetting his balance was as easy as finding a fulcrum and lever. He landed with a thud. When he tried to raise his staff to block another strike, she stomped down on it and brought the end of her pole to rest under his chin.

For several seconds, they remained frozen, not speaking. And definitely not smiling. To win, she had had to resort to a ruse; her triumph tasted bittersweet. She whipped her quarterstaff away and held out her hand to help him to rise.

"You fought fairly, m'lady," he stated, his words hitting the crux of her self-berating. "If attacked, you must use every weapon in your arsenal. Do not be ashamed; I'm not."

She peered into the darkening forest to avoid his gaze.

• • •

After he gave her some time to think on his words, he approached her. "Have you forgotten the wager, m'lady? You have yet to name your prize. Truth be told, I am dearly sorry to have lost this match and the favor of your kiss."

She had turned back to face him, and he gave her what he hoped was a devastating smile. More than ever, this woman intrigued him with her equal measures of strength and vulnerability. The spark from years ago had never been extinguished; it had only smoldered quietly. He'd been dreaming about her for years. Finally finding her, she exceeded his fantasies in every way.

"I make no claim, Larkin. I tricked you." He started to protest, but she cut him off. "Under the circumstances, I forfeit my reward."

"Still, a rematch might be in order," he continued offhandedly. "I suppose that now only your husband will receive your favors."

Once he spoke the words, he regretted them. His opinion of Lord Roger was that he was a cruel and arrogant man. Remembering the sneering lips and cold eyes and imagining him with Aubrianne was infuriating. She must have seen his ire, because she took a step back.

"My husband's lips have *never* touched mine," she averred. "Not even when we stood before God and were married."

If she'd surprised him by winning the match, she stunned him with her words. Her disgust told him everything he needed to know: hers was worse than a loveless marriage; it was one filled with hatred.

And just like that, the final piece fell into place, and his heart felt whole for the first time in his life. He doubted not that eventually he and Lady Aubrianne—Anna, as he thought of her—would come together. But first, he needed her to remember him. He could deal with Roger later; the man's days were numbered anyway.

• • •

Anna waited to see his shock that such a simple gesture as kissing had never passed between husband and wife. His surprise was much too fleeting.

She pulled her gaze away. Too late, she was trapped. Her only chance was to continue with false bravado. She countered with her coolest look, trying to match his smoldering eyes with an air of aloofness. He wasn't fooled.

"As you won," Larkin explained, eyes intent on hers, "you do not owe me a kiss. But you *are* required to claim a prize."

"I say again," she asserted with more courage than she felt, "I make no claim." But she could not look away. His eyes were so magnetic that despite her retreat, she leaned a fraction closer.

His lips curved sensuously. He followed her, stalking, driving her so that she eventually backed into the canyon wall. A mere step separated their bodies. Her hands lifted reflexively to his chest, to push him away or simply to touch him, she did not know.

She felt his heartbeat, felt that it matched her own, as it had once before, years ago. Her dark stranger from the alcove. Her gaze flew to his.

"I would never renege on a bet, m'lady," he whispered. "I offer you the same terms that I would have demanded from you, had you lost. A kiss." He lowered his lips ever so slowly to hers, all the while looking into her eyes, giving her the strength that she needed. Their lips pressed together, tentatively at first, barely making contact.

She exhaled softly, and, as if it were the sign he needed, he pressed his lips again to her slightly parted ones and brushed them lightly against her skin. Lips against lips. Back and forth. Slowly. Gently. Until she joined him in the simple motion. When her lips parted, his tongue dipped between and entered the moist warmth of her mouth. Just barely.

She couldn't catch her breath. She could only concentrate on the feel of him. She'd waited an eternity for this kiss. Her knees buckled, her lashes fluttered. He grasped her waist to support her. Without knowing it, her hands traveled from his chest, upward, to the back of his neck, to that place where his hairline met his nape and his curly black mop was softest. She never imagined a kiss could be so sweet.

• • •

"Breathe, Lady Aubrianne. Breathe," he murmured against her lips. The feel of her fingers twining in his hair moved him more than any kiss could. Pressing his lips to hers again with more insistence, he resisted the urge to move his hands from their safe purchase on her waist.

"It *is* you, isn't it?" she whispered, before her lips came alive, matching her need with his own. And as their kiss deepened, he found that he was the captured party, so entangled were her fingers in his hair. Even if he wanted to, he could not break away.

He moved closer to her, inching forward and pressing his legs against hers. Her hips shifted, and her entire body pressed against his length. They gasped as breast met chest. Their bodies were as sealed as their lips and desperate to merge closer.

He wanted to see her face. To discover if she truly remembered. He slowed the kiss. His tongue retreated, and he heard her moan in protest. She wasn't ready to end the embrace, so he played with her lips, tugging at them with his own, pulling them softly with his teeth, before laying gentle kisses to the bruises on her face. With each pass, he broke the contact a little more. Her eyes fluttered open and met his.

"I wondered if you knew," he murmured. "I've searched for you for years, and now I've finally found you."

"Then kiss me again," she said. And he did.

CHAPTER THIRTY-FIVE

Trespasses and Confessions

As the sun dipped lower, the last bit of light filtering through the thickening canopy of trees faded. The campfire lent little illumination to the canyon floor. Mostly, it was the newly risen moon and stars that provided a soft glow to the evening.

Larkin walked over to where Aubrianne was tending to the mare. "How is she?"

"She's sweating. But she'll make it through the night. Won't you, Rina?" Rina pawed at the ground while Anna stood near her head. "Gilles gave me what remained of his provisions. There's some bread and cheese, a few apples from last year's harvest."

Food was not exactly what he was hungry for, he thought ruefully, as she began whispering soothing words into the mare's ear. "And I have Will's lunch," he managed. "What say you to a picnic, Anna?" She looked up, her eyes wide and full of sadness.

"It has been a long time since anyone called me Anna," she explained with a tremor in her voice. "In fact, the last person to say it was my father when we parted on my wedding day."

"Anna suits you." He put his arm around her and walked her back to the fire. "But if it causes you pain, I won't say it again."

"No. I like it," she replied with a soft voice full of longing for days lost. "I never much cared to be called Aubrianne—too formal. But Roger insisted, for just that reason."

"We should sleep," he suggested. "We can talk in the morning after we've both rested." He knelt by her side and brushed her forehead with his lips, whispering goodnight. For a long while, he listened as her breathing slowed and evened. Then he too fell asleep, knowing his slumber would be light, leaving his senses attuned to any danger. It was very late when he opened his eyes and searched for Anna. She was asleep, peaceful, and he silently added more wood to the fire.

The night was clear, and though the moon had moved on from the slice of sky above their canyon, the stars were bright. With the fire, they offered enough light for him to make his way to check the horses. Tullian and Rabbit stood together.

Rina kept apart, regarding him patiently. "Keep an eye on things for me, will you, Rina?" The mare eyed him and snorted. Lark took it as a yes and left her to check Rabbit. He scratched his horse in his favorite places and then scratched Tullian where he had seen Anna do it. Suddenly, the ears of both horses pivoted.

The hair on Lark's neck rose when he heard a muffled noise. Fool, he thought, to wake and leave the fire without arming himself. He hastened back as soundlessly as he'd left.

. . .

Anna's senses prickled. She and Larkin were not alone in the canyon. She tried to locate him through slit eyes. He was gone. Feigning a restless sleep, she rolled to her side and listened for any noise that might give away the intruder's location.

There. She heard it again. Coming from the direction where her feet pointed. Where was her knife? She chided herself for not taking her usual precautions. With the telltale sound of creaking boot leather, her focus sharpened.

A man, skulking toward the fire. Anna dove for the bag that held her knife and opened her mouth to shout Larkin's name. Before a sound could escape, a hand clamped down on her lips while another grabbed her and yanked her to her feet. *Stupid*, she criticized herself, to have only focused on the threat she had heard. She should have realized that there was another man and that the predators would have split up. Her captor put her in a stranglehold while his hand covered her mouth and nose. She struggled to draw in air.

"Scream, and I'll break your neck. Do you understand?" It was Roger. Anna nodded, and he moved his hand from her mouth and nose. As she sucked air back into her lungs, Roger gave her arm a vicious twist, pinning it behind her back.

He propelled her forward. Submissively, so as not to provoke him, she pleaded, "Stop this, please." Gorman drew a dagger and sliced open her chemise. She died a thousand deaths as the vile beast groped at her.

Then Gorman's dagger slipped between the laces of her breeches and the fabric fell away. She was completely bared to his grasping paws and struggled to get away, but her husband's hold on her was too strong. "I beg you, Roger, don't let Gorman do this." And for a second, after he released her, Anna thought perhaps he would do just that. Instead, he shoved her forward. The last glimpse she had of her husband as Gorman wrestled her to the ground was of his twisted face gleaming in anticipation. She understood then and there that this would be the last time she would be abused. Roger was finished with her. But she would not go without a fight; she would inflict as much damage as she could. And so she thrashed, bit, and kicked.

• • •

Lark crept back to the campfire, his eyes and ears alert to anything that might give away an intruder's position. There was nothing. Crouching, he inched forward. When Anna cried out again, he sprang forward, ready to kill with his bare hands if necessary. There was no one else in the camp save Anna.

She was dreaming. He rushed to her side. "No, please, no. Keep him away!" she keened. "Roger, no. I'm begging you." Her face was contorted in pain and rage and fear. It was too much. He grabbed her shoulders, but she sat up with a jolt, her eyelids squeezed shut, lashing out, scratching and hitting, all the while screaming "No!" over and over.

"Anna, open your eyes. *Open your eyes!*" he ordered.

She fought against him with every bit of strength that she possessed. She came close to tearing his flesh with her teeth. Lark moved behind her and crisscrossed her arms in front of her. His grip was firm but gentle, and he drew her to his chest. He called her name again and again, until she collapsed against him.

"Where did you go, Larkin?" she whispered. "I called for you."

"Anna, it was just a dream," he soothed.

"Just a dream," she panted weakly.

"A nightmare," he amended. "You're safe now. I won't let anything hurt you. I promised you, remember?" He rocked her gently but didn't loosen his hold. "Only a dream."

"A dream…" she echoed, still dazed.

"Can you remember what it was about?" he asked. "It might help to talk it through."

She took her time before answering. Lark waited as well, afraid of hearing what she would say but knowing he would listen. "Remember it? I don't have to try," she finally said. "It's easy to remember one's own life."

Lark wasn't sure what her dream entailed, but from what she had screamed in the throes of her nightmare, he had a good idea. He forced his bile down. "What did he do to you, Anna?"

• • •

Anna didn't want to tell him but found that she couldn't prevent herself. With a great sob, she answered, "Whatever he wanted. Oh God, Larkin, he did whatever he wanted."

And once she began, she couldn't stop. She told him about her wedding night and then all that followed. She told him of Roger's escalating cruelty and his efforts to break her as if she were an animal. "He used those words: 'I'll enjoy breaking you, Aubrianne.' I thought that he had won his sick game," she said with a sigh. "He didn't win. He never can now. You changed that, Larkin. Our kiss changed that. I don't know what will happen upon my return, but I do know he will never put his hands on me again. He'll never break me."

"I will kill him," Lark vowed. "As soon as we return, I will kill him."

She scrambled away from him, evading his hands as he tried to draw her back. He would never understand. She'd been stupid to tell him so much; she should have stopped herself. He spoke of killing Roger as if it were nothing to him. *What gall*, she thought. Killing Roger was not his right. And once back at the keep, she would follow through with her original plan. The only difference: she would stay and face the consequences.

He dropped his hands to his sides, and Anna could tell that he was struggling to check his anger. "Why didn't you leave him? Baldric, the King, your family would've—"

She lifted her hand. "No, Larkin. I don't want to talk about this anymore. It was a mistake to burden you."

"Anna?"

"I need to check Rina," she stated, shutting her heart away from him. She left him alone by the fire and walked to her only solace over the last three years: the horses.

Rina nickered at her approach. "Not long now, is it?" Anna murmured. She smoothed her hand down Rina's side, holding it against the mare's abdomen and waiting for the telltale tightening of muscles that would indicate a contraction. When it came, she began to count. Rina

161

turned her head to nudge her. The next spasm was a long time coming.

"I'll see you in the morning, Rina-girl. You'll be fine until then." The mare shook her head, twisting and shaking her mane like a wet dog.

Anna went next to Tullian and Rabbit; both were alert. Then she left them, too, unable for the first time in her life to find peace with her horses.

She wasn't ready to go back to the fire and face Larkin. So she followed the brook back to the entrance of the canyon. The stone slab had cooled since the sun's rays had kissed it. She sat upon it, easing herself back. There was comfort to be found in the dense strength of the rock.

And because her instincts clamored for her to curl into a ball and hide, Anna stretched out her legs and tilted her chin to the night sky and its thousand glittering stars. She remembered sobbing while Larkin had held her. Now she only wept. It was only after her eyes were dry that she decided to return to camp.

She stood and smoothed her clothing, wiped her face with her sleeve, and turned to the faint light of the fire. Larkin was leaning against a tree not six paces from where she'd rested.

He said not a word as she walked toward him. Only as she passed did he push away from the tree. His fingers found hers, and she looked down in surprise as her own laced together with his. They walked back to the camp in silence.

Larkin did not stop where his bedding was laid out, but walked with Anna to her spread. He sat down and pulled her to him. She was too exhausted to push him away and drifted once again into his waiting arms. They fit as perfectly together as a boot to stirrup. Her back rested against his beating heart, his cheek pressed against her ear.

"Can you forgive me?" he whispered.

"For what should I forgive you?"

"For being an idiot."

Anna remained silent. When he sighed, she pressed her body closer to his. She knew that Larkin had been thinking about what he'd asked. She had walked away from him, angry because he had no right to judge the motives that had kept her tied to her husband. But she had burdened him with her story.

So she patiently waited. When he finally spoke, his words were not those she expected. "You never told me about your dream."

"It was like all of the others," she said. "Except the ending."

"What was different, Anna?" he murmured.

"In this dream, I knew it was the last time. In truth, Roger no longer needs me. And he can't risk keeping me alive. I know too much."

"So you've been training with Gilles, preparing for his final move against you."

"Or against my family," Anna added. "His people have sworn an oath against us."

"His people? You mean soldiers from Stolweg?" he asked.

"Not all of Roger's people are from Stolweg, nor are they from Ragallach." She let her words sink in before continuing. "And even at Stolweg, loyalties are split. Roger can be charmingly persuasive when it suits his needs. My own father was taken in by his smooth promises and, from the number of horses he continues to send us, must be completely indebted to him."

"And if your family could be protected?"

She knew this was the answer he needed. Her response would cement forever how he would see her. Did it matter if she told him? She still felt connected to him but could not imagine them growing closer. Not now. Not after he had heard most of the truth.

Anna took a deep breath to check her anger. "You are judging me, Larkin."

"But I—"

"You are. You're angry with me. I saw it in your eyes as clearly as I now see the stars. And I'll tell you something else, Larkin. I'll answer your question, but for a selfish reason. I need someone to know the truth." She drew a deep breath, then began, "Just as he planned to supplant Lady Isabel with me, so has he found my replacement: my sister, Claire.

"I sent Cellach, our master-at-arms, to warn my family, to give them a fighting chance. For when I return to Stolweg Keep, my family's welfare will no longer be in my hands. I will no longer submit to him," she explained. "And he will try to kill me. If he succeeds, he will force Claire to take my place. I won't let that happen."

Touching the hideous ruby on her finger, Anna pulled hard, yanking it off. She held the ring aloft, staring at the blood-red stone. "Roger forbade me to ever remove this."

Lark examined the gem. "The ruby doesn't suit you, Anna. I think I understand, though. It's a symbol, isn't it?"

"It's my reminder that this life I am caught in is but transient," Anna admitted. "Rubies are fragile. It would take but a little pressure to crush this one to dust." She slipped the stone into her pocket before turning to him. "You can't kill Roger," she forbade him. "I could tell you that I

163

NICOLE ELIZABETH KELLEHER

worry for my family's safety, but the truth is that it is not your right. Nor Baldric's, or even King Godwin's."

"You mean to kill him yourself," he deduced.

"I must. You have to promise me, Larkin. Swear it on all that is dear to you. You will not kill Roger, not while I breathe." Her words were so cold and final, she shivered. But she needed him to understand. If she failed in her attempt, Roger would kill her. Then, only then, Larkin would be free to do that which she could not.

"You cannot fail, Anna," he ordered, and she could hear the struggle in his voice. "I don't understand what is happening between us, but I do know that you already mean too much to me. You've haunted my dreams for over five years. I cannot lose you. Not again."

"But your word, Larkin? Will you give me your word?"

He sighed. "I promise you, Anna. You will have your chance. I'll even help you. I could teach you…" He stopped midsentence when she looked at him as a tolerant parent regards a child.

"Anna?"

"Larkin?" she answered lightly to dispel the gloominess.

The corner of his lip twitched, but then he grew serious. "You have my word. You'll have one chance. I can promise you no more and no less."

Could she ask more? Anna didn't know. But she was done talking. She hid her face in his chest, drawing in his scent as if storing the memory to draw upon in the future. She would always have their one kiss. If it was to be all she could ever have now that Larkin understood the extent of her dishonor, so be it. It would have to be enough.

She moved away. "I need to sleep. Rina will need me in a few hours."

Surprisingly, he pulled her back against him and smoothed her hair. With her cheek against his chest and his arms about her, Anna fell asleep.

CHAPTER THIRTY-SIX

Daybreak

As a soft halo of light stretched over the canyon's sliver of heaven, Anna awoke. The fire had gone out, but its embers still glowed in the shadowy clearing. Larkin was asleep by her side, his arm draped across her waist. He hadn't left her alone, she thought, despite knowing her secrets.

Carefully, so as not to wake him, Anna raised her head to check on the horses. Tullian and Rabbit were dozing, and Rina was awake but calm. When the mare showed no signs that her labor had increased, Anna gazed at Lark's still-sleeping face, and gently lifted his arm and sat up. Just as she was about to stand, he shifted in his sleep and came to rest with both arms about her waist, his head nestled in her lap. Her stomach grumbled softly with hunger. If she tried to dislodge him, he would surely wake. And he looked so peaceful, with his long, dark lashes dusting his cheeks, his mouth and lips for once relaxed.

He sighed contentedly in his slumber with a wisp of a smile on his lips. If she could just stretch far enough, she thought, she might be able to reach her saddlebag without disturbing him. Her fingers snagged the strap on the second try.

While he slept, she pulled out a late apple from the last of Doreen's stores. Though no longer crisp, the fruit was sweet and juicy. With her grandfather's dagger, she cut it into perfect wedges, removing the bits of core.

She was halfway through her meal when Larkin, his eyes still closed, whispered, "You could at least share if you're going to wake me so early."

Anna laughed and picked up a wedge. She touched his lips with the fruit. Her face hovered just above his, and the long tresses of her hair hung down around him like mossy vines. He chewed, his strong jaw working, his lips still smiling. Her body warmed in unexpected places just watching him.

His eyes bored into hers, and her lips parted. She fed him another slice.

"Careful," he told her. "Right now, you're looking at me like I was a piece of your favorite cake." She blushed and tried to look away, but his voice dragged her back to stare at him.

"I was having the most pleasant dream," he continued, his words yet lazy with sleep. "I was lying in a garden with a beautiful maiden. My face was next to—"

Anna quickly shoved another slice of apple into his mouth, stifling a giggle.

When her fingers dipped back to feed him the last small slice, he captured them and pressed them to his lips. He licked her thumb, all the while holding her gaze. Then, slowly, he went from one fingertip to the next. "I wonder if your lips are as sweet as your fingers, Anna."

He propped himself up on one elbow and with his other arm brought her head to his. Then he kissed her, gently, taking her lower lip between his two and sucking. "Sweeter," he murmured, running his fingers through her hair before shifting them so that she was on her back and he was above her.

A low growl emanated from deep within his throat. His hands sought to free themselves from her hair while his tongue played with hers. He dragged himself away from her lips to allow his mouth to move down her neck. His lips laid a searing path down her throat and then back up to her earlobe. He nibbled on the tender flesh while his nose sent little puffs of air into her ear. She turned her face, her lips fought to find his. But he was in control again, and he kissed her slowly.

"Anna," he whispered, "open your eyes and look at me."

They opened, and were glassy. She murmured on an exhale of breath held too long, "Larkin, I don't—" He kissed her soundly to stop her from speaking more.

"We have hours, Anna. And we can stop any time you want." Her hands reached around his neck to pull him down for another taste. His teeth nipped at her lips. His mouth sucked at her tongue. He left a trail of kisses down her throat to her collarbone while his hand skimmed down her arm to her fingertips and back. He allowed his fingers to brush against her breast, and she leaned into him. His lips found hers again as his hand claimed its prize.

Lark loosened the thin ties that held the collar of her chemise. While her hands tangled in his hair, he kissed her breastbone. Through the fine linen of her blouse, he caressed her breast in lazy circles. Finally, the pad of his thumb rubbed across her nipple, and he heard her gasp in pleasure. He could feel her longing. When he pinched her nipple, ever so gently, she groaned with pleasure. His mouth steadily made its way to her breast, nosing her collar aside as he kissed and licked her exposed flesh.

Lark delighted in the delicate panting noises she made; he had never dined on anything as sweet as her skin, and he inhaled her essence: horse and leather and the scent of lavender.

He took his time trailing lips and tongue over skin. When his mouth discovered her breast, she arched in ecstasy. He pulled and teased, his teeth scraping the soft flesh below her nipple, his tongue pushing insistently at her firm, round globe. He raised his head to study its beautiful shape and then bent back to the dark rose areola. He took her nipple in his mouth, sucking and sucking, until he heard her gasping for more. It was only then that he moved his hand to loosen the fastenings of her breeches.

• • •

Deep down, Anna had always known it could be like this. When Larkin's mouth moved away to capture her other breast, she growled her displeasure—until, that is, he suckled her again, plunging her back into the heady abyss. A mounting wave grew deep within. She had never felt such rapture, and, as nervous as she was, a thousand horses could not have dragged her away.

Her body awakened and found its own rhythm. His long fingers inched lower to gently cup her mound. He was tentative, waiting for her response. When her hips lifted from the ground, his hand slid into her breeches, and his middle finger pressed down, stroking her and matching her motion. His finger caressed up and down, up and down, over and over. His head came up, and he was kissing her again.

• • •

As Lark moved his finger inside her, her gaze quivered. He continued pleasuring her, in and out. Her eyelids fluttered closed. "Keep looking at me, Anna. I want to see your face, your eyes."

Again and again, he plunged his hand between her legs; her hips thrummed. Deeper he drove his finger while his thumb dallied with that most sensitive bud. Higher he forced her until she came in a shattering climax. She stared into his eyes, and he watched her focus waver until she saw nothing, her body quaking with pleasure, driven higher by his thrusting hand.

As her breath tripped, Lark kissed her again, whispering words he doubted she would recall. He waited and listened as her body calmed. Her eyes searched his face, and he knew she was with him once more. He thrust his finger again and sent another wave of pleasure ricocheting through her body. She came again, gasping, and moaned his name.

"I want you to remember how I am looking at you, right now, while pleasuring you," Lark whispered. "And later, when we are back at the keep, I'll look at you just this way. You'll remember how it made you feel."

She reached up and brought his face to hers, lips crushing lips once more. His hand was gone from between her legs, traveling up her stomach to capture her breast. After a soft caress, he pulled her tighter to him, not caring if she felt his arousal. He made no move to take her, only held her closer. They clung to each other near the sleeping embers of the fire as the sun's first rays gave life to the day, holding on to the peaceful moment for as long as possible. Each knew that a day's ride away, their friends—Anna's people and Lark's fellow guards—were attempting to find proof of Lord Roger's treachery.

CHAPTER THIRTY-SEVEN

Rivalry

The sun was just rising when Roger and his soldier reached the rendezvous point. His older brother was already there and waiting impatiently. Nearby, the man whom Gorman had sent ahead was waiting with his horse, now refreshed and ready for Lord Roger to take back to the keep. "Brother," Roger said as he jumped from the back of his horse. "I trust you've read the note I sent and are aware of the predicament."

"I have, Roger," he replied. "And for once, you have an idea that is not terrible. Father would approve if he were here."

"There's no time for squabbling," Roger said tiredly. "Do you have what I need?"

His brother handed over a small pouch. "If you dilute it, we'll have time to play with your quarry. In its pure form, death is instantaneous. You need only a few simple herbs to mask the flavor, and one to activate the poison; the list is in the pouch."

Roger had hoped to be quickly rid of Baldric and the guards; he hadn't counted on his brother wanting to witness the execution, and more, taking part in torturing the helpless men. He hefted the pouch in his palm, burning a hole in it with his glare. Oh, would that he could avoid the unnecessary violence his sibling and father loved so much. If he didn't acquiesce, it would be reported to his father that he'd shown mercy to King Godwin's men, when in truth, he simply preferred expediency.

"Right. Now," Roger said, "go ahead and hit me. But make it count, for you'll not get this chance again." His brother peered into the surrounding woods before squaring up, and Roger snickered. "Don't worry, Garamantes is not—" Before he could say more, his brother's gloved fist struck out viciously, catching Roger on his cheekbone. His teeth rattled with the punch, and he blinked to clear his head. He was too late in seeing the drawn blade, and felt a searing pain as the dagger sliced

NICOLE ELIZABETH KELLEHER

through his sleeve and into his bicep.

"You want them to think you put up a fight, don't you?" Leaving Roger no time to recover, his brother coshed him in the temple with the pommel of his knife. Roger staggered and fell to one knee, and his brother knocked him the rest of the way down with his boot. Roger's man stood nearby, knowing better than to interfere. "Much better," Roger's brother said, holding out his hand to pull Roger from the ground.

Roger growled for reply. "There's a clearing in the western woods, less than a day's ride from Stolweg," he seethed. "My man will show you the location. But stay far out of sight until we signal for you."

His brother wasn't used to being ordered about by Roger, and he bristled. "And if I don't, little brother?"

Roger mounted the fresh horse. "You may not like it, but I am more knowledgeable about Baldric and his men than you are," he said. "I don't want you risking this mission because of your bloodlust." Before his sibling could say more, Roger added, "Besides, my actions are not the only ones reported back to father." He pulled his sword and wiped some of his own blood along the blade, then sheathed it. After tying off his wounded arm, he wheeled his horse around and set off for the keep alone.

CHAPTER THIRTY-EIGHT

An Expected Arrival

Nestled in Larkin's arms, Anna watched the streaks of dawn light up the sky and tried to comprehend the miracle he'd given her. Even thinking of it now sent ripples of bliss from the top of her head to the tips of her toes.

"What are you thinking about, Anna?" he murmured into her ear. She blushed. "Oh, I see," he chuckled. "Didn't you say that we have to remain with Rina for three days?"

"Three days, two nights. Why?"

His lips found her neck as his hand reached under her shirt to cup her breast again. "Because there is so much more." His tongue made lazy circles on her neck as he teased her nipple into a hard nub. "If you want it." When she moaned his name, he tipped her face to kiss her again. She hoped there would be enough time. As if to mark the dwindling hours, Rina trilled her lips.

Lark stood and helped her to her feet, bringing her close to him so that he could kiss her. "Later," he promised, and reached for her hand. Together, they walked to where Rina was laboring. The mare waited patiently, nibbling at tender shoots of grass. Anna placed her palm on Rina's back and smoothed the trembling muscles under the skin. The horse pawed at the ground. With her hand on Rina's abdomen, Anna waited for the contraction and counted, marking the time between the tightening of muscles.

"How much longer?" Larkin asked her.

"An hour, at the most," she predicted. She rubbed Rina's velvety muzzle. "You're an old hand at this, aren't you, girl?" The mare struck the ground again as another contraction came.

"Then I'll be right back with something to eat," Larkin promised.

As he walked away, Anna admired his lanky build, and the fit of his leather breeches. She grew warm anticipating the things he would do to her.

She turned her attention back to Rina and ran through the list of items she would need on the off chance of trouble. She was checking that everything was in her saddlebag when Larkin returned, examining the contents of Will's lunch from the day before.

"Cheese, and fresh, crusty bread. Some roasted root vegetables too smashed to eat. There's one small honey cake."

Anna grinned.

"What?" he asked.

"I was just thinking that perhaps," she said, recalling his earlier words and pointing to the pastry, "*that* is a piece of my favorite cake."

He split the dessert into two equal portions. "Well?" he demanded when she finished her portion.

"Well what?"

"Which is better, the cake or I?" When she didn't answer right away, he frowned.

"Give me a second, I'm still thinking. I think I need another taste," and she leaned over and planted a sloppy kiss on his lips, then drew back quickly. Gazing up into the sky for help, she mulled over her answer.

"Perhaps you need another sample." He kissed her hard. "Well?"

"How can I begin anew with no cake with which to compare?" she teased.

"I think I can find a suitable substitute," he stated happily. He plucked out a turnip from Will's bundle and held it above her lips.

"You wouldn't."

"I would. Now tell me."

"All right. All right! You are."

"I am what?"

"You are better than cake."

"Go on."

"I would rather kiss your lips than eat another piece of cake for the rest of my life." His eyes narrowed. "I swear it to be true."

Casting the turnip away, he dipped down again. The soft kiss quickly deepened. Before they could go further, Rina whickered.

"Later," he sighed, and heaved himself away. She smiled as he helped her up.

"You know, I've never witnessed a foaling before," he said. So Anna explained that, barring any complications, it would be fast, with Rina doing all the work. When Rina whinnied louder and shuddered, Anna rolled up her sleeves and positioned herself behind the mare.

"Look, you can just see the hooves," she said. Rina's abdomen heaved, and with a huge contraction, the foal shot out. The baby landed in Anna's arms with enough force to knock her to the ground. In her lap was a newborn filly. Four long legs twitched as Anna quickly removed thick mucus from its nostrils. Then Rina came 'round to lick her newborn clean.

"When you said it was fast, I had no idea," Larkin said, amazed.

"I didn't mean *that* fast. Come, help me up." They carefully lifted the filly from her lap and let Rina take over. Larkin held out his hand and helped her to her feet. He noticed her soiled shirtfront and eased back.

"I said it would be messy," she reminded him. Still, she hadn't imagined being knocked to the ground and completely covered with, well, everything. She would have to wash her clothing in the pool and wear her long overtunic until her garments dried.

The tiny thing managed to wobble on four spindly legs. Tullian came over to sniff at the new filly, then, seemingly pleased, returned to the patch of grass where he'd been grazing.

She felt Larkin's hand on her shoulder. "What are you going to name her?" he asked.

"Why, Honeycakes, of course!" she replied.

CHAPTER THIRTY-NINE

Later

At the pool, the sun's rays barely penetrated the willow's canopy. The air was crisp as Anna took stock of her stained clothing. The shirt was hopeless. Her breeches were not too bad. She stripped to better clean them.

Kneeling on the mossy bank, she touched her hair, and her hand came away with a gooey remnant of Rina's foaling. The pool would be frigid during these early days of spring. She stepped gingerly into the water, allowing her body to settle into the depths. The shocking cold was like an iron fist punching her heart, forcing her to gasp aloud in short, violent puffs. Knowing she would never grow accustomed to the bitter chill, she quickly dunked her head underwater, pulling apart her braid to free her hair.

When she could no longer keep from drawing breath, she resurfaced. Compared to the water, the cool spring air was deliciously warm. She made quick work of scrubbing away the morning's labor before shivering her way from the pool. Her tunic, heated by the dappled sunlight, warmed her skin. Her hair dripped around her, its loose, wet curls hanging wildly. Holding her wet shirt and breeches, she stepped into the full sunlight and saw Larkin near the campsite. A soft breeze gusted just as he noticed her.

• • •

She would be chilled, he'd thought. And wet. He rebuilt the fire so she could sit and dry herself. A soft oath escaped him as she emerged like an apparition stepping through the willow fronds. The breeze had picked up and was blowing her loosed hair in all directions. Her mane was darker when wet, and the normally golden-brown streaks glowed auburn in the sunlight. Now and then he glimpsed a naked leg when her tunic billowed around her.

He could barely swallow. *Later* had come. He made no attempt to hide the desire burning in his eyes. She was watching him, suddenly shy, and he smiled as she found the courage to walk closer. He took her wet clothes and spread them on the grass to dry. Then he pulled her to him and touched her damp hair. He ran his fingers down her proud neck and over her shoulders. His hands traveled back up, cupping her face. She pressed herself willingly against his body.

"You are so beautiful, Anna," he murmured.

He lifted her off her feet and set her near the fire. He removed his shirt, then kissed her, easing her back against the blankets. With forced patience, he unlaced the ties that ran from her tunic's collar to its waist.

He had never beheld such loveliness. He levered himself over her, enraptured by the feel of her nipples straining against his chest. She was following his every move and blushed as their eyes met. He kissed her, deeper this time, and felt her hands come alive, pulling him tight against her.

He dragged himself away long enough to remove his breeches and saw her eyes widen in appreciation. He remembered kissing her that first time. He had thought her to be a woman with at least some experience. She'd been married for three years, after all. But after the admissions of the previous night, coupled with her morning's passion, he now knew better. She was a virgin to the ways of making love.

She was shivering, so he hugged her closer and murmured into her ear. "Are you afraid?"

"N-no, not afraid," she stammered. "I just…"

And he knew. She didn't know what to do. "It's all right. I'll help you." He kissed her forehead. "I'll show you how it can be." He kissed the tip of her nose.

Against her lips, he said, "Kiss me, like you did yesterday. Let me feel your fingers in my hair." He murmured these last words. She responded by twining her fingers through his locks and kissing him deeply. While tongues played and lips pulled, he rolled her onto her back. His free hand roamed over her naked skin, touching her everywhere.

"Ah God, Anna," he said shakily.

He lifted his head to gaze again at her. She was perfectly made: long, sinuous, and curved in all the right places. Her skin was smooth and without blemish, nary a freckle or mole to tarnish the creamy surface. His eyes drifted back to her face; she watched him expectantly. He traced the delicate line of her jaw and stopped at the tiny dimple in her chin. He kissed the small indentation. His finger then ran along the graceful yet proud line of her nose, and he noticed for the first time the little freckle on its side.

He propped himself up on one elbow and let out an irreverent whistle. "Heaven above, Anna, you take my breath away." Her smile tenuous, she remained silent, as if awaiting his judgment. Lark went on, his hand running up and down her warming skin, unable to get enough of the feel of her. "Can you guess what my favorite part of you is?" She gasped as he rolled her nipple between his thumb and finger.

"Not even close," he murmured as his mouth seared a path to her breast. "Guess again." Anna moaned as his lips suckled her. His hand followed the curve of her waist and played over the tight muscles of her stomach before his fingers dusted the springy curls of her mound. He lifted his head from her breast and rose back up to see her face as his hand gently parted her thighs. First one, then two long fingers probed.

"Mmmm," Anna hummed as his fingers slid inside her.

"Wrong again," he teased, balancing himself above her trembling body. "Since you cannot guess, I'll tell you." He kissed the side of her nose and said, "It's this tiny spot on your nose. It's the most perfect freckle I have ever seen." She pulled him to her in a ravishing kiss, and he felt himself losing control.

"Take me in your hand, Anna. I need you to touch me."

As if she'd never felt a man before, her hand hesitantly traveled down his side, then up and over his buttock. When she finally touched him, it was Lark's turn to gasp. "Move your fingers up and down, slowly," he pleaded. She willingly complied, and he matched her rhythm by inserting and drawing his fingers into and from her.

"Oh…" she breathed huskily.

"Guide me in, Anna. Now. Please," he begged. She moved his throbbing shaft to her opening, and he sank deeply into her welcoming body. He strained to go slow, but her hips were driving up against him. He plunged again and withdrew, over and over, burying his face in her hair as if he couldn't get close enough.

He slowed his strokes, changing the tempo that she was so determined to control. He drove into her quickly, then pulled out as slowly as possible. He altered the pace again, refusing to give her a chance to fall into any rhythm. She was wild beneath him. After her gasps turned to moans and the moans to screams, he began to steadily move in and out, in and out, deepening each thrust. He was so close himself, and barely remembered that he would have to withdraw quickly so as not to spill his seed within her.

He again covered her mouth with his own while his hips lifted and plunged, pushing her over the brink. His own release was seconds away when she screamed out his name: "Lark!"

Hearing his name thus pronounced, his body ignored his mind's duty, and he recklessly drove into her again and again until his seed exploded. He acknowledged the risk they'd just taken, but the thought was fleeting. He kissed her over and over, his body sealed to hers, her muscles still grasping and clenching him from inside.

He lowered his full weight upon her. Her hands skimmed his back, pressing his shoulders closer to hers as if she were attempting to draw him nearer. He whispered her name, and she opened her eyes. Searching her face, he found only deep contentment.

The breeze had picked up, gusting with more force, lifting the tendrils of her hair from the ground. She looked, for all the world, as if she were underwater, her locks floating freely about her face. A mermaid.

Large billowing clouds were sailing across the sky like giant ships, while the sun played a game of hide-and-seek behind them, breaking free now and again to bathe their naked bodies with warmth. All around them, great shadows swept over the canyon floor. The long spring greens flushed and rose, caught in each new breath of weather.

He held her tighter, indescribably afraid that the next gust would lift her away to the heavens, for even the grasses strained to maintain their tenuous grip to the earth. And he realized in that instant he could not survive losing her. The pain he felt at the mere idea was so acute it passed over his eyes, dampening the joy he felt at finally finding her.

She must have sensed his melancholy, for she reached up with her hand and smoothed away the worry from his brow. Then, she moved her hand to his cheek, lifting her face so that her lips touched his in a tender kiss. And the sorrowful thought was banished.

CHAPTER FORTY

The Coming Storm

Anna stared up at the piling clouds. Around her, the spring leaves on the maples and poplars were silvery, flipped in anticipation of the coming deluge. The trees would have to wait, she determined. The sky would not open its floodgates until evening.

She held tight to Lark. As naked as she, he was probably feeling the chill.

He looked down at her, the soft curls of his silky black hair falling helplessly in his face. Completely at odds with his dark, dangerous eyes, his hair was that of a cherub.

A vicious wind kicked over them, and Anna sighed; they would have to separate. She kissed him again, softly, like before, and he kissed her back. Finally, Anna spoke. "A storm's coming. We have some time before this one hits. But when it does come, we'd best have shelter."

"Do you have another secret canyon to lead me to?" he asked suggestively.

She smiled at him. "Better—a cave."

When he rolled off her, she grew conscious of her nakedness. Larkin picked up her chemise and breeches. He sat in front of her, his brow creased.

She refused to meet his eyes for fear hers would show him the shame she felt. He had not yet seen the scars on her back. But he opened up her shirt for her, its fabric stiff from drying, and slipped it over her head. Another horrible truth about her marriage went undiscovered.

A gust of wind blew around them as they parted. The tremendous white clouds of the late morning had been overtaken by somnolent gray masses set on conquering the sky. Larkin went to retrieve the horses while Anna rolled the blankets and packed the saddlebags. She strapped her grandfather's dagger to her waist and slung Gilles's bow and quiver over her shoulder. One never knew what game would cross their path. Or what trouble.

Larkin returned, leading Tullian and Rabbit. He had belted on his sword and dagger. If he noticed that she was armed, he didn't comment. "Ready?" he asked, eyeing her thoughtfully.

She nodded, and they left the canyon in much the same way that they had arrived, wending their way in the streambed, only slower now, with a new filly in tow. And when the path became too difficult, Larkin lifted Honeycakes over his lap.

It took two hours to make their destination. Lark scanned the area, trying to find the cave as Anna dismounted. She left Tullian to wander.

Larkin turned to her. "I thought you said there'd be a cave."

"Larkin, if you were any closer, you would fall in."

He turned to study the outcropping to his right but still could not see it. She took his hand and led the way, pulling him around the budding lilacs, into the perfectly camouflaged crevasse.

She explained that it was Tullian who had led her to its location. After drinking his fill from the stream, he'd lifted his head, and his bit had jangled, surprising a rabbit that had been hiding in the brush. Anna had dismounted, hoping to find a warren of coneys. What she discovered instead was that the solid wall of rock was split, the crevice hidden by the lilac.

The fissure was just wide and tall enough to accommodate a person leading a horse. For months she explored the cave and began outfitting it with supplies. No one else knew of its existence until now.

She showed Larkin to the opening and found the torch she'd left months before, ready and waiting. Larkin lit it for her and followed her into the cavern. The ceiling of the cave was high and vaulted. The floor was a combination of flat, solid rock and packed clay. The walls were craggy; sharp rocks and fissures abounded, providing recesses perfect for hiding supplies and gear. Anna set the end of the torch into one such fissure, creating a natural sconce on the cave wall. She turned around, and her breath caught as she gazed at Larkin's inky eyes.

"First things first, Anna." His hands encircled her waist as he pushed her against the cave's wall. She thrilled inside when she felt his lean body thud roughly against her, and she lost all thought as his kiss crushed her lips.

He stepped away just as quickly. "Stop doing that to me," she panted.

"Stop kissing you?" he teased.

"Yes. I mean, no," she replied, flustered from the stirrings he had aroused. "I want you to keep kissing me. But you can't—" He rushed forward again. His lips came down upon hers in another pulverizing kiss, this one longer and deeper than before. A molten heat radiated through her, and she was glad for the rock wall behind her. He pulled at her clothes to reach her breasts and wedged his knee between her thighs, using his leg to lift her against him.

Circling her arms around his neck, Anna cradled him while his mouth teased and nipped her exposed skin. She thrust her hips forward and Larkin shifted his leg higher, helping her to grind against him. His hand came 'round to support her bottom, bringing her forward.

She wrapped her still-clad calves around his waist, seeking desperately to gain purchase, but unable to do so. Again his arm pulled her forward, again she slid back. She wanted him, right where they stood, pressed between the wall and his body. But he was content to guide her forward against him over and over again. An exquisite pressure grew inside her, and the rocking motion was more than she could take. She rode out her passion straddling his muscular thigh while her screams echoed through the cavern.

Pressing his forehead against the cool wall, he murmured into her ear. "You're incredible, Anna. You make me want to keep you within my reach every second just so I can enjoy pleasuring you." Her breath still labored as his tongue darted into her ear. A low, strangled moan emanated from her throat.

"Can you stand?" he asked.

She tightened her arms around his neck and shook her head. Her voice had abandoned her and she was afraid she would melt into the dirt floor if he released her.

"Good." He chuckled, holding her a bit longer. She clung to him as her breathing evened. "Now?" he asked.

He slipped away a little. Her legs felt as wobbly as Honeycakes's, but she could indeed stand on her own. In the flickering light of the torch, she searched his face. "Is it always so intense between a man and woman?"

"I don't think so," he answered.

"Have you ever felt this way before, Larkin?" she asked him, afraid that he would say yes.

He waited and took a deep breath before answering. "Never before, Anna. Only with you. Perhaps it's your reluctant need for me, I don't know. But I've never known the like."

Did she *need* Larkin? Yes, Anna realized, frightened by how quickly she'd come to depend on him. He would leave when his duties called him to his next mission. She stiffened in his arms. "My need, Larkin? Or is it my dependence you seek?"

"Is there a difference?" he asked, confused.

"I refuse to be beholden to another. I have been Roger's…" Anna paused, not knowing how to end the sentence. The only word she could come up with did not even begin to explain how it had been. "I have been his…his *property* for three years. I refuse to be owned by another man."

Lark's eyes glinted in the dim light. "If you think I wish to own you, then you are sorely mistaken. Just the opposite—I can't help but desire to be your slave." He stepped away from her, then stopped. "Do not think to liken me to him again, Anna," he warned, and strode out of the cave.

She hadn't meant to compare him to Roger. She just needed to protect herself. There was too much at stake for her to think that these few days could be anything more than a brief liaison. She would never be that naïve again. But she didn't want to think about the day he would leave. So she did the only thing she could at such a time. She made herself busy readying their camp.

Lark returned with their saddles and tack just as she finished setting the logs in the firepit. Without speaking, they spread out their blankets, overlapping the edges. When they finished, they went outside to check the weather.

The sky had a peculiar yellowish-green brightness to it, a precursor to the violent storm that was brewing. Even the air smelled sharp. Far off, Anna could hear the low rolling of thunder.

CHAPTER FORTY-ONE

Cellach

The ridge upon which Cellach sat offered the best view of the northeastern region of Chevring. From here, he could see its famous rolling pastures, though the lush grasses were oddly absent of the horses Lord Gervaise bred and trained. And to the northwest, he could make out the mountains separating Stolweg and Chevring. Even from this far distance, the sky above the range was unnaturally dark. He thought of Lady Aubrianne, and prayed that she was safe in the keep.

When she'd entrusted him with the mission of securing her family's welfare, he'd readily agreed to help her. He would do anything for her, especially if it meant stopping her husband, Lord Roger. But the farther away from her and the keep he traveled, the greater his misgivings grew. Moreover, he couldn't shake the feeling that she'd said goodbye to him for the last time.

Yet he rode on, sparing little time for rest. His current path would place him east of Chevring, far from any of Lord Roger's men. Thus, he'd been surprised to find so many tracks. One set—two riders, light in the saddle—had ridden hard out of the rolling hills and valleys, to the east. They'd been pursued. From the depth of the hoof marks, those giving chase were heavily armored. The signs of passage were at least a week old, perhaps two. Curious, he followed the trail. It ended abruptly when the pursued managed to hide their tracks in the rocky terrain beyond the fertile hills. Cellach could see where the soldiers had tried to recover the trail. But they'd given up their quarry and turned back.

He was almost to Chevring Castle, and he slowed his mount to approach with more care. Before cresting the final hill, he secured his horse in a copse of willow and poplar. On foot, he skirted his way along the edge of the trees and up the slope. He crouched low so as not to offer a silhouette against the bright sky as he topped the rise overlooking

Chevring. Creeping forward, he peered through the long grasses and into the wide valley. The horrific sight below was one that he would remember for the rest of his days.

The once-beautiful castle had been demolished. The heavy limestone walls had been crushed as if they had been made of mud and straw. The buildings surrounding the castle—stable, servants' housing, and even the chapel—had been razed. Scorched timbers jutted from the rubble like the ancient ribs of some long-forgotten carcass.

A shadow fell upon the grass next to him. He rolled away in time to miss being skewered by a sword. His dagger cleared its sheath but quickly found a new home in the chest of a soldier wearing a strange uniform. As the man crumpled to the ground, Cellach covered the soldier's mouth to staunch any cry for aid.

"I can make your death easy or I can make it hell," Cellach whispered, grasping the hilt of the still-embedded dagger and shifting it imperceptibly. The soldier groaned and nodded.

"Where is Lord Gervaise, and Lady Estelle? Where are the survivors?" he demanded.

The soldier sneered at him. Blood foamed from his mouth and through his final gurgle, he managed to answer before dying. "There aren't any."

Cellach had no time to think about the man's response, for he heard voices just over the rise. He pulled his knife from the dead soldier's chest and wormed his way down the hill. He was painfully aware that his victim would be found in moments and his own presence at Chevring revealed. Finally, he stood and, at the base of the hill, ran as fast as he could to the edge of the trees. Behind him, he heard the shouts of alarm as the men discovered the dead soldier.

Only in the embracing cover of the woods did Cellach risk a backward glance. At least half a dozen men had assembled on the ridge. Several were moving to his location. He didn't worry about hiding his tracks and ran full speed to escape their grasp. Fortunately, the soldiers were on foot. His escape depended on getting to his horse and following the path of those who had fled weeks before. When he reached the copse, Cellach groaned. His horse was gone.

The soldiers closing in on his location had yet to detect him. They were less than thirty paces away. Three against one. Cellach drew his sword in preparation. He scanned the area, trying to find the quickest escape route. He turned left and blinked, not quite believing his eyes.

Not ten feet away stood a young girl. She spoke not a word, but

183

motioned with her hand for him to follow. Cellach looked back the way he'd come. He could take his chances against the soldiers, or he could follow the child. For the first time in his life, he backed down from a fight and raced to the girl.

The ground was rocky, and he covered the short distance quickly. The girl pointed to a small opening in a thick patch of briars. Cellach entered on hands and knees, ignoring the piercing thorns as they grabbed his clothes and bit into his skin. The girl was behind him, sweeping a leafy branch over the ground to cover any possible tracks before using the foliage to close off the hidey-hole they'd just entered. The voices of the soldiers were only yards away. After making sure the child was behind him, Cellach continued to crawl through the thorny tunnel. And then, quite suddenly, he found himself in a clearing.

A spring bubbled from the ground in front of him, its course cutting into the impenetrable morass of brambles across the clearing. He stood and was met by six frightened faces, all children, most of them younger than the girl who had led him to this strange sanctuary. Beyond the children, he saw his horse, standing patiently with its brethren, Chevring steeds to the last. A skinny boy stood in front of the other children, brandishing a small knife. All around them, they could hear the soldiers calling out to search deeper into the woods. Cellach sat on the ground in an attempt to appear as unimposing as possible. The girl walked silently past him and sat down. The boy followed suit but did not relax his grip on his blade.

Finally, the voices faded. "I saw him kill one of the soldiers," the girl whispered. "We took his horse. He would have been killed had I not helped him."

Cellach studied the children. Though malnourished, they were unharmed. The youngest was only a babe. That the children managed to keep the infant quiet was a miracle.

"My name is Cellach. I am the master-at-arms at Stolweg Keep." The boy jumped to his feet, crouching in an attack stance, ready to protect the other children with his woefully small weapon. He watched helplessly as a toddler of perhaps three tottered past him. With arms outstretched, the lad ran to Cellach, and planted his small body in Cellach's lap.

"Lady Aubrianne sent me," he explained in as calm a voice as possible. "You can put your weapon down. I am her friend."

Except for the oldest boy and girl, the other children seemed confused. "Lady Aubrianne," the girl prompted. "You remember. Miss Anna!"

The children charged him. He was knocked backward, tackled by their small bodies. The mere mention of his lady's name earned him their trust.

Cellach nodded to the eldest two. "You've done well," he said respectfully. "Your parents would be proud of you."

"We've stayed here night and day," the boy explained, finally sheathing his blade. "We have fresh water aplenty. Food's been more difficult. The packs we brought are nearly empty now."

"We haven't had meat in days, not wanting to risk a fire to cook it," the girl added. "We take turns foraging for fruit, nuts, and roots. It doesn't always taste good, but we've made do."

She pointed to where the infant was sleeping. "There's but one stale loaf of bread left. We've been softening it with water and berry juice for the babe."

"What's your name?" Cellach asked.

"Sarah. And this is Luke." She motioned to the lad who'd been ready to defend the others.

"Did my brother Pieter tell Anna to send you?" Sarah asked. "He left almost two weeks ago with Miss Claire."

That explained the tracks he'd seen, Cellach surmised. "I saw their trail. The soldiers never caught them." The girl rushed to him and clung to him tightly.

One of the younger children gazed up at him. "You'll take us to Miss Anna, won't you?"

"You have my word on it," he vowed. "You'll have to listen to me, and Luke and Sarah." These children had lost everything—their loved ones, their homes.

"But first things first." He walked to his horse and opened one of his saddlebags. Then, he presented the children with a wedge of cheese, a good amount of dried meat, a loaf of bread, and a few roasted root vegetables wrapped in grape leaves. The last bit he handed to Sarah. "For the baby," he told her.

The food was distributed, and Cellach sat down, motioning to Luke and Sarah to join him. "We can talk while you eat," he explained, knowing they were hungry. He needed answers.

Over the next hour, Cellach questioned them. He learned that Lady Claire, Lady Aubrianne's sister, had left with the stable boy, Pieter. When they did not return as expected, the soldiers were sent to retrieve them. Lady Aubrianne's mother had used the diversion to spread the word to the people of Chevring: prepare the younger children for flight. Luke and Sarah's group was one of the first to leave. They didn't know if the others had left in time.

Cellach asked how they had found their hiding place, and they explained that it was a well-known spot among the children of Chevring. In fact, it was where Miss Anna had often hidden from Miss Claire.

"Did you see what happened to the castle?" he asked soberly.

Luke toed a rock from the dirt. "Machines, sir, ten of them. Some families had taken refuge in the chapel, others in the hall. I stopped watching when the soldiers began using fire." Luke's voice caught, and he buried his face in his hands.

Cellach pulled the boy tightly to his chest. He had seen the ruins where the chapel had stood, and the charred remains of the destroyed castle. No one could have survived. "All right, Luke. We won't talk of this anymore today." The boy nodded and wiped his nose on his sleeve.

"How will we escape here?" Sarah asked.

"We'll go on foot at first, leading the horses. I assume there's a way out of this clearing other than the one we used to enter it. The horses had to get here somehow." Luke nodded.

"You will take us to Anna, won't you?" Sarah asked anxiously.

"I'll try. But it might not be safe for you at Stolweg. I won't know until we approach the keep," he answered. "For now, try to get some rest. We'll travel at night."

Most of the children were able to sleep, having sated their hunger. Sarah waited until the younger children were down before giving in to her exhaustion. Only Luke remained awake.

Cellach sat next to the brave boy. "Luke, if we have trouble tonight, I will do what I can to protect you. But you must be strong awhile longer. Should we get separated, take the others and ride hard, due east." He drew the route in the dust with a stick. "After you cross two streams, turn north. You'll eventually come to a wide road. Follow it east, to Whitmarsh. Lord Baldric is a good man and will protect you. I believe Lady Claire and Pieter were aiming for his land.

"Travel only at night," Cellach cautioned. "Try to find places like this to hide during the day. After a few days, you can risk a fire to cook any game you find. But only in the day—a fire is harder to detect in daylight. And make sure you have a thick canopy of trees above you. The branches and leaves will dissipate the smoke."

He could see that the boy was frightened. "I don't plan on leaving you, Luke," Cellach promised. "I'm only telling you in the event that we are separated."

186

"In case we run into the soldiers tonight," Luke said.

"Exactly. I'd wager that a few have already been posted in the area, hunting for me. I will scout ahead before we leave, and flush them out."

"And you'll kill them," Luke stated. Cellach was chilled by the vengeance in the boy's words.

"As many as I can, Luke," he answered plainly. "As many as I can."

Later that evening Cellach found, and relieved of their lives, two soldiers. Their uniforms bore the marks of Nifolhad. He could detect no more and stole back to the clearing. His young wards had packed their meager belongings and put the horses on leads.

In slow procession, he led the group from the clearing. They picked their way through the woods, coming across no other soldiers. As they approached the place where the ground grew rocky, the hair on his neck rose. Cellach stopped the children and continued alone.

Someone was hiding somewhere ahead; he felt it in his gut. He stalked forward, hunting his prey, and found the man. He neatly slit the throat of his quarry before an alarm could be raised. Turning back to beckon the children forward, Cellach found himself face-to-face with another soldier, the tip of his sword pressed to Cellach's heart.

"Been waiting for you. My captain has a few questions he would like to—" The man stopped midsentence and fell to his knees. With a shocked expression, he keeled forward. A knife protruded from his back. Six paces away, Cellach spied Luke, small and frightened, his arm still outstretched from throwing his blade. Cellach dragged the bodies behind the trees, out of the boy's view. He removed the dagger, wiped it clean, and returned it to Luke. They walked back to the others in silence.

CHAPTER FORTY-TWO

Scars

Later that night, after making love again, Lark collapsed on top of her. She noted that in their passion, they had missed the neatly spread blankets.

"Anna, my Anna," he whispered.

The realization of how much control she had lost hit full force. But instead of being fearful, she felt exalted. "Larkin, my Larkin," she echoed, as he rolled them over to the blankets.

Outside, though the storm raged on, the worst of it had passed. It would rain all night, drenching the land and drowning the streams and brooks, choking the delicate waterways with its spew. Anna grew thirsty thinking of the deluge.

She sat up, her legs astride his, and tugged a corner of the blanket over her lap. Leaning back, she snatched the strap of the wineskin. It tasted sweeter today than before, and she offered it to Lark. He didn't take it; he was too preoccupied with studying her.

"All of you," he demanded, pulling the blanket away, then running his hands down her waist to the gentle swell of her hips.

Anna stretched languidly as his fingers traced down her thighs, then returned to cup her buttocks before resuming the trek up her back. She stiffened. How could she have forgotten?

"Anna?" he asked, and she slid sideways to lie on the blanket.

"Show me," he ordered. "Right now, Anna."

She glared at the ceiling of the cave, then rolled away from him to reveal the cruelly made etching on her back. He reached out to touch her and she flinched, though not in pain.

"One day, he set Gorman on Will," she explained before he could ask. "I was late by six lashes. Will would not have survived fifteen."

"But you could? There are more than nine marks here," he added when she didn't reply.

She shrugged. "Roger developed a taste for it. He told me it had excited him watching Gorman whip me. He wanted to feel the same power. No one else knew about it because I took care of myself. No one else knew."

• • •

Behind her, Lark caressed her tortured flesh, a silvery passage of snails. He placed his palm, fingers splayed, on the worst area, hoping the warmth would soothe her. He applied a gentle kiss to each mark, and, little by little, the tension left her body. Not for the last time, he regretted his promise to give her first shot at Roger.

• • •

Roger was miserable. His arm was throbbing so badly that he was almost able to ignore the pelting rain. All he wanted was to return to the keep, the warmth of his hearth, and, surprisingly, the comfort of his wife's expert care.

"Hell's beast," he swore when his horse stumbled and jarred him, causing his clouted head to ache even more. He should have taken one of the Chevring mares, but had worried that his brother would have confiscated it for himself. The horses were Roger's only advantage when it came to his family. Not Stolweg, or Ragallach, or even Chevring, but the destriers his father so desired.

Lightning arced through the night, followed immediately by a deafening boom of thunder that crushed his skull. Another vicious flash, and the forest ahead exploded, sending burning shards of bark and splinters in every direction. His mount reared, throwing Roger to the ground. Thunder pealed again, and before he could catch the reins, the gelding shot off through the trees. Roger cursed again, then forged on, thoughts of his wife's waiting balm and the pouch full of herbs protected under his cloak warring back and forth in his mind.

CHAPTER FORTY-THREE

A Question of Trust

When Anna woke, the tumultuous rain had ceased. Silence pressed against her ears. The fire had long since devoured its meal, its ravenous crackling but a memory. She was wrapped in the warmth of Lark's arms. His body curved protectively around hers.

In the background, the horses shuffled about. Honeycakes came to explore Anna and Larkin's side of the cave. The filly was beautiful, much like her mother, all grace and form. But she would not be a broodmare. She would be trained and would eventually fight alongside the likes of Rabbit and Tullian. Anna frowned. Trouble was brewing; it resonated in her bones. And it would be much greater than that which surrounded Roger.

"Good morning," she greeted Lark when he buried his face in her neck.

"It will be," he growled. His hands began their familiar trek over her bare skin. When he found her center, she was ready. She turned to him and smiled, knowing they would spend the morning making love. There was naught to do but watch the horses while Rina rested and the filly gained strength. As their bodies joined, all thoughts of the morrow fled.

• • •

It was afternoon when Anna finally took Lark by the hand and led him outside where they could sit in the sun and discuss Roger. She began telling him of the doings of her secret group and ended with the morning the King's envoy had arrived.

"As much as I hate to say this, Anna, we must leave before first light tomorrow. Roger is a threat," he explained. "And although I trust that Baldric and the others can protect themselves—"

190

"I understand," she interrupted. "We both must tend to our duties." Lark looked around for something to do, offering her no information in return.

"I set out snares yesterday. I'll go check them," he said, and then left her alone with her thoughts. Perhaps he did not as yet trust her as she trusted him.

Anna walked over to where the horses were grazing. She ran her hands over Honeycakes, examining the foal to make sure she was sound enough for the journey back to Stolweg Keep. "We have a long trek tomorrow," she said to the filly. "But we'll start early, and take it slow."

• • •

Lark knew she was upset and that he was the cause. So he sat next to where she was plucking the quail they had snared and picked up a discarded tail feather. Spinning it in his fingers, he stared at the ground, trying to find the right words. "I owe you an apology," he stated. "It means more than you can know that you trust me enough to tell me about the past three years."

She spitted the quail and set it over the flames.

"I'm sorry that I haven't told you what I know in return," he added. "I guess I'm trying to protect you."

"From what? What worse could there be than what I've already experienced?" she spouted. He threw the feather into the fire. "Wonderful," she said. "Now it's my turn to say I'm sorry."

"Anna, you don't know everything. You do not know of the friends I've lost. Good men on diplomatic missions. Men whose families will never hear from them again."

"I know that Roger killed his first wife. He staged it to look like she had taken her own life. He will try to kill me next. And I know that he plans on taking my sister for his own."

Lark recognized the fierce anger raging through her. He had felt it himself in his past. She was right. She deserved more from him than his mistrust, so he told her everything. Combined with what she had told him, the picture presented was astounding. With Ragallach, Stolweg, and Chevring, Roger controlled the heart of Aurelia. He shared his beliefs regarding Roger's true parentage.

"The way Roger perceives himself," Anna commented, "as if he is lord and ruler over all…if what you are saying is true, Lark, might not his mystery father be a member of the royal family?"

If what she guessed was true, Lark thought, Aurelia would soon be at war.

• • •

They cleaned up in silence, thoughtful of what was to come the next day. Anna thought about how easily the pieces fell into place when they worked as one. They made a good team.

Lark had retired to their shared blankets. His eyes were closed, but Anna knew he wasn't sleeping. She sat on the tree trunk and pulled off her boots and stockings. She removed her clothes and stretched out next to him.

"Anna?" he asked.

"Lark?" she answered.

"Kiss me." She did. He kissed her back. And they became lost in their need for each other. Anna had only one lucid thought that night: before she went to Roger tomorrow, she would tell Lark that she loved him.

CHAPTER FORTY-FOUR

The Letter

Roger rubbed the goose egg on his temple, trying to ease the headache that had been his constant companion since meeting with his brother. He'd returned from his excursion well past midnight, expecting the courtyard to be deserted and Baldric's men asleep. But no, they were all awake, Gorman had informed him as he strode in, and waiting for him in his banquet hall, drinking his cider and eating his food. At least when the six other riders had returned, Baldric had believed their story. As per instructions, each pair reported finding no trace of any strangers in the Stolweg environs.

Roger's arrival, alone, bruised, and wounded—not to mention filthy, smelling of ozone and caked in mud—lent even more credence to his story. His brother had been right to cut him, just as he'd been right about their father liking Roger's plan. Roger would just have to be careful not to give his brother any chance to take the credit.

As he'd expected, Baldric had interrogated him for hours. And they had believed his every word: he and his man had been attacked, and his man had been killed; Roger had managed to fight off three men, killing two; he had almost killed the third man, but reinforcements had come; he had barely escaped to bring the news back to the keep. Roger had even described the attackers' garb, making sure to include a few items that would indicate that they were Nifolhadajans, allowing Baldric and the guards to draw this conclusion. Several retellings later, Baldric had ordered him to get some rest; they would ride out and together root out the interlopers in three hours' time.

But Roger was too keyed up to rest, so he sat at his desk, making sure the information in his ledgers was beyond suspicion. When he finished, he checked again that his chamber door was locked. Then he retrieved the letter hidden away in his trunk. He sat on the cushioned

NICOLE ELIZABETH KELLEHER

bench near the hearth, and patted the seat next to him. Garamantes lumbered up, sniffed the paper, then dropped his head in Roger's lap, where he promptly began to snore.

Roger fingered the old parchment with reverence. It amazed him how this simple letter had put him on his current path. He'd kept it hidden away, taking it out only once a year to read. Even so, the letter's creases had softened and were coming apart from the passage of time. He smelled it, as if her scent still lingered in the ink.

There was a loud rap, and he tucked the worn parchment into his tunic before unlocking his door and bidding whoever it was to enter.

"Excuse me, m'lord," Gorman announced. "You asked to see me."

Roger handed him the list of herbs and the pouch from his brother. "Gather what we need from the maid's stores, and see that the barrels are marked properly. I want no confusion when the time comes."

Gorman shook the packet. "They won't know what hit them until it's too late. So his lordship liked my idea?"

"Your idea?"

"N-no, m'lord. I misspoke," Gorman blustered, covering his error. But Roger was not interested in punishing Gorman at the moment, and sent the man away.

Everything was neatly tied together; Roger could foresee no trouble. Except that he still hadn't dealt with the frayed ends of his rope yet—the two biggest loose threads being his wife and the guard Larkin. While he'd been racing to see his brother, the man had galloped off to find Aubrianne. To make matters worse, Gilles had returned alone and explained that a mare was unexpectedly foaling. Roger supposed it was true that Aubrianne was best suited to the task of seeing his mare through the early birthing. But no amount of reasoning could help him overcome the rage he felt knowing the guard was alone with his wife. After he finished with Baldric and the others, dispatching the troublesome Larkin would be at the top of Roger's list.

Then, Roger remembered his letter again and pulled it from his tunic with the utmost care. So as not to cause more damage, he gently unfolded the timeworn parchment. The letter always soothed his mind when he was troubled or tense. He began to read.

Dearest Babe,

I write this letter to you as I lay dying. I am weak and will not survive your coming into this world. The midwife won't admit it. She even tries to dispel the notion as foolishness on my part. But in my heart, I know it to be true. Her words are hopeful, but she cannot hide the sorrow in her eyes.

I have carried you these last nine moons and have given all of my strength to you so that you may be born healthy and strong. It is all I have left to give you. My love for you will see you safely into this world.

I have spoken with father and mother—I want to make sure you are loved and cared for after I am gone. At first, your grandparents refused to listen to me, not wanting to believe that I am slipping away from this life. Yesterday, mother finally sat with me while I told her the tale of how you came to be, and my wishes for your future.

Until you are given this letter, you will not have been aware of my existence. I write to you of the facts of your birth because you have a right to know your heritage. I write this even knowing that your world may be shattered by the truth.

First, the man and woman you have grown to love as your mother and father are your grandparents. They have pledged to love you and take care of you when I cannot. They will raise you as their own, and you will inherit everything as their heir. Please understand. This will be done to protect your identity.

Second, you have a brother...

There was another knock on his door, and Roger cursed. "One moment," he yelled. After folding his letter, he tucked it back into his tunic to finish later.

CHAPTER FORTY-FIVE

Resolved

"I've sent Ailwen to awaken Lord Roger," Baldric informed Trian. The guard greeted the others, then swiftly shut the door to Baldric's quarters. He'd just returned from his recent charge: tracing Roger's tracks as far as he could before having to turn back to make the keep by morning. "What did you find?" Baldric asked after relating the claims made by Lord Roger.

"Lord Roger's story is mostly consistent with what he told us. There *were* two sets of tracks going, and one returning. However, he veered southwest, not due west as he claimed. I never reached the point where he was attacked, but I did pick up fresh tracks and followed them. Moving north, and in no apparent hurry. Four men, all told. One heavily armored. Another—I swear—was one of Roger's men."

"Not so dead as our host has claimed. And the others? Were they Nifolhadajans?" Baldric asked.

Trian nodded. "I removed this from one of the saddles. It's the proof we need that Lord Roger is involved in a conspiracy." He opened his hand to reveal a small metal disc. Baldric's eyes narrowed.

Tomas leaned forward to examine the object. "What is that?"

Warin put his arm around the young guard's shoulder. "That, my friend, is the symbol of the royal house of Nifolhad." Warin looked incredulously at Trian. "You say you took this from a saddle. Exactly how close were you?"

Trian's silence was the only answer Warin would receive. "You never cease to amaze me, my friend. How can such an ox of a man be so stealthy? It's beyond my comprehension."

"You fared better than our host," Tomas added. "He was caught in that storm without his horse. Had to walk all day to make it back here."

"I came across a woodsman's croft," Trian explained, "and waited out the worst of it. Fortunately, I found those tracks before the rain hit."

"They're setting a trap," Baldric stated. "The question is: do we play along?"

Warin took the metal disc from Trian. "We do if we want to give King Godwin a prize greater than Lord Roger's head."

• • •

"You think it wise to meet in the open?" cautioned Carrick.

"I think skulking in the stable will only draw more attention. If we are here, in plain view of Lord Roger's men, they won't be suspicious."

"Just the same," Doreen spoke up, "I think we should keep it short." She saw Will approaching. "Gilles," she said, nodding in their son's direction.

Gilles stepped forward to stop his son, but Will walked directly to the group. "You shouldn't have met without me. I have just as much at stake in this as any of you, perhaps more," he stated, reminding them of the lashing he took. "And you'll want to hear what I have to say, for it concerns Lady Aubrianne."

Gilles nodded to his son. "Go ahead, Will."

"Lord Roger's been holding the lives of her family over her head. I heard her ask Cellach to ride to Chevring and warn them. I believe Lady Aubrianne means to put an end to Lord Roger. And she means to leave us when she's finished."

Grainne looked thoughtful. "That fits in with what I discovered yesterday in her hearth: she incinerated her wedding gown. And I can't shake the feeling that she was saying goodbye. We can't allow her to do it."

Gilles addressed Carrick. "As the miller, you are the only one among us who has good reason to be seen with the other members of our group. Can we count on you to spread the word?"

"And the word is…?"

"We end this before Lady Aubrianne has to."

"When?" Carrick asked.

"Before Lady Aubrianne returns," Gilles announced. "Which means today. Lord Roger is taking the King's men into the western woods to hunt for the soldiers who attacked him. But take heed, we do not want Lord Baldric any the wiser." One by one, they returned to their tasks.

Only Will and his father remained behind. "I want first shot," Will said.

Gilles's eyes widened at the sudden ruthlessness in his son's voice. "Just be sure to make it count," he replied.

CHAPTER FORTY-SIX

Preparations

Lord Roger strode into his chamber, Gorman at his heels. "This interference ends today. Is all prepared?"

"Aye, m'lord, the keg is ready."

Roger's mood was much improved. His wife's maid had treated his arm and given him an herbal tonic of some sort to ease his aching head. It was time to replace old blood with new blood. Better blood. Excepting that his wife was alone somewhere in the hills with Larkin, he might have been truly happy.

Two days ago, his brother had assured him that his father's man, Lord Phelan, would soon arrive from Chevring, bringing the men who would fortify Stolweg. Chevring and Ragallach were already under Roger's control. Phelan could be trusted to complete whatever task was set before him, the current one being the transport of the massive weapons from Chevring to Stolweg. Once here, they would prepare for their advance on Whitmarsh.

Roger recalled how his brother had crowed that the testing of the weapons on Chevring had been an utter success. He was supposed to have waited for Roger to be there. And now Lady Claire had disappeared. His brother had probably raped and killed her.

But Roger had found the perfect way to get back at him. Instead of going to the clearing where his brother would be waiting the next morning, Roger would stop halfway there, and take care of Baldric and his men this very afternoon. He couldn't wait to see his brother's face when he found that he'd been robbed of the chance to inflict pain on Godwin's men.

All of their planning would soon come to a head. His brother's forces would join with his, and together they would march on Whitmarsh. Lord Baldric's castle would topple as easily as Chevring's had. The path would then be clear to march on an unsuspecting King's Glen. And this time, Roger wasn't worried that his brother would take all the glory unto himself. For Lord Phelan played no favorites when spying on them for their father.

It was finally within his reach, Roger thought with eager anticipation. Once all of Aurelia was secure, his brother and Phelan would leave. Roger would reign over this side of the Western Sea, his brother the other—but only after he wrested the throne from their father's grip.

• • •

"I've news concerning these so-called attackers from Nifolhad," Carrick whispered to the others. "When I warned Maggie to stay close to the keep because it might not be safe at the mill, she laughed at the idea, saying that Lord Roger would protect her. I told her that he'd been attacked and injured. She told me I must have misheard, because Lord Roger had talked to Gorman about going to meet his brother."

"His brother?" Gilles asked, hoping no one would ask how Maggie had been privy to a conversation between Lord Roger and Gorman.

Carrick shrugged. "Seems we're not the only ones scheming. You're sure we shouldn't wait for Cellach?"

"We can't risk it," Gilles answered. "We must make our move today."

Grainne agreed. "The timing is right. Lady Aubrianne must be spared this act. She'll not return to the keep until the late afternoon. Even if she rides hell-bent to intercept us, it will take her hours. By then, the deed will be over."

"Be cautious," Doreen added. "Lord Roger ordered Gorman to fetch two casks of cider last night. Gorman claimed Lord Roger wanted it on hand to celebrate once they captured the men who've infiltrated Stolweg. If you cannot remain hidden in the forest, do not partake of any drink with the others."

"Do you think the King's men are at risk?" Gilles asked his wife.

"Grainne is better suited to answer that question." All eyes turned to the small woman.

"This morning," Grainne began, "I noticed that some of my herbs were missing. Mixed together in the proper quantities with the right minerals, Lord Roger could certainly poison the cider. We all know how he likes to torture his victims, so I doubt that the drink will be deadly. He'll want Baldric and the guards incapacitated, but aware."

"We'll have to be ready," Doreen stated, "for the King's men will be vulnerable."

"That will be our cue, then," Gilles decided. "When Lord Roger moves against the King's men, we act. Heaven protect us and allow us to save them." Gilles's words were met with nods all around. "Spread the word, Carrick." One by one, the group dispersed.

CHAPTER FORTY-SEVEN

Hours ahead of daybreak, Lark and Anna had eaten a quick meal. Neither had wished to leave the cavern that had become their private sanctuary. What would it be like to just ride away with Lark, she wondered, and start a life together where no one knew them? But she could no more forsake her friends than he could abandon his. So they'd set out while the night yet ruled the sky, riding much too slowly, but having to do so for the sake of Rina and her filly.

When they reached the castle, her husband, Baldric, and the King's guards had already departed. Strangely, the keep was empty of Anna's friends as well. The courtyard and stable seemed deserted save a few servants and a scullery maid. One of Roger's soldiers came out of the barracks. With a little encouragement from Larkin, he finally explained that Lord Roger had been attacked, and he and the others were hunting down the men.

"I'm to tell you that you are ordered to stay in your chamber, m'lady."

"Ordered by whom?" Anna demanded.

"Lord Roger. And you, sir," he added, "Are to stay here as well. As, er, stated by Lord Baldric."

"Very well, then," Anna acquiesced. "But pray, can you tell me where I can find the stable master?"

"Out with the horses, I suspect."

"How about the cook?" Lark asked. "I'm famished." The soldier shrugged.

"Perhaps you could call for my maid," Anna suggested.

"How am I to know the whereabouts of all the servants?" the man grumbled. "Come, m'lady. I'll escort you to your chamber."

"We'll see to our horses first," she stated, brooking no argument, and marched into the stable leading Tullian and Rabbit. Lark went to set

NICOLE ELIZABETH KELLEHER

Rina and Honeycakes loose in the paddock.

"M'lady," a soft voice whispered, and Anna turned to see Rheeta, one of the farmers' wives, hiding in a stall. "A messenger came from King's Glen. I told him that only Lord Roger's soldiers were in the keep when he said that his message was for Lord Baldric only." She pulled a sealed letter from her sleeve, and handed it to Anna. "I told him to wait at the mill, that I would see it delivered when Lord Baldric returned, but something strange is happening here. I'm afraid of the soldiers."

Anna climbed back atop Tullian and whispered, "Stay hidden."

"I will, m'lady."

Lark entered the stable from its rear entrance. "Ready?" she asked.

Lark opened his mouth to say something, then shut it. He mounted Rabbit. "There are more soldiers in the courtyard. It'll be a race to reach the main gate before they close it."

Outside the stable, they could hear men approaching. "It's already closed," Anna informed him.

"The west gate is still open, m'lady," Rheeta said.

Anna nodded. "It will be guarded, but if we charge, they'll fall away like barley under a sickle."

"After you, then," Lark said, and they bolted from the stable, scattering the soldiers who were converging on them. The man posted at the western egress pressed himself flat against the side of the tunnel, not even raising a hand to halt them as they thundered by.

After they crossed the bridge, Anna slowed to a trot. She patted Tully on the neck, an assurance that they would soon run. It had been four days since he'd had a good gallop. She glanced back. Strange— Roger's men were making no attempt to follow them. Anna remembered the letter, and handed it to Lark. "This was just given to me. It's for Lord Baldric from the King."

"We'd best hurry then."

"Before we go, Lark, there's something I need to tell you." Tully pranced in anticipation. "I like to ride." Anna stated.

"Of course you do. You breed horses and—"

"No," she cut in, "you don't understand." Lark and Rabbit pulled up next to her. "I am betimes willful, and usually stubborn."

Lark rolled his eyes. "You don't say?"

"I do say. But when I say that I like to ride, well, there's no easy way to explain." She whispered to Tullian, and he started dancing. "I am what I am, Lark. Try not to worry. If you can't keep up, I'll meet you at the forest's edge." Under the shadow of the bridge, she leaned forward and planted a kiss on his cheek. With a signal to Tullian, her horse shot forward. She didn't look back. Lark would catch up. Eventually.

She and Tullian flew. Moments later she heard Rabbit's hooves pounding into the lush soil near the river. Then Anna lost herself in the feel of the wind whipping past her face and the power of her steed. They raced through the western orchards and into the open pastures that spread before the looming forests. The sea of field barley was already deep, and their path cut through its gentle waves. Lark raced somewhere behind.

Four pounding hoofbeats became eight. Lark rode close enough to her that Anna could touch his shoulder. On they rode, over the fields, pulling up just shy of the woods. Its tangle of brush and briars, as forbidding as the mountains to the northwest, blocked their passage.

"They're following the old road," Anna said, her breath rapid after the hard ride. "The way bends to the south like a bow, then turns back to the west. I'd say they have a good hour on us."

Lark peered into the near-impenetrable forest before turning his dark gaze upon her. "Let's be the bow string and make up some time."

"You think you can find a way through there?"

"Anna, I can find a trail through anything." He smiled cunningly. "If I can't, I make one."

"Lead the way," she said. "This time, we'll follow you."

Lark and Rabbit leapt back and forth to find an opening. Once one was discovered, the horses twisted and pivoted through the trees. It was what the steeds had been trained to do. If in a time of war, they would have to weave their way through battlefields filled with fighting men. For an hour or more they zigzagged through the forest, veering from one deer trail to the next.

Anna noticed a human footprint in the soft dirt to their right. It was fresh. Unfortunately, she wasn't paying attention to how closely she rode behind Lark, and Rabbit's passage caused a thin branch to whip back. It stung her cheek before she could duck.

Rabbit lunged forward and disappeared. Tullian followed, leaping high, and Anna was blinded by bright sunlight. Leaving the wild darkness behind, they had caromed into a sunny clearing. Lark was waiting for her, and she saw him frown.

"You were riding too close." He wiped a drop of blood from her cheek with his knuckle.

"I know. I was distracted," she panted from the excitement of the ride. "Did you see it?"

"It?" he asked.

"The footprint."

His eyebrows raised a fraction. "I'm surprised you saw them too. We were moving fast."

"I saw only one. How many were there?"

"At least eight tracks. Two belong to women. Anna, what are your people up to?"

"I wish I knew," she said. Tullian sensed her urgency and hastened forward. She held him back long enough for Lark to reel Rabbit 'round before hurtling once again into the dense woods.

• • •

They had made good time, Roger thought. With luck, he would be rid of Godwin's men before his supper. His brother was at least a day's ride southwest. "We'll set up a base camp here," Roger announced. "This clearing is central to these woods."

"Shouldn't we be searching for tracks?" Baldric demanded.

"There's enough daylight for hours of searching." He alighted from his horse and ordered three of his men to prepare the camp. "Gorman, send out the remaining men to scout for tracks." They'd already agreed to send the men to retrieve his brother.

"These woods are dense—it could take weeks to find the bastards who dared attack me," Roger explained to Baldric, then turned to give another order. "You there, tap that keg. Let's make a toast to ridding Aurelia of unwanted men, eh, Baldric?" This farce would soon be over, Roger thought. And this would be Baldric's last taste of his cider. He was looking forward to informing his brother and Phelan of this success.

• • •

Ailwen watched the trees. He thought he'd seen something. Several minutes passed without so much as a quiver of branch, and he relaxed, a little. Perhaps it was that damnable mastiff Lord Roger insisted on bringing. No, the dog was still tied to the cart.

Ailwen made note of the soldier removing the cider from the cart. Gorman cuffed him and whispered in his ear. The young soldier stopped and unhitched the other cask. Ailwen was about to warn Baldric when he thought he saw movement in the trees again. He watched, and waited, but saw naught else.

The cask! Ailwen tried to make it back to his group. Unfortunately, Baldric and the others had taken deep draughts from their mugs. Gorman shoved a cup at Ailwen. He took it roughly, sloshing most of the contents before tipping it to his mouth and pretending to drink. Warin grabbed a second cup and drank with gusto.

Ailwen managed to dump his into the grass without notice. If the cider was true, he could always have a second cup poured. If it was tainted, he would feign whatever symptoms the others had. For if poison was in the cards, his best bet was surprise.

• • •

"Are you sure it won't kill them, Grainne?" Gilles whispered.

"Not as long as I can get to them in time." She thought about the missing herbs, broom and devil's bread. "I've prepared a grog to speed their recovery."

Gilles nodded. "Then we wait for Lord Roger to make his move. Stay hidden."

• • •

Hearing voices, Anna and Lark slowed their pace. As the words grew more distinct, they dismounted and crept closer.

Anna touched Lark's arm and whispered, "Lark, before we move forward, there is something I want to tell you. I meant to earlier, but I—" She had wanted to say that she loved him, but the shushing of metal leaving leather stopped her cold.

She and Lark inched forward and beheld the strangest scene. Roger, Gorman, and several of Roger's soldiers surrounded Baldric and the others. They held drawn swords while the King's men did nothing to protect themselves. Quite suddenly, Warin's knees buckled and he fell sideways to the ground. Tomas followed, then Baldric, who managed to stay on his knees. Ailwen, too, fell. Trian, because of his great size, crashed to the ground last and with a painful thud.

She and Lark looked at each other. "Poison," he whispered. Anna nodded, then tilted her chin in Ailwen's direction. His hand was inching to the hilt of his sword.

Larkin signaled with his hand, trying to capture the fallen guard's attention. On the third try, Ailwen noticed the pale flash of palm. He looked directly at them and blinked twice.

"Stay here," Lark whispered. Before Anna could argue, he stepped from their hiding place.

But she did not remain still. She moved away in order to enter the clearing from another direction. Roger spied Lark and placed the tip of his sword at Baldric's throat.

"Lose your weapon," he ordered. "Drop it now!"

Hoping to divide Roger's attention, Anna marched into the clearing and straight up to her husband. "What do you think you are doing? Release Lord Baldric at once," she ordered. "Or have you gone mad?" It was a dangerous ploy, but Lark and Ailwen needed a distraction. Anna knew she was the last person her husband expected to order him around. Lark drew his sword.

She had seen Roger angry before. This was different. There was a feral madness in his eyes. His wide-eyed stare shifted back and forth between her and Larkin. His grip on Baldric's jerkin loosened, but the sword dipped dangerously to Baldric's heart. Anna gave him a satisfied smile, hoping to distract him even more.

"You Chevring whore!" he hissed, his voice pitched and reedy. He moved his steel from Baldric and lifted it to strike her. Anna was ready and dodged the blow. Roger raised his arm again to swing at her.

"Hold!" came a shout from the trees, and Will stepped into the clearing.

"And you'll be next!" Roger yelled, spittle flying from his mouth. Will's arrow sped across the clearing before Roger could act on either threat.

Her husband dropped his eyes, puzzled that there should be an arrow sticking out of his chest. His mouth opened to speak, but no sound came forth. He stared at the boy who had shot him, then looked down again. Four more arrows had pierced him. Ailwen and Lark sprang forward to protect their friends. Roger succumbed to gravity and fell back, gazing uncomprehendingly at the bright blue sky.

• • •

"Drop your weapons," Gilles ordered, standing next to his son. The soldiers did as they were told. Only Gorman had been able to draw blood. Cur that he was, he had attacked Doreen, throwing his mace at her. Had she not jumped sideways, her skull would have been crushed. The weapon's head had only grazed her.

Doreen touched her temple, and her hand came away bloodied. Gilles caught her just before she sank to the ground. Anna saw Gorman draw his sword to finish the job. He was stopped when Carrick's arrow took a notch from his earlobe. Roger's man did as he was told.

Her friends had saved her from spilling her husband's blood, Anna realized, but were leaving the fate of Gorman in her hands. She went to Lark. What was it that she saw in his eyes: disbelief that she had not listened to him or anger that she would put herself in danger? They stood toe-to-toe, and she gazed into his eyes before pulling his dagger from his belt.

She needed to face Roger. His hateful eyes fixed on her as she pulled the ruby ring from her pocket. While her husband drew his last breaths, Anna held the fragile jewel in her palm and struck it with the onyx-inlaid pommel of Lark's knife. Shards of broken ruby rained down upon him. Then, Roger passed into what Anna hoped would be hell.

Gorman, she thought. Oblivious to those around, she walked to where he waited.

"Lady Aubrianne, please. I was only following orders," he begged.

Before another word could be uttered, Anna brought the tip of Lark's knife to his throat. "You are not permitted to speak," she hissed.

"But, m'lady—"

His cowardly plea was cut short as she pricked his neck. "Never *your* lady, Gorman."

Then, using Larkin's knife, she cut away part of his uniform to wipe the blade clean. "I'll give you a head start." She walked with measured steps to the cart, and then cut the rope that bound Garamantes. Gorman fled into the woods.

The mastiff sniffed at Anna, licking her outstretched hand. She thought of Roger's shortsightedness in revealing the beast's kill command. With the bloody scrap of Gorman's uniform at its snout, she whispered a single word into the dog's ear. Garamantes growled deep in his throat, then shot into the woods.

Anna became aware of the others in the clearing. The soldiers had been bound to the back of the cart. Grainne came to her; Anna shook her head. "See to Baldric and the guards. Stay with them. Help them if you're able."

"I am, my lady."

Anna walked to where Lark stood. Holding his dagger, the black hilt covered with the red dust from the shattered ruby, the blade with the blood of Gorman, she handed it to him. "Your blade, their blood."

NICOLE ELIZABETH KELLEHER

"Anna—" he started. His next words were silenced by the resounding echoes of Garamantes's snarls and Gorman's screams.

"We can talk later, Lark," Anna forestalled him. "Right now, Doreen needs me. I'll meet you back at the keep."

"I should come with you, Anna," he said. "It might not be safe."

"I won't be alone, Lark," she pointed out. "Besides, your friends need you more. Follow Grainne's instructions; they'll recover that much faster." She ignored the questions in his eyes and kept her expression fixed. When he pulled her into his arms, a small sigh escaped her lips. She would have to remain strong for her people. Anna finally accepted that even with Roger's death, her troubles were not over.

"Give me but a little time, Lark," she begged, distancing herself from him.

Anna glanced back at the others. Grainne had already enlisted the help of Ailwen. Together, beginning with Baldric, they poured Grainne's tincture of herbs down each man's throat. Grainne told Ailwen to lay Baldric on his side. Seconds later, her first patient vomited. The poison that had managed to seep into his blood would have to wear off naturally.

Anna wanted nothing more than to quit this place. Roger might be gone and Gorman had been removed as a threat, but were there others who would try to exact revenge on her family? Will brought Tullian forward, and she remembered that Will's arrow was the first to fly. She stepped back to study him. There was a new hardness in his eyes.

"After me, you had the most right, Will," she acknowledged.

He nodded and laced his fingers to help her up. Gilles had mounted his horse; Doreen sat in front of him, encircled in his arms. She gave Anna a weak smile. *Good*, Anna thought. She was still awake. Dry blood stained her face, but there was nothing fresh leaking through the bandage wrapped around her head.

The others had loaded Roger's body onto the small tumbrel that had held the cider. It was too short for its cargo. Bent at the knees, Roger's lifeless limbs dangled sans grace. The captive soldiers stumbled behind as Carrick took the reins and set the horse to a fast clip. Will and the farmers brought up the rear.

Anna twisted in her saddle and looked back at Lark. He watched her even as he tried to help Trian. She was the first to turn away. How much time she needed, she didn't know. The shock of being free of Roger was setting in. Too much had happened, too much remained unknown. But first, Anna had to tend to Doreen. Only afterward would she seek the privacy of her chamber.

CHAPTER FORTY-EIGHT

The Clearing

When Baldric tried to sit up, Grainne put a hand on his shoulder. "Take your time," she told him. "The poison will wear off soon." She looked around. Larkin was helping Trian. The big guard could wait. And the young one, Tomas, she thought, was alert; he could wait as well. The smooth-looking fellow would need help immediately. He had downed two mugs.

"Larkin, and you," she said, pointing at the guard who had affected paralysis. "I'm sorry, I don't know your name."

"That's Ailwen," Larkin provided. "You're holding Warin," he added, nodding his head at the man Grainne was propping up.

"He'll need our help first," Grainne instructed.

"What can I do, good lady?" Ailwen asked, hesitantly meeting her gaze.

"You can tilt his head back while Larkin props him up. His mouth is slack enough that there should be no problem pouring this down his gullet."

"Are you sure you can't let him stay that way a bit longer?" Tomas begged. "He's so quiet for once." A few strained chuckles came from Baldric and Trian.

Grainne smiled at his jest. "Sorry," she said, "not unless you would like to carry him back to the keep and plant him there. Much longer and he'll be apt to stop breathing all together. After he swallows," she added with more gravity, "be ready to turn him on his side. And stand back else you end up covered with his breakfast."

She regarded Ailwen. "Ready?" At his nod, she upended her flagon into Warin's mouth. Some trickled down his chin, but Grainne was pleased to see him swallow.

"Make sure he keeps on his side," Grainne instructed after Warin gave a hearty retch. "Let's see to the young guard.

"How came you to not drink?" Grainne asked Ailwen as they tended to Tomas.

"I saw Gorman signal to switch the casks and grew suspicious," Ailwen explained. "I was distracted and couldn't warn the others in time."

"You spied one of us in the woods," Grainne guessed.

"At first I thought it was the dog," he related.

Grainne noticed that the horrible snarling and screaming had stopped.

Lark walked over. "I'm going to make sure the beast finished the job," he stated, his eyes distant. "Can you help the others to Baldric's side? There is much we need to discuss."

"And Warin?" Ailwen asked.

"If he can groan, it's likely he can hear. Just move him closer."

Grainne frowned. Trian was standing, albeit unsteadily, and making his way over.

"I'm coming with you, Lark," Trian declared. "It's no use arguing."

"You'll only slow me down, Trian," Lark complained. "You can hardly stand."

"The only way for me to move faster is to get my blood flowing. Let's go." Trian rounded on his heel and all but reeled to the edge of the clearing. Lark shook his head and followed.

It didn't take them long to find Gorman. The doomed soldier had been intent on escaping the dog, not hiding his trail. It was a gruesome sight. Lark knelt and felt for a pulse on Gorman's wrist. It was impossible to find one on the man's shredded neck. The hand he was holding was missing a finger; another digit hung by a strip of skin. But it was Gorman's face that gave them pause. The dog had ravaged it.

"Too bad about the beast," Trian said as he frowned down at the mastiff. Lark gave up finding a heartbeat and spared a moment for the animal. He was spread over Gorman's chest, staring unseeingly into the forest. Gorman's hand still held the hilt of the knife that was embedded in the top of Garamantes's head.

"We'll bury the dog," Lark allowed. "Let the carrion birds have Gorman."

"Lark, are you all right?"

"No, I'm not," Larkin admitted, "but I will be when this is over." He nudged Gorman's dead body with his toe. "Lord Roger and this man, you cannot imagine. They're lucky to be dead. I only regret that I was not the one doing the killing."

"Lady Aubrianne must be a formidable woman, Lark," Trian stated. "I can't imagine the strength it took to be married to a man such as Roger."

"No, you can't. She is stronger than even she realizes. Stronger than us all, I fear."

Before Trian could ask him what he meant, Lark set to work covering the dog with rocks. After one last look at Gorman, Trian turned to help.

• • •

Lord Baldric and Tomas, Larkin observed upon returning to the clearing, were sitting upright. Warin was lying on his side, and Ailwen was attempting to prop him up.

"Is Gorman dead?" Baldric asked.

"Quite," Trian replied when Lark remained silent. "The dog, too."

Baldric cleared his throat. "We need to talk, men. Why don't you start, Lark? I think Lady Aubrianne has told you much already. If you know more, Grainne, please jump in."

Lark began the story with Anna's arrival at Stolweg and her life over the past three years. His eyes darkened when he hinted at Lady Aubrianne's ordeal.

"We decided to act before we knew your cider was drugged," Grainne explained to the assembled men. Before Baldric could speak, she continued hastily, "Forgive us. We believed our task would be easier if you were out of harm's way. We would never have allowed them to hurt you. Roger and his men were always targeted."

"I wondered how it was possible that you had the exact draught we would need to recover," he commented. "But you should have trusted me. You *can* trust me. We could have spared you from—"

"We did not know that at the time, m'lord," Grainne interrupted. "And we had to move before our lady returned. You see, Lady Aubrianne had reached her end, just as Lady Isabel had."

"Her end?" Baldric asked.

"She was going to pit herself against Lord Roger and would have done so at the expense of her life. We were not willing to lose her."

Baldric looked at Lark for confirmation, and then nodded appreciatively. "So many blows to Lord Roger, it's impossible to determine which killed him. I believe King Godwin will be relieved; it will save him from dealing with a charge of treason. But how did you know that Lady Aubrianne was going to act?" Baldric asked.

NICOLE ELIZABETH KELLEHER

"The morning you came, my mistress was changed. It was much the same with Lady Isabel the night before her death."

Lark caught her eye. "Lady Isabel did not jump to her death as once thought," Lark provided, placing his hand on Grainne's. "She was murdered by Roger, or on his orders. Go ahead, Grainne. Tell us the rest."

She told Baldric of Lord Roger's abuse of first Lady Isabel and later Lady Aubrianne. She began with the story of Will's lashing. "Lady Aubrianne saved Will. He was to receive fifteen blows. Six were dealt. Lady Aubrianne t-took the rest."

Baldric was stunned. "God's oath, is this true?" But Lark's gaze was fixed on some point in the distance.

"Lord Roger," Grainne resumed, her voice cracking, "had summoned Lady Aubrianne to his chamber the night before your arrival. Something terrible must have happened, for she returned much changed. I've never seen her so determined, and so resigned."

"So you deduced that she was going to kill him?" Baldric asked.

Grainne nodded. "We believed she only held back because she was worried about Chevring. Will overheard her asking Cellach to take a message to her parents, to warn them."

"Damn. The message!" Lark interjected. "Baldric, this was delivered this morning, after you left the keep." He pulled out the letter from his tunic.

Baldric wasted no time breaking the royal seal and reading the missive. "Good Lord, no!" he exclaimed. "This cannot be!" He handed the parchment back to Lark.

"Not Chevring," Lark stated, horrified.

"What about Chevring?" Grainne demanded.

"Destroyed, Grainne," Baldric answered. "Every man, woman, and child is presumed dead."

"I have to leave!" Grainne cried. "I have to help Lady Aubrianne. If someone tells her…" She jumped up, hastening to the narrow road that would lead her to the keep.

Lark rose to join her, but Ailwen had already readied his mount and was putting a lead on one of the soldier's horses. "I'll see her back safely," he offered. "Baldric needs you here. You missed much while you were away."

"Tell her I…" he started, then lost his words when he noticed the others giving him peculiar looks. "Tell her that we will return soon." Ailwen nodded, and Lark took his place next to Baldric once more.

"Does the message say how Chevring was destroyed?" Warin asked him, finally sitting up on his own.

"It does not," Lark replied. "Only that it is gone." He stared down the path where Anna had ridden, wishing more than anything that he could be with her.

"You must have a sense of Lady Aubrianne's character, Lark," Baldric said. "Will she survive this news?"

Lark swept his eyes to Baldric and replied, "It will only make her stronger. Baldric, I—"

"We're almost done here, Lark," he interrupted. "I'm beginning to think there is more to Lady Aubrianne than meets the eye."

"You don't know the half of it," Lark told them as they resumed their council in the clearing. "Lady Anna began an unorthodox training when she was quite young. There's a gift that runs on her mother's side of the family. Every few generations, a girl is born with certain talents. Swordplay, quarterstaff, knives, and bow. You name it, she's mastered it."

"But she's only a woman," Tomas scoffed. "Granted, she's tall and quick, but she's thin."

"Not thin, Tomas. Lean," Lark corrected. "She is all muscle and coiled to strike any time. I know. She bested me at quarterstaff."

At their disbelief, Lark expounded, giving them an accounting of their bout.

"So she caught you unexpectedly," Warin interjected.

"Yes, but not in the way that you are thinking. First, she intentionally dropped her guard. I continued my swing, one I thought she would block, but my staff connected with her side. I stopped to see if she was hurt. Before I knew what had happened, I was flat on my back with the end of her pole at my throat. It was a neat little trick. You should ask her to show you, Tomas." Lark noticed a strange look on Baldric's face. "What is it, Baldric?"

"I've heard rumors about such women," he replied. "The Queen has been searching for the descendants of Lady Jeanne for years. Your mother, Lark, has been helping her." Baldric stared down the trail that led back to Stolweg Keep.

"Who is Lady Jeanne?" Tomas inquired.

"Lady Jeanne fought in the Great War against Nifolhad," Warin explained. "The King's scholars claim that she fought better than most men. And tracing further back in history, you'll find similar women in every war. Lady Jeanne was said to have descended from those women. If Lady Aubrianne is a direct descendant…"

Lark turned to Baldric. "Are you going to tell us the rest?"

His mentor drew his gaze from the trail and focused on Lark before speaking. "There is always such a warrior in times of great strife. If Aubrianne is the latest incarnation of her ancestors, then her existence heralds more than a single lord's grasp for power. It suggests that another war is upon us."

Lark turned away and felt Baldric's hand on his shoulder. "Such women are marked, Lark. They have no choice but to be strong. Anything less does not occur to them."

. . .

Ailwen trotted up to the half-running, half-walking Grainne. "It'll take you all day to return on foot. I've brought a horse for you and will see you safely to the keep."

Grainne stopped. She ogled the horse and shuddered. She hesitated but a moment before screwing her courage tighter and putting her hand on the saddle's pommel. If it took her having to ride a beast to help Lady Aubrianne, she would do it. When she lifted her foot to the stirrup, the horse snorted, and Grainne shrieked and stumbled back. Not of the Chevring line, the gelding startled and bolted back the way it had come.

"Are you hurt?" Ailwen asked with concern. When she shook her head, he held out his hand. "Let me take you, then."

Ailwen hoisted her into his saddle. His arm circled protectively around her waist. "You can hold the pommel if it will help," he offered.

"What's its name?" she nervously asked.

"*Her* name is Hellfire." Grainne's hands shot out to hold the saddle horn with a white-knuckled grip, and she heard Ailwen chuckle. He kicked his mare forward. "It's a misnomer, Grainne. I promise. My horse has the sweetest disposition in the world."

"Oh," Grainne managed to squeak.

"I'm going to speed up our pace," he told her. "Just a nice, easy canter to spare you some jarring. We'll reach the keep much faster. Ready?"

Grainne closed her eyes and shrank back into the strong chest behind her. Ailwen held her tighter as Hellfire found her gait. Grainne decided she might not ever like the sensation of such a large creature moving underneath her, but she certainly fancied the feel of Ailwen. They would be back at the keep in no time at all.

CHAPTER FORTY-NINE

Chin High

As they rode into the courtyard and to the stable, Anna and her friends earned more than a few curious looks. Several of Roger's men loitered about, others hurried to the main gate. Only those few who were born at Stolweg remained to face the scrutiny of Lord Baldric. For any of these men, only time would tell. Anna hoped they would redeem themselves.

The sound of the cart rolling into the courtyard caught her attention. After handing over Tullian's reins, she headed out of the stable. Carrick, who had driven the cart, was doing his best to hold back his daughter.

The girl was crying hysterically, beating her fists against her father's chest; she'd seen Roger's body. Everyone in the courtyard had turned to witness the spectacle. When Maggie noticed Anna, she flew at her, hands upraised like claws. "You killed him!" she screamed. Anna grabbed the tiny wrists, easily deflecting the attack.

"Control yourself," she said in a voice too low to be heard by the onlookers. "There are only a few here who know of your shameful behavior. If you continue your ranting, all will come to understand your misfortunate attachment to my husband."

Maggie pulled herself up as if she were a queen. "Your husband!" she spat, caring not that her father was standing next to her. "*Your husband* cared nothing for you. He would have rather seen you dead than be married to you."

Anna slapped Maggie's face with such speed that the young woman was knocked sideways. She'd always thought of Maggie as a victim. Though the girl's words were spoken in misguided grief, Anna no longer cared. She'd had enough for one day. Enough for the last three years. Enough for the rest of her life. "Carrick, your daughter is not herself. Please see her home."

"Yes, m'lady. Thank you, my lady," he said and shuffled his

daughter away.

Anna felt the weight of every eye upon her. She turned on her heel and disappeared into the cool shadows of the keep to tend to Doreen's wound.

Afterward, in her chamber, Anna closed the door for a brief respite. She would have to answer the inevitable questions from Baldric soon enough, and then they would all discover just how deep the roots of Roger's treachery grew.

• • •

Grainne's only thought was to see to her mistress, and to make sure that she heard about her family from a friend. She ignored all else, including the inconsolable Maggie, who passed her as she made her way to the main gate of the keep. She raced to her lady's chamber, then steeled herself before opening the door. Lady Aubrianne was resting near the hearth. "M'lady, there has been news from King Godwin," Grainne began, sitting on the couch next to her mistress and taking her hands. She delivered the news as gently as she could.

"Destroyed?" Lady Aubrianne asked, as if disbelieving. "Destroyed," she repeated with a finality that chilled Grainne to the bone.

"Lady Aubri—Lady Anna, let me…" Grainne started, but couldn't finish. Her mistress stared straight ahead, into the cold hearth. Grainne recognized the haunted look that came to her lady's eyes. She'd observed it over and again for the past three years, only to be squelched by her lady's sheer determination. But Grainne was worried. Lady Anna would believe that she must remain strong for her people. Grainne knew that if her mistress didn't allow herself to grieve, she wouldn't allow herself to be happy. That was no way to live, now that she was out from under Roger's thumb.

"I want to see this message from Godwin," Lady Anna demanded. "As soon as Baldric returns to the keep." Her lady stood up and paced in front of the fireplace. "We must determine if Stolweg is threatened. I will not lose another family."

• • •

By herself at last, Anna stared down at the mortar and pestle that she had used so many times to prepare her healing salves. She would mourn in her own time, in her own way, and only after fulfilling her duty to Stolweg and its people. It was what her grandmother had taught her: face adversity with chin held high, shoulders back, and chest out.

Quite unexpectedly, Anna remembered her sister Claire, and how they would giggle when they puffed out their flat, girlish chests. Their grandmother's *tsks* would have them rolling. Remembering Claire and those carefree days, she felt as if her breath had been knocked from her. Something inside snapped.

She began to shake. Such a rage as never had she felt before swelled inside her. For more than three years, she had survived Lord Roger. She had turned her back on every blow and violation; she knew that to do otherwise would mean her family's destruction. He had dangled their welfare over her head like a noose. And then he'd done the unthinkable. He had slaughtered them. How he must have enjoyed knowing they were gone as he continued to threaten her into subservience.

She remembered the expression on Roger's face when she had crushed the ruby he had given her. With his dying breath, he had sneered at her. Now she knew why. She picked up the crock filled with the balm she had created for the purpose of healing and hurled it as hard as she could at the tapestry depicting the wedding.

• • •

Once Baldric had given him his leave to ride ahead, Lark wasn't long behind Grainne's arrival at the keep. He'd caught up with her in hallway, and she filled him in on Anna's behavior. He'd expected as much. He should have come back with her and not given her a chance to build her walls. But as he stood in her open doorway next to Grainne, he was taken by surprise. Broken crockery and splattered balm dripped from the tapestry across the room.

When Anna turned to them, breast heaving, eyes wild, Lark cautiously approached, then held her as sobs wracked her body.

In one swoop, he picked her up, cradling her in his arms. He strode to the couch near the fireplace and sat with her there, she half in his lap. "You're going to be all right, Anna," he whispered. "I promise. You'll be all right." She lifted her eyes to him several times, as if she wanted to speak, only to bury her head in his shoulder, dissolving again to tears. He continued to murmur words meant to soothe until, finally, her tears subsided.

Lark lifted her chin and she gazed up into his eyes. Gently, he wiped her cheeks.

"How, Lark?" she implored him.

"We don't know, Anna. We only know that every building has been razed."

"When did this happen?" she asked.

"Weeks ago, we think," he told her.

• • •

Weeks ago, Anna thought. Weeks ago, Roger had returned. His elated mood was one that had terrified her. Weeks ago, he had brought additional Chevring horses to Stolweg. Weeks ago, he had spoken of a fire there, but refused her any details.

Anna imagined that she could smell the coppery scent of blood, the stench of burning flesh, sickly and sweet. She was the last of her line now. And she wouldn't rest until those responsible for the destruction of Chevring were brought to justice. And justice meant that every last one of her enemies would die. By her own hand, if necessary. If she was sure of one thing, it was that her late husband had not been alone in his actions.

"I'm so sorry, my Anna," Lark said.

She turned to him then. "Not as sorry as Roger's accomplices will be," she vowed.

CHAPTER FIFTY

Cellach's Return

Cellach marveled at how the children supported one another, persevering without complaint. And although he was proud of them, and told them so, he worried. He'd yet to see a single tear.

More troubling to him, however, was their immediate future. Had he delivered them from Chevring just to lead them into a trap? In a few hours, it would be morning, and they would be near one of Lady Aubrianne's hidden glens. He would have to leave them alone.

As the dawn finally rose, his tattered group heard voices. He gave them a signal to wait while he scouted ahead. He returned moments later to find the children bunched together, their eyes apprehensive. He beckoned them forward.

They were tired to the bone, Cellach realized, after riding all night. But they followed him with trust. He watched their faces as they entered a small clearing where beautiful Chevring mares and foals grazed. Standing in their midst were two men, staring back at the children with identical expressions of disbelief.

• • •

Anna had put off meeting with Baldric far too long. She was the Lady of Stolweg; it was time she acted the part. Her people needed a leader.

She studied her reflection in the tall glass. This day, her stable garb would not serve. "I'll need one of my gowns for this meeting, Grainne," Anna said.

"Of course, m'lady," Grainne replied. "I know just the one." In the meantime, Anna set to work on her hair, plaiting it so that nary a tendril escaped. There was a knock at her door and she heard someone speaking to Grainne.

"A note, m'lady. From Carrick. He found it in the cart," Grainne explained when Anna came from behind the partition to dress.

"I'll have to read it later," Anna said, setting the folded paper on her worktable. As Grainne helped her into her gown, a soft breeze entered through the open windows and played about the chamber. The note slipped to the floor unnoticed by either women.

. . .

Anna was the first to arrive at the appointed place in the courtyard, and waited for Baldric. When he arrived, he walked purposefully toward her, but stopped halfway between the castle and the fountain, his attention captured by some excitement near the main gate.

Upon hearing the familiar beat of horse hooves, Anna turned to see the small herd of mares and their foals enter the courtyard. But their numbers had swelled. Behind the horses rode Will and Gilles. And Cellach! And he was grinning. She raced to them, recognizing at once the children of Chevring. Luke and Sarah, Adele, and another boy. Robbie? He'd been only four when she departed her childhood home.

Anna counted the beautiful children. Seven. Seven survivors. Luke had already slipped from his mighty steed and was rushing to her. She picked him up and swung him around in a circle, his legs flying high into the air. They were crying and laughing at the same time. Sarah ran, protectively holding a bundle. Anna opened her arms to take in Sarah and the baby she held swaddled against her. Robbie joined them, and Adele, then the younger children. Anna looked down at the small boy running to her and called, "This cannot be Adam. You were barely walking when I last saw you. Such a fine boy you are." He beamed back at her, elated that she remembered his name. Anna looked at them all and named aloud those she could. "Luke, Adele, Robbie, and Sarah. Sarah, who is this beautiful girl you hold?"

"M'lady, this is Hannah. She was farmer Daniel's daughter."

Anna's heart broke again, thinking of their loss. These children were orphans. She felt a tug on her skirt. "Know me? Know me?" a little boy asked hopefully.

"How could I not, sweet Paul? I once swaddled you when you were smaller than Hannah."

Anna glanced helplessly at Baldric, and he tipped his head in deference to the greater need. Their conference would have to wait until the children were fed and settled. They were walking to the castle when the children skidded to a stop. Finding Cellach in the crowd that had gathered, they raced to him. Anna saw his eyes brighten as they hugged him before returning to her. She mouthed the words *thank you* to him and bowed her head in respect. Off to the side, Lark was standing with Trian and the others. There was not a dry eye among them.

"Miss Anna, Miss Anna?" Sarah was calling.

"Sarah, it's *Lady* Anna now," Luke corrected in a loud whisper.

"That's all right, Luke," Anna said. "What is it, Sarah?"

"Have you heard from Pieter?"

"Pieter?" she asked, remembering fondly the stable hand who had helped her to evade her mother so many times. How could she tell Sarah that he was lost? "No, Sarah, I am sorry." The young girl was undeterred, and Anna worried about the long road she would have to travel before accepting the deaths of her family.

"I just thought that you may have heard from Miss Claire. Pieter left with her, weeks ago." She was about to ask the girl to explain when Cellach ran to her.

"Lady Aubrianne," he gasped, out of breath. "Your sister—she may have escaped."

"Thank you, Cellach," she said, hugging him fiercely. "Thank you for bringing these children, for giving me hope that not all is lost. And thank you for returning to me safely." As she stepped away, she gazed upon the children. Had she seen Cellach's face, the unwavering devotion in his eyes would have shaken her to her core.

After the children had been settled, Anna found herself with an hour to collect her thoughts before meeting with Baldric. The sun had almost set below the western hills, and Anna decided to walk to the chapel. The cool interior was empty as she entered and proceeded to the altar. Earlier in her chamber, she had prayed for courage and for hope. Her prayers had been answered with the return of the children to her care. And knowing that Claire might still live, Anna was humbled. She spent what was left of her time giving thanks.

When she finished, she walked to where she knew Lark would be standing on the shadowed steps outside. Without a word, for she had none to express what her heart had for so long buried, she pulled him to her. He was so solid, so real, and she drew in his scent as if it were his very essence.

"Thank you, Lark."

"For what, Anna?" he asked.

"For making me feel safe."

"Thank you for letting me." He tilted his head in the direction of the keep. "They'll be waiting for you."

. . .

They entered the great hall, and all eyes turned in their direction. Lark took his seat next to Baldric. It was Anna who spoke first, not Lord Baldric. As the Lady of Stolweg, it was her place to do so. Her voice was cool and modulated. "Cellach, I think it best if you start at the end."

She held up her hand at the puzzled looks from the others. "We all are aware of the circumstances regarding the ruination of Chevring," she put forth. "I would like Cellach to describe what he saw. And we have additional information from the children. Once told, we may be able to draw some conclusions as to the reason for my home's destruction and my husband's treachery." She nodded to Cellach.

Cellach told the others of finding the trail that he now knew belonged to Claire and the Chevring stable boy. He described what he saw from the ridge overlooking the castle. "I was discovered by a soldier. I'm sorry, m'lady," Cellach warned her in advance, "but before he died, I asked him where they were holding the survivors. He told me there were none."

Anna locked eyes for a moment with Lord Baldric, and nodded. Cellach continued. He related the details of the weapons that Luke had described: great rolling machines, ten in all.

"Did the boy say what type of machine it was, Cellach?" Lord Baldric asked.

"No, my lord, he could not name it. His description made it sound similar to a catapult. I even suggested this, and he replied that the weapons were too different."

"Mordemurs," Anna announced, to their collective surprise. Cellach jumped from his seat. "Mordemurs," she repeated, placing a calming hand on his arm. "The machines are mordemurs."

"But how?" Cellach charged. "No one, not even you, should know of such a weapon." He sat down heavily. "What am I saying? It is not yet even a weapon, just a design. A drawing."

"What is this mordemur?" Baldric demanded.

Anna raised her hand again, asking for their patience. "We will explain." She turned to Cellach then. "If you go through your sketches, you will find one missing. I once had an opportunity to search the documents on Roger's desk. He had one of your drawings, and he had stolen a ledger from Chevring. In my father's script was a notation regarding lumber that was to be taken as payment by Roger. A note in the margin, written by Roger, said *Chevring: Mordemur, 10*. At the time, I thought that *Mordemur* was the name of a person."

She saw that Baldric's patience was wearing thin. "Tell them what the word means, Cellach."

"It is not the name of a man," he said to the others. "It is the name of a weapon. Mordemur is not meant to be one word—that must have been Lord Roger's idea. It is three separate words: *mort de mur*, or "death of walls." If they have built ten of these weapons, then Chevring was just—"

"Target practice," Anna concluded.

Baldric rose and began pacing. "Out with it, Cellach. What can these weapons do?"

"A mordemur is to a catapult as a crossbow is to the longbow," Cellach replied. "In theory, my wall killer can pierce any battlement, no matter how fortified. It is stronger and faster and ten times more accurate. I designed them so that they could be dismantled, the base becoming a wheeled wagon for transport. They can be moved easily over any terrain. Hills, plains, mountains." He turned to Anna. "M'lady, when they discover that Lord Roger is dead, they will turn on Stolweg."

"Would ten be enough to destroy a fortress such as Stolweg?" Baldric asked gravely.

"It would take only a few days with that many," Cellach replied. He hesitated a moment before saying more. "The boy told me that more soldiers had returned for the machines. When they departed, they took the old forest road, the one that leads to Stolweg. The machines are already on their way."

"We have one advantage in all of this," Anna proclaimed, and all eyes settled on her. "They do *not* yet know Lord Roger is dead. Until they do, Stolweg is not a target."

"How long will it take them to reach the keep, Cellach?" Baldric demanded.

"From Chevring? Three, four weeks perhaps. They have already had two. The mountain pass will slow them."

"So for now," Anna summed up, "we plan our welcome party."

CHAPTER FIFTY-ONE

Duty

It had been an exhausting two weeks, Anna reflected, and they were no closer to a consensus of what to do than they had been before. She had wanted to launch a force against the men bringing the mordemurs to Stolweg, and do so as far from the keep as possible. But Baldric had argued that they did not have enough men to attack a force that size, and waiting at the keep would allow King Godwin to send reinforcements. Anna saw the logic of his stance, but worried that King Godwin's army would not arrive in time. At least she and Baldric had agreed on one thing: sending scouts to assess the size and whereabouts of the Nifolhadian forces.

Anna stood atop the battlements and searched out into the dusk. The endless councils with Baldric had gone as expected. The few answers they found only served to raise more fears and more questions. But then Anna's life had always been about the unknown. She took a deep breath as she continued to survey the dim land below.

It was strange for her to stand alone, so high above the peaceful fields and pastures below, knowing her land would be thrown into turmoil. The men with whom her late husband had allied himself would soon be at the gate. Anna prayed that they would arrive with no thought of destroying Stolweg.

With that in mind, they formulated a plan. When the Nifolhadajans arrived, Baldric and the guards would ride out to meet them. Anna insisted on joining the sortie with Cellach at her side.

No mention of Roger's death would be uttered in hopes of buying the people of Stolweg a little more time. Upon discovering the cold reception, the strangers would reassess their strategy. Anna estimated that it would be a matter of hours before the construction of the machines commenced.

From memory, Cellach had redrawn the machine for Lord Baldric.

The weapons of the keep would make nary a dent, so well armored were the workings. There was no chance of destroying the mordemurs by conventional means.

But Anna had noticed a weakness in the design. If she and her people were to survive, she would have to take matters into her own hands. This time, she would not tarry. Waiting too long to act had cost her her family. She wanted to go over her idea with Lark before presenting it to Baldric and the others.

He and Warin had just returned. They'd done what they could to slow the enemy's progress but judged that the weapons would arrive in another two or three days. King Godwin's army had decamped for Stolweg but would not arrive in time. Anna's heart ached thinking about the beautiful and peaceful land below marred by the approaching Nifolhadajans.

The air around her cooled as the sun faded, giving way to the deeper blue of the encroaching night. Above her, the stars were already bright in the sky. They gave her hope as she walked back to her chamber. She put aside all thoughts of impending battle and focused instead on Lark. They'd spent too many nights apart, and her heart ached for him.

When Anna entered her chamber, Grainne was there, laying out her sleeping gown. Her maid helped her to shrug out of her dress. "Would you like me to stay awhile, Lady Anna?" Grainne asked.

"Thank you, Grainne, but no," she answered, loving that her friends had taken to calling her Lady *Anna*. She pulled on a robe over her sleeping gown. "It's been a long day, and I'd like to check on the children."

Outside her room, they moved in opposite directions, with Grainne taking Anna's tray to the kitchen. The children were sound asleep. Piles of clothing, toys, and the like filled the room. Anna smiled, proud that her people were so giving.

She was making her way back to her room when she passed her chamber door, and instead walked on to Lark's quarters. She couldn't shake the feeling that he'd been avoiding her. She knocked determinedly on his door and waited for him to answer. When the door remained closed to her, she made up her mind and opened it herself. He was not within. So she sat on the lone chair in the chamber and waited for him. And waited.

The moon ascended, its light flooding the room, marking the time as it cast its cool wash upon the floor. Anna lingered, following the splash of light as it inched away from her. When her impatience grew too great to bear, she stood and paced. Finally, she leaned against the wide, sloping ledge of the window.

A breeze swirled through the room as she bathed in the moon's beam. She skimmed her hands forward along the sill, feeling the cold, hard stone as it inclined to the outside. It was difficult to imagine a weapon that could penetrate the bulky walls of Stolweg.

"Where are you, Lark?" she whispered to the night. She sighed, knowing she'd tarried here too long.

As Anna turned from the window, the air shifted in the dark room. She peered across the dim chamber. There was just enough illumination from the window for her to recognize Lark's familiar silhouette. His head was lowered, and he didn't seem to see her. She waited, breath held, as he lit the candle on the table. It took a mere instant for him to sense her presence. His eyes, though unaccustomed to the dark, homed in on her immediately.

"What took you so long?" Anna asked, barely managing to breathe.

"Another meeting with Baldric," Lark answered, and took a step toward her.

"So many meetings," she said. In the flickering light, she could see the dark desire in his eyes as he approached.

"I went to your room," he told her, his voice tight. "I knocked, and you didn't answer."

"I was tired of waiting," Anna whispered. "So I came to find you." He came closer still.

"So I see." He was so near to her, he needed only to reach out with his hands, and she would be in his embrace.

"And here you are," Anna murmured, knowing that at last they would be together. He took the final step. They stood toe-to-toe, and yet he did not reach for her.

"And, here *you* are," Lark echoed, his voice dripping with need.

"Can you give my mind some respite from the past weeks?" she begged him. "Can you make me forget?" He closed the gap between them and crushed his mouth to hers. Her hands reached up and captured his face.

His fingers touched her cheek, then trailed down the sensitive skin along her neck. His hand came back up, and his thumb pressed gently against her trembling lower lip.

"Should I kiss you again?" he asked and, when she nodded, he bent his head to her.

Her knees, already turned to pudding from when he first entered the room, dissolved. She leaned against the wall for support while his lips devastated hers. "What else do you want?" he asked. "You'll have to tell me, Anna." His fingers played with the ties of her robe. Soon it was in a pile on the floor.

Only his lips and fingers had touched her, and she needed him so much more. Anna lowered her hands from his shoulders and slid them down his arms. He'd rendered her speechless by his kiss, and here he was asking her questions. She would show him what she wanted. And what she wanted was to feel his body against hers. Taking his wrists, she pulled his arms around her. Then, she reached around his waist and settled her hands on his back, drawing his body forward, hard. Lark's arms tightened the circle in which they held each other.

"You haven't answered me, Anna." She gave a muffled response, her face buried in his neck, her mouth kissing and nipping his skin. Lark used his body to press her against the wall, and his hands drew up to lift her face. His eyes searched hers as he insisted, "Tell me."

"You," she replied, blushing deeply.

Lark smiled. "Is that all?"

She had missed him, body and soul, these last days. "I want you," she growled. "Right here. Right now. All of you."

He eased back, just enough to be able to lift her shift over her head. Then he pressed the length of his body against hers, and she marveled still at how well they fit together.

She gasped as his hand found her breast, and her need to feel his skin against hers grew. She fought to pull his shirt over his head, running her hands over the hard planes of his chest and down the laddered muscles of his stomach. And lower, where she could feel him straining for release from the tight leather pants that constrained him.

A deep growl emanated from within him, and his hands left off their exploration of her breasts to reach down and remove his breeches. She stared hungrily at his naked torso. His eyes, too, looked as if he were starving for her.

He lifted her suddenly, his strong hands cupping her buttocks, and she wrapped her thighs around his waist. When he pulled her forward against his body, she found herself sealed against his naked hips. Spinning with desire, she was ready for him.

Lark raised her higher before slowly lowering her body onto his jutting hardness. He groaned in pleasure even as she gasped at the feel of him inside her once again. He worked their bodies, thrusting and lifting, over and over. Anna held his shoulders, keeping him to his task.

As Lark plunged up and forward, she could feel the cool, smooth stone rubbing against her back, unforgiving against her scarred skin. His strokes seemed so much longer when set against the unyielding resistance of the wall.

His head hung over her shoulder and his breath roughened, hot and wet upon her neck. Her fingers twined into his hair, trapping him to her. "Anna, I can't get enough of you like this. Oh God, I need more. I need to touch all of you."

In one fluid motion, he shifted their joined bodies, setting her on the cold windowsill. His eyes, black as night, bore into hers, the intensity of his desire matched only by her own. He thrust into her, and thrust again. And again, until she could no longer focus and threw her head back from the heat smoldering in his gaze.

Then, his mouth found her breasts, his beard rough on her naked skin. All the while, his hips continued to move against her in long stabs. His hand reached between them, and his knuckles brushed her intimately. Anna's cries grew louder as he teased and stroked.

The delicious tension inside her grew and grew, and she begged for him not to stop. Her body exploded. "Larkin!"

Her very essence felt as if it had shattered into a thousand pieces of bliss. And still, she wanted more. She knew Lark would continue until he pushed her over the brink again, until she forgot even herself. So she buried her face against his shoulder to muffle her cries. Her body arched against him, and he gave up her breasts. Leaning forward, he curved his body over hers as her climax continued. His hands gripped her hips, pulling her impossibly closer as he drove into her.

And finally, he shuddered, his own muted cry unintelligible in the mass of her hair. She tightened her thighs around him to ride out his final thrusts.

They stayed there, on the window sill, unable to move, barely able to breathe. He lifted his head slowly, as if it weighed twenty stone, and gazed once more into her sated eyes. She smiled, and wiped the perspiration from his brow before lifting her lips to his in a simple kiss. With her arms and legs still wrapped about him, he carried her to his bed.

• • •

"Well?" Lark murmured.

"Hmmm?" she asked him.

"Did it work?"

"Did what work?" Anna managed.

"Did I make you forget?" he purred against her ear.

"Forget what?" She sighed happily. Lark pulled her tighter to him, and so entwined, they drifted off to sleep.

It was hours before dawn when he woke her with a kiss. She stretched, arching her back deliciously as he stared in appreciation. Out of fuel, the lamp had sputtered to its end. The night was cold, and she shivered against him, before fitting herself closer to his body.

"You're cold?" he said, rubbing his warm hand over her shoulder and down her arm.

"Not cold," she replied. "I just don't want this to end."

He sighed and teased his fingers around one of her loose curls. "Nor do I." Neither wanted to part, but both understood the need for discretion. With another deep breath, Lark sat up and stretched his arms, sitting for a moment before picking up his breeches. Once garbed, he reached for Anna's sleeping gown and robe. Tenderly, he helped her to dress, but only after applying enough kisses to her body to last her through the coming day.

. . .

They sat side by side with their legs hanging over the end of his small bed. She did not want to break the spell they had created but needed to ask him something. "Do I just imagine it, or do the others look at me strangely? Only your regard seems unchanged. I feel, I don't know, I feel…"

"What do you feel?" he asked.

She paused, not sure he would understand, then forged ahead regardless. "I know that people have always thought that I was different. But now the looks cast in my direction worry me."

"You're right, you are different." He placed his finger on her lips before she could protest. "You *are* different. Perhaps because I am closer to you and know the changes you have been going through these past weeks, it did not seem to you that I saw you differently as well."

"But your friends, Lark, they are uneasy around me." Lark frowned, and she asked hurriedly, "What is it? You must tell me."

His hand continued to rub her shoulders as if trying to soothe her nerves. "Do you remember what you told me about the women in your family?"

She nodded, and he continued, "Baldric knows a little too. He shared this knowledge with the other guards. I myself never realized the extent of the coming trouble. You managed to leave out much of your history."

Anna turned away. "I didn't want you to think I was crazy."

"I wouldn't have," he assured her.

"But I didn't know that, Lark. I've lived with this my whole life. I don't think anyone truly realizes what my ancestors endured. What they accomplished and triumphed over. And what they sometimes lost. I didn't even know my own mother was capable of wielding a sword until I was sixteen. I like to think she died fighting alongside my father." Anna lowered her voice. "My mother always tried to make me into a lady."

"Anna," he said, raising an imperious eyebrow at her, "you are more a lady than any woman I know."

"That's not what I meant," she whispered as his hand smoothed her riotous curls. "My mother tried to keep me from learning such skills as were deemed proper only for men—fishing, hunting, fighting. Anything that could help me to prepare."

"But if she knew you were marked, why wouldn't she want you prepared?" Lark asked. "It doesn't make sense, Anna."

"I think she thought that if I eschewed these physical skills, perhaps I could escape fate's grasp. She was trying to protect me."

She took his hands and gazed into his eyes. "Lark, to know that one's existence will coincide with a great upheaval—it is enough to drive a sane person mad. If I did not exist, would the upheaval be averted? I have lain awake many nights asking myself questions such as that."

"Then it's true? Are we on the eve of another great war?"

"I don't know, Lark. I sometimes like to think that it has always been a coincidence or that my ancestors found their true strength because of the turmoil."

"It's the age-old question about the egg and the hen. Answer me this at least. Your ancestors, the women like you, did they survive?"

"As far as I know, always."

"Good to know," he said, kissing the top of her head. "I like having you around. Now, I have a question for you. Why is it so important that you join us when we ride out?"

"I must, Lark. I am the Lady of Stolweg. It is my duty, not Baldric's, to represent Stolweg."

"Let Cellach go in your stead," Lark countered vehemently, standing and crossing the room. "Why put yourself in danger if you do not need to?"

So this was why she'd felt him distancing himself from her. She rose from his bed and walked to him. "Lark, it's *my* duty. *I'm* the leader of my people. Not Cellach."

"Just think about it, Anna," he said. "Please."

"I will," she conceded. "But I can't make any promises." She drifted into his arms and tried to reclaim the peace she'd felt there earlier. But she could no more shirk her duty than she could cut off her arm. If Lark felt this way about her safety when she would be surrounded by five guards of Aurelia, she worried, how would he feel about her other plan? Would she even be able to tell him about it?

CHAPTER FIFTY-TWO

A United Front

The next morning, Anna opened her chamber door, thinking to help Grainne. To her surprise, Lark was just outside, sitting in a chair he had found somewhere.

He smiled up at her. "Good morning, Anna."

"Did you sleep out here all night?" she asked. Grainne came around the corner with an enormous tray laden with food. Lark just grinned and took the tray from Grainne. Anna's eyes widened at the amount of baked goods, cheese, and sausages that Doreen had prepared.

"Come in, Lark. I hope you're hungry," her maid commented with a lilt in her voice.

She was carrying enough for an army, Anna mused. "Are we having a party?"

"Not yet," Grainne babbled happily.

"Come on in then, Lark," Anna said. "Grainne seems to think I'll have company today." She held out her hand to help him from the chair. As he rose, he stretched like an old man.

"It serves you right if you're sore, sitting in that chair all night. You must be exhausted."

"Oh, it's not the chair that has made me stiff this morning." He winked, and then chuckled when her mouth dropped open. Anna checked to see if Grainne was listening. Thank goodness, her maid was preoccupied with setting up the banquet. Before Anna could respond, Lark put his arm around her shoulder and ushered her back into the chamber to the waiting food.

A moment later, Baldric poked his head in the door. "Do I smell breakfast?" he asked. Before any could answer, they heard the sound of feet running down the corridor.

"This way!" cried a young girl's voice.

WILD LAVENDER

"No, this way," called another.

"Where is she?" another pouted.

Suddenly, Baldric was spun like a top as the children from Chevring raced into Anna's room. "Don't look at me, m'lady. It was his idea," Grainne said, tilting her head at Lark. "He asked Doreen to put everything together. With so many people staying in the great hall, it wasn't such a bad idea."

Lark had scooped up little Paul, grabbing a sweet bun for the child before they were gone. Anna caught his eye and beamed at him. Not caring in the least that his tunic was now covered in sticky honey from the boy's messy hands, Lark sat down, the toddler on his lap. He would be a wonderful father, Anna thought, easily picturing him surrounded by his own children.

She realized for the first time that she and Lark had been everything but careful when they had lain together. She resisted the urge to move her hand to her stomach, remembering that she had continued to drink her special tea every day since marrying Roger. Her cycle had come without fail for the last three years.

Lark was regarding her with concern. He was about to set Paul from his lap, but she shook her head and smiled at him.

The children had taken over her room, and the miracle of their survival filled her with joy. Lark relaxed again but continued to check on her every so often.

"Would you like me to take him, Lark?" Anna offered. "You haven't eaten yet." He shook his head and reached for one of the last pieces of bread left on the table. She handed him some cheese from her plate to go with it.

When no one was paying attention, he grabbed her wrist and pulled her down to sit next to him on the crowded couch. She instinctively pressed herself closer to him. "Later," he promised in a whisper only she could hear.

After everyone had had their fill, Sarah and Luke gathered the children about them to explore the keep. Baldric was next to depart. "Let's meet in the courtyard in an hour," he told Lark on his way out.

"Here, let me help you with that," Baldric offered, when Grainne walked to the door with the heavy tray. He escorted her from the room, pulling the door shut behind him.

• • •

Lark was the first to notice that they were alone in the chamber. He leaned forward and planted a sloppy kiss on Anna's lips. "It is just you and me, my sweet. And we have an entire hour."

"Lark, someone could come in. We can't."

"Let's secure the door," he suggested.

"Absolutely not," she contended, though her heart screamed for her to do it. "What would they think upon trying to enter only to have me let them in and find you here?" But his attentions were melting her resolve. His fingers caressed her nape. The determination in Anna's voice wavered as she whispered, "Lark, we can't. We mustn't."

"We most certainly can," he murmured and leaned forward to trap her in his arms. "And we most assuredly must!" His lips did not bother with hers. Instead, they seared a line down her neck and back up to her ear. With a moan of pleasure, Anna gave in to his seduction.

They both heard a resounding knock at the door. Lark stepped behind the tapestry while she went to greet the latest visitor to her chamber.

"Good morning, my lady," Cellach greeted her.

"Good morning to you as well, Cellach. What news? Are the families evacuating?"

"That's just it, Lady Aubrianne," he answered. "They've gathered in the courtyard. They insist on seeing you first. I have heard that some intend to stay."

"How many?" Anna demanded.

"Well, everyone, my lady," Cellach replied. "Perhaps if you were to speak to them?"

"I'll be down in a few moments, Cellach," Anna promised. He bowed, and paused as if he wanted to say more. Anna waited, but he departed, keeping his silence.

Lark came from behind the partition with his arms crossed. "What am I to say to them, Lark?" Anna asked. "They must hie from here, before it is too late."

"Anna, just tell them the truth from your heart; let them decide their own fate. You cannot protect everyone." He uncrossed his arms and pulled her to him.

"Let's go, then," she said, taking for granted that he would be by her side.

• • •

They reached the door that would take them to the courtyard, and Lark hesitated. "I'll be close if you need me," he said, and gestured to where Baldric stood. At Anna's perplexed expression, he added, "Anna, your people need to see you. Only you. Now go, they're waiting."

Lark watched her as she stepped into the courtyard. A hush fell over the few hundred people who had gathered there. Cellach stood by, waiting for her. Lark felt a surge of jealousy as the arms master offered Anna his hand. She took it and stepped up to stand on the wide brim of the fountain to address the crowd.

Anna began by telling the assembly of her husband's duplicitous acts, carried out with the Nifolhadajans. She continued with a description of the great machines that Roger had used to destroy Chevring. Many crossed themselves upon hearing there were no survivors except the few children who had been discovered by Cellach. She thanked Cellach for his steadfast loyalty to her and to King Godwin. She offered a prayer that her sister had survived and was now safely ensconced at Whitmarsh, and that perhaps others from Chevring had also escaped. There was a moment of silence for those who had not.

When she spoke of the impending arrival of the enemy and their mordemurs, her voice lifted to stress her message. "The curtain wall is no match for these weapons, nor are our battlements. I entreat you to leave, please."

Before she stepped down from her dais, she thanked her people for their compliance with her wishes and told them to see Cellach for instructions and supplies. She didn't notice that Carrick had jumped up to take her place.

The irascible man cleared his throat with such volume that all present turned their eyes upon him. "I know most of you here," Carrick called out to the crowd. "If I don't, I'm assured that you at least know me." There was some chuckling at this, and Lark noticed that Gilles, Will, Grainne, and Doreen were now standing below the man.

"First, let me say that was a fine speech, Lady Anna." She nodded to him, but her face told Lark that she was worried about what was to come.

"No one here denies that you love us and only wish to see us safe. And I—we"—he swung his arm wide, indicating the people in the courtyard—"appreciate your concern, and love you more for it. However, with no disrespect intended, we think you must be daft." A few people laughed nervously, others gasped at his audacity. Grainne and Doreen scowled up at him.

"Your pardon, my lady," Carrick acknowledged, unfazed. "Stolweg

NICOLE ELIZABETH KELLEHER

is as much our home as it is yours. Thank you for your protection over the past three years. Don't think we didn't notice. But if you don't mind, we'd just as soon stay and fight for our home." He lifted his fist into the air and shouted. "And our lady!"

A great cheer rose up. "If you haven't a weapon, see Cellach," Carrick shouted above the din. "He'll get you settled straight away." And with that, his rebuttal was over.

All heads turned as a rider came through the main gate. He was one of Cellach's men, Lark realized. Finding Anna, the man dismounted and bowed. She asked him what news.

"Perhaps we should go to the council room," Lark suggested.

It seemed to take forever to reach the entrance of the castle. On the way, Anna was stopped again and again by her people. She knew them all by name and asked small details that she recalled from their lives. Each time, her thoughtfulness was met with an approving nod and, Lark thought, with reverence. A woman—Lia, he heard Anna say— approached holding a babe in her arms. She was crying with happiness, telling Anna that she had named her daughter Brianna, after her mistress. Anna hugged the woman and kissed the child, promising to visit with her later.

Lark finally acknowledged how much she truly cared for her people. And they, in turn, loved her. It was not reverence, it was loyalty. And a complete trust that she would save them all.

In the council room, he caught Anna's eye, and, as the scout reported, Lark saw, for a brief moment, a passing shadow of uncertainty in her eyes. The news was not good. Over two hundred men were moving the mordemurs through the valley with the henge.

• • •

Anna frowned after hearing the report. So little time was left. "Cellach, when we are finished here, see that everyone is safely inside the curtain wall," she ordered. "Then retract the bridge. Dismantle the mill's causeway; we can rebuild it later. Be sure that Carrick supervises."

"These men from Nifolhad will be suspicious when they find both crossings gone," Anna predicted. "They'll move the mordemurs to the southwest, just north of the bridge. Our position is most tenable from that location." She pointed to the map spread on the table. Baldric confirmed her assumption.

"Cellach, describe again how the machines work?" she asked. "I want to know every detail."

"I have gone over the plans a thousand times, m'lady. There is no way to damage them. Even sabotage is impossible," Cellach explained. "All of the workings are underneath, protected by thick planks covered in hammered steel. Once the weapons are assembled, the main body is lowered to the ground. There exists at most two hands of clearance from the ground to the bottom of the side armor."

"Humor me, Cellach. I would like to know exactly what we are up against."

CHAPTER FIFTY-THREE
Cellach Revealed

"What do you think?" Anna asked, as she, Baldric, and the guards studied a map of Aurelia. "Will they try to destroy Stolweg as they did Chevring? Or, do you think they will try to leave the keep intact?"

Lord Baldric rested his chin on steepled fingers to consider her questions. "'Tis the keep they are after. This fortress is too important an asset. No other territory is so strategically placed, save perhaps Whitmarsh. If they can control Stolweg, they can cut off the whole of the west from Godwin's army. We must assume Ragallach to the northwest is under their control. With Chevring gone, only Sterland to the south stands, and Cathmara to the north."

Anna gazed at Lark; he had told her that Sterland was held by his half brother. "Sterland will stand," he asserted, his tone brooking no argument. "They'll not allow this horde to cross to Morland and the southeastern smallholds."

"What say you, Trian?" Baldric asked, for it was Cathmara whence the guard had come.

"My family can ward off Ragallach," Trian affirmed. "Even with the mordemurs, the Nifolhadajans would not stand a chance. Cathmarans have never depended on walls and battlements for safety. The Nifolhadajans would be fools to try my father's hand." The other guards smirked at the mention of Trian's father.

"Trian is the most civilized of his line," Lark explained to Anna. "And the reason his family sent him to King Godwin."

"So, it is to Stolweg they will come," Baldric continued. "They'll do as we suspect, Lady Anna. They'll destroy a portion of the curtain wall to gain access to the castle. We'll place your archers on the battlements."

The rest of the afternoon was spent strategizing. Even with the help of Anna's people, they would be outnumbered four to one. Most of

Roger's soldiers had fled and joined the Nifolhadian ranks. But Cellach had surprised Baldric, and Anna as well, when he called forward the men and women he'd been secretly training. Stolweg's small band of fighters now numbered over seventy strong.

Baldric had just called for a break when a soldier from King Godwin arrived. Mud-splattered from his ride, he delivered more disheartening news: Godwin's army would arrive too late to protect the keep from the weapons.

But no one knew what Anna had refrained from revealing. To save the keep, she intended to destroy the mordemurs. Success depended on the saboteur being small enough to slide under a six-to-eight-inch gap. And she would endanger none but herself. If caught, she could defend herself and, perchance, escape.

If Lark knew, he would never allow her to go. He was barely accepting that she would ride out with Baldric to meet the men from Nifolhad. As the meeting concluded, she worried that the price for her actions would prove too dear. But if she didn't try to save her people from the mordemurs, what future would there be? When Doreen arrived with food, Anna excused herself and headed to the top of the battlements to think through her plan in peace.

• • •

Lark watched Anna leave the council room. On her way out, their eyes met. Something was bothering her. He was about to excuse himself to follow her when the messenger from King Godwin ran back into the room.

The man approached Lord Baldric and Lark. "M'lords, I have a letter for Lady Aubrianne. It's from her sister, Lady Claire."

Lark relieved the messenger of the note and raced out the door. Instinct told him where he would find Anna. Had he been in her place, he would have headed in the same direction. He climbed the stairs three at a time.

• • •

Cellach needed to talk to Lady Aubrianne, and in private. She was not in her chamber, so he returned to the armory. Over the last few weeks, he had finally admitted to himself that he loved her. With the impending conflict as catalyst, he had gathered enough courage to speak his heart. Had she gone to visit the stable or the children? She'd been overly thoughtful when he'd explained the details of his weapon, falling silent near the end of the meeting.

And when the day's council had adjourned, she'd excused herself. His mind struck upon the idea that she was on the battlements. He turned and made his way up the stairs, arriving just in time to see a dark figure grab Lady Aubrianne from behind. Not knowing if she was in danger, he drew his sword. But she didn't react in fear to the man standing so close behind her. To his surprise, she melted into his embrace, for surely that was what it was. In that moment, Cellach realized he was too late. His hand stayed, his sword pulled only midway from its scabbard. Knowing there was no chance to retreat unnoticed, he stepped forward.

· · ·

It had been the unmistakable hiss of metal skimming leather that demanded Lark's attention. He pushed Anna to the side and turned to face the threat, and his heart recognized a rival. Cellach was quick to mask his emotions, but Lark recognized that the man was in love, and with a woman who would never return the sentiment. Anna's heart belonged to Lark.

Cellach coughed nervously, and slid his sword home. "I guess we are both out to protect Lady Aubrianne." His tone was light, but Lark could hear the unspoken regret.

Anna stepped forward. "What brings you here, good friend?" she asked.

"You, my lady. If I could have a moment of your time…"

"Of course," Anna answered. Lark stepped to the wall, but not so far that he could not hear what was being discussed.

"Lady Aubrianne, after this is over, I would like to take my leave of Stolweg. I have family to the southeast that I have not seen in years."

"Take as long as you need, Cellach. If you—"

"I'm sorry, Lady Aubrianne," he interrupted. "I was not clear. I wish to—that is, I do not plan on returning to Stolweg. I will stay until all is organized, and we are sure of your safety and the safety of your people. I'm sorry, but this is something I must do."

Lark gave them a sidelong glance. Anna had taken Cellach's hands in her own. "You need never explain your reasons to me, Cellach," she said. "You've done so much for me already. You once kept me strong when I wanted to die. And you have given me the children, and with them, hope. I would not have made it to this day without you."

"You did it on your own, m'lady," he replied, pulling his hands from hers.

"You know that isn't true, Cellach. After Roger…I needed to feel that I wasn't defenseless. You reminded me of the strength I possess. I will be forever grateful."

Lark winced at that word, *grateful*. It was probably the last word that Cellach wanted to hear. "I hope you'll reconsider," she told her friend, "but if your mind is set, go where your heart leads. We will miss you. I will miss you."

Cellach bowed and bade her good night. Lark walked back with him to the door leading to the stairs. Before stepping through it, Cellach reeled on him, his cheeks ruddy with anger. "I'm holding you accountable for her well-being," he warned. "Her life, and her heart. I wonder, though, if you are man enough to accept her, secure enough to let her do what she will do."

"Of course I accept her," Lark scoffed.

"All of her," Cellach asserted. "She will do things for others. Impossible things. She will not hesitate to sacrifice herself for those she loves." He stared unhappily at Anna as she gazed into the night. "She loves you, that much is clear. But I think in the end, you'll hurt her. You'll hurt her because you are not strong enough for her."

"Stronger than you, I think," Lark growled. "I would not have left her to the abuse of her husband." He regretted his words immediately.

"I'll leave you now. But let me give you one piece of advice, m'lord. Trust her completely, or be prepared to lose her." And with those parting words, Cellach was gone.

Lark returned to Anna, weighing Cellach's admonition. When she looked at him, there were tears in her eyes. "I will miss him terribly, Lark." Lark heard the pain of loss in her words. "Still, I suppose it is for the best, knowing how he feels about me."

Lark had thought Anna unaware of Cellach's regard. "How *does* he feel about you, Anna?"

"He holds so much guilt in his heart," she said. "When we sparred in the hills and woods, I would see fleeting looks of pain in his face. He has never forgiven himself for not protecting me from Roger. I refused his aid over and over. In my heart, I always knew that he would want to leave Stolweg one day. That is why I did not try harder to persuade him to remain."

Lark put his arm around her and pulled her closer to his side. "Argh, I'm such a fool," he cried, "I came to find you and completely forgot the reason why." He reached into his tunic and extracted the letter. "Anna, it's a message. From your sister!"

"She's alive," Anna breathed. She tore open the seal and scanned the letter. Then she read it again, this time aloud.

> *Dearest Sister Anna,*
>
> *I have just received word that you are alive and in the best of hands, with one of the King's most trusted guards.*
>
> *I am well but cannot yet speak of my grief over the loss of Mother, Father, and our people. I will honor them by remaining strong. I know you are doing the same and would not have me do otherwise. I have always tried to be like you, and hope, in at least this, that Mother and Father would be proud.*
>
> *Anna, Mother returned to be with Father. Their love was so great that she could not bear him standing alone against the men who had threatened us every day.*
>
> *The messenger waits as I write. I have heard that King Godwin's army is amarch. My faith is such that I know we will survive the coming trials to meet again. I cannot explain whence this knowledge comes, I only know it to be true. Perhaps it is my faith in you.*
>
> > *Yours in love and hope,*
> > *Claire*
>
> *Post Scriptum: By now you know of Chevring's destruction. I was not the only survivor, dear sister, a small consolation to be sure. Pieter is with me.*

Unable to contain her happiness, Anna spun around the open battlement, arms outstretched in sheer joy. Her prayers had been answered. She was smiling, and growing dizzy. She crashed into Lark's chest in one last twirl. He held her tightly while she caught her breath and balance, and his deep laughter at her happiness sounded like a dream.

The wind had picked up, and when they felt the first few splats of rain, they ignored the weather until it grew stronger, forcing them to race foolishly back to the dark alcove. Lark reached for her, and she gave herself up to his embrace, savoring her joy.

• • •

Later, alone in her chamber, Anna went over what she would need to do the next day. Her plan depended on the Nifolhadajans' ignorance of

Roger's death. They would first see that the bridge had been drawn back and then move to the mill's causeway, by now dismantled.

Thereafter, they would give in to their suspicions, and the situation would escalate. Anna and Baldric had already decided that the best way to gain time would be to ignore them. As a precaution, their captain would be sure to order the mordemurs constructed and put in place. Cellach had assured Anna that it would take at least eight hours to ready the weapons. With luck, the task wouldn't be completed until late in the evening. Sure to be overconfident, the force from Nifolhad would rest before beginning the barrage the next morning.

She was tired and rested her head against the back of the couch, basking in the warmth of the fire. Before long, she drifted off to sleep, only to wake and find Lark kneeling over her. He was frowning at her.

"You didn't hear me enter," he pointed out.

"I may need to adjust the hinges on my door again," she replied, her eyes twinkling. But his face was serious. "Lark, I didn't intend to fall asleep. I just nodded off for a moment."

"Promise me you'll take more care."

"You have my word," she told him.

He sat next to her and took her in his arms. His voice was barely audible as he whispered, "I couldn't survive if I lost you. You take so many risks. Today, in the courtyard, you were surrounded by so many people. Any one of them could have been loyal to Roger."

Anna pushed him back from her. "Look under the cushion, Lark," she ordered. "Go ahead, look." He did, and found her dagger hidden there. "Gilles, Carrick, and the others, they were with me in the courtyard. I was aware of the danger, but what would you have had me do?"

"Stay in your chamber with the door barred whenever we are forced to part," he suggested. "If I could, I would lock you away where no danger could find you." Anna could see he meant every word even though she knew the reasonable part of his brain was telling him it was a foolish wish. "Why are you smiling at me, Anna?"

"I would accept such a cage, but only if you were locked away with me. And that can never be, can it?" She took his hand in hers. "Lark, there will always be risks. And danger. I will always put those I love ahead of myself if it means that I can save them. That includes you," she added when his eyes darkened. "If it meant saving your life, I would throw myself—"

"Stop, Anna. I already know it to be true. I do not need to hear it spoken."

Anna sighed, knowing the next evening would test Lark's love for her. She turned away lest he see some hint of her plans.

"Forgive me," he conceded. "I only want to protect you from all that is evil in this world."

"We should stop talking about this," she cautioned, "at least until this current threat is over."

For the first time in their reckless affaire de cœur, they could not share their thoughts, and held back speaking that which they wanted most to say. Anna did not want the night to end in such a manner. Her heart ached that it should.

"I don't know what will happen in the next few days," Lark said, "but I—"

Anna stopped him by putting her fingers to his lips. "For tonight, can we forget tomorrow?" She didn't want to hear his words, that he would protect her, save her even. And she didn't want him involved in her scheme. There was nothing he could do to help, and his presence would put them in more danger. More likely, she reasoned, he would stop her from going.

By way of answer, Lark hugged her close to his chest and held her for a long time. They reclined near the fire. "Lark," she said. "Do you think there is enough time for *later?*"

"The nice thing about *later* is that there is always time," he answered. Her fears and uncertainties were erased as they fell into each other.

CHAPTER FIFTY-FOUR

Mordemurs

It was late in the evening when Anna was finally free to return to her chamber. The day had gone as they predicted. At midday, word was brought that the Nifolhadajans had made the rise overlooking the Stolweg basin. Unfortunately, after discovering the retracted bridge and the mill's dismantled causeway, they wasted no time assembling the mordemurs. With nightfall, their construction was complete. They were now celebrating across the river. No one came to the keep's gate. No one requested an audience with Lord Roger. As careful as Baldric and the Guards had been in securing those loyal to Anna's late husband, someone must have slipped through their net. The only logical conclusion as to why the Nifolhadajans had constructed the mordemurs was that they were cognizant of Roger's demise.

Anna and Lark had just arrived at her chamber's entrance when Trian hastened to them. "Ah, Lark, I was sent to find you. Baldric has called another meeting," he explained.

Anna turned to go back to the council room. "My pardon, m'lady, but you are not required to attend this council. We'll be discussing how best to protect Whitmarsh. Baldric wants a plan in place to destroy the weapons if they move to his castle. He awaits us now."

"Of course," Lark said. "I'll just make sure Lady Anna's quarters are secure."

Fortune was smiling upon her, Anna thought. She wouldn't have to make an excuse to Lark in order to retire early. In fact, she'd probably return before his meeting was even concluded. She waited patiently in the corridor while Lark entered her room.

"Go," she urged him when he gazed at her with regret. "Baldric is waiting for you. There's always later." Much later, she hoped, knowing how thorough Baldric could be.

She closed her door as he walked away, quickly changed into dark breeches and tunic, and then, after belting on her dagger, she raced to the tapestry. She was through the narrow passageway to the west chamber in record time and dropped into the secret tunnel that would take her to the chapel. Will's assistance had already been enlisted that afternoon, and it was imperative that she arrive before him.

Anna had just reached the altar when Will entered. "Any trouble getting here?" she asked.

"Only a little, my lady, most everyone is in the great hall where Cellach is giving them last-minute instructions." He looked at her with concern. "Lady Anna, what is this about?"

She outlined her plan, explaining that there was only enough clearance under the machines for someone slight. Before Will could volunteer, she raised her hand to arrest his offer. "I won't put any but myself in danger." He didn't look convinced. "Nothing will go wrong," she assured him.

"Then why tell me, m'lady? Why not just go with none the wiser?"

"I don't expect trouble. But just in case, I need you to tell the others what I tried to accomplish. Do you trust me, Will?"

"You know I do, my lady. I just don't like this. How are you going to make it across the river unseen?" Anna moved behind the altar and pushed the carved rosette that opened the panel.

"Lady Anna!" Will gasped. "What is that?"

"It's a tunnel, Will. It goes under the river and comes out in the crypt." She put her hands on his shoulders. "I need you to remain here until I return. If I'm not back in two hours, find Cellach and tell him where I have gone. And, Will, wait near the chapel's entrance. If the enemy should find this tunnel before I return, I'm counting on you to raise the alarm."

"Are you sure you have to do this, m'lady?" he asked.

"Yes," she replied. "I'll be fine, I promise."

She stopped and turned back to him. "Should anything happen to me, though, tell Lark—"

"I won't have to tell him anything, m'lady. You'll be fine. You promised."

Anna grabbed her lantern and ducked into the hole. Racing through the passageway, she ran over in her mind what Cellach had told her of the weapon's workings. The mordemur's throwing mechanism depended on the thick rope cables to give tension to the throwing arm and counterweight. A person could sabotage the weapons only by squeezing under the machine, a gap of less than two hands. Once there, a simple matter of slicing the main cable centered underneath the platform would do the trick. If the rope were not cut all the way through, the weapon would appear to be in working order, at least until the firing mechanism was thrown. The swinging arm would produce too much tension for the damaged cable, and the line would snap well before any payload could be released. If fortune favored Stolweg, the projectiles would crash down into the weapons, demolishing them.

She reached the tunnel's egress, turned off the lamp, and entered the crypt, leaving the secret door open by a tiny gap. If she had to run, she didn't want to waste time searching for the release button in the dark.

She strained her ears for sounds of the enemy outside, thinking her way clear, when the distinct rattle of the iron gate rang through the stone room. From where she had ducked behind the nearest crypt, she could make out the shape of a man. He must have seen the broken lock and seized the opportunity to loot the crypt. The unmistakable sound of the man's water as he relieved himself echoed inside the sacred room. Crouching lower in the shadows, Anna cringed as the pommel of her dagger scraped across the surface of a tomb.

"Who's there?" the soldier called out.

Anna remained silent. The soft steps of his boots betrayed his approach. On hands and knees, she crawled farther away. His sword whispered to her as it was pulled from its sheath.

"Show yourself, and I might spare you," he whispered. Anna felt something under her fingers, a pebble on the cold floor.

She could hear his apprehension and silently drew her blade before tossing the pebble in the opposite direction. The sound of the soldier's boots scraping the cracked stone floor told her that he'd turned to investigate. She came around the tomb and observed him in the dark crypt. She had an advantage over him. Her eyes had had more time to adjust to the limited light.

He was perhaps five feet away, his back turned, his sword held out in front of him. Silently, she stalked him from behind, her blade poised to strike. She took his measure and in an instant was able to determine the best angle of attack. Memories of hand-to-hand combat flooded her mind even as she reached both hands to encircle his face and neck. Her free hand drew his forehead sharply back while her dagger hand sliced across the tender flesh of his exposed throat.

A gush of blood flowed over her arm, and she stood back, her mind numb to the ruthless act she'd just committed. He reeled on her, trying to find the one who had taken his life. His eyes met hers for the briefest moment, then went blank. He died before he hit the floor.

Working quickly, Anna removed his uniform. Her mission would be that much easier if she were disguised as one of the enemy. The tunic was still warm and soaking from his blood. She secured his sword and belt around her waist before dragging the still-warm body into the passageway. Lastly, she donned his leather helmet, and then stepped out into the cool night, ready to tackle the sabotage of the mordemurs.

The Nifolhadajans were overconfident and not expecting trouble. Those not sleeping were well into their cups. There wasn't even a sentry posted near the machines.

Anna slipped through the graveyard and walked to the first machine, trying as best she could to saunter like a man, acting like she belonged there. She noted that the closest soldiers were to her right, some thirty paces beyond the last machine.

She walked to the front of the mordemur, dropped to her knees, then crawled to its far side. Flat on her back on the trampled grass, Anna wormed her way under the gap. There was not much clearance under the mordemur, and absolutely no light.

With Cellach's drawing fixed in her mind, she shimmied to the center of the great wagon. Her eyes tried to compensate for the blackness around her and could not. Reaching up with her hands, she found a tangle of ropes and strained to see which was which.

No, she thought, this was not working. She closed her eyes to shut off the useless sense. Relying only on the memories of Cellach's design, she once again reached up, and this time found the correct cable to slice. Back and forth her dagger sawed at the thickly braided ropes, her fingers gauging what remained. The cords had been plaited of nine strands of thick hemp. With only two of the nine left to be cut, Anna slowed her sawing. She nicked one. The other she left intact to break on its own under the tremendous pull of the counterweight.

One machine down, nine to go. The Nifolhadajans had foolishly placed the weapons in a straight row, a mere ten paces from one to the next. Anna rolled to her stomach and crawled to the next machine to repeat the process.

She was filthy from the grass, dirt, and horse manure. Somewhere along the way, her hand landed in something the consistency of mud. Only it wasn't. The stench was fetid, and human. These Nifolhadajans were disgusting, she thought, wiping her hand on the uniform she wore.

After redoubling her efforts, the sabotage of the second weapon was finally complete. She crawled along the front of each mordemur, hastening to make it back to the chapel before Will alerted the others. Eight, seven, six. Still no soldiers within the immediate area. Five, four, three. Then, voices!

She shimmied under the second-to-last mordemur, completed her work, and continued on to the final weapon. The two voices floated above the rush of the river, the night sounds of crickets and frogs, and the far-off conversations near the campfires. They were at the far end of the waiting machines. As Anna wormed her way back, she could make out what they were saying.

"Where is that young whelp? He left the weapons unguarded."

The other man chortled, his speech slurred from too much drink. "Well, you're late to relieve him. Mebbe he's off looking for you."

"Or to find some drink for himself," the first soldier guessed. They had come closer, and were standing in front of the machine under which she was concealed.

"If thatsh the case, I think I'll follow young John's lead. I'll bring shumthing back for you."

"You'll be sorry if you don't! And if you see him, drag his lazy arse back here. His lordship will have us whipped if he finds out the weapons were left unattended."

The feet of the drunken soldier staggered back to the campfires. The first soldier stood still for a moment. She watched perplexed as he shifted from foot to foot in a little dance, and she rolled away just before her face was splashed with urine. *Animals.* She cursed silently. The watchman continued his slow circuit of the machines before halting again at the first.

Her deadline weighed upon her. If she was to stop Will from raising the alarm, she needed to move. After a moment that seemed to stretch forever, the guard resumed his tour. She waited for him to reach the machine at the very end and step out of view to make his slow circuit around it. Then she edged out toward the opposite direction. The slope to the river was only steps from where she crouched. If she could make it there, she could continue crawling unseen for at least another twenty paces.

A thick mist rose from the shallow marsh near the river. Anna finally stood and, despite her instinct to run, walked with a casual gait to the graveyard. Twenty paces left. She heard a shout behind her.

"You there, John. Halt!"

• • •

Will reckoned that two hours had passed; he'd kept his promise. He raced from the chapel and found his father and mother speaking with Cellach. As quickly as possible, he explained the circumstances. They raced back to the chapel. Doreen went to find Grainne.

• • •

The meeting with Baldric had concluded, and Trian and Tomas exited the keep in time to notice the dash across the courtyard. "Tomas, find Baldric and the others," Trian ordered. "Send them to the chapel." Tomas did not have long to search, for he found Baldric, Warin, and Ailwen on their way to their rooms. He described what he and Trian had witnessed. They too made haste to the chapel.

• • •

Lark had been the first to leave the council room, so great was his need to check on Anna. When he reached her chamber, he knocked. She did not answer, so he opened the door.

"Anna?" he whispered, and was answered with silence. Her bed was yet untouched. Far from worried, Lark imagined that she'd gone to check on the children. He went looking for her, and discovered Doreen at Grainne's door. The two women were upset and fretting over something. Or someone.

"Where is Anna?" he demanded at once.

"She was in the chapel," Grainne answered nervously.

Lark loomed menacingly over them. "What has she done?"

"We don't know exactly. Will said something about sabotaging the mordemurs. She—" Lark did not wait to hear the rest.

• • •

The uniform Anna wore was now stiff and crusted with blood, dirt, and God only knew what else. She could smell the grime on her face and see it on her hands. Almost to the safety of the crypt, she forced herself not to run. Only twenty paces more and she would be in the graveyard. She ignored the first call.

"Ho, John." This time she halted, afraid to cause suspicion. "I want a word with you. Now!"

It was the soldier who had been guarding the machines. If she ran, she could make it to the secret passage. But doing so would raise the alarm. On the other hand, he thought that she was just another soldier.

He called out again, and from the corner of her eye, Anna saw him coming in her direction. But his drunken friend had returned with a fresh supply of whatever they had been drinking. "I see you found him. Did you clout him for leaving his post?"

"Not yet," the other answered. "John, if I have to come and get you, you'll regret it." John must be the name of the soldier that she had killed. She looked down at the dried blood on her hands. He had a name, and possibly a family, too. Her bile rose first, then her stomach tightened. She doubled over to retch. The two men stopped in their tracks and burst out laughing.

"These young pups, they can't hold their drink. Go on, John. Go relieve yourself where we'll not trod upon it," the night guard called.

"Since he's had enough t'drink a'ready, we'll just share his portion. Come on, I'm thirsty. Thish night is too long," the other soldier slurred, and they moved away.

Anna hurried to the graveyard, her hand covering her mouth. Once inside the shelter of the crypt, she hurried into the passageway and, in her rush, tripped on the dead body. Her foot came down on the lantern, kicking it against the stone wall where its thin horn panels shattered and its flame guttered out. She had no choice but to pull the heavy door shut, closing herself in the tunnel with the dead man. The murky darkness groped at her as if it were alive. Terrified, she fought her rising panic and stifled a scream. Closing her eyes against the void ahead, she heard a voice in her head. "Breathe, Anna, breathe." They were Lark's words, soothing her, as he'd done before.

• • •

Lark entered the chapel and crossed the great expanse to Cellach and Gilles. Both were yelling at Will, demanding to know exactly how long Anna had been gone. Why weren't they headed to the gate to bring her back? He skewered Will with his glare, but the young man held firm.

"I swore an oath to Lady Anna. She didn't want to endanger anyone else. I even offered to go in her stead, but she wouldn't have it. She promised to return in two hours' time."

Lark had had enough. "Where did she go, Will?" He followed Will's gaze to a dark opening at the base of the altar. Shoving Cellach and Gilles aside, Lark hissed, "Where does this lead?"

Will lifted his chin in challenge. "To the crypt on the other side of the river. It's not more than fifty or so yards from there to the first mordemur."

"But, Will," Cellach asked, "what in God's name does she think she can do? There is no way to sabotage the weapons. Every cable and ratchet is protected."

"You told her yourself, Cellach. There's naught but a gap of two hands' width from the ground to the bottom of the canopy."

Baldric moved forward. "Impossible for a man to access the underbelly," he stated.

"Pardon me, my lord," Grainne interrupted, having just arrived, "a man may not fit. But a woman, an especially slender woman, could."

"How long has it been since she left?" Lark demanded.

"She should have been back by now," Will worried.

• • •

"You know the way," Anna whispered to herself. "The tunnel is straight. Just keep your eyes shut until you feel the incline. You'll see the candles from the chapel once you start the climb." She unsheathed the soldier's sword—John's sword—and used its tip as a guide along one wall, her outstretched arm along the other. Inching her toe forward to find the corpse, she stepped over it. Then she began walking, slowly at first, then faster to distance herself from the dead man. When the tunnel finally leveled, Anna's foot came down hard, and she stumbled forward, caught herself, and moved with even greater haste.

The change in slope was so gradual she barely registered it. When she did, she opened her eyes to pitch black. Had her egress been sealed?

Of course not, she remembered, for there would be no light until she climbed the stone ladder. She reached out with her hand to find its wooden rails. After scrambling up, her eyes detected a faint glow. All that remained was to crawl under the altar and out the hidden exit into the warmth of the candles. With her sword hand leading, she reached the opening.

• • •

They all saw the tip of the sword as it came out of the secret entrance. Its design was clearly the work of Nifolhad. When the helmeted head of a soldier poked out of the tunnel, Lark grabbed him by the scruff of his neck. He was immediately aware that the man's uniform was covered in blood. Lark drew his knife with one hand while the other clamped around the soldier's neck, pinning him against the altar.

"Where is she? Tell me now, and I'll make your death quick."

Hands were grabbing him, and a few words cut through his fury. "Lady Anna…let her go!"

Through the red haze of his rage, Lark fixed his eyes on the person closest to him, Will. The young man's lips formed the words, "It's her!"

Lark stared at the soldier's hands struggling to break the choking grip. Dread settled in his stomach as he discovered that they were not those of a man. They were infinitely more delicate. He dropped his knife and released her neck at the same time. He pulled the helmet off, and a mass of tangled curls fell around the smudged face. "Anna!"

He could do nothing but support her while she choked, attempting to fill her lungs. "What have you done, Anna?" he yelled. "You're covered in blood—are you injured?"

She still had not looked at him. Her head hung down with her hair covering her face. "Not my blood," she managed to croak.

Hearing her cracked voice, his anger returned. "Damn it, Anna. I almost snapped your neck just now." He could not bear knowing he'd come so close to killing her. When her identity had been revealed, his knife had already pierced her tunic and was poised to stab her heart even as his fingers squeezed her throat.

She lifted her head. The fear in her eyes froze Lark to his soul. He'd been the cause of this terror. She would never see him the same way again. He saw the angry red welts on her neck. Averting his gaze from everyone else, Lark turned from Anna and left the chapel in long strides. Behind him, he heard her trying to call out his name. But his mind was reeling from what he had almost committed; he did not have the courage to face her.

• • •

At her feet lay his dagger. Grainne rushed to Anna's side, and ordered her to sit so she could examine her. Anna protested, insisting she wasn't injured.

"Not injured!" Grainne shot back angrily. "Have you seen yourself?"

The others were gaping at her. "It's not my blood," she told them. After no one spoke, she shouted, "It is not my blood!"

Baldric raised his eyebrows. She could tell he was angry, but he held it in check. He was a practical man, and she knew he wanted to know if she'd been successful.

Before he could ask, she gave him the answer he sought. "All ten machines, Baldric."

"We'll meet in the council room in one hour," he announced. "I want details. Grainne, will that give you enough time to assist your lady?" He looked at Anna ruefully. "Perhaps an hour and a half would be better. You smell horrible, Lady Anna."

Astounded into silence, Anna finally took note of her clothing. She was covered in every vile substance imaginable. Blood from the soldier, her own sweat and bile, urine from the guard who had almost discovered her, mud, grass, and something else she refused to put a name to.

Baldric managed a tight smile. "Trian will escort you back to your chamber." She knew he wanted to say more, perhaps assure her that Lark would come to his senses. But he said nothing and strode to the chapel doors. Tomas and Warin followed.

Anna collected Lark's dagger from the floor. Trian had moved forward to retrieve it, but her words stopped him cold. "I'll return the knife myself, Trian. No one else."

CHAPTER FIFTY-FIVE

Consequences

Lark stalked up the stairs to the battlements. The men posted there gave him a wide berth. He stared out at the enemy, and his anger at Anna grew. He was furious that she'd been so reckless. He felt a steadying hand on his shoulder and knew it was Baldric.

"You have a choice, my young friend," Baldric counseled. "You can forgive Anna and move forward, or you can lose the most important person in your life."

"I have forgiven her, Baldric," he muttered and hung his head. "I can't forgive myself." Lark looked down at the waiting mordemurs. "Did she reach them all?"

"Every last one. We're to meet in the council room to debrief." Baldric's brow was creased with worry. "She cannot help what fate has handed her, Lark."

"Just because she's been trained to be a warrior doesn't mean she has to be one."

"What you don't understand, Lark, is that she is not the way she is because of her training. And unless you find a way to come to terms with this simple fact, I fear that you'll never have a chance with her."

Baldric started to turn away, then stopped. "I do not think Lady Anna would want you to blame yourself, Lark. You couldn't have known it was her. We all thought she was a soldier from Nifolhad. Even I didn't suspect otherwise, not until I heard Grainne."

"You didn't see her eyes when she looked at me, Baldric," Lark said, allowing some of his anguish free. "There was so much fear."

"I may not have seen her eyes at that moment, Lark, but I saw them as you strode away. Her sorrow then was from knowing that she had put you in an impossible situation. You may be unable to imagine it, but right now, she needs you to forgive her *and* yourself," Baldric added. He turned, leaving Lark to his thoughts.

Anna's door opened, and a brigade of bucket carriers entered. Grainne caught her wry expression and backed away. "You really do reek, m'lady."

When the bath was full, everyone but Grainne departed. She helped Anna to strip out of the spoiled uniform and then out of her own clothes. Anna stepped gingerly into the hot bath, then sat and submerged her head. She came up for air and noticed that Grainne seemed to have something on her mind.

"Out with it, Grainne," she ordered as she scrubbed her face and neck.

"Well, m'lady, I don't know what you had to do to accomplish your deed"—she paused to inspect the bloody uniform in a heap on the floor—"but I have an idea."

"Do you?" Anna asked, allowing her temper to flare as she finished washing away the muck and gore from her skin and hair.

"Aye, m'lady," Grainne countered with equal fire. "And don't you worry, I'll get over being mad at you for not trusting me. But I only want to say one thing. If no one else tells you but me, you have to know this: we thank you. You were reckless. And, with all due respect, foolish. But so very brave. You probably saved us all."

"Oh," was all that Anna could think to say. She stepped from the tub, and Grainne wrapped a thick rug around her as they walked to the couch.

"Here, m'lady," Grainne offered, her tone conciliatory. "I've made you some tea."

Anna took the cup from her friend. "Perhaps we are destined to save each other, Grainne."

"That we are, m'lady," she agreed. "That we are."

• • •

Once all were assembled in the hall, Baldric wasted no time getting things started. Anna was asked to relate her story. She did so, sparing little detail.

"So you were able to sabotage the machines without being noticed," Baldric finished.

"Not quite," Anna admitted. "I was noticed." Baldric's men shifted uneasily in their seats. "They thought I was one of their own. A soldier named John." Anna quickly walked them through what came next. How the two soldiers thought she, or rather John, was sick from drinking. She was able to make it back to the crypt unimpeded.

"What happens when this *John* informs the others that it was not he they saw?" Baldric asked.

"He won't," she told him, looking him straight in the eye.

"Lord Baldric," Cellach interjected. "It has been a difficult night for Lady Aubrianne. I believe she has answered all of your questions. Perhaps tomorrow—"

"How does the entrance to the passage open?" Lark interrupted, speaking to her for the first time, but focusing on a point just beyond her. "I returned to the chapel, and there is no sign that the entrance exists now that it is closed. The ability to cross the river unseen could serve us well in the coming days."

"There is a release on the first step behind the altar," she answered as if by rote. "Hidden within the carvings on the riser, you'll find a rosette different from the others. In its center is a rectangle with two wavy lines underneath: the river and the crypt. Press the rosette to open the panel."

Cellach was first to rise, and he pulled out her chair as she rose from her seat. Lark stood and bowed to Lord Baldric. He hastened from the room, not sparing so much as a glance her way. Baldric walked over to her. The worry in his eyes matched that which she felt in her heart. Anna had broken more than the mordemurs this night.

• • •

Atop the battlements, Lark waited. He was sure that Anna would meet him here. There was much he wanted to say to her, starting with the remorse he felt for his actions. But then fear had wormed its way into his heart. He felt crippled by it. And that made him angry all over again.

When she had walked into the council room, he saw the bruises on her neck and wanted to howl. Well, Lark decided, he was through with waiting. He pulled open the door that would take him back into the castle.

He might have missed her if not for turning one last time to see the night sky. She must have come from the opposite direction, for there she stood, in the center of the tower's roof, searching for him. He went to her.

• • •

Though Anna stood next to the man to whom she had given her heart, she felt completely alone. They were more alike than he would ever guess. Both could be lethal if required. She gasped then, and felt Lark tense.

Her darker side shocked her, and Anna discovered that rather than despising this newfound power, her mind embraced it for its strength. She was no longer just a predetermined ideal in someone else's eyes—not in her mother's, nor Roger's, and no, not even in Lark's eyes. She could no more apologize to Lark any more than she could rewrite the past three years.

If they were to have any future together, Anna determined, he would have to be the one to come to terms with her actions. Because if given a second chance, even knowing that she could lose him, she would choose again to save her people.

She straightened her shoulders and lifted her chin. "It's who I am, Lark," she stated, her voice still hoarse from his choking hold. "There was no other way." Then she repeated more to herself than to him, "*It is who I am.*"

Lark continued to stare out at the enemy. She set his dagger on the battlement's merlon and spoke. "In the chapel, I was not afraid of you, Lark. I was afraid of who I had become."

"And who is that?" he finally asked, and it seemed to Anna that this was the one question for which he truly wanted an answer.

"I'm Anna. The woman who has always loved you. I am the people of Stolweg and Chevring—their protector, their guide, their friend. And, I am you: a person who is willing to do anything to protect those he or she loves, even if it means killing another without thought or hesitation. I am Anna, Lark. I am not ashamed of who I am, just as you are not ashamed of who you are."

She'd said her piece and turned to walk away. Reaching to open the door, she heard Lark's voice, and she stopped.

"You already said that you weren't injured, but are you all right?" he asked.

She pondered his question. She thought once more about the soldier she'd slain. "No, Lark," she admitted. "But I will be." Before anything else could be said, she left. She would put aside thinking about Lark until later.

Later. Anna's heart cramped remembering the word they had used in play so oft before. Tomorrow was going to be a grueling day, and she had much to accomplish before the morn. If she were lucky, she might find an hour's sleep.

CHAPTER FIFTY-SIX

Terms

Grainne woke earlier than usual the next morning. Climbing the stairs from the kitchen, she passed one of the windows. The leaden sky of the night before had yet to release its hold over the countryside. *No rain*, she thought. The low clouds were perfect for mourning; she only hoped the coming losses would not include her friends.

When she entered Lady Anna's chamber, Grainne wasn't surprised to find her mistress awake, dressed and meticulously coiffed. She must have taken great pains to secure every tress, Grainne mused; not a single strand dared escape its tight braid.

There was a keenness in Lady Anna's gaze, as if she possessed the same restless energy that Grainne had noticed in the guards. Grainne longed for the raucous noise of the children and the merry company of Baldric. And the chamber lacked one other important guest: Lark.

"Grainne, I need your help." Her mistress opened the largest of her trunks.

"Surely it is too cool for your summer gowns, m'lady," Grainne observed. "Do you wish to change?"

"No, Grainne. I'll wear this today. But I require some accessories."

"Then let's get started," Grainne advised. "The sun's rising, and they'll want you in the courtyard presently. What do you need me to do?"

Her lady removed the contents of the trunk, handing over the folded gowns one at a time. Grainne peered into the empty chest. Then Lady Anna pulled on a small leather strap hidden in the trunk's depths, and Grainne gasped when a false bottom lifted.

Lady Anna gave her an engaging grin. "It's time you learned a little more about me, Grainne, and the line of women from whom I come." Grainne stared with unbridled interest over the edge of the trunk. With reverence, her lady carried the first bundle to her bed.

• • •

Anna stood back, allowing her friend to admire the array of weapons and armor spread before them, each piece precisely sized for a woman. She instructed Grainne on how to attach cuisse and greave, pauldron and vambrace, until all that was left was the breastplate.

Grainne lifted the light piece, set with silver stars and lapis lazuli, to Anna's chest. But her maid was at a loss as to how to attach the armor and fumbled with the ties and buckles. There was a light rap on the door, and Grainne bade whoever it was to enter. She pinched her finger and let out an oath just as Cellach walked in, already suited up.

Anna expected to see surprise on his face. Instead, he regarded her proudly, as if he knew she possessed such treasure all along. She threw him a pleading look, and he quickly took over.

"Look here," he pointed out to Grainne. "You have the backplate upside down. No wonder you could not match the ties." Cellach made quick work of the last few straps. He stood back so that Anna could secure her dagger and sword belt around her waist.

Finally, she slung her bow and quiver over her shoulder and secured her shield over them. She picked up her helmet and held it under her arm. Cellach nodded his approval.

"Shall we go, then?" Anna prompted when her friends could do naught but stare at her. Cellach led the procession, with Grainne bringing up the rear. As they walked through the keep, she kept thoughts of Lark at bay.

"Baldric and the guards are mounted, Lady Anna, and are waiting near the fountain," Cellach provided. "Gilles has Tullian ready for you." They took the back route to the stable, avoiding the crowds of the courtyard.

"Good morning, m'lady," Will greeted, then whistled when saw her armor. "Let me get Tully." When he returned, holding Tullian's lead, he walked to the center of the stable. Anna's eyes fell upon her steed. For a moment, she didn't breathe. Tullian was completely barded, muzzle to tail, in the most beautiful equine plating she'd ever beheld.

"Oh, Tullian, you look magnificent! Who did this?" she exclaimed to her friends. They nodded at Cellach. "Of course it was you," she said, clasping his hand and holding it tightly in hers. "Thank you, my friend."

"Will, a hand up for your lady, please," Cellach ordered. So she placed her foot in Will's laced fingers and, with a bounce, was vaulted into the saddle. Grainne held up her helmet, and Anna waited while

Cellach mounted. He led the way to the courtyard. Tullian, sensing her excitement, lifted his legs high and pranced his way behind.

• • •

The courtyard was crowded with worried onlookers. Their attention was focused on Baldric and his guards, each suited in armor, their deadly weapons glistening. Then Baldric spotted Cellach, noting how the crowd opened a lane for him. They bowed low in respect as if he were Lord of Stolweg. Why should the arms master garner such deference? From his vantage, he could not see Anna riding behind. But then Baldric saw Lark glower, and finally, his own gaze fell upon her.

She had focused her eyes straight ahead and held her chin high, her shoulders back, and her chest thrown out. Cellach moved his horse to the left and stopped in front of Lark. Lady Anna's Tullian was dancing now, flipping his head up and down, his hooves pounding the ground. She drew up to Cellach's right. Lord Baldric studied her before offering a good morning. He'd expected that she would be outfitted in such armor. And he couldn't help thinking she looked more like a queen than a lady. He tilted his head in salute.

"You're late, Lady Anna. But you more than made up for it with your entrance," Lord Baldric half joked. He turned and nodded to Warin, who signaled the soldiers at the gatehouse. A flag was raised to let the enemy know they were riding out to discuss terms. With Baldric leading, and Lark and Trian riding on either side of him, their group rode out the main gate.

• • •

The bridge had been extended for the rendezvous; six riders waited on the other side. Lord Baldric came to a stop ten paces away.

The riders from Nifolhad regarded Baldric and Anna with interest. Finally, their leader spoke. "I am Lord Phelan. You must be Lord Baldric of Whitmarsh." He turned his attention next to Anna, and then grinned wolfishly at his men. "My friends and lords," he announced, "we are honored by none other than Lady Aubrianne of Stolweg. And, I suppose, the Lady of Chevring as well. Tell your husband he does you an injustice in his description," Phelan admitted, as if trying to garner her favor. "And speaking of Lord Roger, why is he not here to welcome us?"

Lark's eyes came to rest on the man to Lord Phelan's right. He wore a full beard, and unlike the others, his head was helmeted. He slouched in his saddle as if he were bored by the entire affair, a sneer on his face. It was an expression that Lark had oft worn himself. This one would bear watching, he determined.

"Your hospitality is lacking, my lady," Phelan accused when no one answered his question. "Why did you draw back your bridge and ignore my captain? Once again, where is Lord Roger?"

"My husband has had a sudden change of heart," Anna replied. "He is…resting."

The helmeted lord lifted his head at her response, and Lark was struck by her reaction to the man. She focused in on him, taking in his lazy moves as he leaned forward to whisper to Phelan.

Lord Phelan dropped all pretenses of courtesy. "Resting? I see," he spat at Anna.

"But I do not," she bit back. "Why are you on my land? You claim to have come here to speak with my husband. You talk of hospitality. What type of guest are you that you assemble your strange weapons and align them in what can only be construed as a threat?" Tullian shifted aggressively as she spoke.

"Return to Nifolhad before you start something that will only end in your demise," she warned. "Leave Stolweg. Leave this realm. Tell the poser-king Diarmait that you have no business here."

Lark could see Phelan's anger rise. "Such strong words from a mere woman. What do you say, Lord Baldric?" he sneered. "Come, let us discuss the terms of your surrender, man to man. Are women allowed such headway in Aurelia?"

"I am of a like mind," Baldric replied pleasantly. "I would only speak as she."

Phelan turned his disgust on Anna. "You should be more polite, Lady—"

"Polite?" she shouted back. "Lessons on manners from a filthy group of murderers! You had best take my advice, Phelan." Tullian stomped excitedly.

The man next to Phelan mumbled something to his friends. Whatever was said caused a burst of raucous laughter among them. Lark calmed Rabbit as his own horse picked up on Tullian's agitation and inched forward. He heard the dangerous tone in Anna's voice as she demanded to know what they found so amusing.

Phelan leered at her before answering. "My friend was merely pointing out that Lord Roger's little Lady Aubrianne is not so broken after all."

Lark, more than anyone, realized the meaning behind the words. He started forward but was too late. Anna beat him to the punch. He caught a glimpse of her before she spurred to action. There was no shocked expression from a woman maligned. Rather, her visage was cold and calculating. And despite the hard set of her face, he noted a touch of glee in her eyes as she signaled her destrier to do what he was born to do.

Tullian charged forward. As her horse closed the gap to the bearded lord, her great steed lifted his knees and chest and rammed the offending man's horse full on. Struck hard by Tullian, the other horse's hind legs buckled, and its body lifted with the impact. The rider, no longer bored, managed to jump free of his saddle but flew through the air and landed with a terrific thud on his back. His helmet was knocked askew.

Before swords could be drawn, shouts of "Hold!" were called out from both sides. But Anna was not finished. There was absolutely nothing Lark could do to stop her as she walked a calmer but still deadly Tullian over to the man on the ground. The man moved to lift his sword but was prevented from doing so when Tully's hoof landed solidly on the blade and imprisoned it in its sheath.

"You dare pull your sword under a flag of truce," Anna hissed. "We already know you to be rude and dishonorable. But we didn't expect a lord of Nifolhad to be so unbelievably ignorant. Go home, you fool. Have your mother teach you better manners."

"You attacked me first, you bitch!" he shouted.

"Tsk, tsk. Such language," Anna chided him. "But you're wrong. Your vile tongue struck the first blow."

Anna was in her element now. "You do not seem to be overhurt. I see no broken bone, no blood. You are supposed to be a nobleman, yet you complain like an old woman."

Lark studied her. Except for Anna, every soldier present stiffened, ready to attack. She shifted subtly in her saddle as Phelan and his men inched closer to her. What amazed Lark more than anything was when he saw her grin. *Damn it*, Lark thought, *here we go.* He tightened his hold on Rabbit.

She clicked her tongue, and Tullian reared. Instead of landing on the prone man beneath his hooves, her stallion twisted sideways into the horses of the enemy. Anna set Tullian into a series of turns and backward leaps, scattering the Nifolhad horses in every direction.

Then she calmed her stallion as if nothing had happened and returned to her place next to Baldric. A satisfied smirk played on her lips.

But Lark kept his eyes on the man she'd unhorsed. As he made his feet, he removed his helmet. "Impossible," Lark said aloud. Except for his beard, the man was identical to Lord Roger.

"M'lady," Cellach warned, and she brought her attention to bear on the man once again. Lark wasn't sure what she would do, and that worried him. His reflexes spurred him to action, positioning Rabbit betwixt Anna and the Nifolhadajans. She managed to keep the shock from her face as the man sneered at her, but Lark could tell that she was badly shaken.

"Get down, you fools," Lord Phelan yelled at the others still ahorse. "Help your prince. Enough of these games, Baldric. You have until noon to find your sense."

"I think you may have overestimated your strength, Phelan," Baldric countered. "And even if you manage to breach the curtain, you will still have to contend with us."

"So be it, Baldric. We will look on this as more practice before moving on to Whitmarsh." When the man who could have been Roger's twin remounted his horse, the men from Nifolhad rode back to their camp.

CHAPTER FIFTY-SEVEN

Fodder

Baldric rode next to Anna. "We oft wondered about Roger's ties to Nifolhad. Not even King Godwin suspected the bond would be so close. What think you, m'lady? The resemblance is so striking, they could be twins."

Anna nodded, thankful that Baldric was speaking to her in such a commonplace way. When her gaze had fallen upon Roger's lookalike, her courage had fled, thinking Roger back from the dead.

"Well, it was quite the surprise," he continued, "I had expected Prince Bowen, but I did not think it would be so soon. The man you so brilliantly unhorsed was none other than Diarmait's son, sole heir to the throne of Nifolhad."

Baldric turned to her. "That was quite a stunt back there. Tullian is a magnificent horse to be able to respond to your commands so well. It is too bad the horses of the Royal Guard are not so trained."

"What do you mean, not trained?" Anna asked. "Your mounts all have the same battle skills. Lark knows this; I've seen him ride Rabbit. Times have changed indeed when the rider of a Chevring steed knows not upon what he sits."

"Indeed." He fell silent until they rode up to the bridge. "Lady Aubrianne, you made a powerful enemy today in Prince Bowen."

"No, Baldric," Anna corrected. "Prince Bowen made an enemy of me, weeks ago, when he and Roger destroyed Chevring." At her signal, Tullian moved a little quicker, pulling her slightly ahead of the others.

At the stable, Will took Tullian. Anna turned and ran right into Lark. He'd been standing behind her, holding Rabbit's reins.

"I would have done it for you, you know," he said. There was a different light in his eyes.

"I know. Rabbit was ready. You were ready."

NICOLE ELIZABETH KELLEHER

"Then why?" he asked. "Why did you not let me?" He was angry. "Who were you trying to protect this time? Surely not your people."

"Is that all that you have to say to me, Lark?" she asked, wounded that he would think so little of her. "Did you not notice who he… nevermind," she ended, for Ailwen and Warin approached. From their excited faces, Anna guessed that the morning's work was yet unfinished.

For at least a couple of hours, Anna was distracted by the enthusiasm of Warin, Ailwen, and the others as she put them through their paces with their destriers. When they were finished, Baldric placed his arm around her shoulder. "It is heartening to know the Chevring line did not end, Lady Anna."

They continued to the castle and walked the flights of stairs that would take them to the battlements. Judging from the sun, the attack was nigh. Across the river, the enemy lay encamped. A single rider approached. He waited nervously before riding back to the large tent erected behind the men and weapons.

"How long, Baldric?" Anna asked, wanting to know when he thought the assault would commence.

"An hour, perhaps. They think the curtain wall is indefensible from the mordemurs. I had once thought they would take their time, but not now. Not since you attacked Bowen." The corner of her lip twitched. "Lady Anna, you could stand to be as direct in other regards as well."

She followed Baldric's gaze to Lark's brooding figure. "Lark made his choice," she replied.

Baldric sighed and searched her face with caring eyes. But her focus remained fixed on her people in the courtyard below.

Cellach came to stand next to them. Across the river, there was a flurry of activity near the tent as the prince and his lords rode to the top of a nearby hill. Then the soldiers began loading the payloads into the buckets of the mordemurs. They turned the great spoked wheels that would pull their missiles into position.

No one atop the battlements asked if Anna was sure of her sabotage. If she wasn't, there was nothing they could do about it. "They're ready, Lady Anna," Cellach stated, interrupting her thoughts.

She turned to Baldric. "What do you think they'll do after?" she asked.

"Let's hope that they will run around like pullets with their heads cut off," he answered.

The firing levers would release the stored tension of the throwing arms, and what remained of the ropes below would snap. Many would

266

be injured, even killed, in the resulting havoc.

"First they'll lick their wounds," Baldric continued. "Then they will reassess. Their numbers are greater, but Bowen will see the futility of attacking the keep without a wall breach. Their scouts have no doubt reported that Godwin's army will arrive in two days. With no siege possible, they'll hasten for the coast, and we'll give chase, scouring them from Aurelia."

The attention shifted back to the enemy across the river. After what seemed an eternity, the signal was given to fire the weapons. The ballast arms on all ten mordemurs were set in motion, one after the other. Atop the parapet, they held their breaths as the spars arced through the air.

Midway through the swing, first one mordemur, then the others, bucked. Anna imagined the sounds of snapping ropes. The giant swinging arms on three wall killers broke away completely, their payloads shooting straight up only to crash down on the machines. Wood splintered and ropes lashed out. Half of the machines' arms continued their arcs but with much less force than the others. The momentum of their payloads pulled their buckets into the ground, causing booms to crash down, splitting the platforms in two.

The remaining five mordemurs unleashed the worst damage. These weapons had just begun to pull their heavy stone balls when their ropes snapped. The payloads shot backward into the assembled soldiers, dragging split timber and whipping cords into the men.

Every weapon was damaged beyond repair. Almost all were rent in half from the uneven pressure. The men of Nifolhad had been taken unaware. As the payloads and the ensuing splintered beams and ropes caromed in their direction, many of the shocked men remained rooted to the ground. Those unlucky enough to be in the direct path of the barrage were knocked away like kindling.

Anna caught Lark's eye as she turned away from the gory scene below. Her people waited in the courtyard, safe from the destruction. But no one cheered knowing death was so near. Many walked to the chapel and disappeared inside its cool grace.

Anna left the battlements to Baldric and the guards. She desired nothing more than to be alone with her thoughts. Only, she could think of nowhere to go. It came as a great surprise when she found herself in Lark's room. He found her there, hours later, standing at the window, peering into the deepening sky.

She was still suited in her armor and was stiff from not moving. She heard him enter and pause at the door upon seeing her. He closed his door and, already shed of his own protective gear, moved nearer. She sensed him standing behind her, then felt his fingers work to remove the ties and undo the buckles of her armor. He lifted it away, setting it on the table.

Anna didn't speak as her body melted into his strong arms. She turned to him, and he roughly took her face in his hands. His lips fought to find hers. Though their anger and fear was forgotten, their embrace was not gentle. Their hunger for each other was intense. There were no whispers of love. No calling out of names. Atop his small bed, they took equally from each other. Afterward, as they lay spent, Anna waited until Lark fell asleep. Then she silently got up and dressed, collected her things, and tiptoed to his door.

• • •

Alone in the dark, Lark wished more than anything that he had called her back to him. But once again, he hadn't been able to find the words. He was still angry, but not for the reasons she suspected. He should not have let her leave, for the words he longed to say, *I love you*, were as yet unuttered. Restless, Lark left his room to seek Baldric's advice.

On the way to the council room, he passed the west chamber. The door was open, and he saw Grainne, busily at work giving orders to a small band of women. Some pounded herbs, others tore fabric for bandages. On the chamber's bed, the children rolled the strips into tight balls. "Lady Anna's orders," Grainne explained to him. "We'll not ignore the injured and abandoned," she added. "Even if they are from Nifolhad."

As he turned away from the scene, Lark finally understood why he was so angry. Anna didn't need him. She was strong enough to protect her people. She was strong enough to defend herself. And now, hearing Grainne give instructions, he discovered that Anna was even strong enough to overcome her bias and give aid to the wounded soldiers of Nifolhad. A very small part of his heart cautioned that he was being petty, but his pride silenced this quiet voice.

CHAPTER FIFTY-EIGHT
Three Days and Three Nights

Three days had passed since the mordemurs had been destroyed. Prince Bowen and what able-bodied men remained with him had decamped immediately, leaving behind their wounded to die on the field. Three nights had passed since Anna's last encounter with Lark. He'd volunteered to track down and capture Bowen.

It was Grainne, not Lark, who had told her. And her maid had heard it from Ailwen. Warin had volunteered to go as well. Two guards and a contingent of Godwin's newly arrived men were to scour the realm of the Nifolhadajans.

Anna sought the quietude of the battlements, gazing out to the northwest. Word had come that Bowen's ships had been able to land on the coast of Ragallach. He and his men had passed unimpeded through Stolweg's western forests, all thanks to Roger, for the lookout points and strongholds had long been manned by soldiers loyal to his cause. These men decamped as soon as Bowen passed through their lines, leaving Lark and Warin to release the families that had been held captive there for years. And Prince Bowen? He was somewhere in the mountains that rose to the northwest, racing hell-bent to the safety of his ships.

Anna walked to the south-facing battlements. The stars were brilliant, and the waxing moon was just rising above the trees. The ground below, illuminated by the heavenly lanterns, was peaceful.

Three days had stretched into weeks, and Lord Baldric asked Anna to travel with him to Whitmarsh, then on to King's Glen. Anna had yet to decide. But as she peered out into the night, just as she did each morning, she realized that she was searching for Lark. She made her decision: wait no more.

• • •

Lark and Warin flushed out small bands of Nifolhadajans, most of whom wanted to fight. The few who swore the oath to never return were stripped of their weapons and sent to the ships waiting on the coast. From there, they would sail for the Nifolhadian city of Sophiana, and be turned over to Lord Ranulf instead of to Diarmait.

Word came to Lark and Warin that Bowen had already set sail, vowing to return and avenge Roger's death. The small contingent that Godwin had placed under Lark's and Warin's command would remain at Ragallach. With their mission deemed complete, Lark and Warin traveled south, to where Stolweg touched the sea.

Lark had worked hard to keep Anna from his mind. He kept himself so occupied that he managed to barely think of her. But then Warin would say or do something that would recall Lark's attention to the void in his heart. He kicked Rabbit into a canter; Warin followed.

The sound of the two great destriers' hooves as they pounded the hard-packed road reminded Lark of the day that he and Anna had raced to save Baldric. He caught himself smiling at the joy she'd found in riding Tullian. The feeling disappeared when he thought of her launch against Prince Bowen.

When they turned off the main road, taking a rutted trail that ran alongside a garden ripe with summer vegetables, Warin began a discourse on how Stolweg was lucky to have had the lands within the river's girth. Lark merely grunted.

"Stolweg is a land of true wealth," Warin prated on. "The horses, the fertile soil, the lake and surrounding forests. I could go on and on."

"Please, don't," Lark retorted.

But Warin remained unchecked. "Its strategic importance to the realm must weigh heavily on King Godwin."

"And *what* exactly does that mean, Warin?" Lark demanded.

"Just that Godwin will want someone he trusts at Stolweg. Oh, I'm sure Lady Aubrianne could manage the keep. And Godwin may consider letting her. But that was before Cellach decided to leave," Warin explained. "Unless Lady Anna can convince the arms master to stay, the only thing for Godwin to do is to find someone he trusts to wed Lady Aubrianne."

Lark gripped his reins until his knuckles turned white.

• • •

Behind Lark, Warin smiled. Baldric had encouraged him to proselytize Lady Anna at every turn, reminding Lark of her many charms. And Warin was only too happy to see his friend twisted in knots. But if he were honest with himself, he wished happiness for his friend. And Lady Anna was Lark's best hope.

"Now, I wonder," Warin mused aloud, "will Lord Herlewin be in the running? It would be a shame to see Lady Anna saddled with such an indelicate barrel of a man."

Ahead of him, Lark stiffened and, without a word of farewell, wheeled Rabbit to the east. So much for the famous fish stew that was waiting at the Cod Monger Inn, Warin thought. With not quite as much haste, he turned to follow his friend.

CHAPTER FIFTY-NINE

Anna and Claire

Over a month had passed since Lark left with Warin, and Anna wanted to be away from Stolweg, far from the memories that haunted her. So she'd accepted Baldric's offer to travel to Whitmarsh. Claire was with Baldric's wife, and Anna needed to be with family. Cellach had agreed to put off his departure until her return. Sarah would travel with her, for the girl was eager to be reunited with her brother Pieter.

Grainne was in a state of panic about which gowns to pack for the trip. When Anna told her that she would just wear what she had always worn, Grainne scowled. "Lady Anna, you cannot mean it. After Whitmarsh, you'll be traveling to court. To see the King and Queen!"

Grainne was so upset by the notion that Anna ceded the responsibility of a proper wardrobe to her maid's discretion. She had but one condition. "I will not ride sidesaddle, Grainne. In fact, I plan to ride the entire way next to Lord Baldric with dagger, sword, and bow."

"Why not full armor as well!" Grainne declared, throwing her hands up in the air. She sighed. "Don't worry, m'lady. I'll pack an extra pair of breeches and a couple of your long overtunics."

"And my armor?"

"Already packed, m'lady. You'll want to be properly attired for a royal audience, won't you?"

Anna nodded, then did the best thing she could do to help—she got out of Grainne's way.

"What's this, m'lady?" her friend asked, and stooped down to pick up a folded piece of parchment from under the worktable.

Anna took the tattered document, then read the contents. "It's the answer to a mystery, Grainne. I need to find Baldric." She knew exactly where to locate him.

With great reluctance, she walked to the north tower. The door was open, and she saw Baldric sitting at the desk in the chamber that had been Roger's. He'd spent the last few weeks poring over the meticulously kept ledgers of Stolweg, Ragallach, and even a few from Chevring. He'd found no traces linking Roger and Nifolhad, not even personal correspondence.

Anna took a deep breath. This was the first time she'd entered this room since Roger had been killed. She stood in the doorway, finally understanding that it was just another place. She squared her shoulders and marched in, holding out the sheet to Baldric. "I believe this is what you're hunting for." She handed him the letter that Lady Ulicia had written to her unborn son.

Baldric unfolded the letter. "Have you read this?" he asked when he was a quarter of the way through. "This confirms that Roger was a true Prince of Nifolhad." Anna nodded and waited while he finished that which she had already read.

> ...He is but one year older than you. But I am jumping ahead of myself. To help you comprehend, I must take you back two years before you were born. To a day when I went fishing on the sea.
>
> The sky was fair, and the breeze gentle, and we caught many fish. But we failed to notice that the wind had picked up and had pushed us farther west than we had reckoned. The sky to the east was churning with a great storm. It fell upon us within minutes, and our vessel capsized.
>
> Somehow, we were able to grab hold of the overturned boat. The current took us west, to Nifolhad. We made our rough landing on their beachhead, our vessel destroyed and sinking. The Nifolhadajans were waiting for us, and they set upon our party. In the space of minutes, my five escorts, all true to Aurelia, were killed. I waited for the blow that would end my life as well.
>
> A young man stepped forward. "Nay, Lady, you have my word that no harm will come to you. I am Prince Diarmait, and King Cedric is my brother."
>
> His voice was deep and full of sorrow for the men who had given their lives to protect me. His face was beautiful and fair. On his cheek he bore a mark, one that only made him more beautiful in my eyes. He led me away from the carnage, telling me that he regretted King Cedric's insistence that we were marauders to be slain.
>
> For my protection, Diarmait hid my existence from his brother. He courted me, and I fell in love. I am not ashamed that I gave him my maidenhead while unwed. It is testament to how sure I was that our love was true.

A month later, I found myself with child. When King Cedric discovered me, he ordered that I be returned to my family. Diarmait countered that they probably thought I had perished in the storm, and that the men who had accompanied me had been dealt with. Confused by what was being said, I chose that moment to reveal my condition.

"You have taken her maidenhead," I remember the King saying. "God be thanked she is of noble birth, for you can marry her, at least. We will not allow one of our own blood to be bastardized."

A strange look fell across Diarmait's face. Had I not been so pleased at the outcome, I would have recognized the anger and jealousy. We were married the next day, and I lived happily in the great palace city of Kantahla while the babe inside my womb grew.

When your brother Bowen was born, our marriage changed. Diarmait forbade me to see our baby, not even to nurse him. I ached for my child. Diarmait's absences from our bed grew, and I gave myself solace by sneaking into the nursery to hold our beautiful boy.

One such evening, I was alone with the babe, and Diarmait found me. He was drunk and dragged me to his chamber. It was the last time we shared a bed. The next morning, he took me to the beach. He told me I was to return home. Alone. I started running back the way we had come. Bowen was asleep in the nursery, and I would not leave him. Diarmait caught me and dragged me to a small boat. He must have knocked me senseless, for I came awake to the gentle lapping of the ocean. I waited for the sun to begin its descent to find my bearings back to Nifolhad. But it was not to be. A strong wind kicked up from the west, and the current sent me home to Ragallach.

I waited a month before telling my parents about my marriage to Prince Diarmait. My father refused to speak with me, so deep was his feeling of betrayal. To his great displeasure, I continued to wear the gem my love had given me on our wedding day. Red as a heart, the stone came to symbolize the blood I'd left behind.

My spirit was as broken as my heart. I grew weaker and sicker, staring out to the west where my child was growing without me.

Then I discovered that I was with child again, with you. I vowed to see you into this world. I only wish that I were stronger for you. I would have liked to see you grow.

Your grandparents know nothing of this letter. I asked the midwife to hold it for you, along with the ruby from your father, until you became old enough to understand.

You have a right to know that you have family elsewhere. Please do not

*be angry with your grandparents. I made them take an oath not to reveal
your true parentage. Show them the jewel, and they will understand that
it was I who broke faith.*

Always remember, I love you, my little one.

Your mother,
Ulicia

Baldric had begun pacing as he finished the letter. He stopped and
met Anna's eyes. "Diarmait will renew his efforts against Aurelia," he
predicted. "We've killed one son and sent the other running. We must get
this to the King at once."

"I have a messenger saddling his horse now, m'lord."

• • •

Anna arrived at Whitmarsh a week later. No sooner were they through
the gate than Anna spied Claire. She raced to her sister, and they held
each other, crying with happiness that they'd been reunited.

"Claire. Look at you. You're as beautiful as ever."

"And you, Anna. You are just as I pictured. I've dreamed for so long
of seeing you again. Now that you're here, I feel someone needs to pinch
me to make sure I'm awake."

Anna motioned to the small girl behind her. "Sarah!" Claire cried.
"But how? We thought all were lost."

"Seven children, Claire," Anna explained. "My master-at-arms
found them. I'll tell you everything later but for now, let me see…Luke,
Sarah, Adele, Robbie, Adam, Paul, and Hannah."

Sarah tugged at Claire's sleeve. "Miss Claire, where can I find Pieter?"

"What can I be thinking? Of course!" Claire exclaimed. Just then
she saw Pieter come forward to greet his old friend Tullian. Claire tucked
Sarah behind her skirts and called to him.

"I have a surprise for you." She stepped aside to reveal Sarah. Pieter
rushed forward and lifted Sarah from the ground, spinning in circles
until everyone was dizzy with the watching.

After the hugging, laughing, and crying finally subsided, Anna
turned to the woman who had accompanied her sister. "Lady Elnoura,"
she acknowledged, curtsying as best she could. "Thank you for taking
such good care of my family."

"Lady Aubrianne," she began.

"Anna. If it pleases you, Lady Elnoura."

"It does. And you must call me Noura." She was so gracious and lovely; Anna could not help but admire her.

"Come now. Claire will show you to your chamber. You must be tired from the journey. And if not, at the very least, the two of you need some private time together."

Claire showed Anna to her room. The two sisters huddled together, sipping tea and sharing what they knew of the fate of Chevring. Baldric had been thorough in his letters to his wife. Except for the surviving children, Claire knew as much as Anna. Perhaps they would discover more when they traveled to King's Glen in a few days. Anna wondered if Lark would be there.

It was during their journey to court that Lady Elnoura brought up that very subject. "I hope you'll not be angry with Baldric, but he's told me of your regard for Lark."

Anna sighed, knowing it was inevitable that she would have to speak of him. "I don't mind," she said. "I'm finally settling my mind over the whole affair and—"

"I'm sorry to interrupt, Anna, but you do not need to pretend to me that your heart isn't breaking. I see it in your face every time I look at you." Her voice was so soft and gentle that Anna could not refute her words. "I'll not have you worried that others see it. You are quite accomplished at hiding your feelings. I suppose being married to Lord Roger made it an essential skill. But I want you to know, nothing is ever hopeless where love is concerned."

"Lark made his choice, Noura," Anna replied. "I can't change who I am to suit his ideal."

Elnoura smiled sweetly at her. "As time passes, you will both come to understand the truths in your deeds. If you can accept his point of view, and if Lark can accept yours, there is always hope. Neither of you should change for the other. Bend, yes. But not change."

CHAPTER SIXTY

To Court and Back

Riding next to his wife on their way to King's Glen, Lord Baldric told Lady Elnoura about the King's missive.

"We knew this day would come, Baldric," she said when he finished. "Godwin must secure Stolweg. Especially now that Chevring has been laid to waste, and Ragallach is unlorded."

"I'd hoped that Lark would have returned by now, as Warin has. Doesn't Lark know that Lady Anna will concede to whatever Godwin decrees?" Baldric asked. "She will marry for duty, you know, as she did before. Even if duty means marrying one she does not love."

"There is still a little time, my dear," Lady Elnoura promised.

"Noura, what have you done?"

"Nothing much. Just a simple letter to Queen Juliana to tell her of her nephew's idiocy. Lark has always held a special spot in the Queen's heart. And, she's a bigger romantic than even you, my dear. I trust she will influence Godwin in regards to Lady Anna. In the meantime, Lark needs to find his own way, and in his own time." She gazed at Anna and Claire riding just ahead.

"You know, Baldric," Lady Elnoura continued, "I, too, hope that Lark will return in time. But if he decides to follow the path of his father, we need to make sure that Anna does not get saddled with one such as Roger."

"Let us hope it never comes to that," Baldric worried.

"Still, if it has to be," Noura mused, "Warin and Anna would make a handsome pair. You said there was respect between them, and a growing friendship."

• • •

When night fell, they found a secure place to rest. Soon, the tents were pitched, a light supper eaten, and in pairs, everyone retired for the night. Claire and Anna were sharing a tent, and were changing into more comfortable sleeping attire when Claire saw Anna's scars and gasped. "Oh, Anna, what happened to you?"

"Roger," she replied, surprised at herself for forgetting the marks.

Claire hugged her tightly and whispered, "Thank you, Anna."

"For what?"

"For surviving. I—I fled Chevring. And I was so afraid. But I kept asking myself, what would *you* do? The thought of you fighting somewhere kept me strong."

So Anna told Claire how she came to have the scars on her back. Afterward, she felt relief, as if one part of her burden had been laid to rest at last. And each day thereafter, she and her sister caught up on the missing years when neither knew what was happening to the other.

When they finally arrived at King's Glen, all at court came out to see the two young women riding unconventionally astride their great steeds. Anna wore her light armor, and she and Claire held their heads high, ignoring the hands raised to lips of the ladies and noblemen as they masked their whispers. But they had expected this. And after Anna dismounted, an audible gasp echoed around the courtyard as she removed her sword from Tullian's saddle and belted it about her waist. Claire stood proudly next to her. Her younger sister had slung her bow across her back, her quarrel at the ready on her hip.

"Are you expecting trouble?" Warin whispered, surprising Anna with a friendly face.

"You tell us, Warin," Anna teased. "It appears that there are a few ladies here who would rather not have you escort us." Warin only laughed.

Following the Lord and Lady of Whitmarsh into Glen Hall, Anna and Claire were led before the King and Queen. Godwin signaled to them to approach.

Anna felt the weight of a hundred curious eyes upon her. She could hear the rustlings of skirts and the soft footsteps of leather slippers as the surrounding spectators spoke in hushed tones. She and Claire ignored their stares, choosing instead to stand proud and focus on the King and Queen. The whispers grew louder, echoing off the vaulted ceiling. Queen Juliana murmured something to her husband. He nodded and immediately ordered everyone from the hall except Lord Baldric, Lady Elnoura, and the two sisters.

He spoke first to Anna, commending her on her heroism at Stolweg.

He'd read Lord Baldric's reports and asked pleasantly, looking at Anna's sword, if she expected to have any adventures while at court.

"I pray not, my liege. We only wear our weapons to pledge the loyalty of the peoples of both Stolweg and Chevring."

"We were saddened to hear of the loss of your friends and family," Godwin stated. "It may be of some comfort to you to hear that reports have been coming in from other areas of the realm. Your sister and the children were not the only survivors. But the messages have been vague. This infiltration by Prince Bowen has caused much confusion and mistrust."

"Thank you, my liege," Anna replied. "We prayed for such news."

He was silent for a moment, as if weighing what to say next. "Know this, Lady Aubrianne and Lady Claire: for your help and loyalty, we promise that Chevring will be restored. But first, let us speak of our plans for you, Lady Aubrianne."

Anna knew that a new marriage was in the offing. Another duty to perform. Not for family this time, but for Aurelia. She listened as the king spoke of the importance of Stolweg. He acknowledged how bravely she had defended her home but that he could not allow one of his strongest keeps to remain unlorded.

"We have decided—you shall marry again. But we are not blind to that which you endured with Lord Roger. Therefore, we will give a list of suitable candidates to Lord Baldric. When the time comes, you will at least have a choice in whom you wed. Baldric will assign two of our guards to accompany you back to Stolweg and to remain there until you are ready to marry."

Godwin turned to Claire. "And you, Claire, are to either remain at Whitmarsh or return to Stolweg with your sister. Once Stolweg is settled, we will to see to your future. You will marry and return to Chevring."

King Godwin looked pleased with himself. He turned to his Queen. "Juliana, have you anything that you would like to add?"

"No, I believe you've explained everything, my dear." She regarded Anna. "Lady Aubrianne, did you wish to add something?"

"Er, no, my Queen, thank you." Queen Juliana arched her pointed eyebrow.

"Pardon, my Queen," Anna blurted out. "It is just that you remind me of someone."

The Queen smiled. "And who might that be?"

"Larkin of Morland, my Queen," Anna answered.

"Yes, I suppose that he should resemble me. His mother, Lady

Kathryn of Morland, is my half sister. Larkin asked that I not reveal our relation. He did not want to be favored for his connection to me. I trust you will hold his secret."

Anna nodded, and the Queen continued, "No one has yet seen the resemblance. I am curious. What gave it away?"

"It is not so much your features, my Queen," Anna explained. "It's in your bearing and gestures. And when you arched your eyebrow at me, I knew there had to be some connection."

The Queen nodded, looking pleased. "I knew your mother," she said. "And your grandmother. They would be proud of you. Tell me, Lady Aubrianne, can you recite the names?"

Surprised that the Queen knew of this secret, Anna answered, "Of course."

"Good. Be sure to teach them to your sister."

Claire stepped forward. "It is not necessary, my Queen. I know my ancestry. I may never be able to fight like my sister," Claire explained, then turned to Anna, "but I can defend myself. And I know my lineage. After you left, Mother insisted on training me herself."

"Good again," the Queen said, and rose with the King, signaling the end of their audience.

• • •

Claire cast her eye over the celebration being held in their honor. She wished she could help her sister to feel more at ease, but this past week at court, Anna had seemed a fish out of water. Oh, she played the part of Lady Aubrianne of Stolweg perfectly. She conversed easily with lords and ladies alike. But when alone with Queen Juliana's ladies, she fell silent and thoughtful. If she spoke at all, she did so warily.

This was the life for which Claire had always dreamed, though having it now was bittersweet. She looked about for her sister. Maybe she was with the handsome guard Warin; she seemed to enjoy spending time with him. Perhaps there was some spark between them.

She finally spied Anna, dancing a lively step with Warin. So she walked over to where several of the Queen's ladies were standing. When her sister's name was mentioned, Claire kept her silence, stopping just behind the women.

"I agree, Lady Aubrianne *is* beautiful. But really, she shouldn't monopolize all of Warin's time. Every evening the same, they talk and talk. And now, he's danced with naught but her." She winked at her friends and whispered, "I have it on good authority that they retire to their separate rooms."

Another lady, whom Claire recognized as Lady Beth, spoke up, "You are only jealous that Warin has not been chasing you, Caroline." The other women tittered prettily.

"Well, it isn't fair that he spends all his time with her," she complained, "especially with Lark being away. Court has been such a bore without the pair playing their games."

"Have you not heard?" Lady Beth asked. "Our Lark has not returned because he has lost his heart." The women all turned their attention to Lady Beth as she nodded her head toward Anna. Claire didn't remain to hear what was said next, and slipped away unnoticed. No wonder Anna felt so ill at ease among these women. Just who was this Lark, other than nephew to the Queen?

Claire had noticed Anna's melancholy, though it was well disguised, and thought it owing to the loss of their family and home. It had not occurred to Claire that another reason existed for her sister's sorrow. The musicians finished their tune, and Warin delivered Anna to Claire, Elnoura, and the Queen. Claire studied her sister. Her happiness was feigned. When Anna turned to speak to her, Claire narrowed her eyes.

"What is it, Claire?" Anna asked in alarm.

"Tell me about Lark, Anna."

Her sister blinked, then took a deep breath. "I would have told you, Claire, but I didn't want you to worry about me. Come, the night is ending. Let us say our goodbyes and return to our room where we can speak in private."

They returned to their quarters, and once comfortably situated, Anna began the story of how she met and fell in love with Lark, and he with her. She told Claire about the night she had sabotaged the weapons, and her return to the chapel where she almost died by Lark's hand.

"That was the beginning of the end for Lark. He could not forgive himself, and he could not forgive me. I've not heard from him since."

Claire thought it amazing that her sister could have found such happiness after what she had endured with Lord Roger. "Do you still love him, Anna?"

"I will always love him," her sister replied. Anna then told her about the oath Lord Roger had imposed upon his men, a vow to kill her and her family.

"So there could be others waiting to kill you," Claire worried. "How terrible for Lark to realize that you may never be safe, even from him."

Claire could see from Anna's face that this had not occurred to her sister. "It's ironic, isn't it, Anna? Lark is responsible for giving you the strength to want to survive Roger's evil. Now, it's that very strength that he cannot accept."

"You amaze me more and more every day. For months, I've been trying to understand him. I haven't been able to put my feelings to words, and you do it in two sentences."

"And Warin?" Claire asked.

"Ah, Warin. He is a good friend, Claire. And a good man, too."

"Anna, Lark will return. To King Godwin. Or to Lord Baldric. Your paths are sure to cross. If he still loves you, as you love him, what then?"

"I don't know, Claire. I was so angry at him for leaving, for giving up. I still am angry."

"Can you forgive him, Anna?" Claire asked, wanting her sister to find happiness.

"I already have. But I'm afraid it isn't enough. And I have to get on with my life, with or without Lark."

"When are we leaving for Stolweg?" Claire asked, knowing she would happily give up life at court if it meant remaining at her sister's side.

"Within the week," Anna replied.

CHAPTER SIXTY-ONE

Knead

The Harvest Festival was upon them, and Doreen had risen early to finish baking bread for the party. Across from her, Lady Anna worked her dough. Her mistress had returned to Stolweg nearly a month ago, along with the guards Warin and Trian, and she had made almost daily visits to the kitchen.

Doreen had come to depend on her assistance, now that she was carrying a little extra weight. She smiled contentedly and rested her hand on her growing belly. Her child would be born in a few months. And her babe wouldn't be the only new arrival at Stolweg, for there were several other women who were with child as well. The children who had survived the destruction of Chevring had been placed with families close to the keep. All except Luke, who had taken to Carrick, and had gone to live in the miller's home. Maggie had been sent to live with a distant relative to the east, and Carrick was only too happy to take on the boy as an apprentice. When Luke made it known that his uncle had been Chevring's miller, it was clear to all that the two fit naturally together.

Growing families were not the only changes. Grainne had told Doreen that two families had approached Lady Anna requesting permission for their older children to wed during the winter solstice. Lady Anna refused to give permission, preferring instead to give her blessing. Doreen looked up to find Lady Anna studying at her from across the worktable.

"Is the baby kicking you again, Doreen?" she inquired. "You should sit and rest. Let me finish here. And Claire, well, she'll find me soon enough. I'll put *her* to work for once."

Doreen smiled at the thought of Lady Anna's sister. Lady Claire had so much energy that she had everyone's heads spinning. After a month, they had come to love her exuberance as much as they loved Lady Anna for her strength. "I'm fine, m'lady. 'Tis true," she insisted when she noted her mistress's skepticism. "Today is just one of those days when I'm filled with excess energy." Doreen laughed as she spoke. "It would be a shame to waste it. Tomorrow, I'm just as likely to want to sleep the morn away."

The cook thought back to the day when Lark had returned to Stolweg, searching for Lady Anna. He'd left as quickly as he'd come when told that the Lady Anna had departed for Whitmarsh. Doreen had assumed he had followed her mistress there. But Lady Anna returned almost two months later and confided that Lark had never arrived.

The King would not allow Lady Anna to continue alone at Stolweg for much longer. Doreen sighed, at a loss for how to help.

Kneading her own dough, Doreen finished and turned to place it in a banneton from the stacked woven baskets they used for proofing. She lifted her gaze to set the basket in the hutch and discovered a man leaning against the doorframe. He raised his finger to his lips, begging silence. Doreen recognized him at once. She put down the dough she'd just started working and said, "I may just rest my feet after all, m'lady. If you truly do not mind…"

• • •

Anna nodded without lifting her head from the task at hand. She continued the process of pushing, pulling, and folding the dough. The repetitive motions were comforting. She needed something, anything, to punch and to pull. With each lump that she kneaded, the ache uncoiled little by little from around her heart.

• • •

Lark waited a long time, just watching her. Her movements were strong and fluid. She was exactly the same as before, he thought. No, that was not quite true. She had lost the dark circles under her once-haunted eyes. And, Lark thought appreciatively, she wasn't as thin as before. With her sleeves rolled up past her elbows, he could see that she was still lithe. Her arms tensed and flexed as she repeated the same motion over and over.

His breath caught in his throat. She was even more beautiful than before. A lock of brown hair, where it had freed itself from her long braid, twisted and twirled down the side of her face as she leaned over the table's surface. He could see traces of golden brown in its soft curl where the summer sun had kissed it. He fought back the urge to walk over and wrap the tress around his finger. She used the back of her wrist to push the escaped lock back in place, succeeding only in dusting her hair with flour.

• • •

As Anna finished working the dough, the mindless process was replaced immediately by thoughts of Lark. She was certain their paths would cross again. What would she say to him? She played the meeting over and over in her mind, perfecting it, imagining where they might meet. In some scenarios, she was already married to another. But just now, Anna was having her favorite daydream. Lark would find her at Stolweg, perhaps in the kitchen, like now, kneading dough. They would gaze at each other, neither speaking, only communicating their hearts' desires with their eyes.

Gracious, she thought. If she were not more careful, she would overwork this boule and it wouldn't rise. Turning to grab a banneton, she registered that she wasn't alone. Anna didn't move for fear her eyes were deceiving her. There, in the doorway, was Lark. He moved closer, and Anna realized he was not an illusion. She was overcome with an urge to run to his embrace.

And just as quickly, she was furious, with herself for being so foolish, and with Lark for assuming that she would be waiting for him. She grabbed another lump of dough and began kneading it. She had to force herself to slow her motions, concentrating on the shaping and reshaping, even as her mind screamed for her to beat the pulp out of it.

• • •

For a moment, Lark saw Anna's eyes grow heavy with desire. And then she composed herself and calmly reached for another piece of bread dough. Lark had planned everything that he would say. He'd rehearsed his speech for days. When Anna's light brown eyes met his, every rational thought escaped him. He stepped forward, keeping the expanse of the worktable between them, using it as a crutch. "You're not going to make this easy for me, are you?" he finally asked.

"*Easy?* I. Don't. Know. What. You. Mean," Anna answered, punctuating each word with a punch to the dough.

Lark picked up Doreen's discarded lump and tore little bits from it one at a time. He'd expected a straightforward answer, not one worthy of a lady at court. "You never played games with me before, why now?" he asked.

"*Games?*" she asked, not bothering to hide the anger in her voice. "Is that what you think I am doing? No, don't answer. I really don't care to know."

"Anna, look at me," he beseeched her. He hadn't meant it to, but his last request came out sounding exactly as it had those many times he had said the same thing to her while making love.

• • •

Anna couldn't take any more, and she released her pent-up fury on him. But this time she didn't shout, instead lowering her voice to a calm hiss, a tone dripping with warning. "Who is playing a game now, Lark?"

"I just want to explain, to tell you why I had to leave. I—" Lark started.

"*Had* to leave?" she demanded. "I heard you volunteered."

"I thought it was for the best," he began, and Anna heard his irritation. She took a steadying breath. They could continue arguing, each becoming more and more angry. But it wasn't what she wanted. And she didn't think that Lark wanted it either. She was a different woman now. There had been a time once when he had let her rail against him, knowing it was what she needed. It wasn't fair to use him like that anymore. She glared at the ruined dough in her hands and threw the useless mass on the work surface, throwing away her anger with it.

"You were the only person in the world I could talk to," she said, her voice raw with pain. "The only person in the world who knew everything about me."

"And I left you," he stated simply. He walked around the worktable, his hand extended as if trying to bridge the gap between them. Anna wasn't ready yet and took a step in the opposite direction to keep him safely away.

"Until I saw you just a few moments ago, I never realized how badly I was hurt by you," she said. He tried to speak, but she raised her palm to stop him. "I *know* you were hurt, too, Lark. I thought one day you would understand," she added wearily. "I am a person who feels responsible. My people were at risk. *You were at risk.* I would and will do anything to protect the lives of those I care for."

He remained where he stood, and Anna sighed. "We knew each other for such a short time, you and I. You imagined yourself as my great protector, my strength. But I believed you would come to love all of me. I had hoped that you cared enough about me to put aside your pride and talk to me. But you left."

She was finished. Anna wanted peace and was saddened that Lark might not be the one to give it. Two ruined pieces of dough sat on the thick wooden slab.

"No games," he promised. "I've been chasing you across the realm, always weeks behind. When I returned here, you had gone to Whitmarsh. So I followed you there. But you had gone to court. And court was the last place I wanted to go to find you," he admitted. "My life there, before I met you…"

He paused, and Anna knew that he was referring to the games he and Warin played with the Queen's ladies. Anna hadn't been deaf to the whispers and intrigues at King's Glen.

"I went there, eventually," Lark admitted. "But I missed you again, though I heard you made an impression on the Queen."

"Your aunt, you mean," Anna corrected. "Why did you not tell me?"

"I guess we both had our secrets," he said wryly. "But she told me that you were giving this Harvest Festival for your people. I returned to Whitmarsh to find that Baldric and Noura were already on their way here. You see," he said, "I've always been a step behind."

When she remained silent, he forged ahead. "You were right, Anna, when you said that I was hurt too. But that's not all. If I had known you were planning to sabotage the mordemurs, I would have stopped you. I almost killed you. So I shut you out to protect myself." He stopped, not sure of what to say next. This was not going as he had planned.

"What do you want, Lark?"

"What do I want? Oh, Anna, I want you to know that I love you. I always did, though I never said the words, and I have never stopped. I want to know that you're willing to try again, that you want the same, Anna. You don't have to answer me right away," he added when she didn't respond. "I'll leave you alone to think about it." He turned and headed to the door.

Anna just could not believe that he was leaving *again*. She picked the largest gob of ruined dough, intent on chucking it at him. Her arm was already raised as he turned around, smiling that small, secret smile that had always devastated her heart.

"Poor choice of words, Anna. For the record, I'm not actually *leaving* you. I won't ever leave you again, unless you order me to do so."

She hurled the dough at him anyway, but he caught it deftly in one hand. Anna backed away as he came at her, only to bump solidly into counter behind.

• • •

Lark placed his hands on either side of her and gripped the wood of the counter until his knuckles turned white. He dared not touch her, instinctively knowing that if he did, he would lose control. He searched her wide, expectant eyes with their little flecks of gold flashing, daring him to make a move.

"I forgot to add that I want you." Her eyes glinted with pent-up desire. His mouth was so close to hers. All he needed to do was move forward an inch…

His need intensified. "My passion for you has never gone away," he murmured, his lips nearly touching hers. "It is always there, reminding me of the times we were together. I can sense you feel the same."

She made no reply, so he leaned closer. "Don't you, Anna?"

A small noise escaped her, almost too quiet to register, a tiny, soft whimper.

"I'll take that as a yes," he murmured, and her eyelids dropped and her lips parted in anticipation. If he kissed her now, he wouldn't be able to stop. "*Later*," he whispered. Then he pushed away from the counter and turned to leave as quickly as he had come at her.

• • •

Anna felt the heat rising in her core, spreading deliciously lower. *Finally*, she thought. When no kiss was forthcoming, she opened her eyes. He was hastening to the door. Before she knew what she was doing, she grabbed the biggest, stickiest chunk of dough she could find and threw it at him as hard as she could. He had just taken a step outside the door when the clump hit him soundly on the back of his head. Before he could turn around, Anna fled through the opposite door leading to the inner halls and rooms of the castle.

• • •

Lark pitched forward into the courtyard, the dough's *thwack* echoing in his skull. With a sucking noise, he pulled away as much amorphous goo as he could before turning around to confront her. The tail of her braid was all that remained of her as she flew from the kitchen.

Lark shook his head. Her aim was as true today as it had been on the day he met her. He strode to the fountain and, without hesitating, dunked his head. The cold water braced him, clearing his mind and cooling his racing blood.

When he turned around, he ran right into Trian. "I'm glad you're here, Trian," he said, draping his arm around the man's shoulder. "It'll save me the time of hunting you down. Come, let's find Baldric. I require your assistance."

"He's directly above us," Trian explained, pointing to the roof of the south tower. Together, they strode off to discuss Lark's scheme.

CHAPTER SIXTY-TWO

Schemes

Anna raced through the passageway, passing a not-so-surprised Doreen. In her chamber, it took only a moment for her to change into her riding breeches before rushing back down the stairs. She reached the courtyard, making sure that Lark was not in sight. Keeping close to the wall of the fortress, she made the short dash to the stable and saddled Tullian.

But Will blocked her escape. "Come, Will, let me pass."

"I'm sorry, m'lady, I can't do that," he stated calmly. Fearing that Lark had seen her and was right now coming to intercept her, she pleaded again for Will to move.

"Oh, I'll move, but only after you promise me that you're not putting yourself in any danger."

Anna mounted Tullian and smiled at her friend. "I swear, Will, no heroic adventures today. I just really need to ride, right now, and as fast as I can."

Satisfied, Will stepped aside. "Hey!" he shouted in surprise when she grabbed his lopsided cap in passing. He stood there with a fat grin on his face, scratching his head as Anna slammed the misshapen hat on her head and called out her thanks before spurring Tullian through the western gate.

As horse and rider exited the shadows of the passageway, Anna turned in to the daylight, directing her steed to the bridge. They cantered hard, Tullian's hooves slamming down on the thick, wood planks spanning the river.

• • •

From the top of the tower, three men heard what sounded like thunder on a cloudless day. They looked down and saw Tullian and Anna coming off the bridge. Then, horse and rider raced headlong through the pastures below. Once-quiet groups of sheep were stirred into action by the blur that streaked through their ranks. To the men watching from so high above, the trotting animals broke from Anna's path as if she and Tullian were a ship and the dividing herds the wake created by their passing.

Baldric, Trian, and Lark gripped the parapet as Anna approached a low stone wall. Lark's pulse quickened as she slowed to take measure of the remaining distance. Then Tullian surged forward again. Lark's heart jumped to his throat as Tully's front legs leapt up, and the great steed soared over the hurdle. It was so perfectly timed that rider and horse appeared fused together.

Lark regarded the worried faces of his friends. An instant later, Anna and Tully made another jump. He felt as if all was right in the world again. Anna had known all along; she was who she was. He could either accept her wild spirit or live miserably without her. He would not repeat his father's error. Grinning, he stepped away and called to his friends to follow him.

They dragged their eyes from the tableau below. "You should go after her," Trian advised. "Aren't you worried that she might kill her herself riding like that?"

"I'd be more concerned if she *wasn't* riding so recklessly," Lark responded casually.

He walked back to the edge of parapet and studied Anna's diminishing form. She and Tullian came to a sudden stop. A few moments later, Tully reared up, and horse and rider charged up the hill, heading south. Thinking about her expectant lips in the kitchen, lips that he had left unsatisfied, he grinned. "Come. Let me tell you my plan."

• • •

Tully was enjoying this ride as much as she. As they charged up the hill, she realized how happy she was at that moment. She had not felt this free in years, not since her days at Chevring so long ago, when she'd gone riding alone.

She tried to ferret out the source of her happiness and discovered that she was no longer angry. The hatred she had felt for Roger had kept her alive for so long. But that same hatred had been a poison eating away at her heart.

Thinking back to the first week with Lark, Anna realized now that she had confused hope for happiness. When he'd left, he took her hopes with him. All that had remained was anger. Anger at Roger. Anger over the death of her parents. Anger at Lark. And, if she was being honest, anger at herself for letting so many others determine her fate.

She giggled remembering the smacking noise the clump of dough had made when it hit Lark's head. "Okay, Tully-boy, let's go," she urged, wanting more speed. Tully let out a long whinny in answer. They reached the top of the rise, and she pulled Tullian to a stop once more. She patted his strong neck and looked for a new destination.

To the south, Anna spied the opening of the first of the three valleys. Along its western edge, past the high golden grasses, a pastel cloud had descended from the azure sky and settled on the ground. "Wild lavender, Tully, and autumn blooming. It will be nice to have an extra supply for the winter months." She spent the rest of the morning gathering her favorite bloom.

By the time Anna rode through the main gate of the curtain wall, her thoughts had turned to the evening's Harvest Festival. All of her friends would be there. And everyone else who had been in their once-secret group, bringing their families as well. Lord Baldric and Lady Elnoura had arrived a week before, bringing Ailwen and Tomas. With Warin and Trian already in residence at Stolweg, what Anna had planned as a simple celebration was now a party for more than one hundred guests. And now, Lark was here, too.

Her sister was in heaven, Anna mused, doing that which she loved best: ordering people about. Claire had commandeered the event, and Anna was only too happy to relinquish control. As she rode through the gate, she felt truly blessed that her sister was alive. They had become closer than she could have imagined. Tullian trotted through the courtyard and into the stable.

• • •

From the shadows of Rabbit's stall, Lark observed her. She'd been gone for over four hours, and giving her time to think notwithstanding, he'd begun to worry. When Tullian trotted into the stable, festooned in purple, Lark squelched the mirth that threatened to escape his lips.

He gazed at Anna as she expertly removed the blooms that were secured to every free space on her saddle. Then she tied the ends together and slung the bouquets over her shoulders and around her neck. Pulling her steed's forehead down so that it touched hers, she whispered words that only her horse could hear. Tullian gave a loud sneeze and then tried to graze on the flowers hanging around Anna's neck. This only made the horse sneeze again. Anna laughed, and the beautiful sound of it made Lark's heart leap. She pulled off the ridiculous hat, tossing it to Will with an elated "Thank you."

"M'lady, if my cap is the cause of your happiness, I would rather you keep it."

Anna smiled as she had never smiled before. "You keep talking to the ladies like that, Will, and come tonight's dance, your parents will be forced to speak with me about *your* nuptials." Her teasing had him turning as red as bee balm. Then, like a young girl, she turned and almost skipped out the stable doors.

Lark came out of Rabbit's stall and stood next to Will. "I, er, forgot you were here," Will said, clearing his throat. "Do you still want me to saddle Rabbit?"

"It's no longer necessary," Lark answered, grabbing a cloth to help with Tully's rubdown.

"May I speak to you, m'lord?" Will asked. "Not as a stable hand, but man to man?"

Lark cast a glance at Will, suppressed a grin, and answered as gravely as Will had spoken, "Go ahead, Will."

Will led Tully into his stall and closed the gate. He straightened his shoulders and faced Lark. "I was the first here to befriend Lady Anna, and to trust her, too." He paused. "I don't suppose anyone has told you about what she did for me?"

Lark nodded. "She took your punishment upon herself."

"Aye," Will confirmed. "Then you know I would give my life to protect her from pain. And from heartbreak. I've—"

"Will, I'm not here to—" Lark tried to interrupt.

"Let me finish, sir," Will insisted, and Lark nodded. "As I was saying, I've seen Lady Anna unsure of herself. I've seen her haunted, and have been there when she was hopeful. She's been both healer and warrior to us. And, she has been my friend for almost four years. Most times, she's been like an older sister to me. Never once in all that time have I seen her truly happy. Not until just now. I think you're responsible for part of that new joy."

Studying Lark a little too shrewdly for his young years, Will added, "You don't need it. Probably don't want it. But for what it's worth, you have my blessing."

"Will, except for Claire, the family that Anna grew up with is gone," Lark said. "So you're wrong, I do need, and want, your blessing. Funny that I didn't think of it myself."

Will's eyes widened.

"I also need your help," Lark admitted. "Are you game?"

"If it will keep Lady Anna smiling as she just was, I'll run through the courtyard with naught but this cap on my head."

Lark let out a good laugh. "Nothing so drastic, I promise." He put his arm around Will's shoulder, and as they walked to the keep, Lark told Will about his plan.

CHAPTER SIXTY-THREE

Dancing Shoes

Anna found Claire in the great hall. As she suspected, her sister was busy ordering everyone about. "You're in charge, Doreen," Claire was saying as Anna stepped up behind her. "Make sure that Gilles puts them exactly where you tell him to. And don't you dare lift a finger to help, not in your condition. Grainne, do you—" She stopped, her mouth open midquestion, and Anna grinned at her. "What have you been up to, Anna? You're a walking garden."

"I was out riding and spied a field of lavender," Anna replied. "What have *you* been up to?"

"Well, you were gone," Claire responded sheepishly, "and we needed to make a few final touches, for tonight's party. And I—"

"What would I do without you, Claire?" Anna interrupted. "You've always been better at organizing than I could ever hope to be."

Claire reached out her arms to embrace Anna but could not get close enough for all the lavender. It was a tradition in their family that each woman chose a signature flower. Anna's was lavender, of course. And their mother's had been the rose. But Claire had yet to pick a bloom, for she loved all flowers equally. So Anna hugged her sister, not caring if the lavender was crushed.

"Now, I have a favor to ask of all of you," Anna stated, and held out her hands to the three women in the great hall. "Can you come with me to my chamber when you finish here?" After securing their promises to join her in an hour, Anna raced to her chamber to bathe.

• • •

Anna paced as Claire, Grainne, and Doreen gathered in her chamber. They took seats near her hearth, and she poured them each a little wine.

She took a deep breath, then a sip from her cup, and began.

"You may have heard that Lark has returned." When they nodded excitedly, she continued. "Well, I need your help with a few things." Their eyes twinkled in expectation.

"Claire, you alone know how to tame this hair of mine. Can you help?"

"Is that all?" Claire exclaimed, a little disappointed.

"Not quite," Anna said, looking at the older women. "I need to know how to seduce a man." Grainne and Doreen regarded each other and winked. "What?" Anna cried to her amused friends.

"It's about time!" Doreen shouted, slapping Anna's knee. "That man has been doing the leading far too long. It's high time that you took the reins, m'lady."

"And I have just the gown for you to do it in," Grainne exclaimed, leaping from her seat and running to fetch the garment from behind the partition in Anna's chamber. She returned, beaming. "I've been working on it for weeks now, ever since you told me about having the festival. I found it in a trunk in the north chamber." She held up the gown.

"Oh, Anna," Claire said. "Mother had that made for you!"

"I made a few alterations so that it would fit you properly," Grainne explained. "I hope that was all right."

Anna stood to admire the dress. "It's perfect, Grainne, Thank you." The gown was the same deep, rich color of golden wheat at harvest. Sewn from the simple homespun linen of a common woman's dress, the cut was far from the usual. Beautiful embroidery in a warm russet brown trailed down the bodice. The stitching was not just for decoration; it served as the stays of the dress. Grainne's amendments included tiny embroidered lavender buds at the hem, around the cuffs, and along the neckline.

Anna lifted her arms as the gown was pulled over her head. Holding her breath, she waited while Grainne tugged the lacing that held the garment in place. Then she glanced down. Grainne had made another, quite unmistakable modification to the dress. The bodice was so tight that her bosom swelled up and over the edge.

"Grainne, I'm sure to fall out," she gasped. "I want to look seductive, not wanton."

"Don't you worry 'bout that, m'lady. You won't fall out," Grainne promised. "Move around. Lift your arms high, you'll see. You're quite secure in there." Anna swayed, lifted her arms, waved, and spun. She was so tightly packaged that there was no chance of escape.

"You're a genius, Grainne!" Lady Elnoura proclaimed, clapping from the doorway. "You'll have to show my maid how you managed that trick with the needle."

But before Grainne could answer, Claire stepped forward. "We have to finish your hair. Hurry, Anna, sit down." Anna settled back as Claire pulled a little here and tugged a little there. Working quickly, Claire made a few final touches and announced that she was done.

"But, Claire, my hair is still loose," Anna exclaimed with worry.

"And you look beautiful, Anna. Let's see what everyone else thinks before you panic."

Anna stood and turned to face her friends. Almost as one, they announced that her hair was perfect. Turning to the tall looking glass, Anna studied her reflection.

Her hair had been pulled back from her face and secured about an inch from her hairline with a fine wire band, and her cascading curls fell back, framing her face instead of falling in her eyes. Ribbons, the same color as the dress, and lavender sprigs were woven into the headband.

"Do you like it, Anna?" her sister asked her a little hesitantly.

"I love it, Claire. Thank you."

"My turn," Doreen stated. "You'd best sit, m'lady."

"What's this all about, Anna?" Lady Elnoura demanded good-naturedly.

"She's going to seduce Lark tonight!" Claire blurted out.

"Well, it's about time!" Lady Elnoura announced. "What can I do to help?"

Anna explained that she was at a loss on how to initiate the seduction. Elnoura smiled. "Leave everything to me, my dear," she said conspiratorially. "Only, be sure to wear your most comfortable dancing shoes."

CHAPTER SIXTY-FOUR

The Dance

Lark paced in the shadows of the large oak in the courtyard. He surveyed the area near the archway where the guests were arriving for the fête. He scanned the crowd. Most of Anna's inner circle had arrived. Only Cellach was noticeably absent.

The musicians, their instruments tuned, commenced playing. This party was the perfect way to celebrate the harvest, Lark thought. Grainne was at the buffet table. Lady Elnoura was there too, helping to rearrange the chargers holding the food. Tradition dictated that the line between noble and commoner be dissolved during the Harvest Festival.

Lark noted with amusement that several girls were vying for Will's attention. Lucky Will, Lark thought and grinned, to be so young. The times of the equinoxes always elicited romance. Tonight, even the air seemed to shimmer. He counted it as a good omen.

It was the pause in conversation that made him turn toward the banquet tables. Though the backs of his companion guards blocked his view of the flowered archway, Lark knew that Anna had arrived. Warin and Tomas stepped aside to reveal Ailwen leading her to the space cleared for dancing. She was smiling at something he had said, and the music of her laughter carried all the way to where Lark was standing in the shadows. As she stepped into the soft glow made by the lanterns strung above the courtyard, Lark's breath caught.

He'd always thought her beautiful; tonight she was radiant, and his blood stirred upon seeing her. She and her partner spun closer, and Lark's eyes widened at the cut of her bodice. Jealous, he swore an oath and stalked toward the dancers, intent on cutting in.

The music changed, and Ailwen passed Anna over to Tomas. She was merrily enjoying herself now, perhaps a little too much. The music switched again, and before Lark could reach her, Baldric stepped in and took Anna's hand. The dancing area was crowded, and Lark was forced to step back to the perimeter so as not to be in the way. He waited for the musicians to strike the next song.

Finally, Baldric and Anna made their way closer. The musicians paused, then struck their instruments again. Lark waited impatiently; unfortunately, fate had different plans. Baldric and Trian switched partners so smoothly that Lark missed his opportunity. And when the musicians struck up a new song, Anna was too far away. Warin, his rake of a friend, took her in his arms. Her laughter tinkled like bells in the clear night, infecting everyone with her happiness.

The latest dance was fast-paced. Warin spun Anna expertly through the other dancers; it was a miracle they didn't collide with anyone. As they danced their way nearer to Lark, Warin winked at him, then twirled Anna a bit too fast. She caromed off the dance floor.

• • •

Anna was having a splendid time. She hadn't had a chance to find Lark, for her surroundings were a blur as she and Warin wove their way through the dancers. Lady Elnoura had promised she would be engaged with as many partners as possible.

Warin was an exceptional dancer but was a bit distracted by her bosom, now heaving for breath. He put her into another fast spin. Too fast. She flew off the dance floor.

She held up her arms to protect herself from the looming oak tree. Someone stepped into her path, and she collided so hard that she immediately fell backward. Two hands shot out and grabbed her waist, pulling her back and saving her from a fall. It was Lark. He held her tight to his chest, and her arms, folded in front of her, were pinned against him. Anna gasped, trying to catch her breath. She lifted her chin and gazed into Lark's eyes.

"Will you dance with me, Anna?" Lark asked, his voice thick with desire.

"We can't." She still hadn't caught her breath. "The musicians have stopped." Lark let out a curse loud enough to be heard by those standing nearby.

"It's just as well," she said. "I need to rest. It would be easier for me to breathe if you would loosen your grip."

Lark leered playfully in the direction of her cleavage, not bothering to disguise his interest. He tightened his hold instead, and her pinned arms pushed her chest higher. Then, he released her, spun her around so that her arms crisscrossed under her bosom. "This is a lovely party, Anna," he whispered close to her ear.

With her back pressed tightly against his chest, she could feel the strength of his heartbeat through their garments. "Everyone seems to be having a good time," she squeaked nervously.

He pulled her crossed arms a little tighter, causing her breasts to swell even more, then craned his neck to better peer over her shoulder and down her bodice. She felt his exhalation, hot and moist along her neck, and a thousand goose bumps rose on her skin. She tried to stop it, had not even meant to do it. But a soft "*mmm*" escaped on a sigh. Anna felt the heat rising in her cheeks.

She focused on the musicians for a distraction. Carrick was pulling out his recorder to play an old tune. From another guest, a whistle joined in. Gilles brought out his dulcimer, and Will broke out his pipe. The different sounds tangled with one another until a beautiful collection of notes drifted up and over everyone in the courtyard. A couple of drums started up, and then Anna heard the lilting tones of a cross flute's accompaniment. Moments later, the sweet sounds of Will's pipe overlapped the other instruments.

No one musician led. All played together to make a beautiful harmony. At least twelve people were now performing, their notes blended and married, layer upon layer upon layer.

It felt wonderful to be held in Lark's arms again. As her friends struck up another tune, this one faster and more complicated, she happened to glance across the dance area. Doreen, Grainne, Noura, and Claire were frowning at her. She remembered Doreen's words about Lark wanting to be in control, and their scowling faces suddenly made sense. If she didn't turn the tables soon, her planned seduction would fail.

Anna tapped her toe in time with the rhythmic beat of the drums. She pressed her back closer to Lark and, so that no one would see but Lark would definitely feel, she moved her hips in time with the dulcimer. It only took a moment before she felt Lark freeze. She dared a quick glance in the direction of her friends and saw them clapping their approval.

Lark's heartbeat pounded through his shirt. A smile spread across Anna's face when she felt his excitement. She rocked slightly forward on the balls of her feet and then bounced up and down, keeping in time with the faster-paced flutes and whistles.

"Do you still want to dance, Lark?" she suggested innocently, swaying against him. "The hired musicians will return soon, but I'm willing to dance to this tune." Enjoying herself, Anna's grin broadened. Finally, she had him!

"I don't think now is a good time to dance, Anna," Lark growled. "If you keep moving against me the way you are right now, we're going to have a problem." Holding her against his chest to disguise his excited state, he marched her to a nearby bench and table. Anna sat down facing outward while Lark sat down next to her, folding his long legs under the table.

Anna leaned back, putting her elbows on the weathered planks behind her, enhancing the fullness of her breasts. Lark cursed again, only to have matters worsen for him when Trian, Claire, and Elnoura joined them.

"Lark, are you all right?" Lady Elnoura inquired. "You seem a little flushed. Trian, pour some refreshment for Lark." Anna turned around on the bench.

"This is wonderful party, Anna," Lady Elnoura complimented her. "There used to be such a strong division between master and servant here." Then, Noura winked.

Anna smiled gratefully at her newest friend. This was the cue for which she'd been waiting. "I was just going to raise that very subject with Lark." Ailwen, Tomas, and Warin joined them.

Warin sat next to Anna. It must have been a little too close for Lark's comfort, for he pulled her tighter to his side. "What was that about servants, Anna?" Lark prompted.

"Well, not servants exactly—rather, slaves." She had not only Lark's full attention now, but everyone sitting at the table's as well. Measuring the interest of her friends, she settled on Warin and explained, "Months ago, when Lark and I sought refuge in a cave during a storm, Lark asked me a question about, erm, slavery, of a sort. I never had a chance to answer him. I've been thinking a great deal on the subject recently and believe I have my reply ready, if he'll hear it."

• • •

Suddenly wary, Lark dared to ask, "And what might your answer be, Anna?" He sensed that she was up to some mischief, but the fact that she was not throwing food at him told him that her anger had subsided. He would be better served to play along with her game.

"Well, all slavery, in and of itself, is abhorrent," Anna stated. She fluttered her lashes over her soft brown eyes and pressed further. "I suppose, though, it would not be so bad if the slave and master took turns."

At the confusion that this conversation was bringing to the faces of his fellow guards, Lark began to laugh. No one here would comprehend that Anna was talking about the offer that he had made those first days they were together, when he told her that he desired to be her slave. They would probably guess, though, if he let Anna continue. She would never have the courage, he thought, and decided to call her bluff. "And how exactly would that work, Anna?"

She swept her eyelashes down shyly, then looked up again at their friends. Turning to him, she cupped her hands around his ear and leaned forward to whisper. Lark was feeling good about himself now that Anna was seated so close to him, their thighs touching, his arm still loosely draped around her.

Lifting his mug of beer to his mouth, he listened as she whispered, "I imagine, Larkin, that it would involve extensive use of my tongue." To prove her point, she darted it into his ear and then ran it lightly around the edge of his lobe.

Lark had just taken a large swig of beer. With her hands discreetly obscuring her mouth from view, Anna murmured again, "And perhaps, my teeth as well." She took his earlobe gently between her teeth and tugged.

Lark choked on his beer and knocked his cup over. Then, as he shot up, pulling Anna roughly to her feet, the bench crashed backward, and Warin with it. The others broke out into raucous laughter. Lark growled a curse before hauling Anna away from the table, away from the dancing, away from the party, and away from his friends.

Only Claire seemed nervous; he heard her question Trian in alarm. "Will Anna be all right?" she asked.

"I'm more worried about Lark at the moment," Trian replied. Lark doubled his pace, pulling Anna along behind him.

"Lark. Lark. Slow down!" she begged, racing to keep up with his long strides. "Where are you taking me?"

Lark slowed long enough to lift Anna off the ground and carry her in his arms. He sighed wearily as this act, witnessed by his friends, was met with hoots and applause. Anna giggled and reached her arms around his neck as he rushed to the steps of the chapel. Only after they reached the doors did Lark rest and put Anna back on her feet.

He stopped and pulled her into the exterior alcove, pressing her back against the wall and out of view of the others. Taking her head in both hands, he lifted her face to his just before crushing his lips against her mouth. She answered his devastating embrace by plunging her own tongue against his. They kissed and kissed, his arms circling lower around her, pulling her to his chest, sealing his loins to her hips. He could not bring her close enough and groaned aloud. Coming up for air, they gazed at each other, neither able to speak.

Their gasping breaths slowed. Anna brought her hands down from Lark's neck. She wrapped her arms around his shoulders. "You still have not told me whether or not you accept my terms to your proposal," she reminded him, smiling innocently.

"Oh, not only do I accept your terms, I am looking forward to the arrangement." He growled and lowered his head to kiss her again.

"And, it will be my turn first?" Anna asked, and he could hear the excitement in her voice.

"If that is your desire, then yes," he offered. "Now, speaking of proposals…"

CHAPTER SIXTY-FIVE

Second Chances

"Anna, will you marry me? Here? Tonight?"

The intensity of Lark's expression robbed her of her senses, and for a moment she was unable to speak. She was lost as she fell into the depths of his midnight eyes, but he was there, waiting for her. She finally found that for which she'd been dreaming the whole of her life. "Yes, Larkin. Yes."

He grabbed her hand and pulled her through the doors of the chapel. Suddenly, Anna realized that he was serious about marrying her right away. She dug in her heels. "Wait. Now?" she asked. "But we don't have a priest. We need…"

"Don't make me pick you up again, Anna," Lark remonstrated. "You needn't fret about the details. I have everything in hand." Before she could protest again, he pulled her down the aisle.

She stared ahead, bewildered by what she discovered. The chapel was dark save for the area around the altar. A score of candles bathed the area in a warm, ethereal glow. Facing them was Lord Baldric, and next to Baldric, a priest. "I love you, Larkin!" Anna exclaimed.

The clergyman shifted and fretted, as if he were mentally checking off the requirements for a wedding. Bride, yes, Anna thought. Groom, yes. Someone to stand for the groom, yes. Someone to stand for the bride…who would stand for her? Anna worried. The doors to the chapel opened and Will, Trian, and Claire came down the aisle to meet them. Anna hugged her sister and then Trian. Finally, she turned to Will.

He grinned at her, holding out a small bouquet of lavender. He turned to the priest, his tone brooking no argument, and averred, "I'm here to give the bride away. She has my blessing to marry this man."

Anna smiled at her friend; it was perfect. She could not have picked a better man than Will for the task. She stepped away from Lark and gratefully took the proffered flowers from her friend. Will made a display of properly handing her back to the groom and then stepped back to stand with the others. The priest launched into the recitation of marriage rites.

This time, Anna heard every word spoken and felt their full gravity. This was not an arranged marriage like the first. This was a union of love. Her eyes never left Lark's as they repeated their vows, all the way until he said, "I will." And then, he leaned in to kiss her. She tilted her head to meet him. It was the most natural motion in the world. Soft and gentle, their lips met.

"You may kiss the—oh!" the priest started, and Anna giggled. Lark's arms circled around her waist as their lips nibbled and courted. They were soon oblivious to all present.

"Come," Baldric ordered, putting his hand on the sputtering priest's shoulder. "Let us all return to the celebration outside. We'll give our newlyweds a few moments alone. And remember, not a word to anyone. They've earned the right to a little privacy."

• • •

Lark heard the door to the chapel open and close. Standing together as man and wife, he was the first to remember that they were in a church, and with regret, he pulled his lips from hers. He clasped her hands in his and brought them to his chest. "We don't have to tell anyone until tomorrow morning," he explained, and saw apprehension in her eyes. "Anna, tell me. What is bothering you?"

"How do you do that?" she demanded. "How are you able to read my thoughts?"

"The same way you read mine. There is no other in this world who can do the like. Now stop stalling and tell me what is upsetting you."

"Our friends will not be the only ones who will hear of our union, will they?" she asked.

Lark remained silent, one eyebrow arched, and waited for her to explain.

"The King and Queen will hear. Godwin told me that he has a list of suitable husbands for me. Well, for Stolweg, really. What if he's angry because he wanted me to marry someone else? What if—"

Lark touched his finger to Anna's lips to stop her from speaking further. "He won't be angry," he assured her. "I realized that the King would want a trusted man in place here, which is why I rode to

NICOLE ELIZABETH KELLEHER

King's Glen first."

"And?" Anna begged breathlessly.

"Apparently, the King's list is quite specific."

"Are you on it? Please, tell me you're on it."

Lark grinned. "Of course I am! I'm curious, though, Anna. Would it have made a difference to you had my name not been included?"

"Not in the slightest," she answered quickly. "It just makes things easier, doesn't it?"

From outside, a gale of happy cheering made its way through the doors of the chapel. "I am *not* looking forward to going back to the celebration," Lark grumbled. "We've wasted so much time, and I don't want to share you with anyone else this evening."

His bride seemed as pleased as a cat that had just caught a fat mouse. "Then don't," she said.

CHAPTER SIXTY-SIX
One Last Secret

"Don't what?" Lark asked.

"Don't share me," she replied, and led him to the devotional candles. "One last secret," she told him as she pressed the button that would give entrance to the tunnel leading to the west tower. From there, she used the passageways to take them unseen to her own chamber.

Once safely in her quarters, Lark made his way to the shuttered windows and cracked one open. Strands of a melody wafted through the air from the musicians below. He held out his hand and beckoned her to join him near the window. "You've made your people happy, Anna. They are so different from when I first met them. Look at Will. There's a line of young maidens waiting to dance with him." Lark wrapped his arms around her. "You spoke the truth to him in the stable today. Doreen and Gilles will have to visit you soon."

"You mean they will visit *us* soon," Anna corrected, leaning back against his solid strength as they took in the revelry in the courtyard. "Wait. You saw me in the stable talking to Will? I must have looked ridiculous, all those flowers. And the hat. Oh, no. And my hair. At least half of my hair had come loose from its braid." She felt her cheeks flame red.

"You looked beautiful, surrounded by all that lavender. In fact, I've been thinking of naught else all day. Picturing you, naked, in a field." Anna gasped, and he pulled her closer. "And it was not half of your hair. Three or four locks at the most." Reaching up, he entwined his fingers into her loose curls, and tugged gently, pulling her back to him.

He took a deep breath and buried his face in her mane, murmuring into her ear at the same time. "I love your hair when it's like this. I have since the first time I saw it down. Do you remember? It was still damp from your bath in the pool." Unwrapping a long tress from his fingers, he gazed into her eyes. "I have spent many hours thinking up creative ways to—"

"Lark!" She'd recognized the thickening voice and that all-too-familiar gleam that came into his eyes. If she did not put space between them right away, she would never have another chance. She slipped from his grasp.

Grainne had thoughtfully laid out wine and food near the hearth. Anna moved so that the small table was between them, determined to hold Lark to his word. After all, it was her turn.

• • •

Lark had hoped that the memory of her first wedding night with Roger would be kept at bay. But she withdrew, positioning the table between them as a barrier. He swept his eyes over the food that had been laid out and picked up a piece of bread, giving her the time he thought she needed. He turned the slice over in his hand and studied it.

"I am glad to see some of the dough made it to the oven," he teased, trying to ease her fears. "We didn't have a chance to eat earlier, with you dancing and twirling with every man in the courtyard. Are you hungry?" The expression on her face stopped him from speaking more. Anna didn't look nervous. Not one bit.

"Were you jealous?" she asked, feigning innocence. "I was only dancing." Her voice was deep and husky. He could barely swallow, let alone answer.

She ignored the food. "I'm quite ravenous myself," she told him. His blood stirred as her eyes raked his body, and he tried to come around the table. But she would not have him closer, and moved to keep the obstacle between them.

Frustrated by her evasiveness, he started to lift the table away. "Wait, Lark," she pleaded, pressing her hands on the surface to keep it to the floor. "If you remember, it is *my* turn."

He took one of her hands and placed her palm over his racing heart. "I think we've waited long enough, Anna."

"I'm serious, Lark. You gave me your word."

So, he thought, his Anna wanted to play the temptress. He was only too happy to go along. After all, he didn't truly believe that she would be able to seduce him. He would wager that she would last only until the musicians struck up the next song before he would have to take over.

"You have my word," he stated, and caressed her cheek. "I won't move until you tell me to." She came around the table.

Anna realized that Lark never gave his word lightly. With a tentative motion, she put her hands on his chest. All evening she had wrestled with whether or not she would be able to play the seductress. She would probably lose her nerve, she thought, and almost made up her mind to stop before she embarrassed herself. Then she studied Lark's face. There it was, though he tried to hide it—his knowing smile. And if that smile did anything, it steeled her determination. The corner of her lip curved, and she raised her brow in amusement. Lark, at least, had the good sense to stop smirking.

Pushing him backward, little by little, she steered him to the bed. *I can do this*, she told herself. She touched the hair hanging over his forehead and pushed it back lovingly. Standing on her toes, she leaned forward and murmured into his ear, her breath caressing his skin.

"Now, what was it I said? Oh, yes. I would have to use my tongue, and perhaps my teeth."

While her lips teased, her hands were not idle. They slid down to his waist, pulling his linen shirt from his breeches. She lifted his arms and pulled the garment over his head. He was so beautiful, she thought, and stared hungrily at his naked torso. Her hands ran over his chest, delighting in the smooth skin over rock-hard muscles. She could do this, she repeated to herself. Oh yes, she could definitely do this.

Her gaze locked onto the planes of his chest as she ran her nails over him, leaving him feverish where she touched. She gentled her hands, as if sculpting him, following the curve of each muscle down the well-defined ladder of his stomach.

Her shaky breath was audible in the quiet chamber as an unexpected feeling of desire surged through her. How did he do it? He hadn't touched her once, and she was already losing her control. She wondered if Lark felt the same when he thought only of her pleasure. "Of course you do," she murmured.

"Hmm?" he managed, sounding lost, and falling silent again as she scratched her fingertip down the center of his chest. She continued lower, pausing briefly at his navel before moving on to the waistband of his leather pants. Trailing her other hand down his chest, following the rippled muscles along his ribs, she brought her fingers together. With her cheek against Lark's chest, she listened to his racing heart as her fingers worked the fastenings of his breeches until they were undone. She took an infinite amount of time to reach around to his sides, hooking her thumbs in the waistband and pushing down until his pants rode low on his hips. Because she wanted him naked, she waited, enjoying how he looked, how his torso was so spectacularly made that it stole her breath.

He was ready for her, she noticed, and felt a warm glow rising deep inside her. She would do this.

Circling around him, never once allowing her hands to break contact with his skin, she massaged his shoulders before running her hands down his back. He exuded raw power. Her fingers traced lower until they dipped into his waistband again, pushing his breeches down over his tight buttocks.

With a shaky breath, Lark whispered her name as a question. "Shhh," she purred, as if calming a skittish horse.

She went to her knees, pulling his breeches to his thighs. Slowly, trailing her nails up the backs of his legs, Anna stood and wound her way around to face him again. With her palms flat against his chest, she pushed him back so that he sat on the bed. She *was* doing this, she exulted. His breeches removed, she pulled him up once more.

She pressed her lips to his collarbone and rained kisses across his skin. Her hands traveled from his chest to his sides, then down his back and lower. His eyes were closed now, his lips sealed, his throat swallowing hard, not knowing what was to come. She quickened inside again, knowing she was the cause of his excitement.

She heard his breath catch as her mouth slid lower. Her hands skimmed his sides as her lips traveled down the taut muscles of his stomach, past his navel, then lower. She veered to one side and kissed his hipbone. Lark gasped when she licked the dimple where his torso met his thigh. Then, with a gentle touch, she took him in her hand.

He sucked in his breath as she pulled him level with her mouth. Then, hearing his urgent moan, she was emboldened and took him between her lips. Concentrating on just the tip, Anna sucked, kissed, and licked before opening her mouth more to allow him entrance. When Lark's knees buckled, she followed his collapse onto the bed. He moaned again as her tongue circled around him, and his hips began their own dance to match her rhythm.

He was at her mercy, and she exploited the motion of his thrusts by taking him in her mouth again and again. And as she continued to lick, suck, and swirl her tongue around him, she saw his hands clench and unclench the blankets.

This was what she'd been waiting for, and she rose up from the floor. Straddling his knees where they hung over the bed's edge, she spoke for the first time since shushing him. Her voice, full of raw hunger, was unrecognizable to her own ears. "Open your eyes, Larkin," she commanded, as he'd once done to her. "Open your eyes and look at me."

• • •

Lark tried to focus. Anna, still in her gown, had raised its hem to her thighs. She placed first one bare knee, then the other, on the bed. His vision cleared just as she kneeled above him, her legs astride his hips.

"I want you to watch me," she whispered.

She reached under her skirts, and finding his shaft, she grasped him in her hand. She lowered herself, taking her time, so he was at her opening. He moaned her name, and she slid her body down the length of him, her skirts pooling around them.

Once enveloped by her, he closed his eyes. But she lifted up again and waited. "Keep looking at me, Larkin," she ordered breathlessly.

At her command, his eyes flew open. She reached for his hands and removed his clenched fingers from the blankets. Their fingers interlaced, she slid down again and gasped aloud.

Twice commanded to watch, Lark could not now tear his gaze away. She moved gracefully. Her skirts rumpled around and over him, refusing him a view to that which he felt. Strong, lithe thighs relaxed as she filled her body with him and then flexed as she rose before driving down again. He helped her along by surging upward, trying to bury himself as deep as possible in her tight warmth. And still, her beautiful face shone down at him, a crease between her eyebrows betelling of her intense concentration. She was panting, and low, gasping sounds drifted in and out of his hearing.

She finally allowed him to set the pace, and he increased his thrusting, speeding himself to his release. He could tell she was seconds away from her own. He thrust upward, as deep as he could, while she dropped down to meet him. She rose again and lifted herself almost completely away, lengthening the stroke as much as possible. He answered her motion by stabbing upward as Anna came back down. Sealed against her, his seed exploded. He cried out her name, holding her hands, while his hips bucked off the bed. He could feel her inner muscles spasm until she rode out her own climax. Finally, during her greatest throes of passion, she broke eye contact, arched, and threw back her head, calling his name in unbridled pleasure.

Her bosom heaved as Lark pulled her forward to face him, making sure she was steady and not at risk of falling backward off the bed. He gazed up at her, astounded. Her chest was rising and falling as she tried to catch her breath. Her skin glistened with perspiration. Lark tugged her hands again, pulling her forward until her head hung over his. He lifted his head and kissed her soundly, tasting the salty sweat above her lip and the sweetness of her mouth.

Neither was capable of speech as she collapsed on top of him. He stroked her neck, and, under the masses of loose curls, she was sodden. His hand roamed down the back of her gown. Here, too, she was soaking wet. More than anything, he wanted to touch her skin, to feel her breasts crushed against his bare chest.

"We need to get you out of this dress," he growled. "Now."

Anna sighed unsteadily and pushed herself up again, looking dazed. He released the tight lacings that held the bodice of her gown in place. She raised her arms, and Lark picked up the heavy skirts, lifting the dress over her head. Her shift was next. Free from the restraining fabric, Anna fell forward once more. She straightened her legs carefully, so as not to dislodge him. Cheek to cheek, chest to breast, hips to loins. Lark managed to pull a blanket over them; soft strands of music smoked upward through the open window of their chamber.

Bit by bit, Anna came back to her senses. *Boneless*, she thought—it was the only way she could describe how she felt. She clung to Lark as he raked in great, shuddering breaths. He rolled them to their sides, an arm and leg draped possessively over her. As the celebration in the courtyard faded, she and Lark fell asleep in each other's arms.

CHAPTER SIXTY-SEVEN

Good Morning

The hour was early when he woke and looked about their chamber. *Their* chamber, no longer just Anna's, he happily reminded himself. The windows were brightening as the sun lifted above the eastern hills, and the rumblings in the courtyard below intruded more insistently into their peaceful haven. Next to him, Anna was slowly shaking off her slumber. When she opened her eyes, he kissed her. "I love you so much, Anna. How have I survived this long without you?"

"I could ask you the same, Lark," she replied.

He held her tightly, and she buried her face in his chest. "You're stuck with me, my Anna, until the end of our days." They cuddled, twisted in the blankets, until the bustling outside grew too loud to ignore. He'd almost forgotten about the promise he'd made to Baldric, Trian, and the others. In return for their aid in Lark's wedding plans, he had promised to take them on a hunt.

With a groan of regret, Lark extricated himself from the bed. He found his discarded breeches on the floor and grinned at his wife. She blushed furiously but was unable to hide her smile. "You may want to dress," he suggested as he walked behind the partition that separated their dressing area from the rest of the chamber. "Else we may never leave this room again."

· · ·

Anna searched the rumpled bed and sighed happily when she spied Lark's shirt. She had just slipped it over her head when there was a knock at the door followed by a screech as it opened. In piled Grainne and Doreen, with Claire trailing after them, begging them to wait.

"I tried to stop them!" she cried, inserting herself between the two women and Anna. There was a collective gasp from the women behind Claire, and Anna smiled as her sister's jaw dropped as well. Lark had just come from behind the partition. His pants, not quite completely fastened, hung dangerously low on his hips.

"Good morning, ladies," Lark offered, unperturbed by the women in his chamber. "To what do we owe this honor?" His question was met with complete silence. He chuckled and crossed the floor to Anna's bedside. "Have you seen my shirt, Anna? I know I had it last night."

When Lark's gaze fell upon her, he stopped, noting that the desired garment was draped around her. "Ah, I see. Well, it looks better on you, my love," he told her. "I'm sure I have more clothes around here somewhere." Anna saw Claire lift her hand to hide her grin.

"Perhaps over there," Anna suggested, pointing to the dressing area.

"Of course," he stated. After donning the rest of his clothes, he walked past the astounded women, then proceeded to the chamber's door. Anna coughed delicately, and Lark returned to her side faster than Grainne and Doreen could widen their eyes. Grainne clucked her tongue as he murmured to Anna while tucking stray tendrils of her mane behind her ear.

"Perhaps we should have secured the door last night," he whispered.

Anna smiled. "I guess we were too distracted."

"Definitely. But I'm of a mind that after this morning, we'll not have to worry about future untimely intrusions." He glanced in their audience's direction. "I think they may just faint."

Lark gave her a kiss that smacked with desire. After the heated embrace, Anna struggled to catch her breath. And lest she forget it was he who had stolen it, he kissed her silly once more. He grinned at her in that way that melted her knees, then stepped away. As he passed Claire and the still-gaping Grainne and Doreen, he called out, "I'll meet you in the stable, *wife?*"

"I'll be right behind you, *husband*," she answered brightly.

"I bid you goodbye as well, sister," Lark added to Claire with a chaste kiss. He nodded to Grainne and Doreen, and then he was gone, leaving Anna to fend off the ensuing interrogation on her own.

She buried her head under the blankets to muffle the din. Shouts of *husband* and *wife* filled her chamber. Peeking from beneath her covers, Anna beseeched her sister with her eyes.

And so it was Claire who put a stop to the cacophony by slamming the chamber door shut. "Come, ladies. We need to help her dress if she's going to join the others on the hunt." Cries of congratulations and demands for every detail of the wedding followed as they fussed about her.

Claire watched as her radiant sister, having finally extricated herself from Doreen and Grainne, opened her chamber door and shooed them into the corridor. If only their parents were alive to see this, Claire thought, they would have been so proud of Anna.

"You seem sad, Claire," Anna noted. "Is everything all right?"

"I just miss Mother and Father," she explained. "They would approve of Lark, you know, for the love you bear each other is so strong. I only hope that when it is my turn…"

"I promise you, Claire," her sister vowed, "you will marry someone you love. King Godwin's list or no." Anna stopped and gave her a great hug. "Oh, here comes Trian."

When Anna stepped away, Claire felt that all-too-familiar disorientation that had plagued her since she was a child. She reached for the wall. The corridor seemed to stretch and expand, then shrink back upon itself. An image crystallized in her mind, and she breathed in relief. She wouldn't black out this time, only swoon, for it was good tidings.

"We're on our way to meet him," she heard Anna explain to Trian. For a brief moment, Claire's eyes focused on Trian's. He saw her distress and rushed to her, catching her before she fell. His arms were strong as he held her, and gentle for such a bear of a man. And he smelled of horses, and leather, and sunlight.

"Claire!" Anna cried.

"I'm all right, Anna," Claire assured her. "I just need a moment. Trian, could you let the others know that we'll be along soon?" He nodded and helped her to stand. Though he walked away, his scent lingered, and Claire breathed deep. The wholesome odor calmed her.

"What was it, Claire?" Anna worried. "There's only one reason that you ever faint. Have you seen something?"

Claire smiled, then whispered in Anna's ear and placed her hand on her sister's stomach. "'Tis true, Anna," Claire said when wonder filled her sister's eyes. They heard the sound of feet taking the stairs two at a time and saw Lark rushing into the hallway, Trian close behind.

Anna gazed lovingly at her husband, and then whispered in his ear. Claire had never seen a smile as beautiful as Lark's in all her life.

"What is it, Claire?" Trian asked.

"I'll tell you," Claire replied gaily, "*later.*"

Acknowledgments

A huge thank you to my best girls: Becca, who listened to the "screenplay" on our walks; Julie, Cheryl and Mary, for never thinking I was crazy for putting pen to paper; and Karen and Laura, who read countless versions, from one thousand pages to five hundred and everything in between. Your encouragements and critiques were always appreciated.

Much gratitude goes to Kae Tienstra, my agent, who told me to call her back if "things didn't work out" with the other agent and then answered when I called a year later.

Before Kae even saw the manuscript, there was Danelle McCafferty, an excellent editor, a plastic surgeon of manuscripts that have been divided in two and then sewn back together.

And to my team at Diversion Books—Randall Klein, editor; Sarah Masterson Hally and Eliza Kirby, production; the fantastic copyeditors; Trent Hart and Chris Mahon, marketing; and Laura Duane, for acquiring my manuscript—I am forever grateful that you took a chance on a new author. To my editor, Randall Klein: hold on to your blue pencils; the sequel is full of dreams!

Finally, a few familial shout-outs: to my sisters, for their support during the difficult times and their company during the good; to Dave and the boys, Patrick and Connor, for giving me time to write and for cooking dinner when I'm locked away in my office; and to my dad, for passing on his love of all literature.

A graduate of the University of Michigan's College of Literature, Science and Arts, NICOLE E. KELLEHER studied French Literature and Language, Spanish and Mandarin while taking classes at UofM's Art School. She moved to France and attended the Université Catholique de l'Œest before relocating to Belgium to complete an internship at a fine arts and antiques auction house. During this time, she travelled throughout the countryside of Europe, immersing herself in its history, architecture, and art. Nicole lives in Northern Virginia with her two children, husband and Tully the Dog.

Connect with Nicole:

www.nekelleher.com

www.facebook.com/Nicole-Elizabeth-Kelleher-854445384602371

@nekelleher1

CPSIA information can be obtained at www.ICGtesting.com
Printed in the USA
BVOW05s1458250116

433987BV00003B/3/P